Praise for
The Ruthless Lady's Guide to Wizardry

"With this winning ensemble adventure, Waggoner again proves her skill at crafting immersive, historically flavored fantasy." —*Publishers Weekly* (starred review)

"Waggoner . . . crafts an excellent historical fantasy that also manages to have a sweet and hot love story at the center. At turns laugh-out-loud funny and heartwarming, this fast-paced book is for fans of romance, historical fantasy, and Theodora Goss's Athena Club series."

—*Library Journal* (starred review)

"Much of the comedy in Ms. Waggoner's story comes from the clash between Delly's Dickensian world, where 'red drip' takes the place of cheap gin, and the Jane Austen realm of arranged marriages, footmen, and careful distinctions between ladies and 'lady-adjacent personages.' . . . There's great fun in figuring out the rules of the game." —*The Wall Street Journal*

"Delly Wells is the best kind of protagonist. Selfish, skittish, anxious and overwhelmed, smart, opportunistic, a good heart under all the bluster, and, yes, ruthless. . . . Waggoner's characters absolutely shine . . . Agatha Christie in design and Pratchett-esque in execution." —*Tor.com*

"C. M. Waggoner's second novel is a dazzling, romantic fantasy quest." —*BookPage*

TITLES BY C. M. WAGGONER

THE
VILLAGE LIBRARY
DEMON-HUNTING
SOCIETY

C. M. Waggoner

Ace

New York

ACE
Published by Berkley
An imprint of Penguin Random House LLC
penguinrandomhouse.com

Copyright © 2024 by Caitlin Waggoner
Penguin Random House supports copyright. Copyright fuels creativity, encourages
diverse voices, promotes free speech, and creates a vibrant culture. Thank you for
buying an authorized edition of this book and for complying with copyright laws
by not reproducing, scanning, or distributing any part of it in any form without
permission. You are supporting writers and allowing Penguin Random House
to continue to publish books for every reader.

ACE is a registered trademark and the A colophon is a trademark of
Penguin Random House LLC.

Library of Congress Cataloging-in-Publication Data

Names: Waggoner, C. M., author.
Title: The village library demon-hunting society / C. M. Waggoner.
Description: First edition. | New York : Ace, 2024.
Identifiers: LCCN 2023059767 (print) | LCCN 2023059768 (ebook) |
ISBN 9781984805881 (trade paperback) | ISBN 9781984805898 (ebook)
Subjects: LCGFT: Cozy mysteries. | Fantasy fiction. | Paranormal fiction. | Novels.
Classification: LCC PS3623.A3533 V55 2024 (print) | LCC PS3623.A3533 (ebook) |
DDC 813/.6—dc23/eng/20240112
LC record available at https://lccn.loc.gov/2023059767
LC ebook record available at https://lccn.loc.gov/2023059768

First Edition: September 2024

Printed in the United States of America
3rd Printing

For Chloe and Emily,
because friends will help you move,
good friends will help you move a body,
but *best* friends will badger you into taking a nap, going on
a walk, and drinking a glass of water before you snap
and commit felony homicide in the first place.

ONE

Sherry Pinkwhistle woke up to the deep silence of snowfall, cozily ensconced in the warmth of her bed and the knowledge that she had just solved another murder.

She'd woken up five minutes before her alarm—it was 6:55—and she wanted to stay in bed for a while longer than she usually would, just for the sake of luxuriating a little. A treat. A thank-you to herself for a job well done. It was no good, though: Lord Thomas Cromwell came into the room at exactly two minutes past seven and started shouting for his breakfast, and there was nothing for Sherry to do but get up, push her toes into her warm slippers, and start her day.

Sherry didn't like to think of herself as a *dull* person, but she did like to stick to her morning routine. Lord Thomas Cromwell had his breakfast—a half can of salmon-flavored wet food: he was on a strict vet-ordered diet (Sherry was as regimented about Lord Thomas Cromwell's health and fitness as she was lax about her own)—before she started the coffee. While the coffee was brewing, she went out to fetch the paper. Then she made her egg (soft-boiled) and her toast (with lots of butter) and poured herself a cup of coffee before sitting down at the kitchen table next to the window to have her breakfast.

While she ate, she read the paper and watched the snow fall

onto the pine trees in the woods past the garden, with Lord Cromwell curled up comfortably in her lap and purring with all his fat, warm strength. It was an early April morning to meet expectations, with the boldest crocuses sitting up straight to spit in the eyes of the snowflakes. In just another few weeks she would be able to start working in her garden again. A few months after that there would be sunflowers, and the deep-green smell of tomato vines, and she'd sit at the kitchen table in the evenings working on new little houses for the fairy garden that she'd started building two summers ago. Maybe she'd add in some toadstools. When she was a little girl, she'd spent a lot of time hoping to spot a fairy in the inhospitable environment of her suburban backyard. After she'd grown up and gotten married, her husband had always rolled his eyes at her being whimsical. Now she was getting old, and she lived alone, and she could have all the toadstools that she liked.

Sometimes, when she was working on her fairy garden, she would think of her best friend. They had had their fairies-and-witches phase together and had tried to make potions out of dirt and berries they'd found in parks and carved magic wands out of twigs long after they both should have grown out of it. Neither of them had ever really grown out of it. Or maybe Caroline had, by now. Sherry hadn't spoken to her in years.

She tried not to think too much about Caroline.

She returned her attention to the *Winesap Herald*. The murder was on the front page, of course. PROMINENT LOCAL REALTOR ARRESTED FOR BUSINESS PARTNER'S MURDER. There was no mention of Sherry's involvement. Sheriff Brown tolerated her helping out with his cases, but he wasn't interested in sharing credit for his arrests with the local librarian. That suited Sherry just fine. She didn't help him with his cases because she wanted fame and glory. She did it because she was good at it.

Sherry took her time with the rest of the paper, paying particular attention to whether or not the advertisement she'd taken out for the upcoming library bake sale had been printed correctly. It had been. She also took note of a cello recital that she'd like to see in Albany. Then, finally and reluctantly, she read the national news. She always read the national news so that she'd be a well-informed person, but she'd noticed more and more recently that she had trouble remembering any of it. The world's affairs seemed very far away, in Winesap.

Once she'd dispensed with the paper and cleaned up after her breakfast, Sherry got washed and dressed and battled fruitlessly with her crop of wild graying cowlicks for a minute or so. Sherry generally thought of authors as powerful and mysterious creatures, like Olympians, but if she ever met one in person, she would feel compelled to speak to her kindly but sternly on the topic of *hair*. There seemed to be a general agreement among authors that unruly hair was a sign of a free-spirited and artistic nature, as if zaniness was extruded through the follicles. *I'm afraid*, Sherry imagined saying to the author (who would have very tidy blonde hair in a chignon and be wearing a cream-colored silk blouse), *that I'm not free-spirited and artistic at all. I'm very cautious and conventional. I clip coupons for laundry detergent out of the monthly mailer, have only ever slept with one man, and never learned how to appreciate poetry. My hair just comes out of my head like this.*

It occurred to her, abruptly, that this was a distinctly *zany* thing to think about. Maybe the authors were onto something.

Sherry gave up on her hair and bundled herself in all her warm winter things. It was just about freezing outside, which wasn't particularly cold, as early April went. Sherry was a sturdy Upstate New Yorker now, firmly removed from her soft and vulnerable Floridian youth, and prided herself on her ability to be scornful about any temperature above zero degrees Fahrenheit. Besides, the sun was out. She passed a few evergreen bushes still clinging on to bright-red berries that stood out like exclamation points against the dark greens, whites, and grays of the landscape. They were the sorts of berries that she and Caroline would definitely have put into their potions when they were little girls. They had a wicked look to them, like something that would poison a princess in a fairy tale. *Snow white, bloodred*, Sherry thought, *and the branches of the trees as black as ebony.* She assumed they were, at least. She'd never known what ebony actually looked like.

A few brave jays and chickadees were shouting salutations or obscenities at each other as she walked across the road and down the long gravel driveway to Alice Murdoch's house. Like Sherry's own driveway, Alice's driveway was snow covered except for a narrow walking path that ran down the left side, and would remain so until she had a guest who needed a place to park. When they'd first met, they'd bonded over the fact that they were two of the only people in town who didn't own a car.

Sherry rang the bell, as usual, and as usual waited for a long time in the screened-in porch for Alice to emerge. The porch was even more cluttered than usual. There were more pairs of skis and snowshoes than Sherry remembered having seen on Friday morning, along with several paper shopping bags from the local grocery store, what looked like an egg incubator, and, inexplicably, a large plastic cat carrier. Alice didn't own a cat. Sherry considered what she might be doing with the carrier. In the sort of book that Sherry felt somewhat embarrassed to admit to reading, Alice would have trapped a boggart in it.

Eventually Alice appeared, her fine blonde hair so full of winter static that it floated in the air between her shoulders and her hat, which was bright blue with a pom-pom on top like something that had been made for a small child. She was already apologizing. "I'm sorry, I just turned on the TV and saw about the murder on the news. Was it you again, Sherry?"

Sherry responded modestly. "It wasn't me, really. I just noticed a thing or two that the detective hadn't quite gotten to yet, and pointed them out to him. He did all of the rest."

Alice nodded, not taken in for a second. Everyone in town knew that Sherry was good at murders. Sherry appreciated the recognition, if not the phrasing. "I *knew* it," Alice said. "I knew it had to be you. Oh, wait a second," she added, and retreated back into her house. She reappeared a moment later with a lumpy little something wrapped in foil that she thrust into Sherry's hands. "Banana bread," she said. "I couldn't sleep, so I got up early to bake it."

Alice wasn't usually the most domestic kind of girl. Generally, she reminded Sherry of a small, damp animal that someone had just found huddled under their front porch and brought inside, despite the animal clearly not understanding how it was supposed to be behaving inside a human home. There was something feral about her, not in the sense that she might lash out, but in the sense that you worried that if you made too much eye contact she might hide under the couch and refuse to come out again. If she was a character in a book, she would be the housemaid who became hysterical when the police spoke to her but calmed down in the soothing presence of Miss Marple. She was the sort of person who normally had the baking done for her by concerned motherly types, rather than doing the baking herself, and the fact that she'd made banana bread to share with Sherry felt somehow as momentous as when a stray cat consented to being petted.

"Thank you," Sherry said, touched. Then she tucked the banana bread into her big quilted bag—it was more than big enough to accommodate her lunch, two paperbacks, and a loaf of banana bread, and *much* more practical than the sort of little purse that she'd almost managed to convince herself that she'd enjoyed carrying when she was younger—and they started to walk down the hill together toward town.

Alice had moved into the ramshackle little house across the road from Sherry's cottage three years earlier, as an even younger, thinner, and more terrified-seeming girl with a few dollars in cash, a giant bruise on her left cheekbone, and a recently revoked driver's license. Sherry hadn't asked any questions. Instead, she'd spent a few weeks bringing Alice casseroles and the local paper folded to the want ads. Soon enough Alice had gotten her job at Alan's antiques store, and they'd been walking into town together almost every morning since. The antiques store opened at ten, but Alice liked to sit in the library in the cozy corner near the door to the locked room that they never used and read before work. Sherry suspected that she didn't particularly enjoy spending too much time at home alone.

They always had nice chats on their morning walks. This morning, they talked about Sherry's latest murder case. It had been a particularly tricky one: the perpetrator, Mr. Wenchel, who was the victim's partner in a real estate firm, had met his victim in an empty house by posing as a potential buyer under an assumed name, and had created an alibi by hiring a man to pretend to be him at the state real estate association's annual dinner. Sherry had only managed to figure out the ruse when she spoke to the other dinner attendees and learned that "Mr. Wenchel" had blundered an extremely basic point of real estate law while chatting with a colleague during the cocktail hour.

They arrived at the library at exactly fifteen minutes before nine, and Sherry unlocked the doors with the specific blend of anticipation and resignation that she always felt in the few quiet minutes before the library opened in the morning. Soon there would be patrons asking for her to find "that book by that lady who was on *Oprah* a few months ago, it had a blue cover, I think?" and old Mr. Agnes getting snippy with Connie the assistant director over an interloper in his favorite chair, and children smacking each other over the head with the Little Golden Books. Soon there would be a prolonged hunt for a collection of local maps from the late eighteenth century, and little girls all bright-eyed over their newfound power to use their very first library cards to check out the complete works of Louisa May Alcott, and long meetings about an upcoming series of evening performances by local folk musicians, and the particular pleasure that came of turning the circulation desk over to her staffer Beth in order to take a peaceful twenty minutes to drink hot plastic-scented tea from a thermos and eat an egg salad sandwich. Soon there would be all those things, but for now there was peace and quiet, and the smell of old paper and ink, and the hum and click as the fluorescent lights came on one after another and the library woke up for another deliciously monotonous Friday.

Alice retreated into her favorite nook by the nonfiction section to read—she was in the middle of a self-improvement phase at the moment, which made Sherry miss the endless Jodi Picoult of last winter—and Sherry finished making her rounds to turn on the lights and make sure that no one had left anything disgusting in the reading room. Then she went to the circulation desk just in time to answer the first phone call of the morning.

The day went on mostly as usual, with a bit of additional chaos introduced by a new library page who had mis-shelved all of last month's periodicals into the wrong parts of the back volume section. Then, finally, it was time for lunch and the relative peace of the sheltered area behind the circulation desk where Sherry was hidden from view by the corkboards where she posted announcements. She had just taken her first bite of egg salad sandwich when she heard someone calling her name. "Sherry! Sherry, are you back there?"

Sherry sighed. She considered hiding and pretending that she wasn't there until whoever it was gave up and left. Then it registered to her that library patrons usually called her *Miss Pinkwhistle*, and that this voice seemed both very familiar and more distraught in tone than even the most melodramatic patrons typically managed to work themselves up to over a library fine. It was unusual enough to pique her curiosity, and when it came to satisfying her curiosity, Sherry was as unable to resist temptation as a woman on a diet in a cupcake shop. She stood up and poked her head around the bulletin board, which today was advertising the bake sale and the Winesap

Dreams of Spring Folk Festival, and saw Charlotte Jacobs standing there. Charlotte was a tall, glamorous Black woman in her mid-thirties who usually looked to Sherry as if she was ready to be photographed by a fashion magazine. Today she looked more like she was ready to be photographed by *Time* magazine as one of the miserable victims of some terrible calamity. Sherry blinked. Whatever was going on, it was definitely worth setting down her egg salad and giving the crisis her undivided attention.

Charlotte had moved to town about two years earlier, and ever since her arrival, she and Sherry had been doing an uncomfortable dance of not being quite sure whether or not they were friends. A step forward and a step back, an invitation to coffee and a long span of silence. Certainly, on the surface they had very little in common. Charlotte had an art history degree from a famous liberal arts college, a mother whom, Sherry had heard, people who were familiar with modern art would have heard of, and a large collection of interesting jewelry that had been handmade for her by her artistic friends in New York. Sherry was a sixty-three-year-old woman who'd taken a decade to get her degree in library science from a third-rate public university, had a mother whom members of the Polish community center in Clearwater, Florida, might have heard of, and cut her own hair in the kitchen sink.

When Charlotte had first come to town, she'd immediately gotten a library card, and at first she'd looked right through Sherry as if she was one of the card catalogs. But then time had passed, and they'd found themselves at the same event at least once a month—it wasn't as if there was such a glut of arts and culture in Winesap, New York, that it would be possible for the library director and the manager of the town's sole art gallery to *avoid* each other—and eventually Sherry'd worked up the courage to strike up a conversation with Charlotte about the latest book that she'd checked out. Charlotte had loved it, and Sherry had had mixed feelings, but just the fact that they'd both read it and formed an *opinion* about it had been enough for them to form the kind of tentative bond based on shared interests that was inevitable in a town with so few prospective fellow travelers. Not quite to the level of having each other over for lunch yet, but friendly enough that Sherry always received a personal invitation when something interesting was happening at the gallery.

Charlotte clearly wasn't here to talk about a sound installation right now. She looked harried. Her clothes were a little rumpled, and her eyes were puffy. "Sherry," she said, "could you come over to the gallery right now?"

"Of course," Sherry said, moved by how shaken Charlotte looked. Then rationality kicked in. "But—why, exactly?"

"It's John," Charlotte said, and then burst into tears.

"Oh, no," Sherry said—it was the sort of thing that she always seemed to say when people cried: somehow it took her by surprise every time—and emerged from behind the bulletin board to dig some tissues from her purse. She thrust them in Charlotte's direction, vaguely conscious of the fact that her appearance tended to trick people into thinking that she was being very kind and motherly when internally she was wondering if the expression on her face looked appropriately gentle and concerned. She wondered whether saying "there, there," was what she should be doing, or if that was just something that authors put into the dialogue to show that someone was being comforting, like when they wrote "harrumph!" to indicate scoffing. She spent half a second in silent contemplation of whether any of the world's pasty and socially maladjusted bookworms had ever said the word *harrumph!* aloud to express indignation. It seemed inevitable that at least one poor soul had.

Charlotte had taken a tissue and was scrubbing at her eyes. Sherry cleared her throat. "John? Is he all right?" John was Charlotte's husband. Her much older, self-obsessed, and extremely pompous husband. Sherry wouldn't be particularly surprised to hear that he'd been rushed to the hospital for emergency open-heart surgery after someone expressed a contrarian stance about the works of Damien Hirst in his presence.

Charlotte's whole body shuddered. "He's *dead*," she said.

An odd feeling passed through Sherry's chest. Maybe it was guilt for having had uncharitable thoughts about a dead man. Maybe it was unease with her own lack of sadness. John had always struck Sherry as an unpleasant person who didn't treat his beautiful young wife with enough appreciation or kindness. Maybe, though, what was making her uneasy was the fact that as soon as she'd heard that he was dead she'd thought of *murder*. It didn't seem quite right that she'd have that thought first, in a nice little town like Winesap, New York. She knew that she had to ask the appropriate question, though. "Oh, no, I'm so sorry. Was he sick?"

Charlotte shook her head and took a deep, wobbly breath. "Someone—*stabbed* him," she said, and incredulity flitted across her face before the curtain of shock dropped down again. "And the police are there, and they're asking questions like they think *I* did it, and I called my friend who's a lawyer and she's driving up from the city but she won't be here for five hours, and I know that *you* know about"—she stumbled over the word as if it was foreign to her—"*murders,* so I thought that maybe—"

"Of course I'll come," Sherry said. "I'll come with you. Let me just—" She darted off to tell Connie that she would be stepping out for half an hour to deal with an emergency. Then she started to stuff herself back into her winter coat and gloves, trying not to think too deeply about the fact that she was on her way to get herself involved in her second murder in under two weeks.

TWO

It was always strange to be in a room that conspicuously lacked a dead body.

Most rooms didn't have any dead bodies in them, obviously. Even most of the rooms that *Sherry* spent time in usually weren't strewn with corpses. Most rooms, though, didn't feel as if every person in them was revolving around a spot where a dead person had just been. The spot was now occupied by a dark stain, and the stain dragged all the attention in the room toward itself like an exhausted child.

The usual crowd was all there, the people from the state crime lab bustling around while the local beat officers tried to look useful. Sheriff Brown just looked tired. Too tired even, it seemed, to make a show of wanting Sherry to get away from the crime scene. A while ago he'd taken to referring to her as the sheriff's office's "researcher and consultant," and at this point even the people from the state knew her. The photographer gave her a friendly wave. Sherry waved discreetly back, then looked around the gallery to try to get a sense of what might have happened in it.

The studio, at the moment, looked exactly like a crime scene. There were canvases strewn across the room as if someone had been rifling through them in search of something specific. Things had been knocked off the table: a cup of paint-brushes had spewed its contents across a frayed Persian rug. A few paintings had been completely shredded, as if the un-known searcher had at one point taken out their fury on the canvases. The chaos didn't do much to distract from that stain. "Charlotte," Sherry said, "do you notice anything missing? Any particular paintings?"

"I don't know," Charlotte said. Her eyes moved around the room like a camera panning. "I can't tell. Everything is—"

"It's all right," Sherry said quickly. "You can— I'm sure that there will be plenty of time for you to take an inventory, or—is there an assistant?"

Charlotte was already shaking her head. "Just me," she said, and then her eyes welled up. Sherry looked away. She always thought that there was something indecent about staring at someone while they tried not to cry.

She decided to give Charlotte a moment to collect herself and wandered sidelong in the direction of Sheriff Brown. He, absurdly, began a sidelong shuffle of his own when he noticed her, as if he wanted to escape her without her noticing that he was trying to escape. They rotated around the stain in the center of the room like they were performing some macabre religious rite. Sherry made a tactical decision and came to a stop to pretend to peer at one of the canvases that had been flung to the floor, which forced Sheriff Brown to continue his rotation in her direction until he couldn't avoid acknowledg-ing her. "Sherry," he said.

"Peter," she said back. She called him *Peter* out loud, and *Sheriff Brown* in her head, because she appreciated the story-book quality of an actual *sheriff* being someone with whom she sometimes worked to solve mysteries. His coworkers, she thought, ought to be Mortimer Mouse the Mortician and Tommy Turtle the Crime Scene Technician. She had to call Sheriff Brown *Peter* out loud partly because they'd known each other for long enough that it would seem strange if she didn't, and partly because if she called him *Sheriff Brown* she wouldn't be able to stop imagining him with furry ears and a tail and an oversized ten-gallon hat.

She and Peter (his name would be Peter if he was a storybook mouse, too: Peter Brown, Sheriff of Mousington) eyed each other for a long and uncomfortable moment. He couldn't, she knew, be the first to ask *her* a question: it would be a way of admitting that he had, at some point over the past few years, lost control over the pursuit of justice in Winesap, New York, and handed the investigative remote control over to an aging librarian who had changed the channel to PBS to watch the latest episode of *Poirot*. The metaphor had gotten away from Sherry. She wondered whether Peter ever imagined *her* as a storybook animal. If he did, she would probably be a fat old badger in a bonnet.

"I wonder," she heard herself saying, "why they didn't take anything from the gallery."

"Mm?" said Sheriff Brown.

Sherry felt herself retreating into a role. Miss Marple: pink and fluffy and unthreatening. "Oh," she said, her eyes wide. "I came for the opening last week and heard all about the paintings in the front gallery, and a few of them are by Charlotte's *city* friends, you know, and some of them are quite *well-known*, so the paintings are *very* expensive. One of them is on loan to the gallery, and Charlotte said that she was a bit worried about having it here because they don't have any security to speak of, because who would hire security in *Winesap*? But

I noticed, as I was coming in, that all of the paintings from the opening were still there, and only some of John's paintings are missing. John's paintings"—she dramatically lowered her voice—"*aren't worth very much at all.*"

She stepped back slightly to observe how Sheriff Brown had taken that. He looked annoyed, which was a satisfying response. Sheriff Brown always looked annoyed when he thought that she'd done a good bit of deducing. Sherry strongly suspected that Sheriff Brown found her talent for solving murders unendurably *zany.* The way that Sheriff Brown looked at her when she identified the perpetrator of a homicide based on a long, quiet conversation over tea and cookies she'd had with the murderer's mother reminded her of the way that her ex-husband had looked at her when he noticed her enjoying a nice Regency romance novel, as if he was embarrassed just to see her engaging in something so feminine and self-indulgent. Sherry was aware of the fact that anything she did, when done by her, became the sort of thing that matronly ladies who enjoyed Regency romances did. Men, in Sherry's experience, despised anything relating to matronly ladies who enjoyed Regency romances with a depth of feeling that she privately found a bit silly of them. What was the real harm, after all, in a woman quietly enjoying herself? They ought to feel grateful that the matronly ladies were peacefully reading novels instead of forming guerrilla organizations for throwing paint on antique cars and disrupting professional football games.

"So you think it was personal, then," Sheriff Brown said. He sounded resigned. "Not a robbery gone wrong." *It's never a robbery gone wrong in Winesap,* Sherry thought. Then she thought, *Isn't it strange that—*

The thought darted through Sherry's mind like a mouse.

She tried to look at it more carefully, but it had already disappeared into a hole in a baseboard.

"Exactly," Sherry said, a moment too late. Then she added, reflectively, "Or a robber who doesn't know very much about modern art. I don't imagine that the very well-informed art robbers would *come* to Winesap, would they?"

"Probably not," said Sheriff Brown, sounding slightly cheered now. "They'd probably stay in *the city*." Sheriff Brown always pronounced the words *the city* as if he were saying *venereal disease*. He, like many citizens of Winesap, thought of New York City as a place populated entirely by people who were all simultaneously wealthy snobs and desperate knife-wielding purse snatchers. *Which is ironic, considering that the murder rate in Winesap is—*

Into the hole in the baseboard again. Maybe Sherry was going senile. She was too young for it, she thought, but probably everyone who'd ever gone senile thought the same thing.

"So it *might* still be a robbery," Sheriff Brown said, with what Sherry thought was somewhat touching optimism. Poor Peter. All he wanted were some nice, normal, uncomplicated criminals to arrest. The man wilted from lack of petty larceny.

"It might," Sherry said agreeably, and then asked, "Do you have a cause of death?" She always felt very intelligent and professional when she asked that sort of question.

Sheriff Brown gave a brief, unattractive grimace. "No," he said, which could mean either *No, we don't have a cause of death* or *No, I will not tell a Regency-romance-reading senior citizen who doesn't even work for the sheriff's department what the cause of death is.*

"Oh," Sherry said, which she was fairly sure that Sheriff Brown knew meant, *There's no use in your being coy: you know that I'll find out eventually.* Then they engaged in a long moment of sustained, challenging eye contact before Sherry was struck by an overwhelming urge to giggle, mumbled something about, "Poor Charlotte, I think that I should . . ." and drifted off in Charlotte's general direction.

Once she got there, unfortunately, she realized that she still hadn't learned what the correct thing to say or do was for a person at that particular stage of grief. Charlotte was no longer crying—she'd moved on to looking quietly and horribly stunned—so tissues were no longer needed, but there wasn't time to bake her a casserole. Sherry took a moment to engage in something akin to prayer. *What would Miss Marple do?* she thought. Then the answer came to her. "Charlotte," she said, her voice very soft. "Why don't we go up to your apartment, and I'll fix you a nice cup of tea, and you can make any phone calls that you need to make." The bit about the phone calls probably wouldn't have been in a Miss Marple story. Sherry was improvising.

Charlotte looked at her for a moment as if she'd never seen Sherry before in her life. Then she nodded. "Thank you," she said. "It's just—this way." She gestured toward the other room, where a door marked PRIVATE led to the stairway to Charlotte and her now late husband's apartment.

Sherry had been in Charlotte's apartment once before, for a cocktail party. She'd gotten a little tipsy and talked very animatedly about fashionable novels with Charlotte's fashionable friends, and not taken note of the décor. She took note now. There were lots of beautiful rugs and vases and interesting African sculptures, oddly juxtaposed with large prints of harshly lit photographs of very young-looking women's very cold-looking naked bodies. Sherry recognized the style of the photographs. There had been an exhibition of them at the gallery a year ago, and Sherry had noticed Charlotte's eyes sliding off them in the same way that Sherry tried to politely look away from other women in changing rooms. Not Charlotte's choice, Sherry thought, to put these particular pictures on her walls.

Sherry herded Charlotte to one of the wingback chairs in the living room before heading into the kitchen to look for a teakettle. She found one on the back of the stove, filled it, and put it on. She heard Charlotte say, "Mom?" and then start to cry. She was making those phone calls, then. Sherry took her time in the kitchen, waiting for the water to boil and then for the tea to steep. She found milk and sugar and containers for them, and then plates and some cookies. Oreos. The Oreos felt somehow out of place in this particular scene, like a boom mike drifting into the shot. She assembled everything onto a tray and carried it into the next room, where Charlotte was sitting quietly in her chair again, gazing into some spot between her face and the wall.

"Tea," Sherry said, pointlessly. Charlotte could see perfectly well that it was *tea*. She was grieving, not recovering from a traumatic brain injury. Sherry set the tray onto an extremely modern glass-and-metal coffee table. The table looked almost as ill at ease in the room as the naked-women photographs and Sherry.

"He was an asshole," Charlotte said. "That's what my mother just said. And it's *true*, he *was* an asshole. He was cheating on me, back in the city. With his ex-wife. And spending money we didn't have. We had to sell our apartment. That's why I agreed to move out here to the middle of nowhere, to make a fresh start away from all of that temptation.

He was *awful*, sometimes, but I still—" She started to well up again.

"Oh," Sherry said, and sat down on the low sofa on the other side of the coffee table, barely taking a moment to contemplate the fact that she would almost certainly struggle to get up again. "I always thought he seemed as if he'd married up. You'd like to think that they could be more appreciative." By *they*, Sherry meant *men*. "You think that John might have been cheating on you now? Or taking on debt?" These might, she realized belatedly, be deeply inappropriate questions to ask a freshly bereaved young woman. On the other hand, Charlotte had brought it up first. Sherry poured tea. It was something to do.

Charlotte took the mug that Sherry offered her, cradling it in her hands as if she'd just come in from the snow and was trying to warm herself up. "I don't know," she said. Her voice was steady. "It's possible. Do you think that's what the police are thinking? That I murdered him because of the cheating? That I—*killed him in a jealous rage*, or something like that, or . . . for the insurance money? I don't know if he even *had* life insurance." A few minutes ago, she'd looked lost, stunned. Now she looked half nervous and half like she wanted to laugh. It was fortunate, Sherry thought, that Sheriff Brown wasn't in the room.

"I don't know," Sherry said honestly. "They might. They always look at the spouse first. I assume that he doesn't conveniently have a special will that leaves everything to an animal shelter? When was the last time you saw him alive?" Then she winced. "I'm sorry. I'm not being very comforting, am I?"

"Not really," Charlotte said. "I don't know if he even had a will. We never talked about it. Oh, God, we never talked about *anything* like that. I don't even know if he wanted to be buried or cremated."

"Well, I don't think that he'll care either way now," Sherry said briskly, and then nearly slapped a hand over her mouth.

Charlotte was staring at her. "You're really not how I thought you were," she said, after a pause so long that Sherry could practically hear it creaking.

"I'm sorry," Sherry said, truly contrite. She was sometimes shocked by herself, too. She spent so much time pretending to be a nice old lady from a book that her actual, somewhat strange and ghoulish personality tended to take her by surprise.

"No," Charlotte said, "I don't mind." Then she very deliberately selected an Oreo from the plate and ate the whole thing in one enormous bite.

Neither of them spoke. Charlotte chewed and swallowed. Then she said, "Do you think I'm a monster?"

"I don't think so," Sherry said. "Unless you killed your husband, which I don't think you did." Not that she had a reason to trust Charlotte, exactly. It was just that Sherry was pretty sure that Charlotte was much too intelligent and modern a woman to go to the risk of murdering her husband for cheating on her when she could easily divorce him instead. However much Charlotte was about to inherit, Sherry highly doubted it would be worth killing a man for, even if it was a man as obnoxious as John had been.

"Thank you," Charlotte said, with what sounded like complete sincerity, "for not thinking that I murdered my husband."

Their eyes met, and the entire conversation suddenly struck Sherry as so completely surreal that it made her giggle. For half an instant she was utterly horrified by herself, and then it registered that Charlotte was giggling, too. Sherry started giggling harder. They kept on like that for a while, each of them setting the other one off again whenever they started to calm down a little. Charlotte was the first to sober and clear her throat. "If the police were here, they probably would have arrested me right away for that," she said. "It's not funny, I know it's not. It just—it feels like I was cast in a bad movie without knowing it."

"Lucky that the police aren't here, then," Sherry said. "I don't think that they train them to be sensitive about the different ways that people grieve. Not in Winesap, at least." Sherry didn't know if *she* was sensitive about things like that, exactly. It was more that she could watch someone crying or laughing or rocking back and forth in a corner and feel curiosity instead of either suspicion or sympathy.

"You're better than the police," Charlotte said, with so much confidence that Sherry felt intimidated by the highly accomplished detective Charlotte was speaking to. "You'll help, won't you? With finding out who did it."

"Of course I will." Sherry took a sip of her tea, suddenly feeling too aware of the sound of her own voice. She always felt a little silly when she had to say very detective-y things out loud. Every phrase always sounded perfectly professional in her head but turned into lines from a very badly written TV show between the time they left her mouth and the time they hit her ears. It helped if she imagined herself as one of her favorite fictional detectives, none of whom would ever feel bashful about their detective-ing. She imagined herself with an enormous mustache, for self-confidence. "You'll have to be completely honest with me, you know. Sometimes people hide things because they're embarrassed or afraid that I'll tattle on them to the police, and I end up running around in circles for no real reason."

"Is *tattle* the professional term?" Charlotte asked, and then gave a very elegant little shrug. Sherry had never been to France, or even met a French person, but she'd always imagined the French people in books shrugging like Charlotte did. "I think you'd have to be an idiot to be more worried about local gossip than being arrested for a murder. I'm not an idiot."

"You're definitely not," Sherry said. "You're a very intelligent woman."

For a fraction of a second, Charlotte's face took on the expression of a precocious little girl who'd just been praised by a teacher. Then the look vanished and she gave another of those shrugs. "I'll cooperate," she said. "I'll be honest. But I don't know if I'll have much to tell you. I have no idea who could possibly want to kill John."

"You do, though," Sherry said. "At least, you very likely do, in my experience. You just haven't realized that you know it yet." She set down her teacup. "I should leave. Give you your privacy."

"Please don't," Charlotte said in a rush. "My mom won't be able to get here until tomorrow morning, and none of my friends will be here for hours. Just— God, I'm sorry, have you even eaten lunch?"

In all the excitement Sherry had completely forgotten about her egg salad sandwich. Now that she'd been reminded, she felt desperately hungry. "No," she admitted. "I'd just unwrapped my sandwich when you came into the library."

"Oh, I'm so sorry," Charlotte said, and looked lost again for a moment before she brightened. "Do you like onigiri?"

"I don't know what that is," Sherry said. "But I'm sure that I love it."

Charlotte smiled at her and went into the kitchen, then emerged again with a platter of food and a garnish of explanation, a soft flow of chatter about how she'd made these for lunch this morning, how her first roommate in New York had been from Japan and taught her how to cook, and how her mom had never gotten over Charlotte having been willing to learn to cook from a near stranger from a foreign country and not from her own mother. "She wasn't a stranger, though," Charlotte said. "She was my friend. We're still friends." She took a bite of one of the rice balls. Then she started to cry again.

Sherry kept her company for another hour or so. Charlotte put on some music, some Spanish guitar by a man whom, she said, she had met in a little bar in the West Village a few years ago. Charlotte was the sort of woman who had an interesting story to explain every part of herself. It made Sherry feel self-conscious about her own self, her own life, which was mostly all secondhand: experiences she'd had only through novels, places she'd seen on television, pieces of art she'd found at the Goodwill.

"You should go," Charlotte said. "I've kept you for too long."

"If you're sure," Sherry said, though her long absence *was* at this point probably severely straining the patience of the library staff. "Do you have anything to distract yourself with?"

Charlotte nodded. "I think I'll paint my nails," she said. "I usually do them every Friday. I know it sounds silly, but it always feels sort of . . . I don't know. *Meditative.*" Then she winced. "God, now I'm thinking about whether or not anything I do other than lying on the couch crying will make me look like an evil witch who just murdered her husband for the insurance money."

"Wear something unflattering while you paint them," Sherry suggested. "Like flannel pajamas. And keep drinking tea from a mug." If Charlotte was a glamorous murderess on *Columbo*, she would wear a marabou robe and probably not even own a mug. Also, she wouldn't paint her own nails. Sherry felt oddly guilty for having assumed that Charlotte must have paid someone a fortune to make her look so lovely all the time, when it seemed that she was actually just an artistic young woman with extremely steady hands. "*Don't*, under any circumstances, buy a bottle of champagne."

For a moment Charlotte appeared to be taking this all in as if it were legal advice. Then she huffed out a small laugh and shook her head. "Or a pink convertible."

They made eye contact, and Sherry felt suddenly as if she and Charlotte had been regularly having tea and Oreos under the watchful gaze of the poor, cold, naked women on the walls for years, as if Charlotte had been a very dear friend of hers all along. "I'll find out who did it," she said, with a confidence that seemed to come from outside herself. "And you'll be able to drink all of the champagne that you like without anyone to stop you." Then she showed herself out and hurried back to the library, where for a few precious hours she would be much too busy to chase any strange, unsettled thoughts about how neatly the recent events of her life reflected clichés that she had watched in rerun a dozen times before.

THREE

For the rest of the afternoon, Sherry attempted to behave herself. This meant that she spent several hours helping patrons with their requests, and no time at all investigating homicides. She always felt a bit guilty for allowing the hard-working taxpayers of Winesap, New York, to subsidize her on-the-clock Sherlock Holmesing. She felt a bit less guilty when one of the pages came to her to inform her that someone had thrown up on the floor of the restroom. At that point she thought that she did more than enough work on behalf of the public, really, and the fact that she wasn't charging them extra for ridding their town of murderers along with helping them with their school assignment about the pyramids was very gracious of her.

Sherry had heard the phrase "The end of the day couldn't come soon enough." It didn't. By the end of the day, she didn't have nearly enough energy left in her to walk home. Fortunately, she didn't have to. It was Friday, and every Friday evening Sherry met her friend Janine at the Temperance Tea Shop on Main Street for their traditional Tea and Gossip. At the moment, Sherry was running late. She ought to just send Janine a quick—

The thought fled her head. She tried to grab hold of it, but it was gone, and a moment later she forgot that she'd had it at all.

The ever-prompt Janine was already seated at their usual table, presiding over two steaming pots of tea and a tiered tray full of tea sandwiches and cakes and scones with the associated accoutrements. Sherry felt herself relax. There was something so wonderfully comforting about a whole tiered tray full of miniature sandwiches and petit fours like little pink and brown birthday presents. It was food that defied anxiety. You were never presented with a tray full of tiny cakes in the face of catastrophe. An elaborate afternoon tea was the emotional antithesis to the canned soups of natural disasters or casseroles of recent bereavement.

Janine, for her part, looked as distant from the grim realities of a homicide investigation as the jam and clotted cream. She was wearing a pair of absolutely enormous red earrings and a very soft-looking cream-colored sweater that Sherry couldn't imagine wearing without immediately covering it in coffee or tomato sauce.

For a moment Sherry found herself wanting to laugh at Janine's outfit, like it was somehow comically out of style. In the next moment she was left feeling baffled by herself. Janine had always been much more stylish than Sherry, and Sherry really had no standing at all to find her clothing choices humorous. Sherry had no standing to critique Janine in general, when Janine was a complete paragon in most ways that mattered. She was the sort of person who demanded adverbs: she never walked when she could stride briskly, and Sherry had never known her to whisper when she could instead confidently declare. Though she was a very kind and generous person, Janine had the sort of naturally pinched and skeptical face that looked as if she would tolerate absolutely no homicidal nonsense. In truth, she had the face of the librarian who hushed boisterous children in old movies, while Sherry herself had the face of the nanny who would give the British children currant buns in one of those old books about boarding schools.

Sherry had barely taken her seat before Janine started to look even more pinched than usual. "Oh, no," Janine said. "Who's been murdered this time?"

Sherry felt a peculiar sinking sensation in her chest. "Oh, no," she said, echoing Janine. "It's terrible, isn't it?"

Their eyes met. There was something strange in Janine's expression. "It is," she said. "Sherry, there's something terrible—"

She stopped. Smiled. Her expression had turned as smooth as an eight ball. "Why don't you tell me about your latest case, Sherry?" she asked, and then poured Sherry a cup of tea and gestured invitingly at the food.

Sherry couldn't remember what they'd just been talking about. Never mind, then. She took a sandwich. "It was John," she said. "Charlotte's husband."

She explained everything that she'd learned, while Janine drank her tea and listened attentively. Janine worked as a counselor and always listened attentively. She was also an extremely practical person who read mostly *New York Times*–bestselling nonfiction and the occasional Jean M. Auel as a treat, making her an excellent sounding board for murder investigations who only *very rarely* went off on a flight of fancy about how some woman's husband probably had another woman trapped in a secret room in the basement or buried under the peonies in the backyard. She ate a scone with lots of jam and cream. Then she said, "Do you think that there's a possible financial motive?"

"I don't know," Sherry said. "It's possible. Even if he didn't have very much money, he was the sort of guy who liked to give everyone he met the impression that he did." She considered that while she ate a petit four. "Imagine killing someone for his money and then realizing that he didn't have any money for you to take."

"I can't imagine killing someone for his money to begin with," Janine said. "Or killing someone for any reason."

"Hm," Sherry said noncommittally. She could easily imagine killing someone for any reason. She contemplated murder all the time.

"There's always sex," said Janine.

"Hm?" said Sherry, who was selecting her next treat from the tray. She decided on a salmon sandwich. "What about sex?" Sherry wasn't a prude, exactly, but she always found the mention of sex somewhat jarring out of its proper context.

"As a motive," Janine said. "You said that there's been infidelity in the past. People can do strange things when they're jealous. Or in love."

"In love with John Jacobs?" Sherry asked, her eyebrows climbing upward. "Mad with jealousy over *John Jacobs*?"

She could tell that Janine was trying not to smile. "*Sherry,*" she said, admonishingly. "I'm sure that . . . many women have been wildly in love with John Jacobs. And he's—he *was*— younger than us."

"I didn't say that he was *old,*" Sherry said, and started spreading clotted cream onto a scone. "A head of wilted iceberg lettuce isn't as old as us, either."

Now Janine really did laugh, and then looked guilty about it. "*Sherry*," she said. "You're *horrible*." Janine was one of the only people in the world who knew that Sherry was horrible. "The man was killed this morning and you're comparing him to wilted lettuce."

"I'm sorry," Sherry said. The words were a bit muffled. Her mouth was as full of scone as her heart was of repentance. She swallowed. "I didn't like John, but he didn't deserve to be murdered."

"John was a bit . . . difficult," Janine conceded. "He struck me as someone who needed a lot of external validation to feel secure."

Sherry drank some tea. "His mother didn't love him enough, and that's why he cheated on his wife?"

Janine didn't even bother responding to that. "I think that the destroyed paintings are very suggestive, don't you?"

Sherry nodded. "It was personal. Someone was angry with him."

"I thought that, too," Janine said. "But it could also be more specific. The anger could be partly directed at the paintings themselves. Maybe someone who resented John's work, or who had reason to want to destroy certain pieces. What if, say, the person responsible was jealous, and destroyed paintings of other women?"

"You mean Charlotte," Sherry said. "I really don't think that she would." She frowned then, thinking. "I think I need to figure out which paintings were taken or destroyed before I look into anything else. If they were nothing but bowls of fruit and sailboats, then at least I'll know that it was just wanton destruction and be able to start looking somewhere else for clues." Then, satisfied with her decision, she ate a chocolate petit four and asked Janine how the poetry class she'd been auditing was going.

The next day was Saturday, which felt like something of a blessing. Saturday was always a busy day at the library, and at the moment Sherry welcomed busyness. She'd found that after she'd first started on a new murder investigation, a day of hard work helped her to digest all the fresh details like a brisk walk after a heavy meal.

This particular Saturday was a rainy one, so the library was even busier than usual, crowded with damp, furious children and their beleaguered parents competing for space with students and retirees. Everything was louder than it should be, and damper than Sherry would like it to be, and the whole place smelled distressingly like wet dog despite the fact that dogs weren't allowed in the library. The sense of discontent was only deepened by one of the staff reporting to Sherry that someone had taken advantage of the cheap lock on the back door and broken into the library the night before. Nothing had been taken, and it wasn't even the first time that it had happened—the creaky, possibly haunted old library building was an enticing place for bored teenagers to explore with flashlights in the middle of the night—but it was the sort of thing that made Sherry uneasy. She didn't like it when crimes happened in her vicinity that she wasn't personally involved with solving, and the lack of evidence made the Mystery of the Broken Lock a case that was as uncrackable as it was boring.

It was a relief to come to the end of the day, kindly but sternly herd out the last straggling patron, and put the library to bed for the night. She was tired. As she, Connie the assistant director, and an eager teenage page finished tidying everything away, she cast a longing look at her favorite spot in the whole library, with the squashy red velvet armchair and old lamp with the stained-glass shade tucked into it. The corner was at the far end of the nonfiction section, near the door to the room that they never used, so that barely any traffic went past it. Sherry always thought that it would be the perfect place to disappear into a novel for a few hours. Not that Sherry ever had time to sit down and read a novel when she was at the library, but just looking at that chair and imagining herself in it made her feel a bit more rested.

Sherry bid a silent goodbye to the wonderful corner, finished locking up, and walked toward Main Street, her head down against the wind and sleet. It felt as if the elements had set themselves against Sherry personally, slapping at her face and trying to drag her umbrella from her hands. Then the onslaught abruptly eased. She looked up, startled, into the smiling face, enormous gray mustache, and even more enormous umbrella of Alan Thompson. "Need a lift?"

Alan, absurdly, was Sherry's . . . she wasn't sure, really. The word *boyfriend* was too ridiculous, and *lover* would be inaccurate. *Gentleman friend*, maybe. Alan didn't seem to mind that she was keeping things to the occasional brief kiss after many months of dating. He bought her dinner once a week, and they drank wine and talked about books together, and she never once had to pick up his socks. It was perfect. And here he was now, heroically saving her from the quarter-mile walk to Marino's in the sleet. That was the sort of man Alan was. You could tell from the mustache. It was, Sherry always thought, the kindest mustache she had ever seen.

"But we're so close," Sherry said, even as she followed him

to his Volvo and waited for him to open the door for her before she clambered inside. It was toasty warm and perfectly cozy in the car, with the sleet tapping against the windshield and classical music playing on the radio. She felt as coddled and pampered as the people in movies looked when they wore thick white bathrobes in hotel rooms.

"Everywhere is far away when it's cold and raining," Alan said comfortably. "How was your day?"

Sherry told him all about it. He told her about his day right back. Alan was a retired lawyer who owned and managed the little antiques store on Main Street. Sherry found him wildly sophisticated, which she was aware only went to show how unsophisticated she was. She didn't mind. He was the first person she'd ever met who'd spent more than three days in Paris. He knew words to describe wine other than *red* or *white*, and he could talk about the sorts of very *Important* new books she never read, even though she knew that secretly he'd rather read a good Western. He was the sort of man who loved hot dogs and Louis L'Amour, but dutifully had his spinach salad and David Foster Wallace because the proper authorities had informed him that both were good for him. Altogether, Alan was the human equivalent of a subscription to the *New Yorker*. Her thinking that would mortify poor Alan, of course. He wasn't a snob; he was the sort of earnest, kindhearted, well-to-do liberal who seemed to truly feel terrible about all his money.

At dinner Sherry drank almost half a bottle of wine and smiled fondly at him as he earnestly attempted to solve her latest case. She'd told him all about it over the appetizers, and now he was working over the details in the same careful, lawyerly way that he'd lifted the flesh from the bones of the rainbow trout special he'd ordered for his entrée. "I know that you don't like the idea," he said finally, "but Occam's razor would certainly suggest that the wife did it."

She liked how he talked. He would have been one of the dweebs in high school, but he'd stayed in shape, kept most of his hair, and wore suit jackets with patches on the elbows, and had thereby managed at the age of sixty-five to achieve *distinguished*. The rules worked differently for women. A young girl had recently called Sherry *adorable*, and Sherry had decided to take it as a compliment. Maybe she *was* adorable. She'd recently seen a segment on the evening news about some panda bears at the Boston Zoo that had featured one of them rolling placidly down a gentle slope. It had been *extremely* adorable. There could be worse things in life than to resemble that panda bear. "I don't make up my mind about my cases ahead of time," she said loftily. "But you're right. I don't think Charlotte did it."

"But no one ever does, do they?" he asked. "No one ever thinks that their friend could have possibly done it. That's why we should look at the facts. *Cui bono?* In this case, it's almost certainly the spouse."

"If there's much to inherit," Sherry countered. "If it's nothing but debts, won't she be worse off with him gone?"

"Not if he was digging them deeper into a hole," Alan said. "When someone dies in debt, the debts are generally paid out of the deceased's estate. She'll take what remains and be able to start over wherever and however she wants. She's young enough that she'll be able to get away pretty cleanly."

"But why not just get a *divorce*, then?" Sherry asked. "That's the ridiculous part. This isn't 1865, and she isn't even religious. Yesterday she was telling me about all kinds of things she's done that her mother doesn't approve of, which rules out family pressure to stay married. If she didn't want to be married anymore, why not divorce him?"

Alan frowned. "I don't know," he said. "But I don't think many people commit murder after they've sat down and done a cost-benefit analysis. It might have been impulsive. In a moment of anger. Or she might have been drunk, even."

"I might believe that about a man," Sherry returned immediately. "Women don't usually drink too many beers and then beat their spouses to death for buying the wrong kind of cornflakes."

Alan blinked. "Men don't *usually* do that, either," he said mildly. "It's been years since the last time I drunkenly clobbered a lady to death over the cornflakes."

She obliged him with a snort, then moodily prodded at her remaining pile of pasta puttanesca. "If it *wasn't* Charlotte, then who are our suspects? Janine and I both think it must have been personal, but that doesn't narrow things down very much. He was the sort of man who probably made enemies easily. A former business partner, maybe?" She sighed.

Alan took a sip of his wine, considering. "When someone is murdered," he said, "I think that the police look at the spouse first. But *then* they start wondering about a lover. Could that be it? A scorned mistress or jealous husband might have motive to murder."

Sherry sat up straighter. "You're right," she said. "Charlotte *did* say that he'd cheated before." She took a sip of her own wine, feeling significantly cheered up by the prospect of a promising angle to pursue that *wasn't* Charlotte. "I should start looking into where he might have had the opportunity to meet young women." Then she smiled, her brain working faster. "Where he had the opportunity to *paint* young women."

Alan raised his eyebrows. "To paint them?"

She nodded and reached triumphantly for the dessert menu. "Those paintings that were destroyed," she said. "They weren't just *slashed*, like you might imagine. They were *destroyed*. Shredded so badly that you couldn't even tell what the subjects were." All the options looked delicious. "Would you like to split the tiramisu?"

"I'll have a bite," Alan said. "What about the paintings?"

"Oh, good," Sherry said, and gestured for the waiter to order her dessert.

"The paintings?" Alan prompted her once the waiter had left.

"The paintings?" Sherry repeated. "Oh, sorry. It's nothing too earth-shattering, really. Just me speculating. They could have all been nothing but ugly pictures of sailboats. I just wonder whether the killer might have been worried about leaving their own face at the scene of the crime."

FOUR

The next morning was Sunday, generally a day that Sherry would spend contentedly eating toast, drinking tea, and reading bad detective novels one after the other as if she was working her way through a bag of potato chips. This Sunday, though, Sherry had a mission. She was an extremely lapsed Catholic whose very occasional ventures to church reflected her appreciation for organ music and Mrs. McGeary's excellent homemade doughnuts far more than they did any particular spiritual concerns, but this Sunday was special. Their little church had just gotten a new priest, which was the sort of incredible social upheaval that arrived in Winesap with about the frequency of a townsperson announcing that they'd been the victim of an unwelcome anal probing on board a flying saucer (this had happened exactly once, three years earlier, and had created a local maelstrom of prurient delight that was rivaled only by the more recent discovery of some scratches on a tree in the woods that might, if you squinted at them the right way, look like mysterious runes carved by the members of a dangerous sex cult). Sherry, as a snoop and gossipmonger of above-amateur ability, could do nothing in the face of such excitement but put on her nicest slacks and sweater, add her most enormous rubber-soled winter boots in honor of the slush, envelop the entire ensemble in a parka that hit her ankles, and head straight to mass.

Sacred Heart was a nice-looking old white clapboard church just off Main Street that always smelled pleasantly like incense and lemon-scented floor wax. Tourists liked to take pictures of it. It was also extremely drafty, so Sherry kept her coat and gloves on when she settled into a pew near the back and prepared to shiver her way through the service. Then the choir struck up and the altar boys started processing in, and Sherry got a good look at the new priest and forgot to fret about her rapidly numbing fingertips.

The first thing she noticed about Father Barry—that was, absurdly, how he introduced himself at the beginning of his homily—was how truly, remarkably *young* he was. He looked like a college student, and not like the sort of scraggle-bearded freshman boy she'd seen desultorily hacky-sacking his way around town on a recent trip to Ithaca. Father Barry looked more like Harvard's star quarterback as depicted in a Hollywood movie filmed circa 1964. There was a wonderful Eagle Scout earnestness beaming out of his blond, pink-cheeked, square-jawed face. It made Sherry instantly suspicious. It was *possible* that he really was an improbably handsome, wholesome, and good-hearted young priest. It was also possible that he had, in the week or so since he'd arrived in Winesap, already convinced an elderly parishioner to add him to her will before smothering her in her bed and burying her behind the rectory. In Sherry's experience, the second option was vastly more likely.

Despite her misgivings, Sherry didn't hesitate to line up with the rest of the old biddies to meet handsome young Father Barry after mass was over. This made it somewhat frustrating when Father Barry seemed to be avoiding meeting her. The young man had an incredible ability to see people who absolutely needed to be spoken to at the other end of the vestibule the instant that Sherry got within cassock-grasping range. Eventually enough parishioners had finished their doughnuts and left that Sherry was beginning to feel self-conscious about the length of time she'd spent lingering near the coffee urn. She was pondering whether it might be better to come back to chase the priest some more next Sunday, when there was a polite little "Ahem!" from just behind her.

She turned. Father Barry was standing next to a picked-over plate of Danishes and looking bashful. "I'm sorry," he said. "Are you Mrs. Pinkwhistle?"

"Miss," she said automatically. She always felt the need to disabuse people of the notion that there might be a Mr. Pink-whistle hanging around as early as possible, to avoid awkward questions later on. Somehow her being a divorcée always took people off guard: she apparently didn't look the part. It occurred to her somewhat belatedly that young Father Barry was probably more interested in confirming her identity and not her marital status. "Oh, yes. Sherry Pinkwhistle."

He leaned in slightly. "The one who investigates the murders?"

"Yes," Sherry said, and tried not to beam too obviously in expectant anticipation of his questions. Her love of answering questions about her investigations was one of her greatest weaknesses.

Father Barry didn't ask her any questions, though. Instead, he folded her right hand in both of his and looked her straight in the eye. "I'm so sorry," he said. "It's wonderful that you've been able to help solve the crimes, but I can't imagine how difficult it's been for you to have to be witness to so much terrible violence." His provokingly unlined young forehead was creased with concern. "Especially in such a small town. I'm amazed by how well everyone seems to be holding up in spite of everything. My door is always open, though, if you ever need a sympathetic ear."

"I'm lapsed," Sherry said automatically. She felt strange. Uncomfortable. *So much terrible violence. Such a small town.* It *was*, wasn't it? It was strange. It was *horrible.* So many deaths. How many murders had they had this year already? Five? More? She couldn't remember. Why couldn't she—

The thought was gone. She'd been thinking something important, but now it was gone. That had been happening more often lately. She needed to hold on to that thought. There was something important that she needed to hold in her head. She needed to—

Father Barry was staring at her. He looked worried, but his expression was gentle. "I'll listen to anyone," he said. "There's no quiz on the date of your last confession ahead of time. And the coffee is free."

"That's how they get you," she said. "With the free coffee."

"Not how we keep them, though," he said. "The coffee is *terrible.*" Then he gave her a smile that showed off a set of very winsome dimples and gave her hand one last squeeze before he released her. "I'm very glad that you decided to come to mass today, Sherry."

Sherry mumbled something indistinct in response to that. She didn't want to make any promises. Part of her wanted to run. "I'm always easy to find at the library," she said, for lack of anything better to say, her eyes firmly averted from the *suspiciously* winsome dimples. Then she made some noises to the effect of, *Goodbye, Father Barry, please don't feel the need to show me out, I know where the door is,* and made her escape. She'd planned on going right home after mass. Now she didn't feel ready for it. There was a strange hum in her body, a steady thrum of energy. Something peculiar in the back of her head. She had forgotten something. What had she forgotten? There was something that she needed to remember.

Instead of heading back up the hill toward home, she walked farther down Main Street and turned left toward the library. There was a cleaner who came twice a week to mop the floors and keep the dust at bay, but there was always more organizing and polishing to be done, and having work to do relaxed her. She'd never been very good at the *ornamental* aspects of womanhood, but she excelled at the bits where you were supposed to remember to dust the baseboards and wipe down the inside of the microwave with a wet sponge. She was the only one at the library who remembered to clean the cobwebs around the door to the room they never used. It sometimes seemed as if the staff and volunteers avoided that part of the library completely.

She started out at her desk and carefully sorted through all the old mail and other things that she'd very sternly told herself she would deal with after lunch before shoving them into a drawer and leaving them there for two months. By the time she'd finished with her sorting she felt significantly calmer and had a thick stack of documents to bring to the paper shredder. It felt like a bit of an affront to her new sense of equanimity when the shredder jammed and she had to shut the whole thing off and open it up to see what the problem was.

She'd expected just a clump of paper that had gotten twisted around in the machine somehow. Instead, what she found was what looked like part of the binding of a book. She had a momentary, hot flare of fury at the thought that one of the newer volunteers had, for some reason, pushed one of the library books into the shredder. Then she looked closer and realized that it was something much more interesting. It was the binding of a *sketchbook*, and Sherry was very confident that none of the library staff who spent time near her desk had any interest in drawing. She remembered then that the library had been broken into at just around the time John had been killed.

There was, obviously, nothing left to do at this point but to dig through the shreds and see what she would find.

It was difficult for Sherry not to feel very authentically detective-y as she set to her task. She imagined that she ought to be drinking an enormous amount of black coffee, possibly while speaking Swedish. This sense of well-being was somewhat deflated by the realization that, unlike the protagonist of a gritty Scandinavian crime novel, she didn't have any ambitious—but *very* attractive—rookie female officers she could force to help her dig through garbage for several hours, and she also couldn't carry the evidence home with her to sort through as she drank whiskey in a melancholic fashion and thought about the estranged daughter she didn't have. She would have to look through everything as quickly and tidily as possible, so she wouldn't end up spending her entire evening on the library floor.

The tidying in Sweden, she thought resentfully, was probably *also* the responsibility of the devastatingly attractive rookie female officers.

The task was more than a little frustrating. As it turned out, if you attempted to reassemble a sketchbook full of pencil drawings that had just been run through a paper shredder, you very quickly ran up against the limits of your own artistic sensibilities. Sherry couldn't tell her asses from her elbows. What she was sure of, however, was that there were asses and elbows among the shreds, once she eliminated a few sailboats and city streets. Vaguely human forms were beginning to take shape. She assembled and reassembled. She accidentally gave a young lady the prow of a stout sailing vessel. In the end, though, she had two drawings that looked close to being fully assembled. They were both of the same person, she thought. A young woman, fully nude, sitting on an uncomfortable-looking wooden stool.

They looked to Sherry as if they'd been done in a life drawing session.

Sherry peered more closely at the pieced-together drawings, trying to get a sense of what sort of woman was depicted in them. Young, certainly. Caucasian, and probably very fair; possibly redheaded. On her cheeks were drawn what might have been pimples but what Sherry suspected were supposed to be freckles. Her equally befreckled shoulders were narrow and sloping, and her downturned eyes suggested that she was either lost in thought or avoiding the artist's gaze. The latter, Sherry thought. The girl—more a girl than a woman, certainly—didn't look remotely as if she was experiencing being nude in front of an audience as an empowering expression of her blossoming young sexuality. She mostly looked embarrassed, and possibly cold. Beautiful, but young enough and unsure enough of herself to enjoy hearing about how gorgeous and fascinating and unlike other women she was from a sophisticated older man, and naïve enough to believe that he meant what he said.

She looked, in other words, absolutely nothing like Charlotte, and in Sherry's experience there was nothing that a certain particularly nasty type of man liked to do more than to sleep with women who were both much younger than and completely unlike their wives.

Sherry took another moment to try to commit the face in the pictures to memory before carefully returning the whole mess to the shredder bin. Then she called the sheriff to tell him that she thought that she might have found some evidence.

This caused the usual sort of uproar and consternation. Sheriff Brown immediately suspected her of having tampered with a crime scene, an accusation against which Sherry felt compelled to defend herself despite the fact that, as usual, it was completely accurate. Eventually she was kicked out of her own office despite her objections and was forced to trudge home, where she wouldn't have access to all the lovely library resources that she would usually use to track down a suspect. She would have to improvise.

First, she called Charlotte, who picked up after only two rings. She had, it seemed, followed Sherry's advice about not immediately buying a pink convertible and hitting the town. "Lying low?" Sherry asked her.

Charlotte gave an uncharacteristically inelegant snort. "As much as I can," she said. "I'm an unconflicted grieving widow whose husband never cheated on her once in his sainted life. I've had to leave the building a few times to stock up on essential food supplies. I got the *family-sized* Oreo pack." There was a bit of softness and looseness to the sound of Charlotte's voice that made Sherry wonder if she might have had a glass of wine or two. "Hey, listen. I cataloged all of John's paintings to figure out what was missing. It was just a bunch of crap. A few un-titled nudes and a couple of boats and things. So I guess they were just smashing up stuff for no reason. Is there any news?"

"There might be," Sherry said cagily. "Did John ever go to any life drawing classes?"

"Every week," Charlotte said. "He was the facilitator. Wednesdays at seven in Albany. He usually had drinks with some of the students afterward and got home late."

Drinks with students, Sherry thought. *A likely story. Frol-icking with his freckled filly, no doubt.* She gave the end of the pen she was holding a brief gnaw of excitement before poising it over a nearby legal pad. "Where exactly were the life draw-ing sessions held?"

"I have no idea," Charlotte said after a brief pause. "That's weird, isn't it? Why wouldn't I know that? God, *were* there even life drawing classes? Was he just seeing some woman down there this whole time while I sat at home like a complete idiot?" Her voice, which had been growing steadily louder, reached a vibrant crescendo on the word *idiot*.

Sherry winced. "There were definitely life drawing classes," she said carefully.

"Does that mean that he was sleeping with a student?" Charlotte asked. "God, I'm sorry, I'm messing all of this up again. I sound *exactly* like a horrible shrieking harpy of a wife who would kill her husband in a fit of jealous rage, don't I?"

"You don't sound like a *harpy*," Sherry said, because she couldn't in all fairness say that Charlotte *hadn't* just shrieked, and *didn't* sound as if she was fully prepared to march down to the morgue to subject John to an additional, postmortem stabbing.

"You mean that I *do* sound like an unhinged murderer,

then," Charlotte said, and heaved a sigh so loud that Sherry could practically feel it on her cheek. "I think I hate him."

"I know," Sherry said, sympathetically. "It's only natural." Maybe Charlotte *had* killed him. The sheer degree to which she seemed to be trying to endear herself to Sherry suddenly struck Sherry as more suspicious than she'd found it a day or so before. She was, surely, much too young and glamorous and interesting to need *Sherry* for her emotional support. "Has your mother arrived yet? Or any friends?"

"*No,*" Charlotte said. "It's been crazy. Her flight was canceled, and then my aunt Charlie had a stroke. And my best friend's dog is sick. Which, frankly, I find a little insulting. People are so weird about their dogs. We've been friends for ten years, my *husband* gets murdered, and your main concern is your cockapoo?"

"Cockapoo," Sherry mouthed, feeling momentarily overwhelmed by the sheer capacity of The Youth to invent impenetrable new slang terms before it registered that the word rang a distant bell as, possibly, the sort of dog that glamorous young women from Manhattan might carry around in their purses. She cleared her throat, mentally setting the subject of cockapoos aside for further study in her leisure hours. "I'm very sorry to hear that," she said, after what was probably a far-too-long cockapoo-induced gap in the conversation. "I hope that the . . . *cockapoo*"—what a joy to say aloud it was!—"will recover. And your *aunt,* of course," she added hurriedly. "I hope that your *aunt* will recover. Obviously."

"I don't," Charlotte said. "She's the meanest old lady I've ever met in my life. I've always been mad that I had to be named after her. When I was eight she slapped me across the face for saying that I didn't like the supper she'd cooked.

Maybe if she was going to be that sensitive about her pork chops she shouldn't have cooked them until you could side a house with them. Oh my God, I'm doing it again, aren't I? Do I ever say anything that *doesn't* make me sound like a serial killer? You *definitely* think that I killed John now, don't you?"

"I'm withholding judgment," Sherry told her. Honesty, after all, was still the best policy. "I'll talk to you soon, Charlotte."

"I'll be here with my Oreos," Charlotte said. "Plotting my next kill, I guess. Promise you won't let them give me the electric chair, Sherry?"

"I don't think that they use the electric chair in New York," Sherry told her. "I could look it up for you, though, if you want."

"Wow, thanks for that," Charlotte said. "I won't worry at all now."

"I'm glad to hear it," Sherry said. Then they both hung up.

"*Cockapoo,*" Sherry said, to the silent and uninterested room.

FIVE

After having spent most of her day of rest on earnest sleuthing, Sherry decided to give herself the rest of the afternoon off. She cooked herself an enormous plate of spaghetti and had two glasses of cabernet. Then, just to make very sure that she would fall asleep promptly, she put herself into a nice hot bath with *Anna Karenina*. She'd barely made it through two pages of Levin holding forth on all the extremely important modern innovations he wanted to bring to nineteenth-century Russian agriculture when she almost dropped the book in the bath. She'd started to nod off. *Perfect.* She'd tried many methods over the years to treat her occasional insomnia, but she'd yet to find one as reliably efficacious as Tolstoy.

The next morning at the library was a quiet one, which was normal for a Monday. She took the opportunity to hide at her desk and make a few phone calls.

The woman currently at the front desk of the main branch of the Albany Public Library system picked up the phone very promptly and was immediately ready to help out a fellow librarian in a time of need. No, they didn't host life drawing classes at the library, but she could check the community board to see whether anyone was advertising one in town. She came back sounding triumphant: there was a flyer on the board for a life drawing session on Wednesday evenings in a local coffee shop called the Night Kitchen. She also, helpfully, provided the coffee shop's phone number.

The first time she called the coffee shop, no one answered the phone. The second time, the gentleman who answered was less than helpful. Who organized the life drawing classes? He didn't know, but he was pretty sure that they didn't do that. They didn't organize the classes, or didn't host them at all? He was unsure. Could she speak to a manager? A heavy sigh. The manager wouldn't be in until three. "Oh, thank you!" Sherry trilled. "I'll call back then!" In response the young man grunted, then hung up on her.

Sherry called back promptly at three and patiently made her way through an aural gauntlet of hostile or baffled teenagers before finally reaching the manager, a harried-sounding woman who nonetheless did her best to help. "The art people? They rent out the back room every Wednesday night. Hold on a second—" There was the sound of an espresso machine in the background, and two teenagers shouting back and forth about whether or not there were any everything bagels left. Eventually the harried woman returned. "Hello? The organizer is a guy named John Jacobs. Do you need his number?"

Sherry swallowed back a groan. "No," she said. "Unfortunately, John passed away last week. I was hoping to contact whoever he was working with on the figure drawing classes to let them know."

The harried woman made the appropriate noises over this lamentable turn of events. Sherry soldiered onward. "Is there anyone else I could speak to? Someone who might know how to get in touch with his model to let her know that she doesn't need to come in?"

"You could try the arts center?" the harried woman suggested. "The one in Troy? I'm sorry, I have no idea what her number is. You could always just show up here on Wednesday night and see if you can catch her."

"Thank you," Sherry said, and hung up, at which point she was forced to actually deal with the needs of the reading public. It really was annoying, she thought, when the job for which she'd been formally trained and which she was paid to perform by the local government got in the way of her unpaid amateur homicide detection. It was incredible that Jessica Fletcher ever managed to find the discipline to write novels when there was so much fascinating investigation to be done instead. Particularly in Cabot Cove, where people seemed to be murdered on a horrifically regular basis. Much like Winesap, really. It was strange. Hadn't someone said something like that recently? It was both horrible and bizarre that people in Winesap were—

A patron was trying to get her attention: he was looking for a book that they didn't have in Winesap. No problem: it should be available in Albany. Sherry made a call. Once she was done with that, she took a quick break to make coffee and chat with Mary, her volunteer for the afternoon. Mary was an energetic octogenarian, a former English teacher and general book enthusiast with an encyclopedic knowledge of popular gothic novels of the late eighteenth and early nineteenth centuries. They chatted a bit about what they'd been up to lately. When Sherry mentioned that she'd met the new young priest, Mary's pale blue eyes narrowed slightly. "Oh," she said.

"You don't approve?" Sherry asked, prepared to be scandalized. Mary always knew everything about everyone in town: she was one of those elderly ladies who'd formed a network with her peers via various book clubs and churches and volunteer organizations that put her exactly one or two degrees of separation from everyone in Winesap.

"I don't know," Mary said slowly. "I just heard a funny story about him the other day. Do you know Pearl Walker?"

"I know *of* her," Sherry said. Mrs. Walker was an extremely rich widow who lived in a big old house on the outskirts of the village in a lavish, vaguely gothic fashion that she thought probably suited Mary's sensibilities. Sherry had been told that Mrs. Walker had once been known for her extravagant parties, but in the past few years she'd mostly taken to her bed and granted only occasional audiences to her most esteemed friends and acquaintances. Her needs were met mainly via the efforts of an assistant named Karen, an inexhaustibly hardworking and cheerful type who wore slip-resistant clogs with flowers printed all over them and talked about her wealthy charge with an air of affectionate exasperation. "I've chatted with Karen. What about her?"

"Just something that Karen said the other day," Mary said. "The priest has been coming by to visit Mrs. Walker sometimes, since she doesn't like to go to church. Karen said that the first few times he showed up she thought he seemed very sweet and considerate, but on this most recent visit she overheard him asking Mrs. Walker strange questions about her finances, and the second Karen walked into the room he immediately changed the subject."

"That does sound suspicious," Sherry said, struck again by her little flight of fancy about the priest bilking little old ladies out of their life savings before he murdered them. "Keep me updated if you hear anything else about it? It's like something out of a domestic thriller."

"I *know*," Mary said appreciatively, just as a large group of mothers with small children walked into the library and began to demand all their attention.

The next few hours were nothing but work, until finally Sherry had more time to make phone calls. She looked up the number for the arts center in Troy, called them, and lied. She was the librarian in Winesap (true), she was hoping to bring more arts programming to the library (somewhat true), and she'd been considering organizing some life drawing sessions (a vile and wicked falsehood) and heard good things about the model used at the café sessions from a young lady who had attended one of them (another sinful lie).

The woman at the arts center was happy to help. Yes, they held occasional life drawing sessions and were familiar with the sessions held at the café, though they hadn't actually been organized by the arts center. Yes, she did have the contact information for a model who she knew had worked at several of the café sessions, and she would be happy to share it: Ruth had mentioned to her that she was hoping to find more jobs to do. She was a sweet girl, very prompt and reliable, and the students found her interesting to draw—when they worked in pastels they had to struggle to get the shade of her beautiful red hair just right. It was so nice that Sherry was trying to organize life drawing up in Winesap. Sherry guiltily acknowledged the praise—she consoled herself with the thought that she *might* really organize some drawing classes at the library, one day—and then hung up.

Next she called the number that the arts center woman had

given her. No one picked up, but the answering-machine message belonged to an authoritative-sounding woman. "You've reached the Cohen residence. Please leave a message for David, Rachel, or Ruth after the tone."

It was strange, Sherry thought. Not that this young woman apparently still lived with her parents. Something else. Something about the phone number, and the answering machine. There was no time to think about it any longer. There was the beep. Sherry put on her sweetest, fluffiest, most pocket-full-of-caramels-and-meeting-my-bingo-friends-at-the-diner-at-five-for-supper voice to leave a message. "Hello, Ruth. This is Sherry Pinkwhistle, the librarian up in Winesap. I've been trying to organize some life drawing classes for beginners here at the library, and I was wondering if you might be interested in modeling for us. They have *wonderful* things to say about you in the arts center in Troy. Call me back whenever you have the chance!" Then she left both her work and home numbers, followed by an extended, rambling dither about when she was at work and when she could be found at home, and *oh, so sorry, there was an event at the library on Wednesday, so she* would *be here a bit later that night,* until the machine cut her off with a curt beep and she hung up. Perfect. No one would ever suspect a nice old lady who left such amusingly flustered grandmotherly messages of being a homicide detective, amateur or otherwise.

Ruth didn't call back immediately. She didn't call back at all, for the whole rest of that afternoon and until the next evening. Sherry was already in her bathrobe drinking a cup of chamomile tea with Lord Thomas Cromwell in her lap when her phone rang. She got up to answer it, to Lord Thomas's enormous indignation. The voice on the other end of the line was very high, almost childlike. "Hello? Is this Mrs. Pinkwhistle?"

"Miss," Sherry said. "Yes, this is Sherry Pinkwhistle. May I ask who's calling?"

"Oh, I'm sorry," the girl said. "This is Ruth Cohen. The model? You left a message?"

"I did!" Sherry said. "It's so lovely to hear from you. I know it's very old-fashioned of me, but would you like to come up to the library for an interview? I always like to meet people in person before we decide whether or not we'd like to work together."

Ruth agreed to this, after a momentary hesitation, and they arranged a time: Ruth would come up that Friday at six, after the library was usually closed for the evening. Then they said their goodbyes and hung up. Sherry smiled and leaned down to pet Lord Thomas, who was standing on her slippers. She was pleased with herself. Winesap was a tiny place, and not a place that most people ever bothered to visit. Ruth hadn't mentioned being familiar with it. It wouldn't be an answer, exactly, but Sherry thought that it would be a fairly significant clue if Ruth arrived on Friday having never bothered to ask Sherry for directions to the library.

Ruth never did call back for those directions. Sherry didn't make any calls, either. There had been times in the past when she'd called Sheriff Brown in advance of meeting a suspect, just in case she was worried that things might get dangerous. She wasn't worried about that this time. The skinny little freckled girl in those drawings didn't look like she would pose much of a physical threat to anyone, even a slightly pudgy senior citizen who got most of her exercise from reading while walking. She also, if she was honest with herself, wasn't completely sure that Ruth was her suspect. Charlotte was really the more obvious and rational choice. All Sherry had to say otherwise was her gut, and Sherry's gut was as convinced that Charlotte hadn't killed her husband as it was, sadly, opposed to dairy products. She fidgeted her way through the day, jerking her head up every time someone came through the door as if she expected Ruth to somehow arrive five hours early. Then, finally, it was time for the library to close, and Ruth walked through the door exactly on time.

Ruth, at first glance, looked very much like she had in John's pictures. She was young—maybe about twenty—and thin and redheaded, though the effect was more attractive in person than it had been in the rather unflattering drawings. She was very tall, like a fashion model, with a long swan neck emerging from the collar of her coat, and came scurrying into the room as if she felt self-conscious about being noticed. The sort of beautiful but naïve young girl that a man like John would enjoy having hanging off his every word. A fawn, a sylph, a long-legged forest nymph of a girl. All in all, an unlikely murderer. Sherry's mind was already skipping ahead to alternative suspects—Ruth's jealous boyfriend, perhaps, or an overprotective parent? That authoritative-sounding mother Sherry had heard over the phone?—when Ruth finally looked up and met Sherry's eyes. She held Sherry's gaze for a long, cool, appraising moment. Then she looked away, then back, and gave a meek little smile, clasping her hands in front of her like a child abut to recite a poem at a school assembly. "Miss Pinkwhistle?"

Sherry thought that she might have underestimated young Miss Cohen. Perhaps John had, too.

"It's so lovely to see you, Ruth!" Sherry said. She'd worn a big fluffy pink sweater today, and an equally fluffy white shawl. She thought that she looked like an extremely non-threatening strawberry cupcake. "I have tea and cookies for us in the event room. Usually I don't allow any food or drinks in the library, but I decided to make an exception." This earned a polite laugh from Ruth, who seemed perfectly at her ease. Good.

The event room was one of Sherry's favorite parts of the library. The library had, at one point, been a family home, and the meeting room had been first a summer kitchen and then a sunroom before the library had gotten hold of it. The many windows and poor insulation made it less than ideal for storing books, but perfectly serviceable for holding local candidate meet-and-greets and chamber music evenings and Sunday afternoon knitting circles, or whatever else it might be rented out for. Sherry loved all the light in it, and the view of the little community garden out back and the bird feeders that one of her elderly volunteers had set up a few years ago and still dutifully kept filled. The only real drawback was that insulation problem, which made it uncomfortably hot on summer days and frigid on winter evenings. Sherry was wearing several other layers under her pink sweater. Keeping the ambient temperature too low for the comfort of the unprepared was a useful trick both for ensuring that groups of chatty knitters didn't stay at the library for longer than the time that they'd booked *and* for softening up the suspect you were grilling in your freezing-cold interrogation room. Sherry had learned that from a true-crime television show.

Sherry made chitchat with Ruth while she brewed the tea. She asked her about the drive, which she was delighted to learn had been *fine*. Then she asked whether or not Ruth had ever visited Winesap before, in response to which she received a firm *no*. Satisfied, Sherry got down to business.

"Ruth," she said, after they were settled in with their tea and cookies and it would be more difficult for Ruth to easily extricate herself from the situation. "I'm afraid that I have some difficult news. I didn't want to tell you over the phone, and I think they've been keeping it out of the papers for now." Odd, now that Sherry thought of it. Odd that there had been journalists swarming the scenes at past murders in Winesap, but not at this one, despite the fact that John was a fairly prominent local citizen. Convenient, though, for Sherry's purposes, when media attention to the crime might have made Ruth warier of a stranger calling her up and asking her to come to Winesap. It was strange, how often convenient coincidences so often seemed to help Sherry—

"What is it?" Ruth asked.

"I'm sorry," Sherry said. "Have you heard about John?"

Ruth's smile froze on her face. "What about him?"

Sherry bit back a triumphant, *Ha!* "John Jacobs, I mean," she said. "The man who ran your life drawing sessions in Albany."

There was a flicker in Ruth's expression now. She'd realized anyone with only a casual working relationship with a man with an extremely common first name should have asked, *John who?* "I know," she said. "Is he okay?" Then, abruptly, her chin wobbled, just a bit. She was avoiding Sherry's gaze.

"He's not, dear," Sherry said. "I'm afraid that he's passed away."

Another chin wobble, followed by a shiver, but not a trace of surprise.

"Are you cold, dear?" Sherry asked. Exactly as planned. "Here, take my shawl." She got up to drape it around Ruth's shoulders, then sat down to nudge the tea and cookies closer to Ruth. "Have some tea. It'll warm you up."

Ruth was clutching at Sherry's shawl. "I'm sorry," she said. "It's just—sad."

"I know," Sherry said. "You and John were more than just friends, weren't you?"

Ruth looked up at her. She was even paler than she had been when she walked in. "How did you—"

"Just a guess," Sherry said. "Would you like to talk about him? You must have been very in love."

An ugly mottled flush flooded across Ruth's cheeks. "I thought that we were," she said, and then looked away again.

"Oh, dear," Sherry said. "Heartbreak after heartbreak. You know, when I was your age, lots of my friends were treated very badly by older men. Was he not very nice to you?"

"No," Ruth said. "No, I mean—he was really romantic. Not like guys my age, you know? He drove me down to the city once. We got a hotel room in the West Village, and he introduced me to all of these really cool guys who ran art galleries and stuff and artists who wanted me to model for them." Her expression lit up a bit as she talked about it. All those glamorous, sophisticated artists in the big city. All those men who Charlotte probably thought of as friends, flattering John's young mistress and winking at John behind her back. Sherry didn't have to feign her sympathy.

"It must have been so exciting," she said.

Ruth shrugged, her expression dimming slightly. "I thought so," she said. "I mean—yeah. It was great."

"But it didn't last," Sherry said. "That must have been very difficult. But you must have known it would be difficult, hm? Because he was married."

Ruth looked up at her again, her face suddenly transformed. She didn't look like a lost little girl anymore. She looked like an avenging Valkyrie. "He told me he was *divorced*," she said. "I'd *never* date a married guy. My biological father cheated on my mom for five years; it ruined our lives. I had no idea until I came up here to surprise him and I saw—" She stopped. Ruth saw a muscle in her jaw flex.

"It's all right, dear," Sherry said. "You don't have to worry about giving anything away. I already know that you were here at the library. The police have the evidence, and they should be looking at it today. My friend also knows that I'm meeting you here tonight, and you're on the security cameras again." This last bit was Sherry being creative, but the broad strokes were true enough.

Ruth didn't look angry now. She just looked tired. "What do you want?" she asked. "Why did you get me to come up here, if you think the cops are about to arrest me? What was the point? You're just playing Sherlock Holmes? Or you like messing with people's lives?"

The question hit strangely. Other murderers she'd encountered had sometimes been given to oddly dramatic pronouncements about her meddling. No one had asked her *why*. It took her a moment before she settled on an answer that she thought might draw Ruth out more. "John's wife, Charlotte, is a dear friend of mine," she said. "He'd cheated on her for years. It's why they moved up here, in part. It crushed her, and now she's the prime suspect in his murder. The police weren't interested in looking elsewhere. It's always the wife's fault, isn't it? I wanted to help. Charlotte's a wonderful woman. Beautiful and smart and artistic, just like you. I think that you'd like her very much, if you met her. And I think that she deserves an explanation of what happened to her husband, as awful as he was to the women in his life. Don't you?" She paused. She was thinking fast. "And you *are* very young. And pretty. I'm sure that if you went to the police of your own accord and explained all about the . . . *mitigating circumstances*, that might make a difference for you."

Ruth stared down at her mug of tea for a long, long moment. "He asked me out after the session one night," she said slowly. "He bought me dinner and we went to a couple of bars. It lasted about six months. I thought we were in love. I really did. I knew he lived in Winesap, but he never brought me up here. It never really seemed weird, since he was down in Albany for class, anyway. But he talked about the gallery sometimes, so I decided one Saturday that I wanted to come up here to see it and surprise him. When I got here he was out for lunch, so I went in and looked around. They had brochures about the gallery. They had this picture of him and his wife right on them. It talked about how they'd opened the place together. So I left."

"That must have been such an awful shock," Sherry said. She said it with real sympathy. It felt very much like any other conversation she'd ever had with a friend who'd just been through a bad breakup. "What did you do next?"

"Nothing for a while," Ruth said. "We usually just made

plans after class. When I wasn't modeling, I'd meet him somewhere after the class was over. So I just thought for a while,
and then I came back up here again. To . . . confront him, I
guess. I came late, because he said he normally painted at
night, so I figured I could catch him. I had a couple of drinks
at that bar down the street. Then after it closed I went to the
gallery. I knocked at the door in the back and he let me in. He
was pretty surprised to see me. I confronted him about being
married and he acted like it wasn't even a big deal. He said that
he thought Charlotte was going to divorce him, anyway; she
didn't even like him anymore. I told him that sounded like
bullshit, but he made it sound really real. Like they were really
going to get a divorce. Then I saw that he had this big painting
of me right there where anyone could see it. A nude one, I
mean. And I was like, *You just leave nude paintings of your
mistress around where your wife can see them?* And he said
something like, *It doesn't matter, she doesn't care about models.*
And I could *tell*, I could *tell* he meant *he* didn't care, like he
meant *I don't care about models.* So I started cursing at him,
calling him a pervert and a dirty old man and stuff, and it was
like this switch flipped and suddenly he was *so* angry. He got
right up in my face, there was spit going everywhere. So I
pulled out my knife I carry and told him to back off, and he
laughed in my face." There was a brief pause. Ruth gave a few
rapid blinks. "And grabbed me by the throat. He started chok-
ing me. I thought he was going to kill me."

"Then you stabbed him," Sherry said. "To get him to let go.
So it was self-defense."

"Yeah," Ruth said, looking right back at her. "Yeah. Self-
defense."

"You're innocent of murder, then," Sherry said. "Should I call the sheriff now to tell him what you've told me? We might catch him before he sees those security tapes."

"Yeah, okay," Ruth said. Then she looked straight at Sherry again. "Thank you."

"You're welcome," Sherry said. Then she asked, "Just out of curiosity—why did you destroy all of those paintings?"

"Oh," Ruth said. "I kicked the big one while we were arguing. The one of me. Then I thought that if there was one painting of me that was damaged with John dead right next to it, that that would look like a clue. So I ruined all of the ones of me, plus a few others to make it look like someone just trashed a bunch of different paintings for no reason."

"I see," Sherry said. "That was very clever of you." Very clever, and cool, and calculated. "I'm going to call the police, now. To let them know."

Sherry went into her office to make the call. She wasn't worried about Ruth running off: she'd have to come past the front desk to do that. She dialed Sheriff Brown's number without having to look it up. "I've found John Jacobs's killer," she said as soon as he picked up.

"Of course you have," Sheriff Brown said. He sounded tired. "Where is he?"

"She," Sherry said. "She's right here in the library. Waiting for you to come here so she can confess to killing John Jacobs in self-defense."

"Right," said Sheriff Brown. "I'll be right there."

"Just a moment," Sherry said. "There were just a couple of odd things that I noticed in her confession to me."

He sighed. "Go ahead."

"The first," Sherry said, "is that she did an awfully deliber-
ate job of attempting to conceal her connection to the victim
after the fact for someone who panicked and killed someone
in self-defense. Also, she's a redhead, and she has such a lovely
long neck."

"She has a *what*?" Sheriff Brown asked.

"Oh, I'm sorry," Sherry said. She was, she thought, suffering from a bit of post-cracked-case giddiness. "I mean that
redheads are generally very pale, and you can see her neck
very clearly in the sweater she's wearing. Bruises ought to be
very visible on her. If she'd been violently strangled just a few
days ago, I mean. I suppose that she *could* be telling the truth.
You'll probably be better at telling that than me. Forensics and
things."

"And things," Sheriff Brown said. "Thanks, Sherry. I'll keep
all of that in mind."

He was being just a *touch* sardonic, Sherry thought. She
didn't really mind. "You're welcome," she said, very sincerely.
Then she hung up and went back into the meeting room. Ruth
had eaten a cookie while she was on the phone. "The police
will be here soon," she said. "I just had one more question, if
you don't mind."

Ruth shrugged. Sherry took that as assent. "I was just wondering about that sketchbook. You could have easily taken it
with you back to Albany and thrown it into a dumpster. No
one ever would have found it. Why did you break into the library just to put it in the shredder?"

Ruth frowned. "I don't know," she said slowly. "I don't—"

The world flickered.

Ruth's expression smoothed over. "I panicked," she said. "I

wanted to destroy it, and I didn't want it anywhere near where I lived. I saw the library while I was leaving and I thought of the shredder."

"I see," Sherry said, and then the sheriff's department descended on the library. Sherry didn't pay much attention to that, though. She was preoccupied. Her stomach felt uneasy. Something strange was hanging in the air. If you wanted to drive back to Albany from the gallery, the library was in exactly the wrong direction.

SIX

Sherry glided through the next few days on the well-sharpened ice skates of self-satisfaction. She'd done well, she thought. Charlotte thought so, too. She bought that bottle of champagne that Sherry had advised her so strongly against just a few days before and invited Sherry over to drink it. When Sherry got there, those cold-looking nude women had been taken off the walls, and Charlotte was full of the sometimes-tearful giddiness of a woman who had come very close to being arrested for a murder she hadn't committed. They got tipsy together, and made morbid jokes that couldn't be repeated in mixed company, and talked about books and cackled like witches. "Is it awful of me to say that I'm so glad that I had this chance to get to know you?" Sherry asked, once the champagne was gone and Charlotte had mixed them up some spontaneous caipirinhas.

Charlotte gave a little shriek, then dissolved into laughter again. "*Yes*," she said. "It's *obviously* awful, *come on*. You can't just say that you're grateful for someone getting murdered because of the *friends you made along the way*. God, poor John."

"Poor John," Sherry agreed. She felt suddenly odd. Frightened, maybe. "Charlotte—I'm probably being silly. But try to be careful, please?"

Charlotte frowned at her over the rim of her caipirinha glass. "Be careful of what?"

"I don't know," Sherry said. Her head was swimming. She didn't usually drink this much. "There's just—something. It feels like there's something to be careful of."

"By the pricking of your thumbs," Charlotte said, and gave another little giggle.

Sherry didn't laugh. "Maybe," she said. It was dark out now, dark enough that she couldn't see Winesap through Charlotte's living room window. All she could see was the reflection of her own pale, anxious face. "Maybe something wicked."

The next day was Saturday, which meant that she would have her date with Alan that evening. She woke up with her head already aching and full of more of that sense of dread that had started the night before, though now she supposed that she could blame it on her hangover. She was annoyed with the world and with herself. She was too old to drink enough to have a hangover on a day when she knew perfectly well that she had to work. Her trying to seem *cool* to her new young friend, probably. Embarrassing. She was embarrassed and anxious and her head hurt so badly even Lord Thomas Cromwell annoyed her. His yowls for his breakfast were too loud.

Alan was as wonderful as ever, at least. He took one look at her when she climbed into his car—their plan had been to drive to Saratoga to see a live jazz performance—and said, "I know that we said we'd go into the city tonight, but what would you think about just having a night in? We could pick up Chinese and eat it on my couch in front of a movie."

"That sounds *perfect*," Sherry said, the words coming out in a big relieved sigh. Then she confessed, "I have a hangover. Isn't that embarrassing?"

"Extremely embarrassing," he said. "I can't stand to be seen with you. Get out of my car." He pulled carefully out of the library parking lot. NPR was on the radio. "I've been tiring myself out over the books for the store all day. I'll probably be worrying about them all night, too, so I thought I might as well take a break for a few and not bother with all of that driving back and forth. Why do you have a hangover? Hitting the clubs last night?"

Sherry blushed, which was fairly novel. Only Alan ever usually managed to make her blush. Most of the time she was almost completely shameless. She tried to evade the question. "Are things not going well with the store?"

She could see his frown reflected in the windshield. "Just some strange things I'm trying to figure out. And I had to talk to Alice about paying attention to what she's doing. She was doing more daydreaming than working today." Then: "You just changed the subject. Do you have another guy on the side who takes you to all of the wild Winesap parties?" He was teasing, obviously, but it made her blush harder, anyway.

"Charlotte invited me over for drinks."

"Charlotte Jacobs?" Alan asked, shifting slightly to look at her. "The merry widow?"

"Don't call her that," Sherry said, her tone more redolent of the scolding wife than what she'd intended. "She's not a *merry widow.*" She then had to immediately amend that for the sake of truthfulness. "She's not an . . . *excessively* merry widow. And, anyway, she didn't do it. Didn't you see the news? They caught the real killer."

"*You* caught her, you mean," Alan said. "Of course I saw. I always check the paper for news about your cases. I'm just mad that I was wrong about one of them again. You'd think that I'd get it right *sometimes*. Charlotte really looked like the obvious suspect."

Your cases. Sherry blushed again. It was nice of him, she thought, to treat her . . . *detective-ing* as if it was real. Something to be taken seriously. "It never seems to be the obvious suspect," she said absently. She was distracted by the fact that they were pulling into the parking lot of Winesap's lone, small Chinese restaurant. "Steamed dumplings?"

"I'll get a dozen," Alan said. "Should I just run in and order? You can stay in the car, unless you'd rather come in with me. It's frigid out there tonight."

"That would be nice of you," Sherry said, feeling warm and comforted and pampered in the way that Alan always seemed to manage. "If you don't mind?"

"Not at all," he said, and kissed her cheek, then clambered out of the car—a blast of cold air carried in a few stray snowflakes—and jogged into the restaurant. Sherry put her fingertips to where Alan had kissed her, like a young girl in an old movie, and then immediately dropped her hand into her lap. Ridiculous. She was being ridiculous.

Alan was always so *nice* to her. Her headache felt like it was easing. She sat in the car and listened to the radio until he returned, laden with bags and looking eager and pleased, his cheeks flushed from the cold. With the gray mustache, it ought to have made him look like Santa Claus. Sherry thought it made him look like the sweet, earnest boy he must have been half a century ago. On the drive he talked her ear off about a Sichuan restaurant down in Albany that he wanted to take her to the next time they went down for the symphony. He seemed to be under the impression that she had never eaten Sichuan food before, and he was very eager to introduce her to the cuisine. She didn't have the heart to tell him that she'd spent a good amount of time while she was living in New York City eating her way through Flushing. Alan was always so happy when he could present her with a delightful surprise. She wouldn't deny him the pleasure for a minute, even if it meant pretending to be overwhelmed by what she expected would be underwhelming dandan noodles.

They went to his house, which was elegant and comfortable, packed with books and antiques and expensive old rugs. He set a stack of documents down on a side table, then showed her a new drawing he had on the wall, a picture of two cowboys with a wild horse that he'd pulled from a set of six framed original illustrations from a book about the American West that his son Corey had brought in a few weeks earlier. "I felt bad for breaking up the set, but I really loved this one. It reminded me of something from a novel." Sherry made agreeable noises. The picture didn't strike her as anything special, but she liked seeing how genuinely excited he looked about it, and the way that he bragged about Corey's talent for reframing old pictures—the frame did look nice—struck her as very sweet.

They sat on his big squishy old sofa to eat their Chinese food and watch a movie. At a certain point in the evening it only seemed natural to start making out like teenagers, which was something that they'd never done before. She'd always wriggled her way out of it before, always gone in for a hug when she'd sensed him wanting a kiss. She didn't wriggle now. She kissed back. It was hopelessly silly. It was fantastic. Sherry blushed and giggled and, eventually, let her head settle on his shoulder to rest between kisses. She held his hand. It was ridiculous of her, she knew that. Even forty years ago she never felt as if she was quite pretty enough to blush and giggle over a boy without embarrassing herself. The main difference, maybe, was that she was even less pretty now and cared much less about being embarrassing.

At about ten Alan drove her home through what was rapidly turning into a blizzard with some leftovers nicely packed up for her—"so you won't have to cook for yourself tomorrow"— and kissed her goodbye on her doorstep. Then he left, and Sherry trudged across the road to offer the leftovers to Alice. She would take them, she knew: Alice hated to cook but was also constantly pinching her pennies, so Sherry had gotten into the habit of giving her food under the pretext that she didn't like reheated food but hated to waste anything.

Alice opened the door a few moments after her knock and accepted the leftovers with a level of gratitude that suggested to Sherry that she hadn't had anything for dinner yet. She very politely invited Sherry inside. Sherry just as politely refused, then spent a stupid, giddy few moments babbling about her date, and how nice it had been, and "Poor Alan's still going to be up for a while working on his books for the shop; I don't think he's very good at running the business end of things, he really just loves the antiques—" when it occurred to her that Alice probably had better things to do than stand in her doorway and listen to her neighbor babble about her *boss*. Alice did work for Alan, after all, and might therefore find him slightly less adorable than Sherry did.

"Aw, poor guy," Alice said, with a sympathetic little grimace. "That stuff sounds awful. I'm glad that *I'm* not the boss:

I'd probably get in trouble with the IRS for messing up all of the records and, uh, not keeping all of my receipts, or whatever you're supposed to do."

Sherry made the appropriate noises of agreement at that: she, too, had never managed to figure out exactly which receipts she was supposed to be saving. Then she made her way back home—the snow was falling so hard and fast now that it took her what felt like half an hour just to creep across the road and up her own driveway—washed her face and brushed her teeth, and joined Lord Thomas Cromwell in bed. She still felt nice and warm from the memory of her evening with Alan. "Lord Thomas," she said aloud, "would you get mad at me if I brought another man home one night?"

Lord Thomas didn't reply. He *did* use his claws quite a bit as he kneaded her thigh with his pointy little paws.

"Jealousy is a very ugly emotion, Lord Thomas," Sherry told him, and then petted his soft head until they both fell asleep.

She woke up again in a drugged-feeling haze and looked toward the clock on her bedside table: 12:12. She thought, *Make a wish, Sherry.* Or was that just 11:11? She wasn't sure what had woken her up, at first, and then she heard another knock on her door, another insistent *drrring-drrring!* from the jangly old bell. She got up and pulled her robe and slippers on to go see who it was, then turned into a frightened old lady and peeped through the curtains before she opened the door, just in case it was a robber. It wasn't a robber. It was Alice, looking very cold and distraught. A small domestic catastrophe! Her electricity had gone out. Had Sherry's? No, Sherry still had power: a line hadn't gone down in the storm. Had Alice checked her fuse box? Alice didn't know where that was, or how to check it. Sherry to the rescue! She located her big heavy flashlight, bundled herself up, and led the way down into Alice's basement to locate the breaker box, then flipped the right switch with a bit of a magician's showmanship. The power back on, Alice exhibited repentance. She never should have plugged in that space heater, she should know how to fix things on her own, et cetera. Sherry, who was enjoying feeling very competent, heroic, gentlemanly, et cetera, dismissed her apologies. "Anytime!" she said, and left the big flashlight with Alice in case of another space heater catastrophe, before she made her way back home. The snow was finally starting to slow a little. Maybe the roads would be clear in the morning.

Sherry got back into bed, and, for once, fell asleep almost immediately. She woke up again before her alarm, feeling still tired but cheerful. It was, at last, bright and blue outside, the morning light reflecting against the snow so that her whole house was soaked with sunlight coming through the east-facing windows. She found some upbeat folk music on the radio and was bopping happily around her kitchen while she made her coffee and soft-boiled eggs when there was a knock at the door.

She blinked, and answered it, then frowned. It was Sheriff Brown. "Good morning," she said, after a moment. She felt uneasy. Sheriff Brown generally did his utmost to avoid Sherry becoming involved in his affairs. Even an unprompted phone call would be unusual. His appearance at her door was unnerving at best. Her body knew it better than her head did. Her mouth asked the question before her mind could catch up. "Someone was killed again, weren't they?"

Sheriff Brown clenched his lips up like a fist, then took a deep breath. "I'm sorry, Sherry," he said. "It's Alan Thompson."

The part of Sherry that was always just outside of everything, the part that was quietly taking notes in the back of the classroom, the part that volunteered to take the photo, the part that stood behind the table at the prom and ladled out the punch—that part of Sherry thought, *I didn't know that someone's knees really could buckle. I didn't know what they meant when they said that their stomach fell through the floor.*

Sheriff Brown caught her by the elbow. He was talking and walking her back into her house. *But I haven't cleaned*, she thought. He was seeing her house for the first time before she'd had the chance to clean. He was still talking, talking. The body was found at seven this morning when the mailman noticed that the front-door glass had been smashed. Sherry was sitting in her favorite chair now. It suddenly felt unbearable to be touching it, as if it was grabbing at her. She jumped to her feet, then fell back into the chair again when she felt as if she didn't have the strength in her legs to stand. "But it can't be," she said. "It can't be Alan." Her throat was tight and achy. "It's never anyone who I—"

She stopped. The horror of it was clear now, clearer than it had ever been. All these people dying. There was death after death, murder after murder in tiny little Winesap, but it was *true*, it had never felt real, because it was never anyone Sherry cared about. A village with a population of under five thousand people, and there was somehow always someone who was new in town or whom Sherry had never spoken to or whom she didn't like very much available to be murdered in an interesting way. And then Sherry would solve it. She always solved it. She'd solved—the cases were starting to come back to her. There were so many. They'd faded into something vague and indistinct in her head, but now she could remember them. She started to count, then gave up at sixteen. Sixteen deaths. Sixteen corpses. It would be an alarming number in a city twenty times the size. How on earth had they all taken this so calmly for so long? It was unnatural, *monstrous*, so strange and callous that it didn't make any sense. Sixteen deaths, and somehow every single time Sherry had ended up involved in the investigation, and every single time she'd been able to crack the case without any particular difficulty or sacrifice. She'd always just been the smartest person involved, always been a step ahead of both the killer and the police. The trouble was that Sherry *knew* herself, and she'd never been that smart. She was just normal. A normal, average, endearingly disorganized librarian for whom odd coincidences always led to her solving murder cases. Like something from a TV show, or an Agatha Christie novel. Like some sort of horrible game.

Something wicked, she'd said to Charlotte the other night. *Maybe something wicked.*

Sheriff Brown was still talking, but she wasn't really listening. She felt out of her mind and more focused than she'd ever been. Something wicked. There was something terrible happening in Winesap, something much bigger than Sherry or Winesap or even each individual death. But what could it possibly be? An elaborate pay-to-kill club for wealthy sociopaths? A serial killer who framed people and then convinced them to confess? A long-running reality TV show with staged murders and Sherry as the unwitting star? Village-wide ergot poisoning causing mass homicidal hallucinations? None of her ideas made any sense, but neither did the reality. She was still running in mental circles when something Sheriff Brown said finally broke through the sound of her own heartbeat. "Will you help investigate?"

She recoiled. "*No*," she said, and gave him what she was sure was a transparently horrified look. "Why would you—you normally don't want me anywhere *near* your cases, and now—isn't it conflict of—he was my—" Her voice cracked. She stopped, looked down, and blinked hard. He hadn't been her anything, really. She'd never admitted it to herself, but it had been all down to her fear of getting herself stuck in another awful relationship that she'd kept Alan at arm's length for so long. She'd been afraid of letting him get too close, but he'd gotten close, anyway. And now he was gone. He was gone forever. All of his kindness and fussiness and pointless knowledge of very serious novels that he never even liked very much. She'd been trying to get him to read more of the sorts of things that he really enjoyed. She'd been tempting him with *Lonesome Dove*. He was gone now. He'd never get to sit in his favorite chair and read a story about cowboys again. He'd never get to imagine himself rugged and brave and riding high in the saddle somewhere under a wide blue sky.

Maybe he didn't have to imagine it now. Maybe he was already there, finding out what sagebrush smelled like.

Eventually Sheriff Brown left. Sherry barely registered his leaving. She went right back to bed.

She stayed in bed for the next few hours. She didn't read or sleep. She just lay there and looked at nothing and thought about nothing. Her head ached. Eventually her phone started to ring. She listened to it ring, dully hating the sound of it. The ringing stopped, then started again. The third time that it stopped and started she got up to answer it, with the vague idea that she might be able to convince whoever was on the other end of the line to leave her the hell alone.

It was Janine, sounding worried and gentle and sympathetic. "Sherry, I just heard, I'm so sorry," she said. "Is there anything that I can do? God, that's a useless question, isn't it. Can I bring some food over? I could make some chicken soup for you."

"No, thank you," Sherry said. "I just—need some time." She wasn't crying. She wondered if that meant that there was something wrong with her. Something about her that was broken or had never formed correctly. She could solve a murder, but she couldn't mourn a death. Not very feminine, maybe. Not the sort of woman who was worthy of a good man, and *God*, how disgustingly narcissistic to turn Alan's death into a referendum on herself. She felt tired and sick to her stomach. She said, "I just need time."

"If you're sure," Janine said after a short pause. "Maybe I could bring you some lunch tomorrow?"

"All right," Sherry said. Maybe if she agreed, Janine would leave her alone.

"Are there any suspects yet?" Janine asked.

"I don't know," Sherry said. Maybe she was going to throw up.

"But aren't you investigating?" Janine asked.

"*No*," Sherry said. She was going to throw up. "Janine, it's *Alan*, I couldn't—do you want me to go look at the crime scene? I was just there last night, we—"

"But you *will* investigate, won't you?" Janine's voice sounded strange. Not flat. The opposite of that, like an actor in a local Winesap production of a too-ambitious modern play. The emotion was spread on too thickly.

"*No,*" Sherry said. "And *please* stop asking. My boyfriend just *died,* Janine." She'd never called Alan her boyfriend before. It was too late to matter now. Too late, too late—

"But you're so *good* at it," Janine said. "Aren't you worried about finding his killer? Don't you want justice? Didn't you love him?" She sounded even less like herself now, harsh and loud and shrill. There was a strange metallic quality to her voice that Sherry didn't think was coming from the speaker of Sherry's old telephone.

"*Stop,*" Sherry said. "*Stop,* you're being *cruel*—" And *had* she loved him, really? Could she have loved him, if she'd let herself? She couldn't anyway now, it was too late, it was too late for Alan, Sherry could solve a murder but she *couldn't fucking well stop one*—

"*You have to investigate, Sherry,*" Janine said. Her voice shrieked like glass breaking and metal tearing. Like a car crash. "You have to, you have to *investigate the crime,* your job is to *solve the murder, you have to investigate the murder*—"

Sherry hung up on her. Then she dashed to the bathroom to throw up until there was nothing left in her stomach.

SEVEN

Sherry had barely gotten herself cleaned up when the phone rang again.

At first she tried to ignore it again, but it went just like it had earlier: the phone rang, then stopped, then started ringing again. She forced herself off the bathroom floor and down the hall to answer it.

"Sherry," said Sheriff Brown. "I was just wondering whether you'd thought at all about who might have a motive to kill Alan."

"*I'm not investigating,*" she said, and slammed the phone down so hard that it bounced off the receiver and dangled pathetically at the end of the cord. She hung up again, more carefully this time, then went back to bed. Lord Thomas jumped onto the bed, and purred, and made himself into a ball on her pillow right next to her head. She petted him and cried into his fur until she fell asleep.

She woke up, for the second time in the past twenty-four hours, to the sound of someone pounding on her door. She jolted automatically out of bed, sending Lord Thomas skittering across the room and into the hall, and then staggered downstairs and to the door, all while harboring the completely unsubstantiated conviction that the person outside was Alice. Needing her help with something, probably. She was working herself into a state of grievance over this idea—How dare Alice always be needing things from her, when Sherry felt so horribly defeated and frightened and sad? Shouldn't Alice have been told about Alan by now? Why did none of their other neighbors bother to check in on Alice and make sure that she had enough to eat and that the electricity was turned on?—when she peeked through the curtains out of habit and saw that it wasn't Alice at all. It was Sheriff Brown pounding on the door with his fist as if he was planning on breaking it down. When Sherry pushed the curtains aside, his gaze shot straight to her as if he'd expected it. She froze for a moment, then instinctively stepped backward, letting the curtains drop back into place.

"Sherry!" he called out. "Sherry, I know you're in there!"

She stepped farther away from the door and the windows. Sheriff Brown kept knocking. *"Sherry!"* he called out. His voice sounded like ice groaning and gravel crunching. Not like the voice of the man she knew at all. *"You have to investigate, Sherry! You have to investigate the crime, your job is to solve the murder, you have to investigate the murder—"*

It was just what Janine had said, Sherry realized, with an abrupt twist in her gut. Word for word.

Sherry didn't answer the door. She went back up to her bedroom and locked the door behind her, then shoved a chair under the door handle the way she'd seen people do on TV. She dug the old rosary out of her bedside table that she hadn't touched in years. She didn't pray, exactly. She held it as if it was a gun. She wished that she'd gone into the kitchen to get a bulb of garlic before she'd come up here to hide. She listened to Sheriff Brown screaming for her outside the door in his inhuman new voice for a long time, for far too long, until the sun started to set. Then, finally, everything went quiet.

Sherry waited for another hour or so, just to be safe. Then she went downstairs, looked up the number for the rectory, and called Father Barry.

"This is going to sound like I've lost my mind," Sherry said.

"I doubt it," Father Barry said. It was seven a.m. and he was sitting across from her in a booth in the Main Street Diner looking as bright-eyed and sun-kissed as a man who'd stepped straight out of an orange juice commercial. "Usually when someone says something that really worries me about their mental health, they don't start off with apologizing for how crazy the story is going to sound. Usually that's the sort of thing that people say when they're about to tell me that they're in trouble." He leaned in a little closer. "Are you in trouble, Sherry?"

She bristled instinctively at the use of her name. The way he used it made her feel as if he'd been reading books about how to win friends and influence people. Then she tried to rein in her suspiciousness. She'd called the poor man and asked him to meet her so she could ask him whether or not he thought that the small town he'd only just moved to was gripped by some sort of mass-murderous madness or dark supernatural influence: the least she could do was refrain from judging the authenticity of his concern because he had *too many social graces*.

"No," she said finally, in response to his question. Then she paused. "Well, maybe. Yes." She paused again. "It really will sound crazy."

"I'll bet that I've heard crazier," he said. "Just try me."

She tried him. She did her best to keep things to the facts, which made everything sound a lot less frightening than it had felt. It was difficult to really communicate something like *his voice sounded like what an iceberg would sound like if icebergs could scream.* "Maybe it was nothing," she said finally.

"I'm so sorry for your loss," Father Barry said. He was quiet for a moment, his eyes on the vegetable omelet the waitress had delivered to him as Sherry told her story. Finally, he looked up at her again. He looked worried. He *definitely* didn't look like a man who'd *heard crazier.* "What do *you* think happened yesterday?"

She could feel herself go very red. "I'm not really sure," she tried, hedging. "Maybe just—the stress getting to the sheriff."

"But you called *me,*" he said. She could swear that he was almost *fidgeting.* "And not a friend, or the police."

"I *can't* call the police, the *sheriff's possessed,*" she said, and then went redder. She'd planned on trying to introduce that idea a bit more delicately. It sounded even more ridiculous now that she'd said it out loud, in a diner, over a plate of pancakes.

"Oh," Father Barry said, looking more nervous than ever. "You think that it's a . . . demon problem."

"I *told* you that you'd think I was crazy," she said, already feeling a sense of rising despair. She was going to be . . . eaten by a demon, or whatever demons did, like the character in the very first scene of the movie who noticed that something strange was going on in the abandoned hospital and decided to have a look around alone in the middle of the night. Father

Barry would be regretful about having not believed her after he saw Sheriff Brown's head spin around 360 degrees, but by then it would be too late for poor Sherry.

"I don't think that you're crazy," he said. He was fidgeting again. "Obviously I take the devil *seriously*, otherwise I wouldn't—" He flapped a hand in the general direction of his collar. "I just, uh. I never took that seminar."

She blinked at him. "What?"

"It's a special seminar," he said. Now *he* was blushing, and practically whispering, as if they were talking about some kind of exotic sexual practice that required you to custom-order the necessary equipment from a single specialty manu-facturer in Baden-Württemberg. "At the Vatican."

"A seminar for what?" Sherry asked, thoroughly baffled. Then it clicked. *"Demon problems?"*

"You know," Father Barry said, and really *did* whisper this time. *"Exorcisms."*

"There's a *seminar?"* Sherry asked, and then started to gig-gle. "Are there . . . PowerPoint presentations?" She imagined a gaggle of priests in their cassocks during their afternoon lunch break on day three of the exorcism conference, eating dry sandwiches and complaining about the quality of this year's speakers. *I can't stand it when these theologians with no real-world experience try to tell actual working exorcists how to do their job,* one priest might say to another, earning a genteel chuckle of professional agreement from a nearby car-dinal.

"I don't know," Father Barry said. He sounded almost as full of despair as Sherry felt. "I've never been. It's sort of—*advanced*, you know? They usually want you to have a degree in psychi-atry before they let you exorcise people."

Sherry blinked. "That's very . . . reasonable of them," she said after a moment. Then: "So if I *did* need an exorcist . . . ?"

"There's supposed to be one for every diocese, I think," Father Barry said. "I could . . . call the bishop and ask if there's one available?"

"Are they usually all *booked in advance*?" Sherry asked. She was starting to feel a little hysterical. She hadn't slept all night, which didn't help at all with her profound sense of unreality. "Is organizing an exorcism like planning a wedding? Is there a *season*?"

"I don't think it's a *full-time position*," Father Barry said. "He probably has to fit the exorcisms in around the rest of his schedule." Then they both just looked at each other for a moment, as the full, bellowing madness of that statement echoed around the red vinyl booth.

Father Barry was the one to finally break the silence. "I was only ordained last year," he said, in a tone that reminded Sherry of miserable childhood confessions of having forgotten her homework.

She allowed herself the smallest bit of softening. "I'd never be able to tell," she told him. "Your homily the other week was very professional."

"Do you really think so?" he asked, brightening. "That was the fifth draft." Then, evidently a bit emboldened, he continued. "You know, there could still be a more"—he flushed slightly—"*earthly* explanation for everything. Your friend Janine acted strangely, but that's really common when people die unexpectedly. People forget how to behave. And Sheriff Brown could just be stressed. We talked about it the day we met, didn't we? How there's such an unusual number of murders around here. It has to be hard on the sheriff."

"But that's *part* of it," Sherry said, leaning forward in her chair until she realized that her sweater was in danger from pancake syrup and was forced to retreat. "It took—it took Alan dying for me to see it. It's not normal. We probably have the highest murder rate per capita on earth, and everyone acts like Winesap is just a sweet, ordinary little village. But it's *not*. Everyone should be fleeing for their lives, but they *aren't*. There's something incredibly strange going on here."

Father Barry was wincing again. "Maybe people are willing to overlook it," he offered. "It *is* a nice little town."

"Father Barry," Sherry said. "Just because you don't want it to be demon problems *doesn't mean that it's not demon problems.*"

He gave a small, restrained sigh. "I just want to make sure that we're not ignoring a simpler explanation."

"Like what?" she asked. "Ergot poisoning?"

"Sherry," he said. "Just because you want it to be demon problems doesn't mean that it's demon problems."

"I don't *want* it to be demon problems," she said, and then immediately conceded defeat. "Right. You're right. I never actually fell asleep last night. I might be a little . . . not at my best."

"No one would expect you to be," Father Barry said, very kindly. "I think that we should both eat our breakfasts. And—I think that I should go with you to talk to Sheriff Brown when we're done."

"Oh," Sherry said, feeling herself relax before she'd even had the chance to register that this was exactly what she had been wanting to hear. "Would you really? That would be so nice of you." If it *wasn't* demon problems, it would be nice to have a big strong young man with her when she went to confront the man who'd spent hours screaming at her front door last night. If it *was* demon problems, then she'd probably be better off to come armed with a priest. If nothing else, if things went truly awry, he'd be able to give her the last rites.

"Of course," Father Barry said, and then started eating his omelet with the energy and enthusiasm of a dog that had finally been allowed to sprint for its food bowl.

Once they were finished with their breakfasts, they walked together toward the sheriff's office. They didn't talk along the way. Sherry was too tired and frightened, and Father Barry looked too nervous. When they got there, the officer at the front desk gave Sherry a shy little wave. "Hi, Miss Pinkwhistle."

"Hello, Cody," Sherry said, in her most grandmotherly tone, and swept on through to Sheriff Brown's office.

Sheriff Brown looked up when she entered. "Oh, Sherry. Did you change your mind about investigating?"

"No," she said, already thrown off. He didn't look at all like a man being confronted by a woman whom he'd screamed at and terrified only a few hours before. He definitely didn't look like a man who'd been demanding that she investigate the murder. He looked just about like he usually did when Sherry saw him, which was to say that he looked a little tired, a little wary, and largely resigned to whatever she was about to subject him to next. "Well, yes, sort of. But I came because I want to talk to you about what happened last night."

"Last night," Sheriff Brown repeated, and then abruptly went very pale. "I don't remember anything. Was I—I don't even remember *drinking* anything." His eyes widened with what looked to Sherry like a frankly *insulting* degree of horror. "Did we—we *didn't*—"

"*No*," Sherry said, feeling exactly as horrified as the sheriff looked. How could she possibly sleep with a *cartoon mouse*? "And even if we had, why on earth would I bring a *priest* along to discuss it?"

Sheriff Brown's whole face went red. "Uh," he said. His eyes darted toward Father Barry. "Why *did* you . . ."

"Sherry wanted me to come along when she spoke to you," Father Barry said. He was standing up very straight, his shoulders back and wide.

Sheriff Brown looked back to Sherry. "About what?"

"You came to my house last night," Sherry said, watching his face carefully as she spoke. She wanted to see his reactions. "You pounded on my door and screamed at me."

He didn't look angry or defensive. Mostly he looked *bewildered*, and possibly frightened. His eyes kept flicking back toward Father Barry. "I don't remember that," he said. "Are you sure that it was me?"

"Completely sure," Sherry said. "I saw your face. And you were shouting about how I had to help you investigate the case. You stayed there for hours."

"My feet were cold," Sheriff Brown said, almost dreamily. "I remember that. I wanted to go home." Then his gaze snapped back to Father Barry. "Does he have to be here?" he asked.

Sherry frowned. "I think I'd be more comfortable if he stayed," she said.

A voice that sounded like wood creaking in the wind emerged from Sheriff Brown's mouth and said, "And what if I'd be more comfortable if you left?"

Sherry jumped. Father Barry sucked in an audible breath. Sherry cleared her throat. "Sheriff Brown?" she ventured. "Are you all right?"

"Sheriff Brown isn't here anymore," Sheriff Brown said.

"Oh," Sherry said. She contemplated saying, *I'll come back later, then!* and leaving immediately. Instead she nailed her courage to the something post—she could never remember how that saying went—and asked, "Who are you, then?"

"Who *am* I?" Not-Sheriff-Brown asked. It sounded almost like a genuine question. "You've brought a priest, so I must be—Lucifer? Yes, *Lucifer.*" His voice changed again, turned deep and gravelly and horrible. "Have you seen *The Exorcist?*"

"Um," Sherry said. She wasn't sure whether it was best to tell the truth or to lie when discussing popular movies with a possibly demonic individual calling himself Lucifer. She wasn't sure why she wasn't more frightened. Maybe she'd worked all her terror out the night before. "I read the book," she said finally. It was the truth. She hoped that Lucifer wouldn't be disappointed.

"Of course," Sheriff Brown said, and then slowly, deliberately started turning his head 180 degrees around on his neck.

"Oh, no, *stop,*" Sherry said, as Father Barry made a sound like, *"Ablaaurgh!"*

The sheriff's head snapped back to the front. *"Fuck you,"* he said, and threw a paperweight straight at Father Barry. A second later he groaned and put both hands to his neck. "What the—did I just—" He was back to using his own, ordinary voice again. "My *neck*—"

"Here," Father Barry said, and thrust a rosary toward him. Sherry wondered whether he traveled with extras. "Hold that."

"I'm a Lutheran," Sheriff Brown said. He sounded dazed.

"Take it, anyway," Father Barry said, and then physically put the rosary around Sheriff Brown's neck. Sheriff Brown didn't scream or fling it away or turn into a giant bat. He just blinked dozily at Father Barry for a moment.

"My head hurts," he slurred out. "I think I'm sick. I think—I should go home." He stood up, swaying slightly. Then he staggered out the door.

Sherry and Father Barry stared at each other.

"Father," Sherry said, "I think that it's demon problems."

EIGHT

The two of them scuttled out of the sheriff's office a few moments later, hoping not to catch the eye of anyone who might ask difficult questions like, *Which one of you was doing all of that horrible demonic screaming in the sheriff's office just now?* Sherry grasped Father Barry's elbow as soon as they were out the door and shepherded him a few yards down the street before it occurred to her that she didn't know where she was leading him and released him again.

"I'm going to call the bishop," Father Barry said. He looked a little pale and sweaty. "I'm *underqualified for this.*"

"You'd think that they'd at least teach you the *basics,*" Sherry said, feeling aggrieved with the Catholic Church all over again. As if there weren't enough wrong with them, they had to bogart all the anti-demon trainings. At the moment she'd give almost anything for a nice, modern, Unitarian Universalist exorcist. The Unitarian exorcist would probably be a Montessori school administrator with a master's degree in social work with a focus in cross-cultural sensitivity in evil-spirit extraction. "You don't have to be a doctor of demonology, but they could at least have given you the hour-long CPR certification course version, just in case there's an emergency."

"Demonology is actually—" Father Barry started, and then stopped, possibly quailing under the force of the look that Sherry was giving him. "I'll call the bishop," he said again. He was rubbing his hands on his thighs. "Do you think that he was really Lucifer? It sounded like he was just making that up."

"It did sound a little . . . improvised," Sherry said. "I'm not sure if we're better or worse off than if I'd told it I was a druid or something. It definitely got more . . . aggressive after it asked about *The Exorcist*. But maybe if I'd said that, we'd end up with some sort of prehistoric Iron Age god in Sheriff Brown's body, and the bishop wouldn't know what to do with it."

Now Father Barry was giving *her* a reproachful look. "God is still God," he said. "And the devil is still the devil, no matter what you call him."

"If you say so," Sherry said distractedly. "Do you think I should buy some crystals?"

"*Crystals?*" Father Barry asked. "What kind?"

"You know," she said. "The kinds they have in the New Age store. For the . . . auras and things. To protect us against the demons."

"*Sherry,*" he said. "I'm a *priest.*"

"Oh, right," she said. "You can't recommend anything that comes from the competitors."

"I'm not a *vacuum cleaner salesman*," Father Barry said. "I have *faith*, Sherry." He paused. "Do they have ones for demons, specifically?"

"I'll ask at the shop," she said. "Would you like to come? We'll probably both want some supplies. Or can you not be seen inside?"

"There's lots of reasons to be in a New Age store," Father

Barry answered after a pause. "They usually sell really reasonably priced candles."

"I wouldn't have thought of you as a candle man," Sherry said, briefly distracted from the thrust of their conversation.

He blushed. "I like to host dinner parties," he said defensively.

"Oh, really?" she asked. "Do you cook?"

"Yes," he said. "Last month I made—" He stopped. "I don't think it's the time to talk about that, do you?"

"You might as well tell me about it," she said as she started walking in the direction of Sun and Moon Boutique. "I could use the distraction." Her head was starting to ache. "And if I keep thinking about Sheriff Brown I might scream."

"All right," Father Barry said eventually, and launched into a description of an impressively elaborate-sounding Tuscan-themed meal he'd recently prepared for five guests. Sherry was intrigued enough by this new twist in Father Barry's persona—she'd envisioned him as solidly a hot dog and meat loaf kind of guy—that it really was a good distraction from what had just happened in the sheriff's office. Really, it was hard to continue feeling anything about what had happened at all: it had been so horrible and so wholly bizarre that it already felt like a nightmare that she'd long since woken up from.

The woman who owned the Sun and Moon Boutique seemed as if she'd been waiting all day for a woman with a priest to walk into her shop and ask, "What do you have for evil spirits?" because when Sherry did exactly that, she sprang into action immediately without taking even a moment or two to gloat. Sherry left laden with crystals and herbs and special candles and bags full of salt that Sherry was assured was *blessed* salt and not just the regular non-iodized natural hippie salt that you could buy for somewhat alarming prices at the grocery co-op in Albany. Then they parted ways, with Father Barry promising once again that he'd call his bishop to ask for help, and Sherry heading straight to the library. She needed to do some research.

The Winesap Library wasn't particularly rich in books about the occult. Sherry grabbed what they had and then ducked behind the circulation desk to check herself out while Connie was in the restroom. She tried to be as fast as she could, but Connie caught her, anyway. "Sherry, I just heard about what happened to poor Alan, I'm so—" Her eyes caught on the cover of one of the books Sherry was checking out then, and she stopped. The title, in eye-catching bright red, read: *When the Dead Speak.*

Sherry felt her face go warm. "Thank you," she said, and then shoved all the books into her gigantic purse and briskly trotted off. She was already well clear of the library when it occurred to Sherry that now she'd have to go back to her own demon-haunted house and spend the next however many hours completely alone.

She occupied herself for about half an hour with placing crystals in their designated spots around her house and pouring the special salt across the windows and doorways, which she immediately regretted. The salt might or might not repel demons, but either way it would get tracked all over her house and she'd have to spend an hour trying to vacuum it out of the rugs. Then she made herself a sandwich and started reading about hauntings and possessions. She'd never been extremely interested in horror stories—they gave her bad dreams—and their sudden relevance to her personal life didn't make them into more enjoyable reading. By six o'clock it was getting dark in her living room, and she was rattled enough to shut all the books, turn on all the lights, switch on the usually neglected television for company, and pour herself a generous serving from her dusty old bottle of brandy.

At some point she must have fallen asleep, because she woke up to the sound of a man's voice very close to her ear. "Woman!" the voice said. "This isn't the time for you to sleep! It's only just gone past six, woman, and I have yet to sup!"

Sherry kept her eyes closed. Whoever was speaking to her was a demon, presumably, and she didn't want to look at it. It was probably hideous and would give her nightmares if she survived this encounter, and opening her eyes wasn't very likely to improve her chances of making it out alive. She'd never been a fast sprinter or learned to do kung fu, and from her experience of reading Stephen King novels, she doubted that either of those skills would do much against an evil spirit, anyway. If she was going to die, she would die without having to look at some horrible monster's disgusting drippy face first.

"Woman!" said the voice again. It was coming from *very* close to her face. It was a deep voice, with a *Masterpiece Theatre* sort of English accent. Not a particularly frightening voice, really. Sort of . . . jolly. "Get up! Time is passing by apace!"

Sherry cracked one eye open. There was no demon. All she could see, a few inches from her nose, was the familiar furry little visage of her fat orange cat. He was sitting on the arm of the sofa where the fabric was already pretty well shredded.

"Lord Thomas Cromwell?" Sherry said, astonished. Then the penny dropped. "Oh, no."

"If you hadn't wanted me here," Lord Thomas Cromwell said, "then you oughtn't have given the beast my name."

"You speak awfully modern English, for a Tudor politician,"

Sherry said. Her heart rate was starting to slow. She couldn't feel that frightened of *Lord Thomas*. Once she'd had to rescue him after he'd gotten his head stuck in a soup can. "You talk like a Tudor whose dialogue is being written by a bad American screenwriter." She was starting to suspect that, whatever sort of creature was responsible for the goings-on in Winesap, it *definitely* watched too much television.

"You're pert above your station, woman," the cat said. Then, more mulishly: "And I want my supper."

"Are you actually the real Lord Thomas Cromwell?" Sherry asked. "What was being executed like?"

"Never you mind," the cat said. He was speaking without his mouth moving, which was a relief. She didn't want to see how the demon puppeteering her cat would attempt to adapt his lipless little mouth to accommodate human speech. "You ask questions above your station, too. Why are you talking when you could be preparing food or investigating murders?"

"You're a cat," Sherry said. She was starting to feel less worried and more as if she was enjoying herself a little. "You don't have a *station*. You can't operate the can opener on your own. If you want to eat, you'll have to behave yourself. Why would the tormented spirit of Lord Thomas Cromwell be interested in a murder investigation in Winesap, New York? Are you sure that you aren't just the same . . . *individual* that I was speaking to earlier, in the sheriff's office?"

The cat was silent for a moment. She couldn't glean much from his expression, because he was a cat. It was possible that he was trying to scowl at her but failing due to a lack of eyebrows. Eventually he cleared his throat, which struck her as somehow an even stranger thing for a cat to do than speak English and demand murder investigations. The sound was definitely too deep to have come from his precious weensy little throat. "It's a bit complicated," he said. Then he stood up onto all four paws and said, "And what of my supper, woman?"

"You won't get any supper if you keep calling me *woman*," Sherry said. "It's *Miss Pinkwhistle* to you."

"Do you really see yourself as fit to make demands of *me*, woman?" the cat said.

"Yes," Sherry said. "Don't you test me, Lord Thomas. I might run the vacuum cleaner."

As far as a cat could be said to ever look alarmed, Lord Thomas Cromwell did. "There's no need to resort to violence!" he said. "I'm sure that we can come to some satisfaction, Miss Pinkwhistle. What do you want from me?"

"What do *you* want from *me*?" Sherry countered. "I'm not the one possessing *your* cat. You can't just come into a woman's home, possess her cat, demand supper, and then demand that she issue demands. Who are you, and what are you doing here? *It's complicated* doesn't count as an explanation."

"Convincing you to investigate the murder," Lord Thomas said. "Why won't you just *do as you're told?*"

"Because I don't want to," Sherry said. "Why do you care so much? What's going on here? Who *are* you? Is it some kind of—human sacrifice cult? But why do you want me to *find the murderer?*" It sounded insane. It *was* insane. She was *talking to a cat*.

"*I* don't care about your petty human murders," said the cat. Then he lowered his voice. "This is all at the behest of *her*."

"*Her?*" Sherry repeated. She found herself almost whispering, which would have probably felt less ridiculous if she hadn't been whispering to her cat. "Who do you mean?"

"She doesn't have a name," Lord Thomas said. "To call her

her is a mere convenience. Creatures like her don't have a sex. When she takes a form, it's often that of a beautiful young woman, but sometimes it's an old man or a lost child. She's an old thing, and a cruel one. She used to steal pretty children or handsome young men and take them as her playthings. Now she has found a new dollhouse to amuse herself with."

"Winesap?"

"Winesap," the cat agreed. "And you, Miss Pinkwhistle."

Sherry resolutely didn't allow herself to shiver. "And where do *you* come in?"

Lord Thomas shifted uncomfortably. It was adorable. Then he said, "She has conscripted me into her service after I, through no fault of my own, unwittingly earned her ire."

Sherry raised her eyebrows. No one used that many words to say that something wasn't their fault when they were completely innocent. "What did you actually do, Sir Thomas?"

He did more shifting back and forth between his sweet little orange paws. Then he muttered, "I tried to eat her."

Sherry blinked. *"What?"*

"She had taken the form of a gleaming white moth," Sir Thomas said with enormous dignity. "I can't be held responsible for my actions."

"Are you *usually* a cat?" Sherry asked, momentarily distracted from trying to find out more about the malevolent spirit who'd taken over the town. Cats did seem as if they struggled to resist trying to eat moths, gleaming white or otherwise.

"I am *Lord Thomas Cromwell*," Lord Thomas Cromwell said grandly, then lowered his voice and said, "I am more frequently a Lord of Cats."

"Oh," Sherry said. She didn't feel as if there was much else that she could say, really. The cat was looking at her expectantly, though, so she tried: "You must be very important."

"I am, yes," the cat said, and took a moment to polish his ears. Then he lowered his voice again and said, "Have you any more of that salt?"

Sherry started to say yes. The cat hissed at her. Sherry blinked. "What—"

The cat shook his head, then nodded, then, surreally, held his paw up to his lips.

"Oh!" Sherry said, then winced, put a hand over her own mouth, and scurried to her bags of New Age supplies to get the special salt. She held it out to the cat, who narrowed his eyes and pawed at the air to remind her that he didn't have hands to take it with. She blushed. He jumped off the arm of the sofa and began trotting around the coffee table counterclockwise. Around and around. She stared. He stopped, gave a disgusted yowl, then stared pointedly at the salt. "Oh, right!" she said. He started trotting in his circle again. She followed him, pouring salt as she went, and thinking sadly about how she was going to have to move the coffee table if she wanted to drag the rug outside to really shake all the salt out. Once the circle was complete, the cat jumped onto the coffee table. Sherry eyed it, then very carefully sat, hoping that the legs would hold up.

The cat cleared its throat. "Now that we have blessed this altar," he said, "we may speak more freely."

"Oh, good," said Sherry. She waited for a moment. The cat stared up at her with his lemon-lime eyes. She stared back at him. "Well?"

The cat hunkered in closer. "I would like to suggest that we strike a bargain."

Sherry frowned. "What kind of bargain?"

"She has tasked me with making sure that you play your part in her game," Lord Thomas Cromwell said. "She wants you to investigate her latest little killing."

"Not little," Sherry said.

Lord Thomas blinked. "I beg your pardon?"

"Not little," Sherry said. "It was *Alan*. His death wasn't *little*." She felt slightly sick. "*None* of them were little. *All* of them mattered. I was just—in a play. In a dream. Until it was Alan. It wasn't real until it was Alan." Shame was dripping down her throat. It should have been real to her before. It was a child's morality to only care about things that happened to her, personally. Her ex-husband had always said that she thought like a child. "Don't call it little again," she said. "None of them. None of them were little deaths."

"Very well," the cat said after a pause. "She wants you to investigate this latest murder. She has tasked me to chivy you into obeying. And what do *you* want?"

"For the killings to stop," Sherry said. "For her to go away." And for Alan back, but she wasn't going to say that aloud to a possibly evil talking cat. There was the chance that he could take her seriously. She shivered.

"Precisely," said the cat. "I know her, as much as a thing like her can be known. If she can be destroyed, that is a thing that *isn't* known. That is a secret that has been forgotten. But creatures like her can be beaten back, for a time, by creatures like you."

"Like *me*?" Sherry asked, and looked down at herself, in a dreadful stupid moment of imagining that her life might have turned into enough of a piece of supernatural fiction for her to have transformed into something special as well, something young and fit and attractive, wearing lots of black leather with a weapon strapped to her thigh. No such thing had occurred. She was still just herself, just ordinary Sherry. Too old and plump and badly dressed to be a heroic demon-fighting protagonist. It was unfortunate that she was the only person around available to take on the role. There was no one in Winesap, as far as she could think, who wouldn't look very silly in leather pants. But maybe the cat saw something in her that she couldn't see in herself? That was the sort of thing that sometimes happened to protagonists.

"Yes," said the cat. "A human creature like you."

"*Oh*," Sherry said, slightly embarrassed. "Human. Yes, I am . . . that. Absolutely. What can I *do*, exactly? I don't have any, you know. Special skills." She imagined herself wielding, possibly, nunchucks. The image was a dispiriting one.

"Have you heard of the creatures called *vampires*?" asked the cat, in the tone of voice of a specific type of man asking a woman if she'd ever heard of a particular very obscure and sophisticated band.

"Yes," Sherry said. "I've read lots of books about them. Why?"

"Oh," said the cat, in the tone of voice of the same man who has discovered, to his great disappointment, that the woman has seen the obscure and sophisticated band perform live on several occasions. "I see. Then you know that they are said to sup upon human blood."

"*Sup upon*," Sherry repeated. "Yes, I know. What does this have to do with me fighting demons?"

"The vampire," Lord Thomas said, "has great strength and the power of flight. But the human has the *blood*."

Sherry frowned. "So," she said, "the human—me—I have something that she wants."

"That she *needs*," he said. "Your mind. Your attention. Your *belief* in her."

"But I *don't* believe in demons, or spirits, or—whatever she is. I mean, I didn't, until the sheriff tried to spin his head around and my cat started talking to me. Should I just *ignore* you? How's *that* supposed to work?"

"You may not *think* that you believe in things that hide in the dark," the cat said. "You do, though. It's in the hollows of your bones. Your heart quickens when you see a shadow through the window. *All* human creatures believe in the older things. All human creatures were raised with their own understanding of them. It is your understanding of such spirits that has altered much of her behavior already. Fortunately for you, I am a creature well-versed in the sorts of fairy stories that you were fed upon as a whelp."

"Now you're just being *rude*," Sherry said. "I don't even know what kind of animal has whelps, but I know that it isn't people. And I have no idea what you're actually trying to *tell* me." It had occurred to her, in a burst of misery, that this could all be nothing but some sort of weird trick or mind game—or, even worse, that she really had simply gone crazy. If that was the case, then she truly was in trouble. Everything about her life had become so strange and frightening that it was difficult to say what, exactly, was likely to be a figment of her imagination, and if she had gone so far as to imagine an entire string of murders that she had solved, then she was so utterly disconnected from reality that there was probably nothing that could be done to help her. Unless it was LSD in the water supply or ergot at the local bakery, she supposed. At this point, she could only hope for ergot.

"I am trying to offer you a deal," the cat said, clearly happily oblivious to the crisis Sherry was undergoing. "You will continue to investigate, so as to appease her. In this way you shall keep her, as the saying goes, *off of my sleek, soft back*. In return, I shall offer you guidance . . . in your *greater understanding* of her."

Sherry frowned. "What does that mean, exactly? What will you do, specifically?"

The cat lowered his voice to a whisper. "Don't speak so loudly! Your emotions call to her. What I will do, exactly, is advise you on how it is that she might be defeated. If you have questions to ask, it might be that I will be able to answer them."

"You know how to defeat her?" Sherry asked. "So tell me, then. Won't that solve both of our problems?"

The cat hissed at her. "Not so loud! No, I cannot simply tell you. To fight a creature like her is a matter of subtlety. The right weapon for one man might be the undoing of another. You must use your own discernment to discover which weapon calls to your hand. I may advise you, but I may not tell you the way."

Sherry had never been an avid reader of high fantasy—she preferred the sorts of stories that involved interesting things happening to ordinary people in the real world, for the slightly embarrassing reason that it made it easier for her to imagine getting to go on an adventure of her own—but she'd been around for long enough to recognize a genre convention when she was fed one by her own fat marmalade cat. "That," she said, "sounds like a very thin plot contrivance."

"I beg your pardon?"

"Prithee, sir," Sherry said, "that sounds like you just made it up."

The cat puffed up his tail at her. "Of course it's *made up*," he said. "As are all things that matter. If you and I stood before a priest and asked to be married now, we would be refused, but had I the shape of a man, the priest could say a few words and bind us unto eternity in the eyes of all laws on earth and heaven. What aspect of that is not made up? My form and yours, the words, earthly law? Belief, all of it. Adherence to convention. A convention much younger than I am, woman, and laws that were made when *she* was already older than most rivers. She hews to more ancient laws. And so must you, Mistress Pinkwhistle, if you hope to have the best of her."

If someone had been there to ask how Sherry had felt as the cat spoke, she would have been forced to admit to how all the hairs on her arms were prickling. She tried to act unaffected. "Or what? What will happen if I just ignore you?"

"Then you shall carry on as you have been," he said. "And labor as a mummer in her little murder plays. Perhaps more of your mortal companions will be the next to die for the sake of her amusement. What is the pinch-faced astrologer's name?"

Sherry was starting to feel sick again. More murders. She might be trapped like this forever: endlessly chasing after killers at the whim of . . . someone. Something. *Her.* It rankled at her a bit to have to take the deal. The problem was that the cat held all the cards, despite his lack of thumbs. "She's a *psychologist*, not an astrologer. And you can quit threatening my friends. I should have named you something else, Lord Thomas. You haven't turned into a more pleasant person over the centuries. Thomas More probably would have made a nicer cat."

"That's what *you* say, Mistress Pinkwhistle," Lord Thomas said. "But only because you've never had to sit through a dinner with Thomas More. The only thing more unbearable than his sanctimony was his halitosis."

"You're just jealous that you never had a flattering Oscar-winning movie made about you," Sherry told him. "And *your* breath smells like cat food."

The cat gave a deep, old-man, "Hm!" which was almost as unnerving as when he cleared his throat. Then he said, "Do we have a deal, woman?"

"*Mistress Pinkwhistle*," she reminded him. His faux-Tudor syntax was weirdly contagious. "And I suppose that we do. Though I'm only agreeing under protest."

"I'll have the stenographer enter your protestation into the record," said the cat. It was a particularly bad bit of dialogue for an English lawyer from the 1500s. Stenographers hadn't even been *invented*, for goodness' sake. Sherry was getting the sense that this Lord of Cats wasn't taking any of this very seriously, which she supposed was exactly what you would expect from a Lord of Cats, when she thought about it. Then, even more absurdly, Lord Thomas held out one little furry paw. "We shall swear our oath on a handshake."

Sherry shook the paw. She managed to keep herself from giggling until after she'd released it, for fear of his claws. "Deal," she managed. Then, because she couldn't help herself, she said, "Is it really a handshake, considering?"

She expected the cat to say something rude and sarcastic in return. Instead, he only hopped off the coffee table and trotted toward the kitchen with his tail held high in the air, pausing only to say, "*Meow*."

Sherry blinked. Then she frowned. "Are you *really* just a cat again?"

Sherry's cat didn't respond to her question. In ordinary

circumstances, this wouldn't have made her feel uncomfortable. She eyed him. "I'm not letting you sleep in my bedroom either way."

The cat ignored her and continued into the kitchen. A moment later she heard him start to scream for his dinner exactly like he usually did.

There was, she thought, not very much difference in the behavior of a cat and a high-handed, chauvinistic Tudor autodidact in the body of a cat. The only thing to truly set them apart was the vocabulary. She sighed. Then she got up and went to the kitchen to open a new can of horrible salmon-flavored wet food.

NINE

The next morning, Sherry started her day by packing her biggest quilted purse with essential supplies. First, she put in a few ugly plastic rosaries she'd been given at first communions and baptisms and had never bothered clearing out of her junk drawer. Next, she added in some crystals. Finally, she went into the kitchen to fill a few small Ziploc bags with salt and empty out the spray bottle that she used to keep Lord Thomas off the counters. She showed the spray bottle to the cat, who was basking in a sunbeam on the kitchen floor. "I'm going to fill this with holy water," she told him. "So don't get any ideas. I'd like my cat to stay a cat. Any funny business and you're getting the spritz."

Lord Thomas rolled over onto his back to show her his soft white belly. She frowned. Either he really *was* just a cat again, in which case her little speech was embarrassing, or he wasn't a cat and was actively *trying* to embarrass her by making her feel as if she'd just been standing alone in her kitchen toughtalking a harmless little kitty like they were a couple of rival mafiosos. She felt her cheeks go warm. Then she shoved the salt and spray bottle into her bag and left.

From her house she went straight to church, where she filled up her spray bottle from the convenient metal container near the font, the purpose of which had always previously eluded her. It hadn't occurred to her to think that it might be there just in case someone had an urgent case of demon problems. Maybe they were required by the church in case of demonic mishaps in the same way that the government mandated sprinklers in restaurants in case of grease fires.

From the church she marched directly back to the sheriff's department, straight past the front desk and into the sheriff's office. Sheriff Brown, predictably, looked extremely irritated. "You can't just barge in here whenever you want, Sherry," he said. "What is it?"

"I'm very sorry," Sherry said, and spritzed him straight in the face with the holy water.

Sheriff Brown made a horrible roaring sound, like something between a T. rex and a garbage disposal. Sherry spritzed him again, more to try to get him to stop making that noise than for any other reason. This time the sound he made was a very ordinary human-sounding squawk. "What the f— *hell*, Sherry?" he said, with a look in his eye like a man who had sublimated his desire to say a curse word into a more respectable urge to slap a senior citizen. Sherry took a step back. "You can't just— Get out of my office, *now!*"

"Only if you take these," Sherry said, and shoved two crystals, some salt, and a plastic rosary into his hand. "And promise to keep them on you."

Sheriff Brown looked like a man who was prepared to argue. He opened his outraged mouth. Sherry cut him off before he could start. "Just take them, and I promise that I'll leave and stop bothering you."

The sheriff gave her a baleful look but didn't projectile vomit or try to break his own neck again. Instead, he took the fistful of items Sherry was offering and jammed them into his pocket. *"Leave."*

"Keep them on you," she said. "Maybe you should put them in a lanyard or something. Like an amulet."

"Get out before I arrest you," Sheriff Brown said, and Sherry got out. She couldn't even blame the demonic possession for getting kicked out of the sheriff's office this time: that had been the very ordinary voice of a more-than-ordinarily annoyed Sheriff Brown. She tried not to worry too much that she'd made a mistake by coming by. She didn't want the sheriff to be possessed, but she also didn't want to be on a very not-possessed sheriff's bad side.

The library was just a quick walk away. She went there, more so she could spend a few minutes breathing in the deeply ordinary and comforting smell of the place than for any other reason. Generally, Sherry spent a lot of time disabusing her bookish friends of the idea that being a librarian was the ideal career for a reader: it wasn't as if the county paid her to achieve her goal of finally getting through *The Guermantes Way* or chatting with her fellow bibliophiles about the latest Jonathan Franzen. Most of the time when she was at work, she was more concerned with keeping the patrons from flushing foreign objects down the fragile old toilet than she was with soaking in the lovely book-drenched atmosphere. Whenever she came to the library on a day off, she found herself startled by how legitimately pleasant a place it was to be.

She wandered through the shelves for a while, avoiding making eye contact with anyone who might want to speak with her, until her feet came to an abrupt stop. A moment later a book jumped off the shelf and landed on her left foot. She'd already been hissing and dramatically hopping up and down for a few seconds of silent agony before she registered which book had just attacked her.

It was a biography of Thomas Cromwell.

For a moment, Sherry considered leaving without the book, just as a way to assert her independence from her demonic overlord. Then she gave in and grabbed it off the ground. If she was going to, in a sense, *live* with the man, she might as well know a bit more about him than what she'd gleaned from *A Man for All Seasons*, which was exactly enough to make her think that *Lord Thomas Cromwell* would be a very funny name for a cat and not a drop more. At the very least she might glean something that she could use to insult him if he tried being rude to her again.

Once she was home, she added the biography to her fast-growing pile of demon-related literature, then went to the telephone to make some calls. First, she called up Janine and managed to make it just long enough for Janine to pick up the phone before she blurted out, "Do you remember calling me?"

"Sherry," Janine said after a moment. "You just called *me*. I picked up the phone. Are you all right?"

"I'm fine," Sherry said. "I mean the last time you called me. You shouted at me about how I need to investigate Alan's death."

There was a longer pause this time. Sherry braced herself for denial and an argument, just like how Sheriff Brown had argued with her. Instead, Janine said, "I've been worried about that for days. I remember calling you to find out how you were, and then everything went hazy. I was thinking about bringing it up at my next physical. I *shouted* at you?"

Sherry, unexpectedly, felt her eyes start to sting. Embarrassing. She blinked a few times. "You did," she said. It came out plaintive. "You didn't sound like yourself. And—" She hesitated, just for a second. Then the whole wild story came tumbling out: Janine's call, and Sheriff Brown standing outside her door the whole night long, and talking to Father Barry and having him witness the absolute madness of what happened at the sheriff's office, and then finally, terribly, humiliatingly, she had to say aloud, in English, to another human being, that her cat had been possessed by the spirit of an extremely rude and even more extremely dead figure from English history.

This time the silence stretched out for so long that Sherry had a miserable moment of wondering whether Janine might have hung up on her in disgust. Instead, Janine said, "Maybe we ought to talk in person."

"Yes," Sherry said immediately, and thought fast. "Eight tomorrow morning at the rectory at Sacred Heart?"

"At the *rectory*?" Janine asked. "Why?"

"So that my cat can't spy on me," Sherry said. She felt a little giddy. "Just make sure that you come. I'll see you in the morning."

As soon as she hung up, she picked up the phone again, this time to call Charlotte. She told the whole story again. Charlotte didn't go silent at least. She gasped and groaned and said things like, "*Seriously? Oh my God!*" that suggested to Sherry that she was taking her story with gratifying seriousness. When people didn't take you seriously, they never demanded to know whether or not you were being serious: they just made subdued noises of agreement as often as possible until they spotted a window in the speeding train of your narrative, jumped out of it, and ran desperately toward the safety of a change of subject.

Then Sherry got to the part about Lord Thomas, and

Charlotte started to laugh. "Oh my God, Sherry, you really got me, I thought you were serious! I was sitting here getting goose bumps remembering how you were talking about *something wicked* coming the other day, like, *this is it!* So how are you, really? I'm so sorry about your friend, by the way. I wanted to call you, but I didn't want to intrude."

"You could have called," Sherry said, oddly touched. "I always like talking to you. And I wasn't joking."

And *there* was the nervous silence. Sherry was the one to break it. "I'd like you to meet me at the rectory at Sacred Heart tomorrow morning."

Charlotte started giggling again. "At the Catholic church? So like—in case one of us gets possessed, the priest is nearby?"

"Sort of," Sherry said. "Father Barry's going to be there. Mostly I want to make sure that the cat can't listen in."

Charlotte giggled even harder at that. "Oh, great! I'm glad that's the reason. That's kind of fun." Then, abruptly: "Do you think the girl who killed John was possessed?"

Sherry swallowed. "I hadn't thought of that," she said honestly. "Maybe."

"Oh," Charlotte said. "Jesus. What does that mean, do you think? I mean—should she go to prison? Do you think she really wanted to do it? You can't plead not guilty by reason of the devil making you do it, can you?"

"I don't know," Sherry said. "I think that people try, but it doesn't usually work. Son of Sam didn't get away with it, at least." She swallowed again. "I think we should try to stop the—whatever it is from hurting any more people before we start worrying about the rest of it."

"Not like worrying about it would make a difference, anyway," Charlotte said. "What are we going to do, call up the governor and go, 'Listen, you might want to sit down, this is going to *blow your mind*.' Wait a second, is that what you're calling about? You want me to help you *fight demons*?"

"I'd *like* you to help me fight demons," Sherry said. She was blushing. "You don't *have* to, though, if you don't want to. I don't want to pressure you. But you're one of the smartest people I know around here, and you've been affected by all of this. I thought that you might want to be involved."

"Are you kidding?" Charlotte asked. "I've just been sitting around crying and eating Oreos for weeks now, and you're telling me that I have the option of going full Buffy instead? Even if you're crazy, at least I'll have to put a bra on to help you investigate whether or not your evil cat's trying to kill you."

"I don't think that Lord Thomas is trying to kill me, exactly," Sherry said, in the spirit of fair play. "Mostly he's just tried to boss me around and get me to open cans for him in exchange for telling me secrets, which isn't that different from how cats usually act. But I don't want him listening in on my conversations."

"Understood," Charlotte said. "Makes complete sense. Should I bring anything tomorrow to the demon-hunting society meeting? Do we need . . . garlic? Stakes? Ingredients for mimosas? Are we doing brunch, or just coffee?"

"The garlic and stakes probably wouldn't hurt," Sherry said. "I've been stocking up on crystals. Every little bit helps, when it comes to demons. And I'm going to bring some pastries." Then she said goodbye to Charlotte and hung up to call Father Barry, feeling markedly more cheerful than she had a few minutes earlier. There was something really bolstering about having Charlotte laugh at her and then promise to come help, anyway. It made her feel as if things couldn't be quite as bad as they felt.

Father Barry wasn't nearly as delighted with her call as Charlotte had been. Mostly he just sounded annoyed that she'd planned to use the rectory as the venue for the inaugural meeting of the demon-hunting society without consulting with him first. "I'm still moving in! There are still boxes everywhere in here, Sherry!"

"Boxes everywhere are better than demons everywhere, Father," Sherry said reasonably. "We won't mind. None of us are the world's best housekeepers, either. I'm going to bring pastries."

"I guess I could make some coffee," Father Barry said sullenly. "Don't expect anything special, though. I haven't even had time to unpack the espresso machine."

Sherry took a moment to marvel over that particular pronouncement before she said, "I don't think anyone will expect a cappuccino, Father. I'll see you in the morning." Then she hung up and returned to her growing pile of library books. She needed to learn everything about demons that she could, with the inaugural meeting of her local demon-hunting society in just a few hours.

Sherry arrived at the rectory the next morning a few minutes after eight. "I'm so sorry I'm late," she said, as Father Barry ushered her into a completely spotless living room with no evidence of so much as a packing peanut anywhere in sight. "There was a line at the bakery." She deposited her greasy bags of doughnuts and Danishes on Father Barry's gleaming coffee table and then blinked at Charlotte, who was seated on his couch dressed in knee-high boots and some sort of cargo vest, and drinking what looked suspiciously like a cappuccino. "Uh. Good morning."

"Good morning!" Charlotte said. "Do you want a coffee? I was just showing Barry how to do some latte art."

"She's so talented!" Janine said from her spot in a nearby armchair.

"I found the espresso machine," Father Barry added, and then trotted off. Sherry made strained small talk with Charlotte until he returned in triumph with a foamy little drink in a dainty little cup, and there was a bit of collective exclaiming over how well he'd made the foamy little tulip on top.

"Well," Sherry said, after the excitement had died down. "I'm glad to hear that you've all been enjoying yourselves." It came across, she was afraid, less than entirely sincerely. "Are we all ready to get started?"

"Oh, definitely," Charlotte said. "I'd like to call this meeting of the Village Library Demon-Hunting Society officially to order!"

Barry waved his hand a little. "Shouldn't it be the *Rectory* Demon-Hunting Society?"

"Definitely not," Charlotte said. "We're a nondenominational organization. And, anyway, our fearless leader's the librarian."

Everyone looked at Sherry.

"Er," Sherry said, suddenly self-conscious. "Right." She sat down on the couch next to Charlotte and went digging into the bag of doughnuts for a moment to buy time. She picked out a chocolate glazed. Then she said, "Well. I guess—the problem is that we have a demon in town. Or an . . . ancient spirit, I guess. My cat has been calling it just *her*. I think I've bought some time with her by promising to investigate Alan's death, but that's not really a long-term solution to a demon infestation. I thought that maybe if we all got together, we could come up with some ideas about how to stop her."

"Honestly," Janine said, "I'm only here because I'm worried about you, Sherry. I know that you're upset about Alan, of course you are, but you can't let yourself get sucked into some wild conspiracy theory." She looked at the other two for confirmation. "Right?"

There was a moment of silence. Janine frowned. "You two aren't in on this, too, are you?"

Father Barry cleared his throat. "I know that I might be, uh, expected to take a certain stance, professionally. But I was with Sherry when she went to see the sheriff the other day. I guess that there could be some other explanation for what happened, but I'm not sure what the explanation could *be*." He looked unhappy. "I do trust that God won't give me anything that I can't handle, but I definitely wasn't *hoping* for demons. It just . . . looks like it might be demons."

"I believe her, too," Charlotte said abruptly. "I've been thinking about it since Sherry called yesterday. There's been weird stuff happening to me for a while now. Like right after John died. I found his body, and the cops came, and the next thing I knew I was at the library asking Sherry for help. I guess I just thought that I blacked out for a second from the shock. But—no offense, Sherry—why would I go to some lady I've only met a few times before I called my own mom to tell her what happened? It was like something was making sure I followed the script. And my lawyer friend I called hasn't been able to make it here this whole time. Every time she tries, something crazy happens to keep her away. Last night her *car* caught on fire. Like, it just blew up in the parking garage. It doesn't make any sense."

"That's not evidence of anything," Janine said. "This is all just a bunch of confirmation bias. I believe you that you can't remember much after you found John's body, Charlotte, but I think that your gut was probably right originally when you thought that it was just the shock. Our memories are *incredibly* fallible, especially when it comes to trauma. And your friend not showing up when you needed her is awful, but sometimes people are just flaky. I know someone whose fiancé left her at the altar in 1987, and as much as I'm sure she would have preferred thinking that the devil made him do it, I'm pretty sure that he was just a jerk."

"Wow, *condescending*!" Charlotte said.

"Janine," Father Barry said, "I don't mean to be rude, but you have three completely sane people all suddenly telling you that they think that we might be having"—he flushed—"demon problems. Couldn't you at least *consider* the idea that we could be right?"

"No," Janine said. "*Come on*, Father. This is *exactly* how people join cults." Then she swallowed. "There has to be a logical explanation."

"So we'll *figure it out*," Sherry said. "Let's say that this is some sort of—mass psychosis that's making people in Winesap kill each other and also making the three of us think that maybe it's because of some evil spirit. Do you know anyone who might be able to help figure that out? Call them up! If we can solve this mess with therapy and medication, then I'd rather have that than try to play Van Helsing. I can barely bend over far enough to weed my tomato beds. I'm not exactly prepared to fight the armies of darkness."

"I don't know if any therapists are qualified for this situation, Sherry," Janine started.

"Why not?" Charlotte chirped. "Because it's *supernatural*, maybe?"

"There are more things in heaven and earth, Horatio," Father Barry murmured.

"I'm Jewish," Janine told Father Barry, in the same tone of firm but polite warning that she usually used to tell waiters that she was a pescatarian. Then she sighed. "I have a colleague who wrote his dissertation on culture-bound syndromes."

"Great!" Sherry said, triumphant. "Give him a call. He can study us!"

"Not if the demon is keeping people out of Winesap," Charlotte said. "If it wants Sherry solving the murders, then it makes sense that it would keep my friend out, right? Like, if I was a demon trying to do my demon thing in a town, I would do it like in *The Truman Show*. Put a big bubble over the whole place. Otherwise you'd get people wandering in and going, like, wait a second, what's going on here? What's with all of these murders? Why hasn't anyone gotten the FBI up here? Shouldn't there be a Republican running for governor talking about how he's going to crack down on the upstate violent crime wave? It doesn't make any sense that we've got a murder rate like the apple farmers have been forming cartels to ship coke over the Canadian border and *no one's noticed*."

"Hm," Sherry said, and then looked toward Father Barry. "Has the bishop gotten back to you?"

"Well," Father Barry said after a long moment. "No. But that might not be . . . a demon problem. Exactly." He cleared his throat. "Sometimes he ignores my calls."

"*Barry*," Charlotte said. "Did you *piss off the bishop*? What did you do?"

"I didn't do anything!" said Father Barry. "I mean—I think I might have frustrated him a few times by mixing up my heresies. And I might have called him a little often when I first got here. But I needed advice! And there's also, uh." He cleared his throat again. "Todd."

Charlotte looked like a woman watching her new favorite reality show. "Ooh, *Todd*?" she asked. "Who's *Todd*?"

"My brother," said Father Barry, with a nearly imperceptible sigh. "I introduced him to the bishop's niece, and he brought her to Cancún. She apparently had a really good time."

Everyone in the room except for Charlotte winced. Charlotte looked delighted. "You have a brother who takes nice Catholic girls to Cancún? Older or younger?"

"Twenty minutes younger," Father Barry said. "And yes, before you ask, we're opposites but still close, just like the twins on TV. We talk on the phone almost every day. He's not a *bad guy*. He's, uh. Figuring things out."

"Oh my God," Charlotte said. "*Identical?*"

Father Barry looked pained. "Yes. Can we please stop talking about Todd?"

"We don't have to talk about Todd," Sherry said. "Listen, I have an idea. How about we *all* try to contact someone from outside of Winesap to ask for help? It would be killing two birds with one stone. If none of them get back to us or can make it here, then we can probably assume that Charlotte's right about this being like *The Truman Show*, and we'll know that we have to figure this out on our own. If they do get back to us, then we'll have some extra help, which will be even better."

Janine was frowning. "Won't the sheriff object to you bringing in a bunch of outsiders, Sherry?"

Sherry's cheeks warmed slightly. "We don't have to tell him," she said. "And he's kicked me off of the case. Or at least— he's gone back and forth between screaming at me to investigate and telling me to stay away from him, so I've decided to investigate independently for now." She lifted her chin a little. "If you don't feel comfortable with that, then you don't have to help."

"I don't feel comfortable with *any* of this," Janine said, and then sighed. "I'll call some colleagues."

"I've got a friend who's a witch," Charlotte said. "Just as a side hustle, I mean, not full-time in a cottage in the woods. She's a project manager for a management consulting firm. I could call her and see if she knows anything about evil spirits."

"She probably knows a lot of them in management consulting," Sherry said.

"I don't know how I feel about working with a *witch*," Father Barry said. "I'm sure that your friend is, uh, a *good* witch, but it's all dabbling with the same bad stuff, isn't it?"

"Oh, come on, like the Catholic Church has this amazing record of not being evil," Charlotte said. "She's not going to open up a gate to hell or something. As far as I know, she mostly just burns herbs in people's apartments after they get dumped to get rid of the bad ex-boyfriend energy."

"She sounds like a lovely young lady," Sherry said firmly. "You should call her. It's all hands on deck in a crisis, Father. And I'll . . . keep investigating. That's what the . . . spirit thing wants me to do, and I don't want to push it too much. It got a bit . . . threatening the other night." She suppressed a shiver. For all that she'd been sassy at her cat—it was just a *cat*, for God's sake—she couldn't erase the memory of how she'd felt while she was hiding in her bathroom and listening to that monstrous voice howling just outside her door.

"Don't you have anyone to call, Sherry?" Janine asked.

"No," Sherry said, and then blinked. "Well—maybe. I'll think about it." She didn't know anyone with expertise in evil spirits, but the question had made her think of one person who owed her an extremely major favor. She didn't want to call her, though. Her stomach tightened up from guilt just thinking about it. She drank some more of her fancy coffee and took a big bite of her doughnut. Then Charlotte piped up again.

"I think that we should all be equipped with stuff to protect ourselves," she said, which launched the whole group into a fairly spirited discussion of rosaries, holy water, garlic, salt, rowan wands, et cetera, until even Janine was lobbying in favor of the usefulness of her collection of anti-evil-eye charms brought back from Grecian vacations. This devolved, over the next few minutes, into discussion of vacations in general. Father Barry, unsurprisingly, had spent a lot of time in Italy.

Sherry drank her coffee and ate her doughnut, letting the sound of the conversation wash over her. It was comforting, for a second, to be able to imagine that a group of competent adults had taken over and would solve everything for her. Then she finished her cappuccino, licked the last fleck of chocolate off her thumb, and stood up. "I should go," she said. "I have to keep investigating. Thank you all so much for meeting with me."

"Wait," Father Barry said. He fidgeted slightly in his chair.

"I know the coroner. I could ask him to meet you. In case there's anything that you need to know about the body. About Alan's body, I mean."

Sherry flushed. Alan was dead, but it still felt indecent to talk about his body. "Thank you, Father," she said. Then she said her goodbyes and left. She needed to go to Alan's house.

TEN

Months ago, Alan had gone away on a trip to visit a new baby granddaughter and asked Sherry to water his plants for him while he was away. He'd told her that he kept a spare key under the garden gnome that his younger son had given to him for Christmas when he was nine. The gnome in question—a battered, faded object that had accompanied Alan for twenty years and through multiple moves—had the normal white beard and red cheeks, et cetera, but was wearing a Red Sox cap instead of the traditional pointy hat. It was the tackiest thing that Alan owned, and so obviously hadn't matched Alan's otherwise completely unremarkable and unwhimsical front yard that Sherry had thought that it would probably be the first place that anyone would look for a spare key. Alan had shrugged at that and smiled dotingly down at the gnome. "He's been guarding my keys for twenty years. He's done a fine job so far."

The sweet gnome-gifting younger son, Corey, had apparently grown up to be a bit of a ne'er-do-well. He had, according to Alan, fallen in with the wrong crowd, though the sort of *wrong* that would be more likely to get Corey featured in the gossip pages as a factor in a nasty society divorce than to get him killed as a factor in a drug deal gone wrong. The type of people whose money papered over their vices. Maybe the gnome was a reminder of happier times, or at least times when Corey was less likely to call his father from a bar in Tribeca to drunkenly ask for yet another cash infusion. Alan had apparently recently charged him with using his wealthy New York and European connections to source antiques for Alan to sell in his shop. He had, it seemed, been successful at it. He'd gone to art school and ran in very wealthy social circles, and had a knack for finding prints and sketches by previously underappreciated artists that Alan could then turn around in his shop for a substantial markup. Alan himself didn't know very much about fine art—his expertise was weighted more toward historical memorabilia, autographs, and furniture—so Corey's contribution was useful for diversifying his offerings. Alan had relayed this to her with relief: he sometimes seemed mildly concerned that his younger son would never find a career to settle into, but now it looked as if he might want to take over the shop one day. Or at least, it *had* looked like that, for a while.

She found the key underneath the gnome, exactly where Alan must have left it last. It was cold and gritty from the ground. She wiped it off on her blue jeans, leaving a dirty smear, and let herself in.

She'd expected it to seem different inside. There should have been a smell of bleach or blood. Instead it was cold and slightly stuffy. It smelled like he'd eaten Chinese food, shut everything up, locked the door, and gone away. Fried garlic and a few days of settling dust. The entryway was as it always was, neat and tidy, his bulkier coats and snow-drenched boots and skis and similar items banished to the back porch, where guests couldn't trip on them. To the right was a small side table with two books about World War II stacked on it, marked with a Post-it note on which he'd written neatly, *Return to Greg*. He always did that, with things that someone had lent him or left at his house: everything was marked with a reminder and placed in the hall to be promptly returned. It made her throat go tight.

She went to the living room, where she'd eaten dinner with him a few nights before. The crime scene. She kept her eyes away from the discolored spot on the rug and tried to pay attention to the details of the room and compare them to what had been there before.

The first thing she noticed was something that was missing: the documents that Alan had left on the side table were no longer there. He would have moved them to the kitchen table to work on them, probably: she'd check there later. The next thing she noticed was the mugs. When Sherry had left Alan's place, the coffee table had still been covered with the detritus left over from their dinner: greasy napkins, paper cartons, splintered disposable chopsticks propped up against the rims of dirty plates. Now the table was clean and wiped down, cleared of everything except two still-full mugs with the tags of teabags dangling off their sides. The wood of the table was stained white in an uneven patch around the mugs, as if tea had splashed onto the table and soaked into the varnish.

Sherry considered that. Alan was a devoted coffee drinker who had offered her a cup of after-dinner decaf more than once. He sometimes also had a glass of whiskey before bed. She'd never seen him drink tea. So, after she'd left or in the early hours of the morning, another guest had arrived, someone whom Alan had been friendly enough with to let into his

home and settle onto his sofa, someone for whom he'd dug
into the back of his cabinet to find a lone box of tea. Someone
who needed sobering up, maybe, or calming down. Possibly
someone with a bit of a drinking problem or someone already
very agitated. Or, perhaps, someone who wouldn't strike him
as a whiskey drinker due to age, sex, or ill health.

She moved on, looking for anything that struck her as out
of place. The murder weapon was obvious: the brass lamp that
usually sat on the end table was missing, probably taken away
as evidence, and there was a scratch on the wood floor behind
the couch where something heavy might have been dropped.
Sherry took a moment to try to imagine what it must have
looked like. Alan's guest would have been standing behind the
couch. They'd been pacing around the room, maybe. Alan had
come back from the kitchen with the mugs and stood in front
of the couch to carefully put them down. As he bent over, the
guest had grabbed the lamp and swung it hard down onto his
head, causing the tea to slosh out onto the table before Alan
fell to the floor and died. Sherry swallowed back nausea. If she
spoke to the coroner, she would know whether or not her theory was correct. If it was, then the killer really could be anyone Alan knew well. You wouldn't need to be a strong, tall
man to bring a heavy lamp down hard onto the back of the
head of someone who was leaning over and vulnerable. Sherry
could have easily done it. Maybe not hard enough to kill him
immediately, but possibly hard enough to stun him, to send
him to the floor, where he'd slowly die, alone in his living
room, with the tea he'd made for someone he'd trusted cooling
a foot or so above him.

She forced herself to step away, to move on. She went to the
side table that held Alan's phone and answering machine. For

a moment she felt a flash of something strange and vertiginous, as if something was deeply out of step with the way it was supposed to be. Then the feeling vanished and she could focus again. She checked the answering machine. No messages. Not surprising, she supposed: a message that said *Hello, this is Karl, I'll be by in fifteen minutes to murder you* would have been a bit too much to hope for. She made a circuit through the living room, but there wasn't much else of note, besides all of Alan's books and tasteful art photography prints and other things that made her chest clamp up from missing him.

She went into the kitchen. No documents. Taken away by the police, maybe. The kettle was still on the stove, but it looked like he'd had time to wash up the plates from their dinner. The trash can contained nothing but ordinary trash. She put the lid back on quickly—it stank—and then noticed that he'd written a note on the pad on the refrigerator. *Call Susan.* She frowned. Susan, she knew, was his ex-wife, but she had thought they weren't in contact. He hadn't written down her number on the note. She set out to search through the rest of the house for anything else out of place, hoping that she might also find some sort of little black book. She moved quickly through his bedroom and bathroom: there was nothing obviously strange in either of them, and they made her too sad to linger in for too long. She was making another loop of the living room—were those library books?—when a photo caught her eye. Alan from two summers ago, in costume for a community theater production of *The Pirates of Penzance*. She smiled reflexively at it, charmed by the sight of him looking so happy in his eye patch and red bandanna, surrounded by aging light-opera enthusiasts. Then the little Alan in the picture shifted his face, looked Sherry in the eye, and opened his mouth in a silent, agonized scream.

Sherry stumbled backward a few steps, her hand shooting up to cover her mouth. Her heart was pounding. The picture was still now, as if nothing had happened at all. Just a normal photo. She wiped her sweaty palms off on her jeans. Then she left as quickly as she could, barely remembering to lock up and hide the key under the gnome again as she fled. It hadn't really been Alan. It *couldn't* have been Alan. It was like her cat talking. It was magic, or the devil playing tricks. Kind, smart, gentle Alan wasn't trapped somewhere in agony. He couldn't be.

Maybe it was all in her head.

She walked home. Almost jogged home, really, trying to move fast enough to make her heart pound from exercise instead of from fear. By the time she got close to her house, she was still so full of nervous energy that she had the abrupt impulse to turn around and walk back to town. The idea of going home to be alone was unbearable. Instead, she took a hard right and headed up the driveway to Alice's house.

She could easily rationalize it to herself, at least: Alice had been Alan's only full-time employee at the antiques store. It was at least conceivable that she might have noticed something odd going on with Alan, or that he might have mentioned something to her that could serve as a clue. Maybe the ne'er-do-well young Corey had been dipping into the company accounts, or maybe Alan himself had been pulling some creative accounting. Technically, she supposed, Alice could even be a suspect, though that seemed unlikely. For one thing, Alan's death had put the potentially cash-strapped Alice out of a job. For another, Alice was small, timid, and had no motive that Sherry could think of to kill a man who had only ever been kind to her. Still, there was a chance. That chamomile tea was exactly the sort of thing that people in general tended to feel compelled to offer to Alice. It was within the realm of possibility that Alice had, for some reason, gone to visit Alan that evening and something had gone terribly wrong. Sherry tried to imagine the scene. Alice, weeping over her financial woes in Alan's living room. What might he have done? Sherry winced at her first thought: an offer of a raise, his mouth near her ear, his hand on her thin, fragile thigh.

She wouldn't expect that from Alan, but people were endlessly surprising. Something like that might have been enough to set off a terrible turn of events. The death had all the trappings of the usual sort of stupid, sad, spontaneous killing: a split-second decision after an argument, not an elaborate plot. She couldn't let all the ghoulies and ghosties distract her from the very simple basics of the case: the person most likely to have killed Alan was the person who, even for a split second, had the strongest reason to want him dead. Sherry sighed as she mounted the steps to Alice's front porch. This was the worst sort of case to try to crack. Very few people would deliberately plan a murder, but given the right moment, the right degree of rage, and a heavy enough object within arm's reach, almost anyone could find themselves a murderer.

The first thing she noticed when she got to Alice's house was that Alice had tidied up her entryway a bit. The useless cat carrier was gone, along with most of the other clutter. Alice's winter boots were lined up neatly next to the door instead of lying on their sides exactly where guests would be most likely to trip over them. The relative tidiness of the entryway made for an odd contrast with Alice herself when she finally appeared in the doorway after Sherry knocked. She looked even more flustered and bedraggled than usual, in a stained T-shirt with her hair unbrushed. "Oh my God, Sherry, I'm so sorry," she said the second she opened the door. Then she burst into tears.

Sherry held her and patted her back as she cried, trying not to feel affronted by what felt like a bit of a reversal of their proper roles. *Sherry* was the grieving girlfriend, not Alice. *Grieving employee* wasn't a position generally accepted as worthy of consideration by wider society. That seemed rude to point out, though, so Sherry made comforting sounds and waited for Alice to pull herself together, which she did eventually. "I'm so sorry," she said again. "I'm making this all about me, I'm the *worst*. I'm just—I'm *really* sorry. Would you like to come in? I could make coffee?"

"If you don't mind," Sherry said, choosing not to engage with the *I'm making this all about me*. "I was hoping that we could talk." She followed Alice inside. The tidying efforts had apparently not made it past the entryway: the living room was as messy as ever. Alice spent a few seconds dashing around to clear the clutter off the coffee table and move it onto the dining room table, which was so covered in stuff—books, unopened mail, half-drunk bottles of Diet Coke, coffee mugs, et cetera— that Alice would really be better off giving up on the table concept altogether and replacing it with some nice open shelving. "Your porch looks nice," Sherry offered.

"I was trying to get organized," Alice said. "Before I found out, I mean." Her voice wobbled. "I'll make coffee," she added, and vanished into the hidden realm beyond the dining table clutter mountain.

As soon as Alice was out of sight, Sherry got up to do a

quick snoop around the room. She wasn't sure what she was looking for, exactly, and there wasn't much to see, anyway. It wasn't a very nice room, and Alice hadn't added much in the way of personal touches. There were the white walls and ugly sailboat prints that had been there when Alice had first moved in, and there was the kind of clutter that tended to build up in the homes of poor people who were nervous about throwing anything away just in case they'd have to eventually buy a replacement. Pens and notepads from banks and plastic water bottles given away at street fairs. Some of the mail on the table looked like past-due bills. Nothing that made Sherry feel particularly good about herself when she went creeping around and peeking at it. The purr and crackle of the coffee pot started up from the kitchen, and she retreated to the ugly maroon couch to wait for Alice to come back into the room.

Eventually Alice reappeared with a mug of coffee in each hand. "I was going to ask if you wanted milk for it," she said. "But I'm out."

"Black is fine," Sherry said, and took the mug that Alice offered in both hands. It felt comforting to hold it. She took a sip and suppressed a wince: it was both watery and full of some awful artificial flavoring. Hazelnut, maybe. "Would you mind if I asked you a few questions about what happened?"

Alice shook her head. "I don't know anything, though," she said. "I mean—I just went to work and opened the shop like normal. I only found out what happened when the cops showed up." Her voice was wobbling again.

"That's all right," Sherry said. "That's fine. Have the police talked to you already?"

Alice nodded, then sniffed. "Yeah."

"Then maybe you could just tell me what you told them,"

Sherry said. She was doing her best to be calm and patient. "Can you tell me what your day was like on Saturday?"

"Nothing," Alice said. "It wasn't like anything. Just a normal day. Not too busy. The only weird thing was that Alan got a personal call at the shop. That's never happened before."

ELEVEN

"A personal call?" Sherry repeated, and sat up a bit straighter. "Did he say who from?"

Alice grimaced slightly. "The cops kept asking that, too. But like, it really wasn't a big deal, I don't think. I mean, I barely even noticed it when it happened; it wasn't some big dramatic thing. He talked for maybe five minutes, and then he came back out of the office and talked to a customer about an old French lamp. He didn't act weird or upset or anything. Just *normal.*"

"And he didn't mention who he'd been talking to?"

"No, and she didn't say who she was when I picked up, either," Alice said.

Sherry blinked. "You were the one who picked up the phone?"

Alice did something that looked like an eye roll that hadn't quite made it out of its larval stage before she squashed it. "Yeah, that's how I knew that it was a personal call. She called the shop and asked for Alan, then said it was personal when I asked if I could help her instead. I told him that he had a call and he said he'd pick up in the office. That's it. Nothing else happened."

"I see," Sherry said. "Did you notice anything unusual

about her voice?" As soon as she said it, she felt ridiculous. Like *what*? A thick Russian accent?

Alice's expression suggested that she found the question just about as ridiculous as Sherry did. "Like what?"

Sherry was blushing. She improvised. "Like—did she sound worried? Annoyed? Did she sound young or old?"

"Oh," Alice said. "No. I mean, she didn't sound upset. She just sounded normal. Not like a kid. Maybe middle-aged? I dunno. She didn't have, like, that old-lady voice?"

Sherry decided against asking whether or not *she* had that old-lady voice. She didn't think she did. She wondered whether most women noticed when they started developing it, or if they sounded to themselves exactly like they always had. She decided to drop the subject of the phone call for now. She had an idea of who it might be, anyway. *Call Susan.* She cleared her throat. "What happened next?"

"Nothing," Alice said. "Alan sold that lamp. A few more customers came in."

"Anyone who stood out?"

"No. Mostly browsers. That's most people who come in, usually. One guy spent a lot of money, but we know him. He owns a shop in New York City and comes up every couple of months to look for stuff he can resell. I already told the cops about him."

"I'm sorry to make you repeat yourself," Sherry said, though she wasn't all *that* sorry. "Do you have his name? Phone number?"

"His name's Mike Kaminski," Alice said. "I don't have his number, but he always leaves his business cards in the shop. I could get you one if you want. I don't think he did anything, though. He's just a normal guy. Sometimes we get resellers who want to rip Alan off, but Mike isn't like that. The worst thing he's ever done is get kind of annoyed that Alan took one of the pictures in this set of framed prints he wanted to buy, but that was pretty normal. Rich people and collectors like to buy complete sets of things. He was nice to me about it, though."

"I'd like to get his number, anyway, if you don't mind," Sherry said, and took note of the man's name, with *remind Alice need number*. Alan's ex-wife, his only employee, a rival antiques dealer. So far her list of suspects wasn't particularly impressive. No one stood out as having a strong motive. Still, she had to follow up on every possible lead. "What happened after he left?"

"Nothing," Alice said. "*Really* nothing. We closed for an hour for lunch. I ate a sandwich in the back and Alan went out. To the diner, I think. Then it got slow, so Alan said I could go home early and he would close up on his own. So I went home and watched TV, and then you came and gave me that food, and a while after that my power went out. That's it." She swallowed audibly. "Sherry, my rent's due in a week."

Sherry made a note to ask at the diner whether or not anyone remembered if Alan had come in for lunch on that day, and, if he had, whether he'd eaten alone. Then she took a beat to consider what Alice had told her. She'd noticed that Alice hadn't mentioned that Alan had had to talk to her about her performance at work that day. Not that Sherry would have mentioned it, either: it didn't seem like the sort of thing that any normal person would bring up when their employer suddenly turned up dead, and from how Alan had phrased it, it might have been a minor enough conversation that it could have slipped Alice's mind after all the chaos.

"Did Alan owe you a paycheck?" she asked, switching over from investigating detective to helpful-friend mode. She'd always liked being the friend that people came to when they were in trouble. It had led to what might have been the biggest mistake of her life. She stomped down that thought. That was back then, and in an extremely unusual circumstance; this was now, and nothing but helping out a young lady in dire financial straits.

"Yeah," Alice said. "I mean—normally I get paid every other Monday, because he did the paperwork on Sunday afternoons. So that's two weeks of work."

Sherry grimaced in sympathy. "I'll see what I can do," she said. "You might want to speak to his lawyer." She wrote down the name and number for her. "There has to be some sort of procedure for when this sort of thing happens. And I can always lend you the money for your rent." She drank some more terrible coffee as a bid to avoid eye contact and immediately regretted it. *Hazelnut.*

"You don't have to do that, Sherry," Alice said. That meant that she definitely wanted Sherry to do it.

"It's fine," Sherry said firmly. "I have the money. How much are you short? I'll write a check."

Alice was blushing, a blotchy flush that stretched down her neck. Sherry immediately felt bad for her. It must be frustrating to have a body that included a built-in billboard for displaying your emotions.

"Five hundred?" Alice asked, in practically a whisper.

"That's fine," Sherry said, very briskly. She didn't want any pity to leak out into her voice. "I'll bring it by tomorrow. And I'll ask around town about a job for you." She braced herself, took a big swallow of the awful coffee, and set the mug down. "Thank you for the coffee."

Alice's eyes had gone shiny. "Thank you," she said. "You *really* don't need to."

"I'm going to, anyway," Sherry said, slightly too loudly. It probably wasn't the right thing to say. She hated this kind of conversation. She stood up in order to escape it more quickly. "I'll see you tomorrow," she added, and then picked up her bag and bolted toward the door. On the way down the driveway she noticed those bushes again, their red berries gleaming against the dark green. Somewhere in the back of her mind there was a very soft hum.

Sherry's little house felt even quieter than it usually did when she got home. She put the radio on immediately, then stood in the middle of her living room for a moment. Her heart was still beating fast. From the shock of that horrible photo in Alan's house, she thought, until it occurred to her that she'd been drinking coffee all morning and only eaten part of a chocolate doughnut. Now it was almost lunchtime, and she wasn't hungry, just nervous and miserable. "This is stupid," she said aloud, and marched herself to the kitchen, where she set out to assemble a tuna salad sandwich.

The sound of the can opener, as always, summoned Lord Thomas, who came trotting up on his cotton-ball feet and gave a decorous little "Prrrow?"

Sherry smiled at him instinctively, then remembered that he wasn't to be trusted and frowned. "Are you really my cat," she asked aloud, "or are you an evil spirit or the ghost of an extremely unpleasant historical figure? Because I'm only going to give you the can to lick if you're my cat."

"*Mow!*" said Lord Thomas, in a way that she interpreted to mean *Stop being difficult and give me the tuna, woman!* She eyed him for a moment. "The problem with you is that it's hard to tell if you're a rude person or an ordinary cat," she said. Then she gave up and gave him the empty tuna can. The two of them spent a pleasant minute or so together, her assembling her sandwich—the secret was dried dill and celery salt—and him licking out the can so vigorously that he bumped it with his little nose all the way to the other side of the room. Then he sat down to polish his whiskers while she sat down to enjoy her lunch. This peaceful interlude lasted until Lord Thomas hopped up onto the chair next to Sherry's and said, loudly, "And how are those investigations going, woman?"

"*Ngah!*" said Sherry, who had been lulled into a false sense of security by his extremely un-demonic tuna-can licking. She pressed a hand to her chest in a way that she was conscious of being a bit dramatic even as she was doing it. "You *startled* me!"

"I do apologize," Lord Thomas said, unconvincingly. "And what of the investigation?"

She glowered at him. "After I've finished my lunch," she told him, and made an extremely elaborate and protracted meal out of her final bites of whole wheat crust. After the last few crumbs were gone, she risked a glance at Lord Thomas. He was staring at her. She sighed. "I have a short list of suspects. None of them are all that impressive, but more interesting stuff usually comes up after I've been digging for a while. And now that I've given you that, you owe me some information, too, don't you? Isn't that how the deal is supposed to work?"

"Indeed," said the cat, and stretched one of his front legs

forward and pointed his nose toward the ground as if he was maybe planning on grooming his belly. It took her a moment to realize that he was trying to bow. "I am at your service, Mistress Pinkwhistle."

Sherry found herself momentarily at a loss. "I don't know what to ask. How is this supposed to work, exactly?"

"How would you expect it to work," the cat asked her, "in a tale of this nature?"

"In a tale of this nature," Sherry repeated. "I don't know. Maybe for you to give me a magic sword or something."

"I am Lord Thomas Cromwell, not Lord Merlin," said the cat, a little more testily than Sherry thought was completely reasonable, considering that he'd *asked*. "This is my counsel: Attend to what particularly strikes you as you go about. Attend to the resonances of things. In the deepest human heart there is a memory of ancient enemies, and a knowledge of how to defeat them."

Sherry watched him expectantly, waiting for more. No more came. That was, apparently, it. "That's it? Just *attend to the resonances of things*? I've been working hard on investigating, and all you have for me is *resonances*?"

The cat drew himself up, which—even though he was a tubby fifteen pounds—wasn't nearly as impressive as Sherry suspected he wanted it to be. "I have advised you in matters ancient and sacred, woman! Take care not to dismiss me so easily."

"Oh, *excuse me*, Your Highness," Sherry said. "I just thought that maybe with all of your drama about making a deal, you might be a little better at holding up your end of it."

"*My lord* will do," said Lord Thomas. "Or *sir*. And there's no need for you to pretend that performing your investigations is such a great trial. Don't act as if you aren't enjoying yourself, woman. This is what you like to do, isn't it? Meddle in the doings of the dead?"

Something about the way he said it made Sherry regret having finished her whole sandwich. She pushed the empty plate away. "What's that supposed to mean?"

"You know exactly what I mean," he said. "She doesn't *force* you to take such an interest in her murders. Her powers are the stuff of unquenchable lusts and blinding rages, not the cold-blooded gathering of clues. She can influence the killer, not the detective. You must *enjoy* snooping around in the blood and guts, for her to have chosen you. You must feel as if you have a talent for it, and look forward to the opportunity to practice your art. Thinking about corpses gives you a little thrill, does it?" The cat's eyes, normally green, were glowing a dull red.

"*No,*" she said. "And that looks stupid."

"I beg your pardon?" Lord Thomas said, in a tone of genuine uncertainty that made Sherry feel as if she'd regained a bit more of an even footing with him.

"Your eyes," Sherry said with authority. "You might be able to get away with it if you were a black cat, but as it is, the red clashes with your fur. It just looks silly, on a marmalade cat."

"Oh," Lord Thomas said, and his eyes promptly started to glow green. "Is that better?"

"Yes, much better," Sherry said. "You look very nice. And stop accusing me of being a pervert. You know perfectly well that that's ridiculous."

"Indeed!" Lord Thomas said, triumphantly this time. "You do like it, though, don't you? You like feeling very clever and important, and saving the day when no one else can. What a hypocrite you are, Sherry Pinkwhistle!"

"I don't know what you're talking about," Sherry said. She was reaching for her purse.

"Oh, yes, you do," the cat said. "Aren't you ashamed of yourself, woman? All of that meddling in other people's secrets when you won't confront what you've done, when your secrets remain buried, when you *arrrllghh!*"

Sherry smiled at him smugly over the barrel of her plant spritzer. She'd gotten him right in the face with the holy water, and he'd leapt straight up into the air and landed on all four paws on the kitchen floor, all his orange fluff standing on end. "When I *what*, Lord Thomas?"

Lord Thomas hissed at her and ran off to hide under the living room sofa.

"That's what I thought!" Sherry called after him. Then she got up to wash the dishes.

She spent the rest of the day doing lots of things that were, essentially, wasting time, while still preserving a tiny scrap of pretense that she was working hard on the investigation. Mostly she just read some more from her stockpile of books on the occult. Some of them seemed like thinly veiled excuses for the authors to breathlessly report on the scandalous personal lives of nineteenth-century spiritualists. One of them, at least, Sherry thought might actually come in handy: it contained a lengthy section on the sorts of objects and symbols that various pagans and occultists found generally important and powerful while going about their . . . occulting. She was reading along contentedly enough when a passage suddenly struck her. *In matters pertaining to death, there is no plant with stronger and older magic than the yew.*

The matters Sherry had been dealing with recently certainly pertained to death. *Yew.* Maybe that could be helpful.

More helpful, perhaps, if she knew what on earth a yew tree looked like, or how to find one. She didn't know very much about trees—she liked to garden, but she mostly stuck to things she could eat, and wildflowers. She made a mental note to look up *yew* in the encyclopedia the next time she was in the library.

She jolted awake the next morning before her alarm went off and spent a few moments frozen in place, terrified of something that hadn't happened yet. What would it be this time? More men screaming outside her door or shouting at her through her cat's mouth? Something horrible transforming her mother's face in the photo on her bedside table? Then she got ahold of herself, got out of bed, and answered the phone. The ringing had woken her up.

"Good morning, Sherry," said Father Barry. He sounded *repulsively* chipper. "I just ran into the coroner when I was out on my run. He'd like to meet you at the diner in an hour, if you have time."

Sherry blinked, then looked at the clock on her bedside table. "Father," she said after a moment. "It's *five in the morning.* You ran into the coroner at *five in the morning*? It's still *dark* outside. Does he have an assistant at the morgue named Renfield?"

There was a brief pause. "I don't know if Matt has an assistant," he said finally. "I think that technically he's the assistant medical examiner, so you have to be sure not to tell anyone that he's talking to you about the case. He could get fired."

"Right," Sherry said. It was too early in the morning to explain her references to a disgustingly youthful and energetic priest. At least she could feel fairly confident that he wasn't possessed. There was no way on earth (or any unpleasant adjacent plane) that the demon wasn't familiar with the main characters in *Dracula*. "I'll be at the diner at six. Thank you, Father."

"You're welcome," Father Barry said. Then he added an extremely cheerful, "Have a nice day! God bless!" before he hung up.

Lord Thomas Cromwell had slipped into the room as she talked on the phone, and gave her an imperious meow. "Good morning to you, too," she said, and yawned. "Maybe I should take up running." Then she added, very hurriedly, "Just joking." The last thing she needed was her possessed cat trying to hold her to her flippant promises to start exercising.

She rushed through getting ready and writing a check for Alice, shoved the check through Alice's mail slot, and made it to the diner just after six. Then she took an awkward moment to scan the room for the medical examiner. Despite her having run into him in passing a few times before in the course of her sleuthing, she always imagined him as a man in a black tailcoat, which was definitely an image from Dickens and wrong both for the job and for the century. The disappointing reality was a tall, lanky, balding man who was usually wearing either a baggy sport coat or tight running gear that made him look even more Gumby-like than he otherwise would. He spotted her first and did one of those awkward half-stand-and-waves that people did when greeting an acquaintance who'd just walked into a restaurant.

She approached the booth, and he jolted back up into an uncomfortable booth-constrained crouch to shake her hand. "Good morning, Sherry," he said.

"Good morning," Sherry said, and slithered her way into the other side of the booth. "It's so nice of you to meet me."

There were already two menus on the table. It seemed rude to launch directly into questions about the dead-people business. Besides, she wanted to order some coffee. She tried to catch the waitress's eye. "I was so impressed when Father Barry said that he bumped into you on a run this morning," she tried. "I could never be that disciplined! Don't you get cold, running so early in the winter?"

"No," he said. "I just layer. I leave for my run every morning at four, then come here at six. It's not hard if you go to bed early. The priest said that you wanted to talk about the Thompson case?"

Matt McGuire, it seemed, wanted nothing more than to talk about his dead-body business before Sherry had had the chance to put her coffee order in. The waitress, whom Sherry had never seen before—Sherry had never in her life gone to a diner before eight a.m.—saved her by coming over with the carafe of her own accord. "Coffee?" she asked. Then, after Sherry had answered in the affirmative, "Youknowwhatyou-want, hon?"

Sherry took half a second to panic over this unanticipated demand for her to make a decision. Then she said, "Ba-coneggencheese," with the confidence she'd developed from shouting her order at the surly owner of her local bodega during her brief sojourn in New York City. Then she tacked on a more polite, "Please."

"Be right up," the waitress said, and ambled off.

Sherry blinked at McGuire. "Did you want to—"

"She knows what I want," he said. "I always get the same order." Then he said, "Alan Thompson died of an epidural hemorrhage following blows to the frontal and parietal bones."

Sherry flinched. She couldn't help it. She prided herself on being unflappable, but she was unmistakably flapped. *Alan.* Poor Alan. She took a sip of coffee and tried to gather herself. Multiple blows didn't square with what she'd imagined when she looked at the scene. "The frontal and parietal bones?"

"The front and upper back of the head," McGuire said, and indicated with a finger where he meant on his own head.

She frowned. "So someone hit him from the back, then ran around and hit him in the front as well?"

"No," he said. "The pattern of injury was consistent with his having been struck on the back of the head with a blunt instrument, then hitting his head again on another object as he fell forward."

"A blunt instrument like a brass table lamp, and another object like a coffee table?"

"I wouldn't be comfortable making that determination," McGuire said. "But yes, possibly."

"Right," Sherry said. That squared perfectly: she just hadn't factored in that coffee table. The back of her mind whispered, *Poor Alan.* "Right," she said again. "Do you have a time of death?"

"I've put it at sometime between ten p.m. and midnight," he said.

"Ten thirty," Sherry said absently.

He frowned. "What?"

"He dropped me off at my house after ten," Sherry said. "I didn't check my watch when we arrived, but I remember noticing that it was almost ten before we left his house. Then he needed time to drive back home, greet a guest, and make two cups of tea before he was killed. It probably couldn't have been before ten thirty." An hour and a half was a nice, tight time frame for her to work with, much better than cases she'd dealt with where the victim was long since cold. Just a neat, tidy hour and a half or so to account for, and not whole days or weeks or longer in which people had a dispiriting tendency to not remember where they'd been or who they'd seen or what they'd had for dinner.

The new timeline also took care of one of Sherry's few suspects. Alice had been home when Sherry went across the road to give her the leftover Chinese food, and they'd chatted until about ten thirty. She'd still been home at just after midnight when she'd walked to Sherry's house to ask for help when her power had gone out. Alice didn't own a car, which meant that in order for her to have killed Alan within McGuire's estimated time of death, she would have had to walk all the way to Alan's house in a raging blizzard in the dark, knock on his door to be invited in for tea, kill him, walk back, and then go to Sherry's house to ask for help, all in under an hour and a half. The walk to Alan's house in good weather took forty-five minutes at least, and the walk back up the hill to Alice's took longer. In a blizzard, Sherry was fairly sure that making it to Alan's house, killing him, and then getting back up to Sherry's in time to ask for help with her electrical problems would be beyond the capacities of one skinny little retail assistant. Besides, Alice still didn't have a motive. Sherry was pleased with this realization for the moment it took her to register that she now didn't really have any suspects at all. A mysterious woman who might have been Alan's ex-wife. Some perfectly pleasant antiques dealer. Then it hit her, and she blanched. She didn't have any suspects. But to the police—to any uninterested observer—the most likely suspect was the last person who had seen him alive, and the only person who could testify that he'd still been alive for any time between ten and midnight.

It wasn't just because of the demons that Sherry would have to solve this one quickly.

TWELVE

Their food came then, and Sherry and McGuire ate their breakfasts in a silence that was less companiable than it was forged out of a mutual understanding that neither of them was remotely interested in chitchat. Then she went straight to the library and to her favorite enormous old encyclopedia, which she kept partially just as a decoration—it was one of those nice leatherbound sets—and pulled out the volume for Y. She looked up *yew* and read the description. Evergreens with fleshy red fruits.

Bright red, standing out against the snow.

Sherry stared at the black-and-white illustration. The shape of the berry was right, too. This was exactly the plant that had been tugging at her attention lately on her walks.

The back of her neck went spiky. The cat had gone on about *resonances*. Well, maybe. Maybe there was something to it, though she didn't know exactly what. She put the encyclopedia away, still feeling vaguely uneasy. It was an hour before the library would usually open, and she was technically on leave. She started vacuuming. Some strange, wild corner of her brain felt convinced that, if she was a good and responsible librarian who kept the place clean and organized, the police wouldn't suspect her of murder. She hung around for the rest of the day, even, ignoring the baffled looks and timid questions of the staff members who'd clearly been told not to expect her. Everything went smoothly and utterly comfortingly until a little boy came up to the desk with several books of Greek mythology to check out.

"Oh, these look interesting," she said encouragingly. She always felt a sort of kinship with small children who checked out big dry books on the sorts of topics that peculiar, uncoordinated children tended to be interested in, like wild horses and dinosaurs and ancient Rome.

The little boy looked up at her. "Sherry," he said, in Alan Thompson's voice. "Please, God, *help me*."

Sherry gave a muffled, strangled scream and stumbled backward, then frantically grabbed for her purse to try to fumble for the spray bottle full of holy water. It was too late, though: by the time she'd found it and looked up again, the boy was gone. He'd left his books behind. Sherry placed her hand on the pile as if she was swearing on a Bible, right over Athena's breastplate on the cover. The books were real. It was all real.

"I'm not crazy," she said aloud, to the immediate and obvious alarm of a passing page.

She hung around until the library closed, then went back to the diner. She told herself that she had business there: she'd forgotten to ask about whether anyone had noticed Alan eating there on the day he'd died. Really, she'd do almost anything to avoid having to go home and be alone with Lord Thomas Cromwell. She used to love petting her cat when she was unhappy and in need of comfort, but it wasn't very pleasant anymore to think that he might sit in her lap and purr.

She'd checked out a Georgette Heyer before she left the

library. She tucked herself into a corner booth with the lords and ladies, then ordered a cup of decaf to drink while she read. When the coffee arrived, it came with a very nice-looking slice of cherry pie. "From Jason," the waitress said. "We all heard about your friend Alan. We're really sorry."

Sherry looked up. Jason, the cook, gave her a small smile and a wave from behind the counter. "Thank you," Sherry called out, touched. He did a different wave, the "it was nothing" kind. Sherry waved back. Then she looked up at the waitress. Jessica, Sherry thought was her name. "Speaking of Alan," she said. "Do you know if he ate lunch here at the diner this past Saturday?"

Jessica frowned as if she was giving that some thought. "I think so," she said. "Yeah, I think maybe he did. Holly had the table—she's new—but I think I remember seeing him, unless I'm getting the day wrong. I'd have to ask Jason which day we had the chicken Florentine."

"That would be lovely of you, if you could," Sherry said. "Do you remember if anyone was with him?"

Jessica looked uncomfortable. "Yeah," she said. "That's why I noticed him. He was with a woman who wasn't you, and she didn't look like she was from around here, so she really stood out."

"*Oh,*" Sherry said, and felt her stomach sink in a way that really wasn't reasonable at all. She'd been insistent about Alan never having been her boyfriend. "Right. Can you describe her?"

"Older," Jessica said. "I mean, uh. Not *old*. About Alan's age." About *Sherry's* age, she meant. "She had this kind of ashy bob, that kind of transitional color for when you're trying to grow the gray in gracefully? I used to do hair, so I always notice if someone has a really good or bad dye job."

"And was this one good or bad?" Sherry asked. She hoped that it was bad.

"Definitely good," Jessica said immediately. "She probably spent a ton on it. She definitely didn't get it done around here. I was trying to guess in my head what she was doing up here. I thought maybe some fancy interior design lady who was meeting Alan to buy special antiques from him or something. That's what she looked like. She was wearing this long camel-colored coat. No one from around here dresses like that. I remember feeling bad that it was touching the floor and probably getting mud on it from people's snow boots."

"That does sound memorable," Sherry said. It was the most neutral thing she could think of to say. "Could you ask Jason about the chicken Florentine? I'm sorry to be a bother."

"It's no problem; it's dead in here, anyway," Jessica said. Then she lowered her voice slightly. "Are you *investigating*?"

Sherry nodded. "*Yes*," she said, lowering her own voice even though there was no one around to possibly overhear. People loved to feel as if they were helping with a murder investigation, and the more dramatic you managed to make it seem, the more they loved it. If there were a seedy dive bar in Winesap, Sherry would arrange to meet all her witnesses there just to take advantage of the atmosphere. Unfortunately, all there was that came close to fitting the bill was a bar and grill next to the gas station that served soggy hot wings and played a constant rotation of Tom Petty's greatest hits, which wasn't exactly an environment where you'd expect to see Philip Marlowe meeting with a beautiful young widow. "It really would be a huge help if you could confirm that he had lunch with an unidentified person on the day he was killed." She managed not to flinch at the phrase *the day he was killed*. It was the sort of phrase that she needed to use to get the information that she wanted: people seemed to find it impressive, along with *our main suspect*, and *the estimated time of death*, and *motive and opportunity*.

Jessica was already nodding. "I'll ask," she said, and trotted off. A moment later it was Jason, not Jessica, who came walking over to Sherry's table. It took him a while: Jason had a fairly pronounced limp. When people asked him about it, he came up with a different ridiculous story every time: Sherry's favorite version was that he'd been trampled by a bull in Pamplona. She'd heard that the actual explanation was that he'd fallen off a ladder while working as a roofer in his twenties, but that wasn't nearly as much fun.

"Thank you for the pie," Sherry said again.

Jason shrugged this off. "You're having a bad week," he said. Jason was a stocky man with warm brown eyes and an easy smile. He'd once told Sherry that he'd moved to New York from Los Angeles as a teenager, and he still wasn't accustomed to the winters. Now he was in his early forties or so, a relative newcomer to Winesap and the diner, and the proud father of two very polite and princessy little girls who sometimes did their homework sitting on stools at the counter. His much younger and very sweet wife was a Winesap local who worked at the hospital in Schenectady, where they'd met, as a nurse's aide.

Sherry had gotten to know Jason because, as one of the few regulars who often hung around the diner after the dinner rush on weekday evenings, she'd had the chance to chat with

him when he'd occasionally emerge from the kitchen. He liked
Ray Bradbury and Tolkien and was currently working his way
through *Dune*. He drove a rusty red pickup, and she'd deduced
from things he'd mentioned to her about his home that he and
his family lived in one of the modest little former summer
homes around the lake. The lake houses had been built back
in the 1920s, when little towns in the nearby countryside were
still attractive summer home destinations to the people of
Schenectady and Albany. The tourist industry had died for
decades and was now being reconstructed by the determined
populace, but the lake houses were far too small now to meet
the needs of the wealthy vacationers who had once owned
them. They were perfect, though, for the ordinary working-
class people of Winesap. You could have your own dock with
a boat there, as long as you didn't mind living shoulder to
shoulder with your neighbors.

Sherry smiled at him. He was such a nice young man. "I
don't suppose you remember which day this past week you
had the chicken Florentine?"

"Saturday," he said immediately. "I remember because we
ran out before noon, but Holly forgot to wipe it off the specials
board, so she kept giving me tickets with the Florentine on
them until I went out there and erased it myself."

"Thank you, that's very helpful," Sherry said. "Did you happen to notice whether or not Alan Thompson was here? If
you'd recognize him, I mean."

He shook his head. "I know what he looks like, but I only
came out of the kitchen long enough to fix the board. We were
slammed my whole shift Saturday."

"I see," she said. "Thank you, anyway. That was very helpful of you."

"No problem," he said, then hesitated before he said, "I was sorry to hear about Alan. I never spoke to him, but he must have been a pretty smart guy, to be a lawyer. I hope you catch who did it."

"Thank you," Sherry said, and then Jason went back to the kitchen. It took her until she was halfway through her pie for it to occur to her how odd it was that he'd mentioned Alan being a lawyer, when he'd said that he'd never talked to him, and Alan had retired from the law a few years before Jason came to Winesap. She looked up to see if he was still behind the counter, so that she could maybe ask him, but he'd vanished back into the kitchen again.

Once her pie was finished, there was nothing for her to do but head home. She did so grudgingly, trudging her way up the hill in the cold, the road illuminated only by very rare streetlights and the lights of houses flashing briefly through the bare trees. She jolted at a sudden blast of noise: it sounded like a motorcycle driving through the village. Strange, at this time of year. A few steps later she caught a flash of red in the corner of her eye. *Blood*, she thought, and turned to look. The red of the yew berries shone dully in the light spilling from the window of a nearby house. She remembered the description from the encyclopedia. It had called the berries *fleshy*. They looked fleshy now, like freshly cut beef. She shivered. Then she took a few quick steps toward the bush, reached out to grab hold of a branch, and tugged and twisted until it came off in her hand. Then she hurried off, shoving the branch into her coat pocket the best she could. She'd sweated a little, and now she shivered. It was awfully cold.

She thought longingly of Alan then, of the way that he always seemed to know when she was feeling particularly tired

and beaten down and would pull up in his car to whisk her off
to something pleasant. Not today. Not ever again, and wasn't
she selfish for thinking about herself when a good, kind man
had been killed? She'd be suspicious of herself if she was
someone else. The odd old woman who lived on the outskirts
of town and was the last person to have seen the victim. The
old woman whose evil cat knew she had something to feel
guilty about.

She'd avoided thinking about it for years. She'd left Florida
to try to escape from it. Here she was, though, with some—
person claiming to be the devil trying to use what she'd done
as leverage.

She was still a few minutes away from home when she decided that she needed to talk to Caroline.

As soon as she arrived, she started stalling, of course. She
made herself a cup of tea. She turned the radio on, then turned
it off again. She used the bathroom and took a long, hot shower,
and bundled herself up in her cozy bathrobe. She poured herself a glass of brandy. Then, with no more delaying tactics
available to her, she got out her old address book and found the
number she wanted. Even as she dialed, she found herself hoping that it would be a wrong number. They might have moved
away. She remembered being in the car with Caroline six years
ago, how she'd told her over and over that everything would be
all right. She was very good at comforting other people, at
tricking them into thinking that she was the wise, protective
older sister or mother or grandmother they'd never had, when
really she was just as baffled as anyone. She didn't seem capable of applying the same skill to her own racing heart.

A woman answered. There was the sound of a TV blaring
in the background. "Hello?"

Sherry swallowed. "Linda? This is Sherry."

Part of Sherry expected her to say, *Wrong number.* She *hoped* for it. Instead, she said, "*Sherry?* God, it's been years. How are you? *Where* are you? I heard that you moved to New York City."

It was like getting into a time machine. Linda's voice had barely changed, the same warm smoker's rasp. "I did, for a while," Sherry said. "Then I left." The city had been awful. She'd never been the sort of woman who stood out, but the city had made her more invisible than she'd ever been. Men kept walking straight into her on the street. She'd wanted to live somewhere where she wouldn't be looked through with the same blank-faced not-quite hostility that she'd seen directed at a gentleman ostentatiously playing the panpipes on the subway platform. "It wasn't for me," she said. "I'm upstate now. Up in the Adirondacks."

"*Upstate,*" Linda said, in the same way she might have said *Tokyo.* Linda, as far as Sherry knew, had never been farther north than Tallahassee. "Is it freezing?"

An unpleasant part of Sherry was tempted to say something like, *No, it's sweltering. I'm wearing shorts on the piazza right now.* "It was just about freezing today," she said instead. "It's warming up. Last month it got down to twenty below."

"What does that *feel* like?" Linda asked, and Sherry found herself unable to resist trying to describe it: how she had to wear tights underneath her pants to keep her thighs from going numb, and the essential nature of thick socks, and how on really cold mornings she had to cover her face so that the snot wouldn't freeze inside her nose. She'd never had the chance to explain her new world to someone from back home before.

She'd made too clean a break. It felt better than she'd imagined it would.

Eventually, though, Sherry had to bring things around to her reason for having called. "I was hoping to get back in touch with Caroline," she said. "Do you have any contact information for her?"

Linda didn't say anything for a while. There was just the sound of the television in the background. A sitcom laugh track. "Maybe she doesn't want you to talk to her," she said finally. "If she didn't give you her number herself."

"She couldn't have," Sherry said patiently. "I moved just after she . . . left. Remember? I don't know where she is, but she doesn't know where I am, either." She frowned into the phone. An issue had just occurred to her. "Do *you* know where she is?"

"I'm her *sister*, Sherry," Linda said, as if she was offended. Then she abruptly changed her tone. "Aw, Christ, you know *Caroline*. She won't tell me. I think it might be Costa Rica, though. Her plane was headed for Mexico, but I don't think she'd stay there with the authorities knowing she'd been there. She used to talk about wanting to go to Costa Rica."

It was jarring hearing Linda so casually mention the authorities in regard to Caroline. Their two brothers and most of Linda's boyfriends over the years had all had their run-ins with the law, but Caroline had always been the good daughter, the one who'd done everything right, up until the day she'd done absolutely everything wrong. "Costa Rica," Sherry repeated. "I remember that, too." It had been one of the things that had made her and Caroline friends: their fondness for shared daydreams about travel. When they were still in high school, they'd made dream collages from pictures they'd cut out of magazines, mostly pictures of gorgeous models posing in front of famous monuments or on romantic cobblestoned European streets. Costa Rica had come later, from TV nature documentaries. Caroline had wanted to see a howler monkey. Even after everything, part of Sherry was glad to think that Caroline had really, finally gotten away to somewhere better. Maybe she was drinking a cocktail on a beach somewhere right now, with howler monkeys crying out from the jungle just behind her. She cleared her throat. "You're in contact with her, though?"

There was a sudden crackling sound from Linda sighing into the receiver. "I have a number for her," she said. "It changes pretty often. I have to wait for her to call me first. Then when she calls, she always lets it ring three times and then hangs up, so I know it's not a telemarketer and pick up the next time."

"Wow," Sherry said, impressed despite herself. "Like James Bond."

"I know," Linda said, sounding as if she was possibly a little more impressed than she'd admit, too. "It's just like Caroline, isn't it? She was always something else."

Sherry made an agreeable noise. Caroline was certainly *something*. "Could you tell me the number? It sounds like with all of the spycraft I won't be able to learn much about where she lives from it, anyway. And she could always choose to ignore the message, if she doesn't want to speak to me. I promise not to harass her. I just want to talk to her about something, that's all."

Linda hesitated for a second. "Do you have a pen?"

Sherry did. Linda rattled off a number. Sherry wrote it down, then had her repeat it, just in case. She had the feeling that if she called back and asked for it again, she might get a different answer. Linda had always been prone to sudden shifts in mood. It had made her exciting to be around when they were teenagers, especially with the air of glamor and sophistication that had come from her having been learning to be a hairdresser while Sherry and Caroline were still in high school. "You should come up for a visit sometime," she said spontaneously. "Escape the heat this summer. Or sometime around the holidays. You could see the snow. I have plenty of space here."

The pause before Linda responded told Sherry the answer in advance. "That's nice of you, Sherry," she said. "Maybe I will." She wouldn't, of course. "It was good to hear from you." She would probably never call Sherry back.

"It was good to hear from you, too," Sherry said. Then she wished Linda good night and hung up.

THIRTEEN

The call with Linda left Sherry feeling strangely drained of energy. She knew that she should do what she'd set out to do and call Caroline. Instead, she pulled the yew branch out of her coat pocket and turned it around in her hands. It didn't have the same air of menace in the warm light of her living room. Still, there was something about it.

She got the salt and poured a circle, like Lord Thomas had made her do the last time. Then she looked around for her cat. There was no sign of him. Of course there wasn't. He was a cat, and she wanted to find him, so obviously he was nowhere to be found. "Lord Thomas?" she said aloud, feeling, as ever, self-conscious over the fact that she was speaking to her cat. "Lord Thomas Cromwell?"

A moment later a little orange head pushed itself out from under the sofa. "May I be of some assistance, Mistress Pink-whistle?"

She smiled. She couldn't help it. "What were you doing under the sofa, Lord Thomas?"

"I was at my repose," the cat said with enormous dignity. "And I cannot cross your circle. You must lift me inside."

She picked him up, avoiding eye contact—she felt suddenly, strangely aware of the fact that her cat wasn't wearing pants—

and set him quickly down again inside the circle of salt. He sat on his little haunches, his tail neatly curled around his front toes, and looked up at her. "You have need of me?"

"Y-es," she said, though she felt uncertain now. "I was just wondering about this." She gestured vaguely with her yew branch, feeling sillier than ever. "I was wondering—I don't know. I think that maybe it has *resonances*? But I don't know what's supposed to happen next."

"You may not know," the cat said. "But your hands are sure even as your mind is uncertain."

"My hands?" Sherry asked, and looked down at the appendages in question. They looked normal. It took her a second to realize what he meant: she'd been fiddling with the branch, nervously stripping off the twigs and needles to turn it into a stick. "I don't get it," she said. "I'm just . . . fidgeting."

"You are crafting something," the cat said. "You know that you are."

"I don't know about that," Sherry said, but looked again at the stick. It looked like a stick. Or like— "Can you stop a demon by driving a stake through its heart?"

The cat tilted its head to the side. "*Can* you?"

"That's what I'm *asking*," said Sherry, with a small flare of temper. "I don't know how it works, I'm not *Van Helsing*. Can you just answer the question?"

Lord Thomas remained annoyingly unruffled. His fur lay smooth across his back. "I asked you a question in return. You spoke of the demon's *heart*. She is a heartless creature. To have a heart she must take human shape. When she takes a shape, she takes that of a mortal. She rides a mortal body like a hunter spurring on his horse. Here, she will pick someone she finds at hand to ride. One of the people of your little village.

Can you look one you know in the eye and drive a stake of yew into their beating heart, Mistress Pinkwhistle?"

Sherry swallowed. Then she shook her head. "No," she said, but even as she said it, she felt her hand tightening around the stick. No. No, of course not. But— "Maybe," she said. "Maybe. If I had to."

"Very well," the cat said. "If you had to. If your need was great enough. If your conviction was strong enough. If you looked your friend in the eye and drove the stake home with the intent of banishing her back to her cold home—then yes. I think that she might accept this as a killing blow, and leave you, at least for a time. She is a gameswoman and a lover of tales. She does not attend to any human law, but certain rules and rituals are older than even she. But you must enter into the spirit of what you plan to do. You must act without detachment, without doubt or irony. There can be no hesitation in your hand."

Sherry nodded. She had already entered into the spirit of the thing, she thought. Her ability to be flip and ironic felt as if it had long since run out. "If I craft it," she said, "with intent. If I sharpen it alone and quietly, and rub it with some sort of sacred oil and—" She swallowed again. "Should I pray?"

The cat's eyes gleamed. It didn't look stupid at all. "Yes, Mistress Pinkwhistle. You should most certainly pray. To whatever god will have you, you should pray."

Sherry nodded. She thought, *Enter into the spirit of it.* Then she bowed. "Thank you, sir, for your counsel."

He inclined his head. "You are most welcome, mistress."

Sherry went to bed and had strange dreams. She dreamed that she was waiting in a stand of huge white trees, in the middle of a circle of hooded figures whom she knew were druids.

Beside her was a masked figure tied to a stone altar. One of the druids handed her a wooden dagger. "Strike true," he said.

"I don't think I can," Sherry told him.

"You must," the druid said, "or she will eat your heart."

She was in a ballroom then, wearing a velvet gown. Someone tapped her on the shoulder. She turned. It was a man in a black cap, with a beaked nose and dark, sad eyes.

"You're Thomas More," she said.

"Pray," he said. His breath was horrible. "Pray to whatever god will have you."

She woke up with a jolt and checked the time. Just after four. She stayed awake, not moving, her eyes on the window, waiting for the dawn. At about five there was the thump of her cat jumping onto her bed. She scratched his ears and let him push his little head into her palm. "You were right," she said, "about his halitosis."

Lord Cromwell purred smugly. Sherry closed her eyes and tried to pray.

An hour later Sherry woke up with the sense that she had just gone on a very, very long walk and was still tired from the journey. She knew that she ought to call Caroline, or work on what she'd started to think of as her yew dagger. Instead she made excuses to herself about how it was too early for a potentially emotional conversation *or* for any kind of ancient ritual magic. Then she gulped down some coffee before pouring the rest into a thermos, tromping her way down into town, and letting herself into the library an hour before it would usually open. It had occurred to her over the past few days that there were more things about Alan that she didn't know than she had realized. Maybe the records in the library would be able to fill in the gaps.

The Winesap Library, though small, was an absolute trea-sure trove when it came to any sort of local history. Every is-sue of the *Herald*, its predecessors, and every other publication and periodical that optimistic locals had launched before their inevitable folding a few months later had been duly collected, cataloged, and stored on microfiche. Still, trying to dig up some theoretical scrap of information that might possibly be relevant in some way to a current murder case would take some time, particularly when there was no guarantee that there would be anything at all to find.

Sherry tried to be methodical about it. She remembered that Alan had had a fifth-anniversary sale at the shop the pre-vious autumn, which meant that the grand opening would have been in September or October—she couldn't remember which—five years earlier. A new shop opening up in the vil-lage was exactly the sort of thing that their tiny local press corps covered in lavish detail. She pulled all the issues of the *Herald* from the relevant time frame, plus the ill-fated re-gional alternative weekly based in Albany that had been in print at the time and then folded not long after Sherry had moved to town. She went straight to the Life and Style section in each paper, working under the assumption that the opening of an antiques shop would be there and not under Business.

She'd skimmed her way through a month's worth of papers when she found it. It was a nice long article, with a picture of a smiling Alan in front of his shop, and the excessively allit-erative headline, LOCAL LAWYER LAUNCHES LIFELONG DREAM SHOP. It included all the bits that Sherry had expected: Alan's years of drawing up wills and doing other essential legal work as the only lawyer in little Winesap, and his childhood inter-est in antiques spurred on by a grandfather who was an ardent collector of Revolutionary War artifacts. Then, something that startled her: "After leaving his first legal job as a public defender in Schenectady . . ."

Sherry frowned. She'd known that Alan had grown up in Schenectady and gotten his degree from Albany Law before he'd moved down to the city for a few years to work in some sort of financial law, but he'd never once mentioned having been a public defender. That immediately struck her as something that might matter. People tended to talk about their first jobs, especially if it was something as inherently worth talking about as defending people who'd been accused of crimes. If anything, it would have come up while Sherry was talking to him about her cases. She felt her face go slightly warm. He must have known things that she didn't, and he never said. She must have sounded like an absolute idiot sometimes. She couldn't help but feel embarrassed, despite the fact that he was gone now and no one else would ever know. "Sorry, Alan," she said aloud.

Once she was over her embarrassment, she could focus on this new twist in the case. This, finally, might be a fruitful direction for her investigation. There were probably few occupations that were richer soil for making dangerous enemies than criminal defense attorney. He could have gotten someone off after they'd sinned against someone with a violent temper and a long memory. More likely, she thought, given the time frame, was someone Alan had *failed* to get off blaming him for the many years that they'd spent locked up. That would fit perfectly well: Alan's former client tracking him down after his release and appearing unexpectedly at his home. Alan, wanting to be kind or perhaps truly feeling some sense of guilt or responsibility, had invited him in and made him tea; possibly because the man—in Sherry's imagination this person was certainly a man—had been drunk, or because Alan knew that his former client was supposed to be on the wagon. Maybe the former client had been agitated: maybe he'd demanded an apology for a perceived wrong or asked Alan for money or a place to stay. Maybe they'd argued, or Alan had gently refused his request. Then a terrible, stupid, impulsive moment: a flash of rage, grabbing the lamp, bringing it down onto the back of Alan's head.

It fit. It fit perfectly. It also presented a problem. Alan had been a defense attorney *decades* ago, and he wasn't around to ask about which of his former clients might have a grudge against him. She was, unfortunately, going to have to do some actual detective work, so far as she was capable of such a thing. Lately she'd grown skeptical of her own abilities in that quarter. If a murder wasn't really a murder if the devil made you do it, surely the same principle held true for a murder investigation.

She pulled out her notebook then, and drew a small chart to organize her thoughts.

SUSPECT	SUSPICION LEVEL	METHOD OF INVESTIGATION
Alice	*Low. No clear motive; second-to-last to see Alan alive.*	*Probably cleared. Could not have walked to Alan's house and back in time. Check to see if any strangers with cars in town? Could have had co-conspirator? (Unlikely)*

SUSPECT	SUSPICION LEVEL	METHOD OF INVESTIGATION
Blonde woman (possibly Alan's ex-wife) seen with him in diner on day of death	Moderate. Spouse/ ex-spouse always a suspect; saw Alan on afternoon of death. Financial motive?	Find Susan to confirm/deny it was her he met. Ask alibi for time of murder. Find Alan's will?
Antiques dealer	Low. No clear motive. Fraud? Interacted with Alan on day of death.	Get number from Alice, call to confirm alibi.
Possible aggrieved former client/victim of former client	Low/high. Such person may not exist. If exists, most likely suspect.	Check Schenectady papers for articles re: Alan. Talk to ex-wife? (How?) Contact former colleagues? Might have to drive to Schtdy: ask Janine to borrow car.
<u>Me</u>	Low/high. Low: I know that I didn't do it. High: was last person to see Alan alive. Probably police's #1 suspect. Might have done it while possessed by demon.	<u>Find whoever actually did it.</u>

Sherry stared at what she'd written for a while, feeling a headache start to build behind her eyes. Then she sighed, put away everything that she'd pulled, and went to the front desk to call Alice.

The phone rang for a long time before Alice picked up. When she did, she sounded groggy, as if she'd been asleep.

Not unreasonable, since it was still only about eight thirty. Sherry pretended not to notice. "Good morning! Did you get a chance to find one of Mr. Kaminski's business cards?"

"Huh?" Alice said.

"That antiques dealer," Sherry said, with what she thought was very admirable patience. "The one you said spoke to Alan the other day. Mike Kaminski. You said that you'd get me one of his business cards."

"Oh," Alice said after a pause. "Right. Uh, hold on." There was the sound of the telephone clattering down onto a hard surface, then another, longer pause. Eventually Alice spoke again. "I found it. Do you have a pen?"

"Yes," Sherry said, and Alice read off the number. Sherry wrote it down, thanked her, and hung up. Then she immediately picked up the receiver again to make another call.

This time it was picked up almost immediately. "Hello?"

"Mr. Kaminski? This is Sherry Pinkwhistle," Sherry said. "I'm with the sheriff's office up in Winesap. I'm calling about Alan Thompson." In her experience, it was best to load a whole stream of very crisp, professional-sounding words at the front end of a conversation, to lull your interlocutor into the mental state of a person on an airplane being told what to do by the flight attendant.

"Oh, I heard about his having been killed," said the man who presumably was Mr. Kaminski. "Awful to hear, he was a great guy. So how can I help you?"

"I just had a few questions," she said. "Did you notice anything off about him when you spoke with him the other day? Anything he said, or anything unusual about his behavior?"

"Yeah," Mr. Kaminski said immediately. "He was definitely off."

Sherry blinked. She hadn't expected that. "He was? In what way?"

"He was worried about the shop," Mr. Kaminski said. "Stressed about the finances. Said he was glad I'd come by because he couldn't guarantee that it would be around in a few months, between how the books looked and his ex wanting to talk to him."

Sherry was glad she wasn't talking to him face-to-face: there was no way for him to see her expression. *What were you up to, Alan? Why didn't you tell me that you were worried about the shop?* "He said that his ex wanted to see him? Did he mention why?"

"Said he didn't know. Thought she probably wanted to ask for money, though."

"I see," Sherry said, and furiously underlined *Find Susan* in her chart. It had definitely been her, then: now the question was what she wanted, and whether or not she had an alibi. "Thank you, that's very helpful. And I apologize for asking, but where were you between ten and midnight Saturday night? Just so that we can eliminate you from our investigation." She was proud of herself for getting that line out so smoothly: she'd learned it from TV and thought it sounded very convincing.

"Club Sixty-Three," Mr. Kaminski said. "It's a cigar lounge on the Upper East Side. I have three friends I meet there every Saturday night. I took a cab home after. Will you need the receipts? Or numbers for the guys I was with?"

"That probably won't be necessary," Sherry said. He'd started out as her weakest suspect, and nothing that he'd said had moved him even slightly farther up her list. "Thank you for your time, Mr. Kaminski. I'll call back if there's anything else."

"No problem," Mr. Kaminski said. "I hope you catch the guy."

"Me, too," Sherry said, with feeling. Then she said goodbye, hung up, and made some changes to her chart with a different pen.

SUSPECT	SUSPICION LEVEL	METHOD OF INVESTIGATION
Alice	~~Low.~~ **Moderate.** No clear motive; second-last to see Alan alive. **Account of Alan's mood day of death conflicts with Kaminski.**	Probably cleared. Could not have walked to Alan's house and back in time. Check to see if any strangers with cars in town? Could have had co-conspirator? (Unlikely)
~~Blonde woman (possibly Alan's ex-wife) seen with him in diner on day of death~~ Susan, Alan's ex-wife	Moderate. Spouse/ex-spouse always a suspect: saw Alan on afternoon of death. Financial motive? **Kaminski thinks ex-wife may have wanted money.**	Find Susan to confirm/deny it was her he met. Ask alibi for time of murder. Find Alan's will?
Antiques dealer **Mike Kaminski**	Low. No clear motive. Fraud? Interacted with Alan on day of death.	~~Get number from Alice, call to confirm alibi.~~ **Probably cleared. Offered evidence was in city. Check back if other leads fall through.**

She looked over her chart for a moment, feeling a bit tired and overwhelmed. There still wasn't very much to go on.

What *was* there, unfortunately, seemed to be pointing her toward a drive to Schenectady followed by several hours in a basement somewhere digging through newspaper archives. She sighed. Then she closed her notebook and marched off to find Janine.

Sherry knew Janine's schedule well enough to know that she would be home when she dropped by. It only occurred to her after she knocked that Janine might not appreciate Sherry suddenly appearing on her front porch without any forewarning. She wasn't sure where her mind was at the moment. It was as if she was doing things without planning on it, the way Charlotte had described finding herself suddenly at the library without remembering having decided to go there. The skin on the back of her neck felt frostbitten despite her thick woolly scarf. Maybe she was just distracted and overwhelmed. Maybe she was being *puppeteered.*

The door opened, and Janine's expression indicated very clearly that Sherry's presence was a less than completely welcome surprise. "Sherry? Is something wrong? I was just getting some paperwork done." She ushered Sherry inside, anyway, and closed the door behind her to keep the cold wind out.

"Sorry," Sherry said quickly. "I know I should have called. I don't know what I was thinking. But something's come up, and I was wondering if I could borrow your car for a few hours."

Janine crinkled her nose at her, then quickly uncrinkled it. Nose crinkling probably wasn't the sort of neutral-but-supportive expression that Janine was supposed to make in her professional life, but people could be forgiven for slips made while off duty. Sherry was frequently guilty, in her personal life, of dog-earing paperbacks. "It's pretty last-minute,

Sherry," she said finally. "I was hoping to run some errands this afternoon."

"I'm sorry," Sherry said. "It's just that I think I might finally have a lead in the case." This was a gamble: Janine had been fairly negative in their meeting the other day, but historically she'd found it difficult to resist discussing Sherry's cases when the opportunity came up.

"Oh?" Janine said, her eyes lighting up very slightly. Then she went pinched again. "Do you need to drive to meet a warlock?"

"No," Sherry said. "I need to drive to Schenectady."

Janine raised her eyebrows. "Schenectady? Why?"

Sherry explained. Janine, finally, looked interested. "That *does* sound like it would make sense," she said. "Psychologically, I mean. Not that there *is* a former client out for revenge. But if there *was* one . . ."

"It would fit," Sherry said. "I agree. Alan letting him in and everything."

Janine hesitated. "Do you think you could have the car back by five?"

"Definitely," Sherry said immediately. "Can I pick anything up for you on the way back? You said you had errands to run."

"Could you?" Janine asked. She looked relieved now. "That would be great, if you could. Just my groceries. The list is on the fridge, I'll just—" She darted off. Sherry waited patiently. Janine was the sort of person who liked you to take your shoes off before you ventured farther into her house than the foyer, and at the moment Sherry didn't feel like bothering with that. Janine was back quickly enough, anyway, with the car keys and a neatly written shopping list in hand. "Thanks, Sherry," she said, having apparently forgotten that it was Sherry who'd shown up on her doorstep to ask for a favor in the first place. "I'm really swamped; I was *dreading* having to go to the store."

"Thank *you*," Sherry said, feeling much more magnanimous than she deserved to be. "I'll fill up the tank before I bring the car back." Then she hurried off before Janine had a chance to change her mind.

She took a moment to sit in the car before she started to drive. This happened every time now: the wave of anxiety, her heart beating faster. She took a deep breath and flicked on the radio. Janine had it tuned to NPR. Sherry let the droning voices wash over her without paying attention to the words. Then she started the car and very slowly and carefully backed out of Janine's driveway. She tried to ignore the quiet chattering voice in her head reminding her of the last time she'd gone on a long drive, the rain beating against her windshield and the sudden jolt of impact. She'd been cocky and sure of herself back then, but it had been easy to feel that way around Caroline. The woman had always known how to spin up a kind of gleaming magic around herself, and Sherry was exactly the sort of very small, dull, ordinary person who headed right for that gleam like a moth slamming into a screen door.

It wasn't the right time to think about Caroline, and the things that Sherry was almost certain that she'd helped Caroline do.

She just drove for a while, slowly and carefully enough that she annoyed a few people who got stuck behind her and ended up huffily passing her on the narrow country road. She couldn't stop thinking about the chance that she could get into an accident. That had happened on that night with Caroline. Only a fender bender, really, but it had been a nasty shock: someone rolling through a stop sign and not seeing Sherry's car through the rain. Sherry had wanted to wait for the police, but Caroline had insisted that they had to go, that she had a plane to catch, that she couldn't miss it, that she wouldn't be safe if she had to wait any longer. Sherry had done what Caroline had wanted.

Sherry was so wrapped up in thinking about Caroline that at first she didn't notice the body in the road.

FOURTEEN

Sherry slammed on the brakes instinctively when she saw the body, and there was a horrible, heart-stopping moment when the car skidded out before rolling to a stop a few inches from the drainage ditch. A moment after the car stopped moving, there was a terrible, creaking groan, and a massive oak tree came crashing down across the road just a foot or so in front of Janine's car, some of the branches close enough to brush against the windshield. Sherry just sat there in the car for a few moments, her heart pounding and her brain taking up a nasty, spiteful chant. *It happened because you got in the car, you shouldn't have done it, you shouldn't have done it. You lost the right to drive yourself. This is payback for what you did.* An iced-over twig from the tree dragged itself back and forth across the windshield with a soft hiss.

She took a few deep breaths. Then she turned the car off and got out to look for the body. There was nothing there, nothing at all where she'd seen it lying just a few moments before. She squatted down to try to peer under the tree, on the stray, awful chance that the body had been flattened underneath it. Nothing. Then she peered into the woods, with the vague notion that there might be someone out there, someone who'd dragged the body out of the road or made the tree fall down to cover it. Some sort of top-hatted villain holding a saw and cackling. There was nobody, though. Just snow, and ice, and then, out of the corner of her eye, movement. She turned to look. A man. Alan.

It couldn't be him. It wasn't possible. It was him. He wasn't dressed the way he'd been the night he'd died. He was wearing the outfit he'd worn when they'd gone snowshoeing together last winter, bundled up in a big puffy jacket and waterproof pants with thick, woolly socks pulled up over the cuffs, like a little boy whose mother had sent him out to go play in the snow. His face was pink from the cold. There were icicles in his mustache. She'd laughed at that, last time. He'd had to break them off before they went inside for hot chocolate.

"Sherry," he said. "You can't leave town."

He didn't sound like a ghost. He wasn't wailing and moaning. He just sounded like Alan. Kind, gentle. Maybe a little tired.

"Hi, Alan," she said. Her throat had gone tight. "I really miss you. I wanted to go to the library in Schenectady to see if I could find out anything about your old cases. How come you never told me that you were a public defender?"

He just shook his head. "You can't go, Sherry. You have to stay in town."

"But *why*?" Sherry asked, wanting Alan to help her, to explain what was going on, even though she *knew*, rationally, that this wasn't Alan. This couldn't be Alan. Either this was another trick from whatever . . . force was causing all the strange things to happen in town, or she was losing her mind. Or both. Maybe all of this had been in her imagination. Maybe she was the evil thing that had come to Winesap.

"You just *can't*," Alan said, but even as he spoke, his face was shifting, changing, the mustache fading away, his whole body growing shorter and wider, a double chin ballooning under his face, his eyes turning pale and suspicious, his blue beanie transformed into a big floppy velvet thing, until—

"Oh, *no*," Sherry said. "*Go away.* Leave me alone!"

"I wouldn't have to appear if you would only do as you're told, woman," Lord Thomas Cromwell said. "It isn't in the spirit of the thing for you to leave the field before the tourney has been completed. *She* won't allow it."

"What a stupid metaphor," Sherry said. "I really wish I could have imagined a better ghost to bother me all the time. You talk like a twelfth grader is playing you at a seasonal haunted house. I'll bet that hat was rented from a costume warehouse."

He sputtered at her for a moment, which she found satisfying. She knew that she shouldn't antagonize him, but in this particular moment it felt like the only thing in the world that she was capable of actually doing right.

"You're a fractious, hardheaded creature," he said. "And you won't leave this place before she's had her satisfaction." His expression shifted then. He looked her in the eye. "She's a stronger thing than either of us, and she likes her game to be played by the rules. You'd best stop trying to bend them, before you risk worse than a fright on a country road." Then he vanished, all at once, and the winter silence filled in the space where he'd been.

Sherry got back into the car, where she shivered pathetically for a while before it occurred to her that she would be less cold if she turned the engine on. She did that. Then, eventually, she managed to convince herself to turn around and drive back toward town. To the grocery store. She had promised to do Janine's grocery shopping.

She made her way systematically through the grocery store, back and forth through every single aisle, picking up everything on Janine's list as she came to it without trying to rush straight to it. It was nice. Comforting. She liked looking at all the colorful packages lined up in orderly rows on the shelves. She liked watching the nice young couple in the spice section trying to decide whether it would be better to buy a jar of mixed Italian herbs or to get the basil and oregano separately. She liked the terrible music piped in through the speakers. When she checked out, the youth and disinterested politeness of the pimply teenager at the register nearly made her cry. It would be nice, she thought, to be a pimply teenage girl who worked at a supermarket and hadn't yet had the chance to do a dozen things that she would regret for the next thirty years.

She drove back to Janine's house, parked, and carried the groceries to Janine's porch. When Janine answered the door, she looked baffled. "Sherry? What are you doing back already? I thought you were going to Schenectady."

"I couldn't," Sherry said. "There was a body in the road."

Janine blanched. "Oh my God. A *body*? Whose body? Did you call the police?"

"It disappeared," Sherry said. It felt as if her mouth was doing the talking without her consent. "Then a giant tree fell across the road."

"What?" Janine said. "Sherry—*what?*"

A hysterical little giggle bubbled up out of Sherry's chest. "Alan's ghost appeared and started telling me that I couldn't leave town," she said. "Then he turned into the ghost of Lord Thomas Cromwell. He's *insufferable*."

"Sherry," Janine said, and took the bags of groceries from her. She was frowning. "I think you should come in and sit down."

Sherry followed her inside, obedient, and sat placidly on Janine's expensive cream-colored sofa to wait for her to finish up in the kitchen. She didn't think about anything in particular, just soaked in the comfort of sitting in a nice, tidy, well-appointed room with no ghosts or demons evident. Then Janine appeared again, with a lovely tray with tea and teacups and chocolate chip cookies, and after she'd settled in with everything and Sherry had had her first sip of tea, she looked at Sherry over the rim of her own cup and said, with enormous seriousness, "I'm afraid that you're losing it."

Sherry choked on her tea, which was unfortunate, because it was some of Janine's very fancy Russian Caravan that she stocked up on once a year at that expensive little shop in Manhattan. When she'd finished hacking, she said, "Is that your professional opinion?"

"No," Janine said. "It's just my unprofessional opinion as your best friend that I think you're stressed-out and mourning your boyfriend, and that you're losing it a little. I think you need to get out of Winesap for a while, Sherry. My friend Kathy has that little place in Key West that I told you about, and it's just standing empty right now. I'm sure she'd let you stay there for a few weeks."

"Key West," Sherry repeated. It sounded insane. Like Janine was proposing that she climb into a rocket ship and head to her vacation home on Neptune. "How am I supposed to make it to Key West when I can't go to *Schenectady*?"

Janine made a face. It was subtle, but definitely a *face*. Then she smoothed out that expression like someone running a spatula over a badly frosted cake. "I don't know that you *can't* go to Schenectady, Sherry."

Sherry didn't think of herself as a person who got angry easily. The opposite, really. She'd put up with a lot before she got angry. She was angry now, though, in a sudden hot rush that felt more *exciting* than unpleasant or uncomfortable. There was a sort of power in feeling righteously outraged. "I know that I can't," she said. "I know what happened to me. I know what I saw. And I think that you're being ridiculous. You're so scared of admitting that something strange is going on that you won't admit that *something strange is going on*. I'm not *crazy*, Janine."

Janine was holding her hands in the air. "Sherry," she said. She kept using Sherry's name over and over in that infuriating way. They probably taught them to do that in therapist school. "I don't think that you're crazy. I *promise* that I don't think that you're crazy." The way that she was holding her hands up as if she expected Sherry to reach out and smack her only made Sherry angrier. She'd never hit anyone in her life.

"That's just *semantics*, though, isn't it?" she said. "You probably say that to all of the crazy people because it's offensive to call people crazy. I don't want you to say that you don't think I'm crazy, I want you to *take me seriously*. And stop acting like you think I'm going to hit you!"

Janine sighed and folded her hands in her lap with what looked like a certain amount of conscious effort. "I promise that I'm taking you seriously," she said. "I'm not talking about how crazy you are behind your back. I believe that you've been experiencing things that you can't explain. It's just *hard*. You understand, don't you? Haven't you ever tried very hard to believe in something but not been able to believe in it, anyway?"

It was exactly the thing to say to smack Sherry's rising dudgeon right back down into the dirt. "I went to Catholic school," she said after a moment. "For a while I couldn't believe but still thought I was going to go to hell for not believing. I used to pray to a God I couldn't believe in to *make* me believe in him. I *wanted* to believe. But now I'm starting to believe in all kinds of things that I don't want to believe in at all. As soon as you start believing in demons and things, then you have to worry about them coming after you. And they *are*. I swear that they are. They won't *leave me alone*."

Janine didn't say anything. She just leaned forward, took Sherry's hand in hers, and gave it a gentle squeeze.

Sherry burst into tears.

She stayed there for a while longer, letting Janine hold her hand and pat her knee and feed her cookies and comfort. Then she left, trudging back up through the snow to her lonely, haunted house. She was beginning to hate being alone in her own home. She hated that she hated it. Lord Thomas came to wind around her ankles and purr. She eyed him suspiciously and hated that she felt suspicious of a creature who lived in fear of the vacuum cleaner. She gave a sudden, furious scream into the quiet of the house, as loudly as she could for as long as she could. When she was finished she didn't feel any better. She just felt like a very silly woman with a sore throat. Lord Thomas, the poor thing, who seemed as if he really was just a cat again at the moment, was hiding under the sofa in a state of fairly reasonable terror.

The screaming having not worked to make Sherry feel any

better, she resolved to do some sleuthing instead. So she couldn't go to Schenectady. Fine. She could still get things done. She poured herself a big glass of bourbon and put on a strange old record of Gregorian chants she'd bought at a yard sale a few years earlier, on the theory that it might remind Thomas Cromwell of Thomas More and keep him hiding under the sofa for a bit longer out of remorse.

It was strange. She'd never particularly liked Gregorian chants—did anyone? She supposed that *someone* must, and they probably threw extremely strange dinner parties—but the sound of them now seemed to soothe her into a sort of trance. She found herself going to the table where she'd abandoned the yew branch, picking the branch up, and carrying it to the kitchen table with her bourbon. Then she fetched the sharpest paring knife in the kitchen and set to whittling. It was nice. Meditative. She drank her bourbon. She prayed. Not any prayer in particular, just half-formed thoughts and phrases that tumbled around and around in her brain—*I believe, world without end, have mercy on us, now until the hour of our death, deliver us from evil.* At the last phrase she felt herself, as if from a distance, shiver. "Deliver us from evil," she said aloud. Then: "Deliver us." She didn't know whom she was speaking to. To the God she'd prayed to as a child, maybe. Maybe to someone else. *Hear me, protect us, deliver us.* The chanting rose around her like a warm blanket. "Protect us," she said, as the wood took shape under her hands. She'd had to cut away a lot of the branch for being too thin and whippy to be useful. It still didn't look like much of a stake. It was only about the size and shape of a chopstick. A very sharp chopstick. It would have to work. The chanting was still playing. She went to the shopping bag that held all the things she'd bought in the New Age shop and pulled out something she'd bought on impulse. Now she thought that maybe it had the right sort of resonance. Oil of frankincense. She rubbed it into the wood. "Protect us," she said aloud. "Deliver us." The smell of it was heady. For a moment she felt as if there were other people in the room, gathering around her, sitting by her side, kneeling. Then the record ended. Sherry blinked. Her little weapon sat on her kitchen table, looking like nothing but a bit of scrap wood you'd find in someone's shed. It looked like that, but it looked like more than that, too. Sherry stared at it. She let herself see that it gleamed.

"Thank you," she said aloud, and lifted it to kiss it. She didn't let herself feel silly. She carried it in both hands to tuck it carefully into her coat pocket. Then she sat again and gulped down the rest of her bourbon. The sudden silence was oppressive. There was the quiet of the very early morning in the room, even though it was only about three in the afternoon. She double-checked the time. Early enough to get more work done, and the need to get work done was the excuse she needed to justify how desperately she wanted to hear another human voice right now. She took a deep, steadying breath, trying to shake off the strangeness of the last hour. Then she called up one of her favorite regular library patrons.

Lois picked up on the second ring, as brisk and alert-sounding as ever. "Feldman residence, Lois speaking!"

"Hi, Louie," Sherry said. Lois was *Louie* to her friends and had bestowed this honor upon Sherry a year earlier, after a spirited chat on the relative merits of Ian Rankin versus Patricia Cornwell. Louie was almost ninety years old, preferred her detectives hard-boiled, and was the chief editor—and only full-time reporter—of the *Winesap Herald*. She refused to retire on the grounds that if she did, no one else would be willing to run a newspaper in a little town like Winesap, which Sherry had to admit was probably an accurate assessment of the case. "It's Sherry Pinkwhistle."

"Oh, Sherry!" Lois said. "I'm so sorry for your loss. Did you get the flowers?"

"I think so," Sherry said vaguely. There *were* flowers piling up in her entryway: she'd just been bringing them in off the porch whenever she saw them. There might also be a casserole or two out there. It was a wonder that Lord Thomas hadn't eaten one of them and gotten sick all over the living room rug. "Thank you, it was very kind of you." There must, she thought, be an appropriate and delicate segue between receiving condolences over her boyfriend's—even if he hadn't really been her boyfriend—death and making indelicate inquiries about him. If there was, she wasn't a sensitive enough person to know it. "I actually wanted to ask you some questions about Alan."

"*Oh?*" Lois said, with an increased perkiness to her tone that made Sherry smile despite herself. "You're not investigating, are you?" There was nothing Lois liked more than a good murder investigation, except for, possibly, a *serial* murder investigation.

"I'm afraid that I am," Sherry said. "I was hoping that you could help me."

"I'll certainly do my best," Lois said with relish. "What questions did you have?"

"They're not very specific," Sherry admitted, already feeling a little foolish. Lois was the sort of person who always knew exactly what questions she was going to ask in advance. Sherry was positive that back when she was a young reporter on the mean streets of New York City, Lois hadn't based *her* investigations on *a funny feeling I had about why he never mentioned his old job*. "I just found out that Alan was a public defender in Schenectady for a while. He'd never mentioned it. I don't suppose you know anything about that?"

"Not a thing," Lois said. "That *is* a little strange, isn't it?"

"That he never mentioned it?"

"Well, that, too, I guess. But I was thinking more that it's an unusual choice of career for a guy with that kind of family background. Maybe it was his way of being rebellious."

Sherry felt a little as if she was watching a foreign film with badly translated captions. "His family? His father was a doctor, wasn't he? Not a cop." A public defender from a family of cops *would* have been unusual and rebellious, though probably not motive for murder.

"Oh, no," Lois said. "I meant how wealthy they were. His grandfather was an executive for GE, left Alan a small fortune in his will. He was the one who got Alan interested in antiques in the first place. Alan told me about him when I wrote about the shop opening way back when. Anyway, in my experience, when dad's a doctor and granddad's an executive, they usually want to see junior making more money than he would as a public defender in Schenectady, at least back when Alan was a kid. These days they probably want their kids to go to fashion design school so they can send expensive sneakers to poor African villagers who never asked for new shoes to start with. Kids like that are like racehorses: if you can afford one, everyone knows you're *really* rich."

"Oh," Sherry said in response to all that. She felt—she wasn't sure. Odd. It wasn't as if Alan would have been obligated to tell her that he was sitting on a pile of inherited wealth. They weren't *married*, for God's sake. They'd never even formally dated, if such a thing was really possible at their ages. They lived in separate houses and kept fully separate accounts. It just felt . . . odd. Another tile falling out of a once-familiar mosaic. A former defense attorney. An heir to a fortune. A bunch of bits and pieces that she couldn't make fit together with the image of a man she'd thought she'd known as well as she knew anyone.

As well as she'd thought she'd known Caroline.

She cleared her throat. "How much money are we talking about, exactly? That Alan inherited from his grandfather, I mean."

"I don't have an exact number," Lois said. "If he told me how much, I've forgotten. But if you're wondering if it was enough for someone to kill for, then I'd say you've found one hell of a motive."

FIFTEEN

As soon as she'd hung up the phone, Sherry sat down again to update her suspect chart. She added one new row, but two new suspects, bringing the total up to seven.

SUSPECT	SUSPICION LEVEL	METHOD OF INVESTIGATION
Alan's sons, Eli and Corey Thompson	High. A huge inheritance is always a strong motive.	They both live far away. Might be in town for funeral? Find out if they have alibis for time of death.

She stared at her chart for a while, trying to extract some sort of sense from it. The results weren't very encouraging. A growing list of suspects, but nothing concrete: just vague motives and half-formed suspicions and shadowy figures who might not even be real. What she needed, what she really needed, was something more solid than a call with a nonagenarian and a few hopeful spritzes of holy water.

She sighed and rubbed at her eyes, then made two more calls. The first was to the public library in Schenectady, where she introduced herself as the librarian up in Winesap and asked, very humbly and apologetically, whether they had any-one there who'd be willing to dig through their local newspa-per archives for her. She then spent five minutes on hold before she was transferred over to a very enthusiastic-sounding young intern, from whom Sherry just as humbly and apologetically requested that she fax over—she stumbled slightly over the word *fax*, for some reason—any news articles they might have available from about thirty years earlier re-ferring to a public defender named Alan Thompson. The en-ergetic young intern had apparently never wanted to do anything more in her life than she wanted to hunt down some antique trial reporting, especially since it was for a *fellow li-brarian*. Sherry refrained from asking whether the intern had, as yet, earned this level of collegial familiarity, and instead thanked her as if the intern was giving Sherry one of her kid-neys. Then, confident that the kid was buttered up thickly enough to reduce any friction she'd encounter while trudging through the *Gazette* archives, she hung up.

She looked up at the wall clock. Five thirty. Perfect. Then she checked her address book and called Greg Walbrook.

The phone rang and rang, then went to voicemail. She tried again. This time Greg picked up, sounding just as baffled by the universe as usual. She'd only ever called him twice before, in the course of arranging Alan's birthday parties, and he al-ways managed to answer the telephone as if he'd never used such a device before and was surprised to discover that he owned one. There was a faint, distant, "I—yeah, hold on a sec-ond." A brief moment of scuffling sounds, as if he was wres-tling the phone away from someone and then dropping it repeatedly onto the ground. Then a much louder and clearer: "Greg Walbrook."

"I know, Greg," Sherry said. "That's why I called you. This is Sherry. Pinkwhistle," she added, just in case he thought he might be speaking to a Sherry he'd known in second grade.

"Sherry," he said, with evident surprise. Then, in a tone that felt as if it matched Sherry's own grief in its sheer, miserable bewilderment: "Alan's dead."

Sherry's throat tightened up. "I know," she said. "That's why I wanted to call you. Do you think we could meet up for dinner and talk?"

"For dinner? Oh—sure. Where? Uh. The diner okay?"

"That would be fine," Sherry said. As far as she knew, Greg never ate out anywhere other than the diner and the dive bar near the gas station. "Can I meet you at six thirty?"

Greg agreed, and Sherry got off the phone with him and hurried to get bundled up and head down the hill. It was a bit warmer out than it had been the previous evening, which was a relief. Getting in and out of town had been so much easier when Alan was driving her back home every so often. It was so much easier to be stubbornly independent when it was nice outside. It was so much easier to desperately miss someone when you lived alone.

Greg was already at the diner when she arrived, which wasn't surprising: he lived just two doors down. When she walked in, he peeked at her as if he thought it was rude to look at her too directly, then ducked his head and handed her a menu, only saying hello a beat later. It was a little strange, but so was Greg, and he and Alan had had a strange friendship. Greg was about as far from a retired attorney as he could get: he'd spent twenty years in the army and did odd jobs to make ends meet. He and Alan had met because Alan had needed someone to rewire and repair the old lamps and record players and things at the shop, and Greg had a special talent when it came to small appliances. He had a special talent when it came to a lot of things. He was also a handyman and a house painter and had an encyclopedic knowledge of everything World War II. He was notorious for asking local landowners if he could set up a deer blind on their properties and then not bothering to bring a gun along with him when he visited; he just liked to sit up there and take pictures of the deer. He was also, according to Alan, an excellent fly fisherman, and the two of them seemed to have formed a friendship on the basis of standing side by side in streams together in nearly unbroken silence.

From what Alan had told her, it wasn't the sort of friendship that involved the two of them pouring their hearts out to each other. Probably not the most promising ground for mining Alan's darkest secrets. Still, they did go out and have a beer together from time to time, and Greg was probably Alan's closest friend who lived here in Winesap. It would be investigative malpractice for Sherry to not at least *talk* to him.

She couldn't push it, though. Greg was skittish, like the delicate creatures of the wilderness he liked to spy on from his deer blind. Instead, she perused her menu with elaborate care while Greg did the same. When the waitress arrived, Sherry ordered the chicken Parmesan, and Greg ordered a meatball sandwich and a glass of milk. For some reason the order made Sherry's throat clench up for the second time that evening. Maybe she was just getting old.

Sherry gently nudged Greg into talking to her about fishing until their food arrived, then let the man finish the first half of his meatball sandwich before she said, very quietly, "I miss Alan."

He ducked his head and wiped his mouth with a napkin. "Yeah," he said. "Me, too."

"Did he say anything to you?" she asked. "Before he died? Not *right* before, I mean—did he mention anything that was bothering him?"

He shook his head. "No," he said. "Not really."

"Not really? So—a little?"

He shrugged. "Everyone worries about something sometimes."

"I guess so," Sherry said. "I worry about my cat getting a urinary tract infection. I used to worry about politics. I was wondering if maybe Alan was worried about something more serious than that."

"He woulda told you if he was, wouldn't he?" Greg asked. "You were his girlfriend. We were just fishing buddies, mostly."

Something about the way he said that didn't settle well atop the chicken Parmesan. Sherry decided to chase after what her gut suggested. "But there are some things that a guy will tell his fishing buddy that he might not tell his girlfriend. Right?"

Greg shifted in his seat, looking deeply uncomfortable. "I know he's dead," he said. "But I still don't like talking about his business."

"He's dead because someone killed him," Sherry said. "If they killed him, they had a motive. I'm trying to figure out who might have wanted Alan dead."

He was shaking his head. "I don't think it was that serious," he said. "Just his wife. Wives're like that," he added, with all the authority of a lifelong bachelor. "She wouldn't leave him alone. It bugged him, that's all."

"His ex, you mean? Susan?"

He frowned. "He had an ex, too? Susan was his wife, wasn't she?"

Part of Sherry already knew where this conversation was headed. One piece after another falling out of the mosaic, the whole image of the man she'd known crumbling to pieces. Another part of her was still busy trying to parse out the individual words Greg was saying. "He only ever had one wife, Susan. They got divorced right before he moved to Winesap."

"They weren't divorced, that was the whole problem," Greg said, and then his face went red again. "Aw, shit, I'm sorry, Sherry—"

"It's all right," Sherry said quickly. "It's all right. I didn't know. I'm glad that I know now." She took a deep breath, then let it out. It was a relief, in a way. Rage was a big enough emotion that it managed to almost blot out the sadness. "So Alan was still married. Separated, though, obviously. Unless—he didn't *Mr. Rochester* her, did he?"

Greg looked baffled. "What?"

"Sorry, sorry," Sherry said. "I'm being ridiculous. Do you know why they weren't divorced? What was the holdup?"

"First it was that she didn't want to get the divorce," Greg said. "So he just took off, anyway, without bothering to deal with the paperwork. Then she agreed to the divorce, but I guess she wasn't happy about what he wanted to do with the money. She wanted to split things down the middle, but he wanted to keep the money he'd gotten from his granddad. The store was more a hobby than a moneymaker, and he was using his inheritance to keep it running in his granddad's memory, kind of, but she wanted to take half of what he had left. From what Alan said, it was getting pretty nasty."

Sherry's first thought was, *poor Alan*. Then she caught her-self. *Was* it poor Alan, really? Maybe Susan had been awful for years, made his life a misery, refused to let him go, and then tried to take away his retirement nest egg once he finally escaped. Or maybe she was a loving wife and mother who treated Alan like gold for two decades, raised both of his strap-ping sons to adulthood, and had the rug pulled out from under her when he suddenly decided to run away from his family and leave her with nothing. Sherry didn't know. She'd never been a part of her boyfriend's marriage. Assuming that he'd been the wronged party in his dispute with his wife would only mar her judgment when it came to considering her sus-pects. "Divorces can be so awful," she said. It was a bland enough thing to say. "Do you know if he saw her often?"

Greg shook his head. "I don't think so. I'm pretty sure she was supposed to come up here and see him, though. He was hoping that she was ready to, you know, agree on how the money would get split up."

"And do you know if they ever actually met?"

He shook his head again. "No. He never said."

"Okay," Sherry said. They had, of course: Susan had been seen in the diner. The question was whether or not she'd gone home after that meeting to sleep peacefully in her own bed. "Thank you, Greg. You've been really helpful." She paused. "You were a really great friend to him, you know. He talked about you all the time."

He didn't say anything for a moment. Then, finally, he said, "He talked about you, too."

He was a nice man, she thought, even if he was a little odd. Maybe nicer than Alan had been. She'd always thought before that Alan was being very kind to spend so much time with him. Now she thought that maybe the charity had been extended in the other direction.

They finished eating. Sherry insisted on paying over Greg's protestations, then dawdled over coffee and a slice of pie after he left. She was dreading the idea of going home. The walk back up the hill, the quiet in her house, the fear of the voices that might come out of the dark. All of it. She still *intended* to go home, though, once the staff in the diner started pointedly putting the chairs up onto the tables and mopping the floors. The plan was to go home. Instead, she found herself walking toward the church, trying the door—it was unlocked—and slipping into one of the back pews. There was someone praying near the altar, but she left after twenty minutes or so, leaving Sherry alone.

The quality of the silence felt different here than it did at home. The church seemed to wear the quiet more comfortably than Sherry's little cottage did, like an old married couple who no longer felt the need to fill in the gaps in the conversation. The smell of old wood and incense was comforting, and the air had a cave-like coolness to it that felt the same now in April as it usually did in August. She'd just planned on sitting there, for a moment, until she worked up the energy and courage to walk back home. Then she realized how tired she was and thought that maybe it wouldn't be so bad if she lay down in the pew for a while to rest. She could remember thinking about how badly she'd wanted to do that sometimes as a bored child on Sunday mornings, still groggy after having been dragged out of bed bright and early for mass. She lay down and remembered more of those childhood Sunday mornings: the atonal drone of the parishioners trudging their way through a hymn, the low buzz of their parish priest giving his homily, the slow churn of the ceiling fans stirring through the thick air of the room, her mother grabbing at her knee to make her stop wriggling. She was thinking about all that when she fell asleep.

"Obviously you're always welcome here," Father Barry was saying. "But a pew can't be a comfortable place to sleep."

For one strange, unsettling moment, Sherry thought that she had somehow fallen asleep in the middle of confession. Then she remembered that she hadn't been to confession in several decades, and a moment later the rest of the strange previous evening dropped into her head in a solid clump. She jolted upright, groaning as her body registered displeasure at having spent the night—and it *had* been the whole night; there was light streaming in through the stained-glass windows— on a hard wooden pew and then noticed that Father Barry was holding two coffee cups. She took the one he held out to her, blushing hot. "I'm so sorry," she said. "I just wanted to lie down for a minute before I walked back home."

"You don't have to apologize," Father Barry said. He looked odd. It took her a few seconds too long to realize that it was because he was wearing blue jeans and a Notre Dame sweat- shirt, no clerical collar to be found. It felt a little like seeing him in the nude. "There's a cot in the vestry, though. You could sleep on that next time." He paused. "Is it because of your haunted cat?"

"No," she said, then winced. "Partly. I don't know. I think I'm just . . . tired."

"That would make sense," he said, and looked at her for a moment in an annoyingly thoughtful, priestly sort of way. "Janine told me that she offered you her friend's vacation home, and you turned her down."

Sherry blushed again. "You've been *discussing* me?"

"Janine's worried about you," he said. He took a sip of his own coffee. "I think I would have said no, too. But it's my job to look out for my—flock." He said the word *flock* as if he felt slightly self-conscious about it, the way that some newly married men hesitated over the phrase *my wife*. "But you didn't make any vows when you became a librarian. If things get too bad, I don't think anyone would judge you for making a break for it."

"Wouldn't they?" she asked. "It sounds like something the villain of a novel would do. Run away like a coward as soon as things get scary."

"Sure," he said after a second. "People talk like they'd be prepared to die for the cause when most of them won't even take half a Saturday to volunteer for it. They're just doing . . . backseat heroism. Maybe they *would* judge you, but that doesn't mean that if we start getting demons pouring through the windows that you shouldn't get in the car and get out of Winesap. You never signed up for this. It's not your job to sacrifice yourself for everyone else just because the devil thinks you should. Or whatever that thing is that's been bothering you. You don't have to believe in the devil to believe that maybe whatever it is might not have your best interests at heart. I think you should reserve the right to walk away from this and enjoy a nice peaceful retirement somewhere."

She blinked at him for a second, taken aback. Then she swallowed. "Thanks, Father," she said. "That's really"—her voice cracked—"nice of you."

He smiled at that, as if he was pleased to have had his success at his pastoral duties recognized, then visibly caught himself and made his expression go graver. "I'm still always here if you need to talk."

Part of her wanted to laugh at him. He seemed particularly young when he said things like that. Instead she just thanked him again for the kind words and the coffee and finally set off on the long walk back home.

SIXTEEN

S he was greeted at the door by Lord Thomas Cromwell, and her initial reaction was to respond to him with the same level of suspicion that she usually leveled at strange men on her doorstep wearing matching short-sleeved button-downs. She fed him his breakfast, anyway, maintaining a wary distance the whole time, until finally he started winding around her ankles and purring and she was forced to scoop him up and give him a cuddle. "I missed you being your usual self," she told him, whereupon he gave an almighty wriggle and jumped down to the floor. He'd never been very patient about being carried around like a baby.

While she took her shower and got ready for the day, she contemplated how completely unnerving it was to live with someone who might, at any moment, be someone else. She'd never experienced anything quite like it before. Her ex-husband, despite his flaws, had been resolutely the same person every single day that she'd known him. The closest she'd ever come to this had been with Caroline. She'd had a strange habit of sometimes, when they were out in public, pretending to be someone else. One particular favorite was a bohemian heiress named Phoebe. Sherry had taken it as a harmless quirk back then, just as something funny that Caroline liked to do sometimes. It was only much later that it had started to feel sinister. As if what Caroline had enjoyed about it wasn't the fantasy but the part where she got other people to truly believe in her lies.

Once she was thoroughly washed, dressed, and hastily fed on a breakfast of slightly stale cornflakes, she gave Lord Thomas one last pat and headed down to the library. She felt more refreshed than she probably ought to be after a night of sleep in a pew. Then, after she arrived at the library, she had another turn of good luck: there was a small stack of papers waiting for her on her desk, with a Post-it note from Connie stuck on top. *For you from Schenect. PL.*

Sherry sat down to read what the intern had dug up. The first few pages were nothing special: Alan's name popping up in his father's obituary and his own wedding announcement, or in a brief and very old piece about his having advanced to the state high school wrestling championship. A few brief references to his having been the defense attorney in cases of minor note, in particular a local official who'd eventually been convicted of embezzlement. Sherry checked the dates: the man in question would be in his nineties now. If he was still alive, he was unlikely to have the energy and upper-body strength to travel to his former attorney's house and bash his head in.

Then, at the bottom, something that looked important. The article was three decades old, and the events it described had apparently made enough of a splash to merit a front-page headline. ORELLANA RULING OVERTURNED. Sherry read on to learn that the name in the headline referred to a teenager named Salvador Orellana, who had been convicted in a homicide case five years earlier. He had appealed the conviction on the basis of ineffective assistance of counsel, and his appeal had been successful.

His defense attorney had been Alan Thompson.

Sherry sucked in a quick breath and let it out slowly. She'd already felt a little frustrated with how the suspects with good motives kept piling up, but this might be the strongest suspect yet. It had all been a long time ago now, but five years in prison for a crime that you hadn't committed might be a rare example of something that almost anyone could stew over for thirty years. At the very least, she needed to try to track down Salvador Orellana, if only so she could conclusively rule him out as a suspect.

There was a photo at the top of the article of two men standing in front of a courthouse. Orellana and his new attorney smiling jubilantly toward the camera. It was dark and blurry, a copy of a copy of an antique newspaper. Sherry couldn't make much of it. Orellana was just a small, indistinct figure in an oversized suit, with a face that could have belonged to any number of vaguely nice-looking young men. It felt impossible to imagine such a lifeless little picture as being something connected to Alan's murder.

She folded the relevant page up and slipped it into her pocket, just as Connie walked in to open up the library for the day. Sherry felt oddly as if she'd been caught doing something wrong. "Good morning," she said, a little too loudly. "Thank you for the faxes."

"Oh," Connie said. She was clearly surprised to see Sherry there. "You're welcome. Were you—did you want to work today?"

"What?" Sherry asked. Then, impulsively: "Yes, actually. I thought it might—take my mind off of things a little."

Connie's expression softened. "That's a good idea," she said. "Just tell me what you need. It's been a zoo around here without you."

Sherry doubted that very much. Connie was a model of efficiency. If she'd been employed at an actual zoo, she'd have it very quickly functioning exactly like a library. "I don't believe you," she said aloud. "If you worked at a zoo, you'd have all of the monkeys reshelving their own toys by the end of the first day. How about you tell me what you need, instead? You're the one who's been holding down the fort here while I've been . . . at home." It occurred to her, very belatedly, how incredibly strange it might have looked to Connie that Sherry was having librarians in Schenectady send her articles about her recently murdered boyfriend. Hopefully she'd assume that Sherry wanted them for a memorial service.

Sherry's stomach abruptly twisted. A memorial service. She'd been so wrapped up in the investigation, she hadn't even bothered to think about who would be responsible for organizing poor Alan's funeral.

Connie must have seen something of what Sherry was thinking in her expression, because she stepped in close and gave Sherry a quick, tight hug. "Thank you," she said. "I will, if you don't mind. You'd been planning on a new display for the children's section, weren't you? Maybe you could get to work on that? I wanted to try to process some late fees before everything gets too hectic."

"The rainy-day display," Sherry said. "Yeah, thank you." Then she took a moment to rub at her eyes, squared her shoulders, and got to work.

As soon as the day got started, she knew that she'd made the right choice to say yes to working. Putting together book displays was one of her favorite parts of the job—she loved seeing people shoot straight toward a new one when they came through the door—and she always found the arts and crafts aspect of it oddly meditative. She put on a pot of coffee in the office and hunkered down to work, letting herself get absorbed in cutting raindrops and tulips out of her supply of colorful construction paper, then selecting a collection of picture books to suit the theme. By the time the display was ready, it was almost time for lunch, and the rest of the day flew by in the same way, all the worries chased out of Sherry's head by the ordinary demands of the library.

It was just before closing time when a group of people walked in who looked very out of place in their cozy little library. In the lead there was a tall, elegant-looking blonde woman in a long camel coat, with the sort of expertly done makeup that made her look much younger until she got close enough for Sherry to realize that they must be close to the same age. Along with her were three young men.

The first was thin and gentle-looking, maybe forty years old or so, wearing horn-rimmed glasses and a blue ski jacket. The second was taller and broader, a rather strikingly handsome young man in a sharp black peacoat, with a shock of dark wavy hair artfully draped across his forehead. She took them all in instantly and recognized them just as quickly: Alan's family. His wife, Susan, and his sons: Eli, the soft-spoken married father of two, and Corey, the aspiring painter with the revolving door of unsuitable boyfriends. It was the fourth person in their group who made no sense, whose presence was making her gawp at them like a hopeless redneck who'd never seen a group of nicely dressed city people in her life. He'd not only changed his clothes since she'd last seen him—she

couldn't imagine him owning such an expensive-looking
coat—but changed his haircut, and, apparently, changed his
perspective on his vow of chastity, considering the way he and
young Corey were looking at each other.

"*Father Barry?*" she burst out, utterly confounded.

He visibly recoiled. Then he threw his head back—she'd
thought people only did that in books—and laughed. "*Jesus,*
that's weird," he said. "The last time someone got us mixed up
it was before he was a *father.* I feel like I'm sinning already!"
He gave her a big, sunny grin.

She smiled back at him instinctively. He had a *lovely* smile.
"You must be Todd," she said, enormously relieved to have
cracked the case and restored order to the universe. The world
continued on its usual route around the sun. She could appreciate, now, how different the two of them looked, once you
knew to expect that there was a pair of them. Just the way that
Todd held himself was different. He moved like a man who
knew he was handsome and was delighted to provide you with
something nice to look at, whereas Barry held himself like he
suspected he might be handsome and wanted to apologize for
any carnal thoughts his good looks might have caused in advance. "I'm so sorry, I should have known. Barry was just talking about you the other day." Then she looked toward the rest
of the group. "And you're Alan's family."

Susan stepped forward and held out a hand. "Susan
Thompson."

Sherry shook her hand when it was offered. "Sherry Pinkwhistle," she said, utterly pointlessly. Susan clearly knew perfectly well who she was. She wasn't looking at Sherry as if she
wanted to get revenge on her husband's dumpy mistress and
slap her in the middle of a public library. Her blue eyes were

calm, clear, and unreadable. Within a few seconds of with-standing her gaze, Sherry cracked. "I didn't know," she said. "That he was married."

Eli visibly winced. Susan appeared unmoved. "I know," she said simply. "He told me that you didn't, and I believed him. Alan was always telling little lies to avoid uncomfortable con-versations. Being divorced was easier than being married, so he lied about it." She shrugged.

Sherry felt almost as if Susan *had* slapped her. It made sense; that was the problem. It made everything fit together just a bit better. Alan wasn't some horrible villain. He'd al-ways been incredibly kind to Sherry. It was just that he was the sort of man who sometimes told little lies to try to smooth things out and make hard things easy and keep everything calm and pleasant. A little lie like, *I'm divorced*, when he was actually only separated. A little lie like, *Of course that paper-work's completed*, when he was defending someone in a mur-der trial. Little lies about his bank account. Little lies that he got away with, until he couldn't anymore. "Yes," she said, a bit faintly. "That makes sense."

Susan's expression shifted into something that looked alarmingly like sympathy. "Anyway," she said. "I'm sorry to ambush you at work. I just wanted to meet—you. And let you know that we're here in town to make the funeral arrange-ments, and for the reading of the will tomorrow."

"Thank you for letting me know," Sherry said. "Will you—I'd like to go to the funeral. If you won't mind too much."

Susan's eyebrows shot up. "Of course you can come," she said. "You were his girlfriend. You didn't do anything wrong. All of his friends should be at the funeral."

"She's right," Eli said, speaking up for the first time. The sound of his voice made Sherry jump. He sounded exactly like Alan. "Dad talked about you all the time. He'd want you to be there."

"And you might want to come to the reading of the will, too," said Corey. "Just in case Dad decided to disinherit all of us and give the cash to his mistress."

Sherry felt her whole face go hot. Corey quite clearly didn't feel as charitably toward his father's girlfriend as the rest of the family. Todd elbowed him. "I can't believe that I've only known you for three days and I already have to keep you in line," he said.

"How exactly did you meet?" Sherry blurted out. She knew that the likely answer from Corey would be a spirited *none of your business*, but she couldn't help herself. The sheer unlikeliness of the coincidence was making her itch. Either there was some sort of scheme afoot—with that amount of money in play, all sorts of strange people might want to attach themselves to this particular domestic tragedy—or her demon friend was up to new tricks.

Fortunately for her, it was Todd who jumped in to answer. "Me and Corey met a month ago at a party. We just happened to run into each other again because it turned out we were all coming up from the city to Saratoga on the same train," he said. "I was just heading up to see my brother, and when Corey told me about what had happened with his dad, I told them that Barry would do a good job with the service, if they didn't mind a priest. I'm going to take them to meet him next."

"I'm sure Barry will do a wonderful job," Sherry said, slightly too late. "Alan never got the chance to meet him, but I think he would have liked him very much." As soon as she said it, she was sure that it was the wrong thing to have said, and that Corey would insult her again. Instead, they all seemed to accept this, and departed with a smattering of polite goodbyes. Then there was nothing to do but provide a brief explanation to a lurking and obviously curious Connie, help close up the library for the evening, and consider her next move.

She went to the library phone without planning on it, and dialed without realizing that she'd memorized the number. It was already ringing when it registered how creepy that was, and she gave a brief, full-bodied shiver just before Charlotte picked up. "Hello?"

"Hi, Charlotte," Sherry said, the heebie-jeebies outweighed by the sudden pleasure of hearing Charlotte's voice. Her new friend, who laughed at her and still took her seriously. "I think the demon just made me call you, so I don't actually have anything important to say. Do you want to go out for drinks with me?"

"Yeah, okay," Charlotte said immediately. "Can we get some food first? I'm starving."

"Definitely," Sherry said. "Marino's?" It was the Italian restaurant where Alan had liked to take her for dinner. Right now she liked the idea of reclaiming it for herself and Charlotte.

"Yeah, great," Charlotte said. "See you in half an hour?"

"Perfect," Sherry said, and hung up, then took her leisurely time getting her things together and then ambling down the road to the restaurant. She was there early, so, in honor of the oddly rebellious mood she was in, she ordered a predinner martini. By the time Charlotte arrived, she was already starting to feel comfortably detached from her surroundings.

"You won't believe this," Charlotte said, before she was even fully seated. "My witch friend I told you about? The one

who was supposed to come up to help out? She got into an accident basically the second she pulled out of the rental lot.
Now she's in the hospital in Yonkers. That's two out of two for
people trying to visit me up here and having some sort of horrible accident happen."

"So we can't get out, and they still can't get in," Sherry said,
the alcohol making it feel more interesting than terrifying.
She briefly explained to Charlotte about how an enormous
tree had abruptly ended her attempt to drive to Schenectady
the day before, though she left out the bit with the ghosts.
Then she said, with a bit of dramatic flair, "And after all that,
guess who came to visit me at the library today?"

"The angel Gabriel?"

"Alan's *wife!*" Sherry said, triumphantly. "Not his *ex*, his
wife!"

"His *what?*" Charlotte said, with a gratifying display of
shock and horror.

Sherry backed up then and told her everything that had
happened since they'd last met, which carried them through
another order of drinks and a round of shared appetizers.
Charlotte, as usual, was an excellent audience for a long and
extremely bizarre story. By the time Sherry'd gotten her up to
date through the Thompson infestation at the library, Charlotte was shaking her head. "First of all," she said, "how bad is
it that I'm feeling kind of relieved that Alan was an asshole,
too? Like, I was feeling like a dumbass for picking John, but I
guess some guys will just cheat until they die, no matter
what."

Sherry winced, then took another bite of arancini. "I think
that's the sort of thing that everyone thinks but you're not
supposed to say out loud," she said. "Like how right now I'm

feeling better about having trusted Alan because you reminded me of how bad *John* was."

Charlotte gave a restrained little cackle of a laugh. "Cheers to schadenfreude," she said. "The only thing getting us through this mess."

"Cheers," Sherry said, and clinked glasses with her. When she shifted in her chair she felt her pocket crinkle. "Oh! Would you like to look at that article I told you about?"

"About the guy who got out of prison? Sure," Charlotte said.

Sherry handed the now slightly crumpled article across the table. Charlotte looked at it for a moment, then frowned. "Does he look familiar to you?"

Sherry frowned, too, and leaned in closer. "Who? Orellana?"

"Yeah," Charlotte said, and brought the picture up closer to her face. "I swear I know him." Then her eyes went wide. "Oh my God. Isn't that *Jason*?"

SEVENTEEN

Sherry felt her own eyes widen. "Jason *Martinez*? *Our* Jason? From the diner? Are you sure? I don't think that they look that much alike, do you? Could it be just that they're both . . ."

"I can tell two Hispanic guys apart, Sherry," Charlotte said. "Once I dated a Guatemalan DJ with four brothers who all got their hair cut at the same place; that could have gotten *crazy*. And yeah, I think it's him. The picture's blurry, but look at his ear." She stabbed at the photo with a fingertip. "Ears never change. I notice ears. They're hard to draw. Jason's have this funny fold thing at the top. It's him."

"Jason," Sherry repeated, truly gobsmacked. "It can't be him, though. He's such a sweet young man."

"He's got to be in his forties," Charlotte said. She was still squinting at the picture. "And, anyway, the conviction was overturned."

"I didn't mean that," Sherry said. "I meant—can you imagine Jason whacking Alan over the head with a lamp?"

Charlotte put the article down. "No," she admitted. "But I can't really imagine anyone I know doing it. It seems like such a dramatic way to kill someone."

"How would *you* kill someone?" Sherry asked, curious.

"I don't know. I've thought about it. On TV, pushing people down the stairs works really well to avoid suspicion, but on TV, everyone seems to fall down a few steps and then die instantly. In real life I think they're more likely to just sprain their wrist or something, unless they're about ninety years old. You'd probably have to push them down the stairs once a day for a month until you got lucky and they banged their head at the right angle, and that would *definitely* look suspicious. Or I thought about hiring a hit man, but then you have to rely on the guy you hire not being either completely incompetent or an undercover FBI agent. Really, I think the best way to kill someone and get away with it is to buy an unlicensed gun from a criminal, wear gloves while you shoot a stranger in the middle of the night, and then throw the gun into the Hudson. It would have to be a stranger because as soon as you have a decent motive, you're a suspect. But I wouldn't have any reason to *want* to kill a stranger, so now there's no point to killing someone in the first place. You might as well skip the whole thing."

"You *have* thought about this," Sherry said, impressed. "And you're right. It's the motive that always catches people out. That's why serial killers who get away with it aren't particularly impressive. Killing poor ladies of the evening who you've never met before and no one cares about isn't much of a trick, when there's nothing to connect the two of you and no one's hounding the police to solve the case, anyway. A woman who tells everyone about how much she hates her middle-class husband, kills him, clears out the bank accounts, and gets away free and clear, *that's* smart." An image of Caroline flitted through her head. Caroline, crying over her husband's cruelty, shedding what looked like real tears. Sherry blinked the thought away. "The diner's still open," she said abruptly. "Should we go talk to him?"

Charlotte looked skeptical. "Talk to *Jason*? Like an interrogation? Would that be safe?"

"We're not going to cuff him to a table and shine a light in his eyes," Sherry said. "Just talk to him. He won't murder us in the diner."

"He *might*," Charlotte said, and then threw back the rest of her third glass of wine. "All right. Let's do it."

They had a brief battle over the check—Sherry won—and then marched off toward the diner in the cold, both giggling a little from the combination of wine and nerves. "If he's not there, we should get pie," Charlotte said. "They have great pie."

"We should get pie either way," Sherry said firmly. "Or cake. To avoid suspicion."

"Is cake less suspicious than pie?"

"No," Sherry said, after she'd suppressed her latest fit of giggles. "I meant we should order something either way, so we don't look suspicious just skulking around the diner and not eating anything."

"Obviously," Charlotte said. "Ooh, maybe I'll get pie *and* French fries."

"As long as you stay *focused*," Sherry said severely. Charlotte seemed to be enjoying herself *slightly* too much to take helping with Sherry's investigations seriously. Then they arrived at the diner and swept inside like an entire post-prom limousine's worth of excited giggling. It was only once they were settled into a corner booth—it was a good position for keeping an eye on everything going on in the rest of the diner, though Charlotte complained about having to face the wrong direction—that it occurred to Sherry that she was, perhaps, slightly too tipsy to be engaging in sensitive conversations with a murder suspect. It was too late now, though: they were here, and Sherry was exactly tipsy enough to feel as if they would therefore be forced to complete the mission. She ordered a coffee and a slice of coconut cake. Charlotte ordered a plate of French fries and a chocolate milkshake, the idea of pie having apparently been mutually abandoned. Then they tucked in and waited.

They didn't have to wait for a particularly long time. The diner patrons of Winesap preferred to eat early. Sherry was only about halfway through her coconut cake when Jason emerged from the kitchen, wiping his hands on his apron and leaning over to say something to one of the waitresses to make her laugh. Sherry gave him a small wave, and he noticed and smiled at her. She gestured for him to come over.

"Are you waving at him?" Charlotte hissed. "What's going on? Is he coming over?"

"He's walking over," Sherry whispered back. "Just act normal!"

"I can't!" Charlotte said, then lapsed into silence as Jason appeared next to their booth.

"Evening, ladies," he said. "Is everything okay?"

"Everything's perfect," Sherry told him. "We were just wondering if you might have time to talk."

He raised his eyebrows. "To talk? Hold on, let me check." He headed back to the counter, consulted briefly with the waitress, then returned. "Yeah, I can take a minute. What's going on, Miss Sherry?"

"I've been looking into Alan's death," Sherry said, "and digging into his past a little. To try to figure out why someone might want to hurt him." She paused, watching his expression. He looked calm. Not upset. Not confused by where this was going, either. "You knew him before you moved to Winesap, didn't you? He was your defense attorney."

Jason nodded. "Yeah. I guess you know the whole story, huh?"

"I do," she said. She was still paying close attention to his expression. "If I were you, I would have hated him."

He laughed. There was no hesitation when he responded, as if he'd anticipated the question and thought through his answer many times before. "Yeah. I hated him the whole time I was in prison, and I hated him for years after I got out, too. He really screwed me over. But it's been thirty years now. I got a wife and two great kids and a good job. It freaked me out a little the first time I recognized him in here, but I just stayed back in the kitchen and out of his way. I spent five years locked up for looking like some other dude; I'm not about to go back to prison for popping off at a customer in the Winesap Diner. No way would that be worth it."

"You have to realize that it seems like an awfully strange coincidence that you happened to move here not long after Alan did," Sherry said. "How exactly did that happen?"

"I just saw a want ad posted up outside a grocery store in Schenectady while I was visiting my folks," Jason said. "They're getting older now, and LA's too expensive to raise a family. I had my girls in this little apartment we couldn't afford. I came up here to check it out and I thought, man, Tiff and the girls would *love* it here. Tiff likes that *Gilmore Girls* show, you know? That's what it's like up here. So we moved. I knew I was probably going to run into someone who was involved in my case back then eventually. I just figured it'd be in a bar in Albany or something, like maybe the judge was going to be a senator or something now."

"And you really weren't feeling angry with Alan anymore?" Sherry pressed. "Maybe you were surprised to find him here. But once you did see him here, you really never had a moment of thinking about getting back at him? It's not a small thing, someone messing up at their job so badly that you end up in prison for years. You'd have the right to be angry."

He raised his hands slightly. "I don't know what to tell you. It was a long time ago, and the older I got, the more I started feeling kind of bad for the guy, like, damn, he kind of messed *his* life up, too. You know he wrote me a letter after I got released? I threw it away without reading it, but when I moved here I found out he'd quit being a defense attorney and moved to the city after he fu—sorry, ma'am—messed up my case. I figure he was probably writing to apologize, right? I mean, if he knew he messed up so bad he straight up just quit his whole job and moved away to where no one knew him."

He seemed to Sherry to be genuinely asking, as if he truly was hopeful that Alan had felt remorse for his colossal mistake. "I think he really did feel ashamed of it," she said. "He never even mentioned to me that he'd been a defense attorney once. I think he probably didn't want anyone to know." Whether that was from a true sense of remorse for his failures or the baser desire to protect his good reputation was harder to say.

"Yeah, I thought so," he said, nodding. "And like I said, even if I didn't think he already felt bad about it, I have it really good now. I mean, my life is great. No way would I mess it up just to get back at Alan Thompson. I've barely even thought about him for the past ten years."

"I believe you," Sherry said, looking him right in the eye as she said it. "But you know that the police are going to ask you where you were last Saturday night."

For the first time in the course of the conversation, Jason paused before he responded. "It was Tiff's birthday, and she asked me to take the night off so I could cook something special for her instead of the customers. I spent most of the afternoon at home cooking, then we had dinner after the kids were in bed and watched a movie I rented. I was home with her all night."

"I'm sure she'll confirm that for you," Sherry said, keeping her voice conversational. "Thanks for your time, Jason. And oh, one more thing. Do you know of anyone else who might have had reason to be angry with Alan?"

He shook his head. "Like I said. It's been twenty years since I've cared enough about the guy to keep track of what he was doing." Then he gave her a quick nod clearly meant to end the conversation, and headed back toward the kitchen.

As soon as he was out of sight, Sherry looked back toward Charlotte, who had sucked down half her milkshake as she watched the conversation like a tennis match. "So what do you think?"

"I don't know," Charlotte said. "He sounded like he might have meant it about not caring about Alan, but the guy would have to be a saint to not still be mad, wouldn't he? And that alibi was garbage. What kind of wife asks to stay home for her birthday on a Saturday night?"

"A frugal wife, maybe," Sherry said. "Or a wife who's

exhausted from her full-time job and two small children and would rather just stay in. Or a wife who's helping her husband with an alibi."

"So you think he did it," Charlotte said.

"I didn't say that," Sherry said. "But no matter what he said about how he feels now, his motive is stronger than his alibi. And—I don't know. He sounded convincing. But he also sounded as if he was prepared for the questions."

"I probably would be, too," Charlotte said. "If a guy who'd screwed me over that badly suddenly showed up dead, I'd be practicing my lines in the mirror."

"You're right," Sherry said, after a moment of reflection. "He's not stupid, is he? It would be the smart thing to do to practice a bit." She chewed on the inside of her cheek for a moment. "All the same. A strong motive and a weak alibi."

"A really awful alibi," Charlotte agreed. "Kind of embarrassing." She ate a few more French fries. "What are you going to do?"

"Let the police know, I suppose," Sherry said. "Let them follow up. They'll be able to do things like check—" She paused, and blinked. There was something that the police should be able to check, something that might be able to confirm whether or not Jason really had spent all night at home, but she couldn't remember what it was. She huffed out a frustrated breath. "I forgot what I was just about to say. Anyway, I think that with a lead this strong I really should hand it over to them."

"Hm," Charlotte said, after a pause.

Sherry frowned. "What?"

"Nothing," Charlotte said. "I was just thinking about how it doesn't feel right."

"What doesn't?"

"Jason being the killer," Charlotte said. "It just feels wrong. Narratively, I guess."

"*Narratively,*" Sherry repeated.

"Yeah. I mean, think about it. This demon's been freaking out for ages about how you have to investigate, you need to investigate. So you poke around a little, and the librarian in Schenectady sends you that article, and I recognize Jason in the picture. Then we come over here, and he's pretty polite over the whole thing, and you decide you want to tell the cops and let them sort it out. It just feels kind of . . ."

"Anticlimactic?" Sherry suggested. She was thinking about it, too, now.

"*Right.* I took a class on short story writing a while ago. There was this guy who wanted to write noir stories in the class. He got the vibe right, with the detectives and the dames and everything, but the plots all went like that. Like, the guy looks around for a while and then he finds who did it. No twist."

"But we're not in a book," Sherry said. "There's not always a twist in real life. Most murders are straightforward." Even as she said it she knew that she was kidding herself. Murders were never straightforward in Winesap.

It was as if Charlotte had read her mind. "Not in Winesap," she said. "And now we know that there's something supernatural involved. I don't know, I just think it doesn't feel right."

"You're right," Sherry said. "It doesn't work, narratively speaking. I wasn't particularly necessary. Why badger me into investigating when the whole thing could easily unravel on its own?" She paused. "Maybe the demon's like your classmate who wrote the bad noirs. Like a sort of—scriptwriter, for all of these deaths and investigations." She bit her cheek again.

"That would make sense, wouldn't it? If what it's after is the investigation itself, and not the person being caught at the end. But why?"

"I don't know," Charlotte said. "Maybe it's about the"—she waved her hand through the air—"energy. You know? Someone dying, and then all of this energy goes into catching whoever did it, or not getting caught."

Sherry blinked. It sounded oddly plausible. Plausible in a context in which they'd already established that they were suffering from an acute case of demon problems, at least. "That makes a lot of sense," she said. "As much as anything, at least. Too bad your witch friend can't come to test the theory. She does energy things, didn't you say that? With crystals? I don't think poor Father Barry would know how."

"Poor Father Barry," Charlotte said. "He always seems so stressed-out. So is the twin hot?"

Sherry squirmed slightly. "Todd? He looks like Father Barry," she said. "But more . . . fashionable."

"Oh, God, he *is* hot," Charlotte said. "Barry's so hot. They should have rules about that, for priests. They should have to have lazy eyes or something. If Barry was my priest I'd go to church just to sin in my heart the whole time."

"*Charlotte*," Sherry said reprovingly, even though she really wanted to laugh. "Don't say that around Father Barry, the poor thing would probably have a heart attack."

"I wonder if he's a virgin," Charlotte said, a little dreamily. "Too bad Todd's gay."

"*Charlotte!*" Sherry said, truly somewhat scandalized this time. Speculating about a priest's virginity! "That's his private business. And, anyway, I don't know if Todd is gay. I just thought he looked like he was being very flirtatious with

Corey. He could just be . . . friendly. Or diverse in his interests." Somehow, speculating on whether or not a priest's twin
brother might be bisexual felt inappropriate by proxy.

"Diverse in his interests," Charlotte repeated. "That sounds
like one of those old euphemisms. *He appreciates Grecian
marbles.*"

"I'm just trying to be respectful," Sherry said. Her cheeks
felt warm. "Why don't we talk about *you*. How have you been
feeling? Have you decided what you want to do with the
gallery?"

"Run it," Charlotte said promptly. "Which is going to be
hard if I can't leave town. I need to go down to the city and talk
to some of the people I know there. I've been thinking, I have
all of this extra space in the building, and there's that little
kitchen downstairs in the studio. I could set it up as an apartment and bring artists in to do residencies."

Sherry expressed interest—she really was interested—and
just let Charlotte talk for a while, prompting her with more
questions whenever the conversation lagged. It felt almost
possible to be optimistic about the state of Winesap and the
world at large when she was eating coconut cake and listening
to Charlotte being very enthusiastic and charming about her
plans for art exhibitions. By the time she'd finished the last
bits of her cake, the sleepiness from the drinks they'd had earlier had caught up to both of them. They paid and left, then
hugged at the door before they went their separate ways.

Sherry trudged back up the hill to home, the evening feeling even darker and quieter than it usually did, the silence
broken only by the sound of a motorcycle driving through the
village. The lights from the streetlamps and the few other
houses seemed muted, as if everyone on her street had

collectively decided to turn off the lights and go to bed early. It made her uneasy. Her home didn't feel any stranger, at least, and the cat's demands were of the usual cat variety. She dedicated five minutes to petting him, then brushed her teeth twice—she knew her breath would smell like alcohol in the morning—drank a big glass of water, and went to bed. She expected to wake up in the middle of the night with the start of a hangover. She didn't expect to be woken up at eight in the morning by the police knocking on her door.

EIGHTEEN

Sherry squinted blearily at Sheriff Brown, clutching at the front of her bathrobe to try to keep him from getting an eyeful of the stained, worn-out old pajamas she'd gone to bed in. It had given her a quick jolt of unease when she'd seen him on her front step, but he'd greeted her just like he usually would have, without any strange demands or horrible demon voices. He just looked very, very serious, which immediately kicked off a different kind of dread. "Peter? What are you doing here? What happened?" The thought hit her stomach like a gulp of ice water. "Has someone else been killed?"

He gave his head a hard, firm shake. "No. No, nothing like that. Don't worry. Everything's been quiet. Not even any kids breaking into garages." He paused. "I need you to come into the station with me, Sherry."

Her head gave an involuntary shake of its own. "What? Why?" Then, very stupidly: "But I'm still in my pajamas."

He gave a sympathetic wince. "I just need to talk to you about a few things relating to Alan's death. There's some stuff that we need to sort out."

She recoiled slightly. "Am I being arrested?"

He shook his head again. "No, no, of course not. We just need you to come in to answer a few questions."

"So you're bringing me in for questioning," she said. "Because I'm a suspect. Well, I knew that, I guess. I had myself on my own suspect list for being the last person to have seen him alive, just in case a demon possessed me and I did it without realizing it or something. Only I couldn't figure out how I possibly could have gotten down the hill and back up again and back into bed in time, especially once you factored in the time to change in and out of my pajamas—" She stopped. She was babbling. Sheriff Brown was frowning.

"Have you been drinking, Sherry?"

She flushed hot. "I had a few drinks with Charlotte last night. Can I—make some coffee, at least? And get changed?" And make sure that she had all her holy water and crystals and things hidden around her person before she went anywhere with him.

"Sure," the sheriff said. "I'll just wait in your living room, if you don't mind."

Sherry wanted to ask him what he'd do if she said that she did, in fact, mind. Crab-walk backward up her stairs while screaming in Aramaic, maybe. Just in case he might, she said, "I'll make coffee," and showed him inside. She went through the basics of her usual morning routine robotically, hyperconscious of the sheriff's presence in her private space. Even feeding her cat felt like too intimate a task to perform in front of him. She was grateful when the coffee was ready and she could politely pour him a cup, then escape upstairs for a few minutes of privacy to drink it while she pulled some clean clothes on and ran a comb through her hair, then shoved some anti-demon supplies into her pockets. She checked herself in the mirror. She looked tired and worried. Tired and worried and old and haggard. For the first time in what was probably months, she found herself digging through the drawer where she kept her makeup. She put on lipstick, then immediately wiped it off. She looked stupid with it on, like a child playing dress-up in her mother's high heels. At least her own frustration and embarrassment with herself had brought a little brightness to her eyes and color to her cheeks: she looked marginally less dead and resurrected.

Eventually she couldn't come up with any more excuses to delay the inevitable, so she dragged herself downstairs and meekly went with Sheriff Brown to ride to the station. He let her sit up front, at least, which was nice of him. At the station, he put her into a room she hadn't been in before. Once she'd accompanied the frantic daughter of a victim into a different room in the station, because the girl hadn't wanted to talk without her there. That room had been fairly pleasant and comfortable, like the waiting room in a doctor's office. This one was gray and spartan, just three chairs and a table that was bolted to the floor. A real interrogation room for a real suspect.

"Sherry," Sheriff Brown said, "I'd like you to go over everything that you did last Saturday evening after you got off work."

Sherry did, with as much detail as she could muster. Alan picking her up, deciding against their previous plans, going to pick up Chinese food, his house for dinner and a movie, the drive home and bringing Alice her leftovers. Then going to bed, and being woken up by Alice, and the whole saga of having to go to her house to help her with the fuse box. The wave of relief that passed over her as she talked through that last part took her off guard. "That's my alibi," she said aloud. "I'd realized that it was Alice's alibi, but I didn't think about myself. She can confirm that she saw me twice, once at about ten thirty and then again at midnight. I couldn't have walked down to Alan's house, killed him, and then gotten back up to bed in my house in time."

Sheriff Brown's face was expressionless. "You were the last to see him alive. You could have killed him, left his house, walked up, then gone to bed."

"But that would mean that he was killed at nine," Sherry said, before immediately realizing her mistake.

Sheriff Brown's eyes narrowed. "What makes you think that he wasn't?"

"Nothing," Sherry said quickly. She didn't want to get the medical examiner in trouble after he'd been willing to speak with her. "I just heard a rumor. That he was killed closer to midnight."

He didn't respond to that. Instead, he said, "When did you find out that Mr. Thompson was leaving you his house?"

Sherry's whole brain stuttered. "What?"

"He left you his house in his will," Sheriff Brown said. "Including everything inside it, plus two hundred thousand dollars to cover taxes and maintenance. Almost a million dollars' worth of cash and property in total. He owned a lot of valuable antiques."

"*What?*" Sherry said again. She couldn't process it. Alan's *house.* He had a beautiful house. He also had two beautiful sons, and beautiful grandchildren. "But—why not his sons?"

"A million in cash each," Sheriff Brown said. "Your boyfriend was a very rich guy. Plenty of reasons for someone to want him dead."

"I didn't know," Sherry said. She could feel her heart in her chest. "I had no idea. We never talked about money. We talked about books we'd been reading."

"You're not doing well financially, are you?" the sheriff asked. "They don't pay you much at the library. Your rent on that little house is pretty high. Doesn't seem like you have much put away for retirement."

"So you think I gambled on my boyfriend having left me something in his will and *killed* him?" Sherry said. Her voice sounded too high-pitched. "If I'd wanted to live in his house, why wouldn't I have just tried to *marry* him?" Her voice broke at the end of the sentence, and, to her horror, she started to cry.

Sheriff Brown leaned across the table just enough to hand her a tissue that he'd pulled out of his pocket. She took it, then just held it in her hand, nervously rolling one corner between two fingertips. He still looked calm. Not like a cartoon mouse at all right now. It seemed strange that she'd ever thought there was anything funny or cartoonish about him. "You wanted to marry him?"

She shrugged and swiped at her eyes. "I didn't think that I did. I don't know."

"There's nothing wrong with wanting to get married," the sheriff said. "Nothing strange about being angry when you find out that the guy you want to marry already has a wife."

It gave her a jolt. She snapped her head up to look at him. She'd never felt slow around Sheriff Brown before. Now she felt as if she'd wandered right into a trap. "I didn't know that he was married until after he died," she said. "You can ask anyone. I didn't know. I only found out when I talked to his friend Greg the other day and he accidentally told me. Alan always told me that he was divorced, and I believed him. Why on earth would I ever think he was still married? It wasn't a situation where we met at hotels. He told me where he kept his spare key so I could go into his house and water his plants while he was away. Where would he have *kept* a wife? It never occurred to me for a second, before Greg told me." Was she saying too much? Overexplaining? There was a camera in the room, she assumed. She had to force herself to keep her head still and not let her eyes dart around to look for it. Would this be the part of the video where the prosecutor paused the tape and asked the jury whether *they* believed her?

Sheriff Brown's expression remained impassive. "You're a smart lady," he said. "I honestly just find it hard to believe that you can solve murders left and right but couldn't figure out that this guy wasn't being honest with you." He paused. "Why'd you break into his house after he died, Sherry?"

Another jolt. "How did you know?"

"One of the neighbors was pretty spooked by Mr. Thompson's murder. He went out and bought three security cameras the next day and had them up and running by that evening. He saw you going in and out when he was reviewing the tapes and gave us a call. Why'd you do it, Sherry? What were you looking for?"

"*Evidence*, obviously," Sherry snapped. "I was *investigating*. Like I always do."

"You don't always break into victims' houses, though," Sheriff Brown said.

"You keep saying *breaking in* like I smashed in the window with a brick," she said. "I had access to the house whenever I wanted it. I just went and got the key." She paused then, and blinked. "And—if he left me the house, how could I break into my own property?"

She immediately knew that it was the wrong thing to say when his eyebrows lifted. "I wouldn't get too ahead of myself, if I were you," he said. "His estate's going to be in probate for a while longer, since there was a lot of it."

"I'm not getting ahead of myself," she said. "I have my own house to live in, I'm not desperate to have to take over a whole new one. I'm just—I know what you're *getting* at."

"I'm not getting at anything," he said blandly. She abruptly felt very aware of how horribly *irritating* all the suspects she'd spoken to over the years must have found her. "Walk me through what you did once you were inside of the house."

She told him, though a bit tersely. There wasn't too much to tell: she looked around, she got an idea of the scene of the crime, checked the rest of the house, then left. She didn't mention how the photo had screamed. It didn't seem like a useful thing to mention. "I didn't disturb anything or take anything out of the house," she said. "And it isn't as if my DNA and fingerprints wouldn't have been all over the place either way. You *asked* me to investigate." Then she remembered that there was something she needed to ask him. "Speaking of things being taken from the house. Were the account books from Alan's shop taken as evidence?"

He was, at this point, starting to look slightly irritated. There was something almost comforting about that. There was something frightening about a man who stayed perpetually and perfectly calm. "I'm just asking questions so we can try to figure out what happened to Mr. Thompson. You know how this works, Sherry. I'm not the enemy here." He paused. "And no. We didn't find anything like account books at the scene."

"Yes, I do know how this works," she said, and found herself standing before she could think better of it. She felt reenergized by the knowledge that she'd been right to think that those missing documents might be significant. If the police hadn't moved them, then the only other people who might have done it were Alan himself, just before he died, or the murderer. "So I know that I'm free to go unless I'm under arrest. Am I under arrest, Sheriff?"

"No," he said, after a moment. "Though you could be, for the breaking and entering."

"Is that a threat?" she asked. "Never mind. I'll be going, then. Let me know if you change your mind and decide that you want my help with investigating again." Then she added, with a flourish, "You might want to look into Jason Martinez at the diner."

"Because Mr. Thompson botched his defense?" Sheriff Brown asked. Sherry had to give him credit for how successfully he managed to seem only *slightly* smug. "We're very aware of his connection to Mr. Thompson. I've spoken to him and his wife already."

Sherry felt her whole face go hot. He sounded like a big-city police officer in a television press conference. When had Sheriff Brown learned how to talk like that? "Oh," she said. "Well—that's good. His alibi's weak."

"Thank you for letting me know," the sheriff said. It sounded sincere, if you didn't pay any attention to what seemed like the suggestion of a smirk lurking around the corner of his mouth. Then he said, "Just one more thing."

Like Columbo, she thought wildly. Somehow whoever was running the TV detective series she was trapped in had rewritten the character of Sheriff Brown. Before, he'd been the blundering local police sergeant who couldn't keep up with

Poirot's deductions, and now he was Columbo. He had his suspect, and now he was circling around her, cornering her, fixing it so that she couldn't wriggle out of the trap. She sat, just the way that Columbo's suspects always stayed to answer more questions no matter how much they complained about him. Was she being compelled to do it? She couldn't tell. Maybe she just wanted to find out how the episode would end. "What is it?"

"I wanted to ask you about Howard Hastings," he said. "You were questioned in relation to his disappearance six years ago. What can you tell me about that?"

For a moment Sherry's mind felt utterly blank. Howard. Caroline's husband. She'd left Florida and come all the way to little Winesap to get away from the memory of him and Caroline. They'd followed her here, anyway. She licked her lips. "If you've been talking to—" Her voice came out in a dry rasp. She stopped. Cleared her throat. "If you've been talking to the Tampa police, you already know everything. I told them everything that I knew."

"I'm sure that you did," he said. Implacably. He felt implacable, like there was no way for her to escape from this conversation, even though the unlocked door was just a few steps away. "But they talked to you years ago, and the detective I spoke to wasn't the lead on the case. I'd like to hear it from you now."

She swallowed. "Caroline had been telling me for months that her husband was abusive," she said. "At first it was just him wanting to tell her when she could see her friends and family, but then it got worse. He changed the PIN for her bank card so she had to ask him for money. He would turn off the water in the house just so he could control when she took a shower. It was horrible. She cried like a little girl when she first started telling me about it."

"And you believed her?"

"Of course I did," Sherry snapped. "Do you know how many women I've known over the years whose husbands have treated them like dirt? My own mother—" She stopped. Her own sad childhood wasn't any of his damn business. "And he was an awful guy. Really nasty and pompous, the kind of guy who'd be really rude to a waitress and then leave a nickel as a tip. Always talking down to her in front of other people. And *cheap*, too. She got married to him too young, and he was fifteen years older, so he managed to impress her with roses and teddy bears before she was old enough to know better, then never bought her another present. I still don't think that she was lying about *everything*."

"Cheap enough to have saved up a million in cash by the time he vanished," Sheriff Brown said, in an irritatingly *knowing* sort of way. "So, you believed that she was being abused. What did you do then?"

"Like I told the detectives in Tampa," Sherry said, "I really didn't do much. I was a listening ear. I told her that I thought she should leave him. Then, when she showed up at my house with her bags one night, I drove her to the airport. That's all. It never occurred to me that I was doing anything other than helping a friend." When she said it aloud, it all really did sound very ordinary and reasonable. Like what any good friend would do. The problem was that it was hard to maintain a secure sense of one's own innocence while being interviewed by the police, for the second time, about a possible homicide.

"So when you drove her to the airport, you weren't aware that her husband was missing?"

"No. Why would I be? He wasn't reported missing until days later, and she told me that she'd snuck out of the house while he was out at a bar."

"Right," the sheriff said. "So you drove her to the airport, and then a few days later you heard that he was missing. Did you call the police right away?"

"No," Sherry admitted. "I tried to contact Caroline first. I waited until I knew for sure that she wasn't going to get back to me before I called the police and let them know what I knew. They were already planning on talking to me by then. They knew that Caroline and I were best friends."

He leaned forward slightly. "Why wait and try to contact her first?"

"I don't know," she said. "I'd never had anything like it happen to me before. I felt like maybe I was being dramatic. Or maybe he'd gone after her and hurt her. I didn't know what to think. I was worried about her. And I thought that the police wouldn't care about what I had to say, anyway. I didn't *know* anything. I just drove the car."

"And then a few weeks after the police spoke to you, you filed for divorce and left the state. Why?"

Her cheeks warmed again. "I wasn't trying to—" she started, and then stopped. "I'd been thinking about a divorce for years. With my best friend gone in awful circumstances, there wasn't much else keeping me there."

He nodded slowly. "It's a strange coincidence, though, isn't it?"

"What is?"

"Your best friend's millionaire husband vanishes, and a day after he's last seen, she clears out all of their joint bank accounts and flees to Mexico with your help. A few years later, your millionaire boyfriend turns up dead, and you end up inheriting a million dollars in assets. You have to admit that it's a weird kind of thing to be involved in *twice*."

"So you think I'm some kind of black widow?" she asked, her temper flaring. "And an incompetent one, apparently. If I'd planned on helping my friend bump off her millionaire husband, you'd think I would have gotten something out of it so I could retire to Acapulco instead of working full-time at the Winesap Library." She stood up. "I really am done with this now. I assume that you'll let me know if you decide that you're going to actually arrest me, instead of just waste my time asking a bunch of leading questions about something that a friend of mine did a decade ago."

He nodded, completely unruffled. Then he said, in a voice that wasn't his, in a voice that was older and colder and darker than the water at the very bottom of a deep lake, "You've been dawdling with this investigation, Miss Pinkwhistle. I don't think that you're free to go after all."

NINETEEN

Sitting alone in one of the jail cells in the back of the sheriff's office gave Sherry plenty of time to think about all the truly terrible decisions that had led her to this point. There were lots of them. In reverse chronological order, off the top of her head: Not demanding a lawyer while she'd had the chance. Agreeing to investigate Alan's murder instead of taking her shot to get out of Winesap. Getting involved with Alan at all. Adopting a murder victim's fat orange cat named Garfield and renaming him Lord Thomas Cromwell purely because she'd thought it was a funny thing to call a cat, thus dooming her to be haunted by who it turned out was one of history's most obnoxious personalities. Investigating her first murder case, when she could just as easily have minded her own business.

Sherry hadn't been completely honest about Caroline.

She hadn't lied, either. Not exactly. Everything she'd told him was true. She'd just left things out.

Unflattering things, mostly.

Sherry had been twelve years old when she met Caroline. Caroline had been ten but seemed much older: even that young she'd had a preternatural confidence to her that made her seem vastly more attractive and sophisticated than could come across in pictures. Sherry had learned that over and over, through the almost half century of their friendship. She'd bring out a photo of them together to show off her best friend, and whoever she was speaking to would say, "She doesn't look anything like what I imagined when you described her." She was tall and sturdily built, with hazel eyes and an enormous amount of thick dark hair that she liked to wear loose down her back, even after it started going gray. When Sherry described her, she always came out sounding like some sort of beautiful sorceress. In reality, she was just an aging hippie who worked as a receptionist and told wonderful stories that sometimes, in the end, turned out to be lies.

There were a few things that Sherry had not exactly lied about. The first was how confident Sherry had been that Caroline's husband was really, truly abusing her in the way that she said that he was. She had understated things a bit, with the sheriff. Some of Caroline's claims had been . . . dramatic. At one point she'd made a wild accusation about Howard plotting to kill her for the life insurance money. Normally Sherry had to be away from Caroline for a decent amount of time before the mists cleared and she was capable of noticing which bits of her stories didn't actually make much sense, but that had sounded odd immediately. Howard was a retired dentist who had made excellent money and never spent any of it. Caroline was his younger, healthier wife who made a fairly meagre salary working part-time at a local chiropractor's office. It had occurred to Sherry even in the moment that the financial incentives for murder there all very clearly ran in the opposite direction.

She'd never thought that Caroline *would* murder her

husband, of course. It hadn't even crossed her mind as a possibility. Murder hadn't been a constant in her life back then. And she had believed that awful old Howard was making his wife's life a misery, so it hadn't exactly been a shock when Caroline had shown up on her doorstep one rainy night with suitcases in tow and asked Sherry if she could drive her to the airport. She'd dragged herself across town on foot, she said, because she wanted to be well away from Howard before he noticed her gone, which meant that her car would have to stay in the driveway. It had all seemed reasonable enough. Even if it hadn't, Sherry would have done what she asked, and not because of any particular nobility on her part. It was because it was *exciting*. It was exciting to feel like she was helping to rescue an innocent woman from her brutish husband on a dark and stormy night, and not very many exciting things had ever happened to Sherry.

The first thing that had given her pause was the suitcases. They'd been very, very heavy. Much heavier than what you would expect for suitcases packed by a Floridian who was flying to Mexico. Even Mexico itself hadn't raised any particular alarms to Sherry—Caroline had been on vacation there once years earlier and hadn't stopped talking about how much she'd loved it ever since—but the suitcases had bothered her. Days later, when the police turned up at her door, she'd had an awful, hysterical moment of thinking that maybe the suitcases had held Howard's chopped-up body. She'd come to her senses almost immediately, of course—why on earth would Caroline have taken his body to the airport with her?—but the image had stuck with her for a long time afterward, appearing abruptly when she was trying to fall asleep at night. She even dreamed about it. Those too-heavy suitcases in her car, something dark leaking from a seam. Later, she heard through the grapevine that the suitcases had been full of cash, that Caroline had spent years withdrawing money from Howard's accounts one small bit at a time, killed him, and gone on one last spree of withdrawals before she escaped to Mexico. This, in retrospect, sounded extremely convincing to Sherry. After all, she had direct evidence.

The second odd thing that she hadn't mentioned to the sheriff was the incident that should have let her know that there was something off about Caroline's story. They'd gotten into an accident on the way to the airport. It had been dark and rainy that night, rainy enough that Sherry hadn't seen the other car come rolling through a stop sign until it was too late. They hadn't been moving fast enough for it to be a serious crash, thank goodness, but the force of it was enough to knock the breath out of Sherry for a moment, to leave her rattled and too aware of the sound of her own ragged breathing. The rain was still pounding hard against the windshield.

They were on a quiet residential street, on a block where a bunch of houses had just been razed, so there was no one else there to see it. Sherry had wanted to do the usual things: to exchange information, to wait for the police to arrive. Caroline had immediately been against it. She'd become almost hysterical for a moment, wailing that she'd miss her flight, that she'd have to go back home to Howard, that she'd never be able to get away from him now. Sherry tried to plead her case with the other driver, to no avail. The other driver was apologetic but firm: she couldn't afford to fix her crumpled fender without insurance covering it.

Caroline had changed then. The tears had dried in what

seemed like half a second. She'd reached into her purse and pulled out a roll of cash. "How much?"

Sherry had wondered, briefly, if she'd hit her head in the crash. The other driver's eyes went wide. It was like a drug deal in a movie: the two cars pulled up close together so that they could speak to each other through the open windows, the rain pouring down, and Caroline—ordinary, middle-aged Caroline—peeling hundreds off a roll of bills. Five hundred, one thousand, two thousand, more. Much more than the woman would need to replace a fender for a beat-up old sedan. Eventually the other driver told Caroline to stop counting and took a wad of cash that Sherry was confident she could use to replace her car completely. Her eyes met Sherry's as she took it. They both knew, in that moment, that they were now complicit in something bigger than a fender bender on a rainy Wednesday night.

Neither of them said anything about it. The other driver took her money and drove away. Sherry drove, too. She was almost at the airport before she spoke. "I won't be able to afford the repair on my own, either."

Caroline didn't say a word. She just pulled out another wad of bills and silently tucked it into Sherry's purse. Sherry had left that money there for months after, part of her half hoping that she'd be mugged and the problem would turn into someone else's. She didn't give in and count the money until she got the job in Winesap and needed the cash to pay a deposit on the rent for her cottage. Ten thousand dollars. A stack of hundreds an inch thick. There was no aboveboard explanation for Caroline, a receptionist at a chiropractor's office, to be flying to Mexico with at least twenty thousand dollars' worth of cash in her purse. There was no aboveboard explanation for Sherry to have taken ten thousand dollars in cash under extremely suspicious circumstances, not asked a single question about it, and refrained from mentioning it to the police when the money was still in her bag hanging by the door when they came to speak with her.

It had stuck with her, that money. That whole night stuck with her. She'd never liked driving since. Every time she got into a car, she was brought back to that night: the sickening crunch of the impact, the rain hammering against the roof like heavy fists against a door, that moment of understanding that had passed between her and the other driver, the money sliding into her purse and mingled guilt and pleasure sliding down her throat. Her daily walk up the hill to her cottage in Winesap felt like a sort of penance. The remaining six thousand dollars in cash that could have gone to a used car stayed locked up in a suitcase under her bed.

She was lying down on her cot in the cell now, and drifting in and out of a doze. It was better when she was asleep, because when she was awake, she couldn't stop thinking about Caroline. She'd managed to keep most of what had happened with Caroline in the back of her mind for a long time now. It was easy, when she avoided the things that reminded her of the whole awful incident the most. Driving, or the smell of Shalimar, or the pounding rain. All easy enough to avoid, here in Winesap. It was a little strange, maybe, that she'd never been bothered by being around murder investigations.

"It's because the investigations give you a purpose," said voices in the cell.

Sherry's head jerked up. There was no one else in the small, bare room. "Who is that?" she asked. "Who's there?" She immediately felt like a cliché. Some sort of horrible evil demon creature, of course. At this point in the movie she should know better than to go looking for the comforting, logical explanation.

There were three flies buzzing around the cell. Which was strange, considering the season. They buzzed closer, looping lazily around each other in the air. "You like to feel as if you matter, don't you, Sherry?" Their voices buzzed, too, a horrible whining Greek chorus.

"Oh, stop," Sherry said, and lay down on the hard little cot, curling up on herself to face the wall. "Leave me alone. I can't investigate while I'm stuck in here. Why did you have the sheriff throw me into a cell if that's what you wanted me to do?"

"Because we wanted to talk to you, Sherry," the voices said. "To encourage you to focus your mind on the issue at hand. You've been trying to do things your way again. You've been thinking about running away. But your way isn't any good, is it, Sherry? You wasted all of your youth, your way. *Your* way made you into someone who never did a single thing that mattered, until *your* way let you take money to help a killer escape from justice. You've done so much better since you've played by our rules, haven't you, Sherry?"

Sherry swallowed hard. That was what she hadn't wanted to think about this whole time. It was true, was the problem. She'd been doing much better since she came to Winesap. In every way, really. Before she'd come to Winesap, she'd felt irrelevant, inconsequential. Nearly invisible. The feeling had been there since she was very young. She could still remember a few early instances. Her father reading his paper and not looking up when she tried to show him a drawing she'd made. A teacher ignoring her raised hand, even after she'd practically squirmed out of her seat with excitement over knowing the answer. A classmate reapplying her lipstick and remarking, with casual authority, about how annoying it was for *us girls* to always have boys bothering us for dates. Boys very rarely bothered Sherry: boys didn't notice her at all. She'd married the first one who did notice her right after high school, and then regretted it almost immediately. His noticing her, it seemed, only lasted as long as it took for him to install her in the little house at 184 Coconut Grove so that he would have someone to iron his shirts for him.

She'd gotten herself out of that house after what happened with Caroline. As awful as what she suspected Caroline had done was, something about the sheer, swaggering finality of her exit had spurred Sherry on to make an exit of her own. She served her husband with divorce papers and sold everything she owned in her own name, then used the proceeds to buy a bus ticket and a few nights at a cheap hotel. Eventually, she'd made her way to Winesap, where, after a few weeks of rural village peace and quiet, she'd stumbled into her first murder scene. Everything had come to her after that. She'd met Janine when one of two rival orchid fanciers from her gardening club killed the other with a pair of pruning shears. She'd met Alan when she solved the case of the mysterious body found in the alley next to his shop. Everything here had been born out of death, all her triumphs and successes, all the respect and friendships she had earned. It had all come out of evil, and she'd taken it as her due, as the universe finally shifting in her favor. She'd thought of herself as the protagonist. She hadn't thought of what it all had meant to everyone who'd been hurt so that she could take her starring turn.

"You know that it's true," buzzed a fly, very close to the shell of her ear.

She slapped at the side of her head. The fly hummed lazily out of reach. "Leave me *alone*," she said. "I don't understand what you *want*."

"For you to play your part," said the flies, buzzing in chorus again now. "Winesap has been nothing but good to you, Sherry. All we ask is that you take that into consideration. We would hate for Winesap to need a new detective to save it from itself."

"But Winesap shouldn't need saving," Sherry said, despite her better judgment. "There's no reason at all for so many people to be killed here. *That's* the problem, not who solves the murder cases after the poor people are already dead."

The buzzing of the flies changed then. A louder, thicker, meaner sound. Sherry could see more movement from the corners of her eyes. A dark cloud. "That isn't your role, Sherry," said the cloud. "That isn't the job you're here to do. Do you not find yourself arrogant, Sherry, to think that you ought to change the course of things? It's your job to be the detective, Sherry. *Shut up and investigate.*"

The buzzing was getting louder. There were more and more flies. Sherry couldn't see or hear. She felt as if there were insects in her ears, in her nose, climbing over her eyelids. She opened her mouth to scream and flies poured down her throat. Then, in the distance, she heard a man's voice.

"Excuse me," Father Barry said, and then cleared his throat. "Um. In the name of—Christ. I . . . abjure you!"

The buzzing eased for a moment, and Sherry hacked a few times and spit out a fly. It had only been one, maybe, which had felt like a whole lot of them. The flies, when they spoke, sounded affronted. "You *abjure* us? In the name of *Christ*?"

"Yes," Father Barry said, a bit more firmly this time. Then he said, "Take that!" and some water splashed against Sherry's face.

"Why are you splashing water around?" the flies asked. They sounded genuinely baffled this time.

"It's *holy water*," Barry said. "You—are you the same demon as last time? Because if you are, you might remember that Sherry is a *Catholic*."

"I am!" Sherry said immediately, opening her eyes to a squint. The cloud of flies had reduced enough for her to be able to see a group of people standing outside the cell, though she couldn't see many details. "I'm devout! I believe very strongly in the power of holy water to discourage demons!" She wasn't sure how convincing she sounded. *Very,* she hoped.

"Oh," said the cloud of flies disconsolately.

"And I'm a pagan," said a woman. Charlotte. Charlotte had come, too. "And I've brought, uh. Some extremely powerful crystals and things, that I believe in *a lot*."

A cloud of flies couldn't sigh, so it definitely didn't do that. It made a sort of loud, collective buzz. Then it faded away from moment to moment, vanishing like fog on a mirror, until suddenly it was just Sherry alone in her cell again in what felt like ringing silence, blinking owlishly at the small crowd of people standing just outside the bars.

"*Barry,*" said Todd. She could tell that he was Todd because he was the one of the two of them who wasn't wearing a priest's collar and also didn't look extremely embarrassed. "That was *badass.* You abjured the demons, bud!"

"I *tried*, at least," said the bashful Father Barry. "I think that Sherry was better at it."

"Aw, shut up, you *killed* it," Todd said. He had his arm wrapped around his brother's shoulders and looked absolutely delighted. Charlotte, who was looking at him, *also* looked delighted. Sherry couldn't really blame her. Todd was wearing a blue scarf that made his eyes look very bright.

"Sherry," Father Barry said, "this is my brother. Todd."

"We've met," Sherry said. "It's nice to see you again, Todd."

"Same," Todd said. "So what did you do to get arrested?"

"I was brought in for questioning about Alan's murder," Sherry said. "I thought that the sheriff was going to let me go, but then things went strange again. With, you know. The . . . demon things. The sheriff talking with a different voice." She winced, conscious of how ridiculous it sounded when she said it aloud, even though all of them had just witnessed something strange happening in the room. "How did you know to come look for me here?"

"Process of elimination," Charlotte said. "I called you a few times this morning to see if you'd talked to the sheriff yet. When you didn't pick up, I called the library, then I called here when no one there knew where you were, either. When they said that you were being held, I called Father Barry for reinforcements, just in case we had to fight our way out or something. I figured you wouldn't want me to call Janine. I feel like she'd be really judgmental about this."

"Todd was having lunch with me when she called," Father Barry said, in a vaguely apologetic tone of voice. "He wanted to come along."

"For moral support," said Todd. "So are we breaking her out of here? Did anyone bring a hacksaw?"

"Thank you," Sherry said to Charlotte. "I don't think that Janine would like this very much, no. And I don't think that a hacksaw should be necessary. Maybe one of you could go and ask Sheriff Brown if he could let me out? The possession might have worn off by now."

"This town is *crazy*," said Todd, with what sounded like extreme satisfaction.

TWENTY

I'll go look for the sheriff," said Todd's more helpful brother. The instant Father Barry was out of sight, Charlotte and Todd started making eyes at each other. Sherry watched, fascinated. She'd always found it remarkable to see how attractive people seemed to have a sort of secret password that let them pass directly through the parts of socializing that involved trying to convince people that you were worth speaking to and move directly on to the fun parts. It reminded her of how very young children made friends by asking another child if they'd like to be friends. In the past few minutes, it seemed that Charlotte and Todd had become very good friends indeed, based on how close together they were standing.

"So," Todd said. "Your husband was murdered, huh?"

"Yeah," Charlotte said. "His mistress stabbed him to death in his studio."

Todd made a sound like, "*Eurgh,*" before he recovered himself and cleared his throat. "That's awful. I'm so sorry."

Charlotte shrugged. "It's complicated," she said. "So . . . what do you do for a living?"

The two of them made uncomfortably flirtatious small talk for the duration of Father Barry's absence, until he reappeared with Sheriff Brown in tow. The sheriff took one look at Sherry and stopped dead. "Sherry? What the—what are you doing in there?"

"Not much," Sherry said. "You didn't leave me any magazines to read." It seemed pointless to bring up her visitation from Beelzebub. Then she added, helpfully, "You locked me up. I've been here for hours."

Sheriff Brown went pale, then shook his head. "No, I *didn't*."

"It must have been someone else, then," Father Barry said, in the tone of voice that someone might use to soothe a child who'd just woken up out of a nightmare. Maybe that was fair: maybe it was exactly how Sheriff Brown felt right now. Like a child caught in a terrible dream. Sherry couldn't blame him, if he did. She'd felt like that for days. "She really is locked up in there, though. We checked the door. Do you think that you could let her out?"

Sheriff Brown nodded and pulled a key from his pocket. Sherry couldn't see his hand from where she was standing, but she could hear the key rattling against the lock when it shook. "I can't," he said. He looked ghostly. "I can't do it." He lifted his hands up so that she could see them. The skin looked almost blue. "*I can't feel my hands.*"

Sherry had heard of skin crawling, but right now she felt like her skin wanted to sprint right out of the cell without the rest of her. She knew that she shouldn't, but she reached through the bars to grip his wrist. He looked so *lost*. "It's all right," she said. "It's not your fault."

He flushed, blotchily and unattractively, all over his face. He didn't jerk away, though. He let her hold his wrist, just for a moment, until she released him. Then his hand shot out to lock onto *her* wrist. "Nothing like this ever used to happen around here," he said. He was looking her right in the eyes, as if he was trying to really make her listen, to force someone to understand him. "This all started after you came to town. There's something *wrong* here."

"I know," she said. "I know. It might be my fault. I'm trying to stop it. I promise I am. Do you think there might be another way to get me out of here?"

"Not until you've thought about why you feel the need to be so insolent," said a snake's voice coming out of Sheriff Brown's mouth. "We'll be holding you here for twenty-four hours. You'll be released in the morning." Then—"*Oh*," he said, in his own, miserable voice. "*Ugh*. That felt like puking backward."

Everyone in the room gave a kind of instinctive writhe of sympathy. Then Sheriff Brown locked eyes with Sherry again. "Sherry," he said, suddenly urgent. "*What happened to the internet?*"

Reality sneezed.

"What?" Sherry said.

"What?" Sheriff Brown said, looking just as confused as she felt. Then he wandered out of the room without saying another word, like a man who'd gotten as far as the refrigerator before remembering that he was running late for an appointment and needed to be on his way.

Todd waited until the sheriff had left the room for about half a second before he said, "I'm going to go look for a hacksaw. Does anyone need anything else?"

"If we're going to break her out of jail, you might as well steal me an expensive car or something," Charlotte said. "Since we're doing serious time when we get caught either way."

"I need someone to break into the antiques shop," Sherry said.

"I'll do it," Todd said. "Do you need me to pick a lock? Did someone open an evil box that I have to get back so Barry can exorcise it?"

"Oh, wow, *is* there an evil box?" Charlotte asked.

Sherry considered that for a second. "Maybe," she said finally. "It's as likely as anything else. Keep your eyes out for anything with a mysterious glow, I suppose. But I really just want to know if the account books are in there. There's an outside chance that Alan could have run them back to the shop before he died, and I want to see them." Really, the specific contents of the shop's books mattered less to her than the thought that someone else might have gone out of their way to try to *hide* them.

Todd visibly deflated. "Oh. Yeah, okay. I guess I could find those. Would they be in a safe? Do you have a key or a code or something?"

"Todd," Barry said. "I don't know if you getting involved is a good idea. Aren't you still on probation?"

"Oh, no, you're a criminal?" Charlotte asked. The look on her face suggested that their blooming jailhouse romance might be about to come to an abrupt end.

"It was just weed," Todd said, looking as if he was making some rapid calculations in his head. He gave Charlotte an admittedly beautiful smile. Sherry could see how a man with a smile like that could get away with all sorts of things. "I promise that I've grown out of my rebellious phase. I'm a nice boy who takes the train upstate to visit his priest big brother every month now."

"I'm only *twenty minutes older*," Barry mumbled.

Everyone was ignoring him. Charlotte and Todd were back

to smiling at each other. "I'll come with you," Charlotte said. "Sherry, is there a key?"

"Alice had one, I think, but the police might have taken it," Sherry said. "She might be at the library right now, if she isn't at home. You could run over and check. And ask her about the safe."

The two of them took off, looking like two middle school best friends who'd convinced the teacher to give both of them a hall pass. Sherry had to call after them to secure a promise from them to meet at the diner at noon the next day. If she hadn't been released by then, she would really start to worry.

Father Barry stayed behind. "I'm sorry you're stuck in here, Sherry," he said. "Can I bring you anything?"

"Some books and snacks would be nice, if you don't mind," she said. She looked him in the eye. "Was it just weed, Father?"

He grimaced and gave his head a quick, tight shake. "Fraud," he said. "But I know what you're thinking, and I don't think he'd ever be involved with a murder. I don't think he'd see anything wrong with trying to catch a wealthy widow, but he's not a monster. He can be a really nice guy."

"Or widower," she said, purely to make herself difficult. Then she felt a little ashamed of herself. It must be hard to be a kind, well-meaning priest with a criminal playboy for a twin. It wasn't as if priests didn't have enough public relations difficulties on their own. "Thank you for telling me. I don't think that Todd seems like a monster at all."

He nodded, then cleared his throat. "I'll get you those books and snacks," he said. Then he pushed a small bottle between the bars. "Holy water. Just in case."

"Thank you," she said again. Then he left, and she was alone.

For a while, she felt stuck in a horrible psychic waiting room, constantly alert for her name to be called and the next awful thing to happen. Nothing awful happened. Time dragged on. Eventually, Father Barry reappeared with a collection of books. "I wasn't sure whether you'd want something to fit the theme or something completely different, so I got you *The Count of Monte Cristo, Rita Hayworth and Shawshank Redemption, Bridget Jones's Diary,* and a travel guide for Barbados and Saint Lucia. And some drinks and snacks."

"How thoughtful," Sherry said, really meaning it, and spent a strangely pleasant few hours planning her imaginary vacation to the Caribbean. Maybe she *would* go on vacation, once she made it out of all this.

Eventually she fell asleep on the thin mattress on the narrow metal bed, and somehow slept harder and longer than she had for a long time, even though that made no sense for the early hour and the uncomfortable place. She didn't even dream. She woke up to the sound of keys jangling and the metal door creaking open, and sat up. She was thinking vaguely that maybe she ought to buy a metal bunk for her own home, just for the sleep quality, before it occurred to her that there might be a supernatural component to her unusually heavy rest, and she gave an uncontrollable little shiver.

"Are you cold?" Sheriff Brown asked as he pulled the door open. He couldn't even look her in the eye.

"I'm fine," she said with dignity, even though she didn't feel dignified at all. She knew that she stunk. "Thank you for letting me out."

He opened his mouth, then closed it again and nodded. His expression was closed and wary. "You're still a suspect," he said.

"I know," she said. "I'm going to find whoever actually did it, though."

He just nodded again at that, and she collected her personal items and left. Everything outside the cell felt suddenly brighter and more vibrant than it had been before. Her mind felt clearer. It was seven in the morning. She hurried back home, fed Lord Thomas, showered, and made herself a big, elaborate breakfast, with eggs and toast and bacon and sliced fruit. Then she sat in her favorite armchair, closed her eyes, and had a good, long, sleep-fortified think.

Sex, revenge, or money. Those were the three main reasons for someone to commit murder. She needed to narrow the possible motives down to one.

In this case, Sherry thought that sex could be eliminated. She'd already found the other woman, and the other woman was currently sitting in her living room racking her brain over who might have killed Alan. She'd also met the wife, and whatever Mrs. Thompson's faults, Sherry found it hard to envision her bashing someone over the head with a brass lamp in a fit of mad jealousy. If she *had* killed Alan, it wouldn't have been for that reason.

Next up. Revenge. This was where Jason came in. Sheriff Brown had said that he was also looking into him, which meant that she and Charlotte weren't alone in thinking that he had a substantial motive. She needed to check up on his alibi, which would mean doing a bit of old-fashioned detective-ing. She would have to talk to his neighbors to see if anyone could confirm that he'd been at home with his wife all night.

Money. This was where the Thompsons entered her calculations. Based on how they'd all been dressed when they came into the library, the bunch of them were accustomed to a certain standard of living. She knew for a fact that Corey had been in the habit of asking his father for loans to fund his Manhattan lifestyle, and that his intermittent work for his father was probably his steadiest source of income. Eli, with his wife and children, was the more successful and reliable brother, but she doubted that his income as an architect could provide the sort of life that he'd grown up with. Susan cared enough about money to have spent years fighting over it in their divorce proceedings. If Sheriff Brown had been right about the amounts of money that they'd each be about to inherit, they would all have a very good reason to want to kill Alan. There were also three of them, so they'd be, in theory, capable of either providing alibis for each other or of potentially ratting each other out, if it came to that. She'd never gotten the impression from Alan that his sons were particularly close, so it might be possible to play them against each other. She would need to look into them all, though she wasn't sure where she would start. None of them lived in Winesap, and Sherry now knew from unpleasant experience that she wasn't able to leave. She'd be restricted to what she could glean from talking to them, and possibly to Todd. She would have to work quickly, starting with seeing if she could attend the reading of the will.

Money was at the crux of another question, too, one that Sherry found a bit more difficult to untangle. The problem of the antiques store's account books. Alan had said very clearly that he'd planned on continuing to work on the accounts after he'd dropped off Sherry that evening, but when she'd gone through his house after his death, they hadn't been anywhere in sight. True, there could be some alternate explanation. The most likely one was that the police had taken them as evidence.

It was also possible that he'd simply decided against working on them at all, or finished with them quickly, and tidied them away somewhere where Sherry wouldn't have spotted them on a brief nose through the house. The other option was more troubling: that whoever killed him had taken the accounts with them.

Who would care about the financial state of the store? His heirs, most likely. Corey, with his part-time work for his father, which might give him access to the shop's accounts, was particularly suspicious. He could easily have used the job to take money from his father when the loans weren't enough to cover his expenses. Alan had also sometimes worked with an accountant and a financial adviser: if one of them had been skimming off the top, then they'd have a vested interest in keeping Alan from finding out. Then, of course, there was Alice.

Alice was a strong suspect, in some ways. She'd seemed genuinely distraught over losing her job after Alan died, but she was in dire financial straits, and if she had been stealing from her employer, it was possible that she could have done something stupid in a moment of panic. Alice had an alibi, though, and one that Sherry had provided personally: there was no way that she could have made it to Alan's house and back on foot in the narrow possible time frame unless she had either a secret car that Sherry didn't know about—in which case, where would she have parked it so that it would have escaped Sherry's notice? She would certainly have noticed tire tracks leading through the snow around to the back of Alice's house—or outside help. Someone driving a getaway car. This struck Sherry as, if within the realm of possibility, definitely in one of the most distant and heavily wooded counties of the realm. Alice was practically a hermit: as far as Sherry knew, she didn't have any friends in Winesap outside of Sherry, let alone anyone who'd be willing to be her accomplice in a murder plot.

If there *was* such a person, Sherry didn't feel at all guilty thinking that it would be a man. She'd been working under the assumption from the day that she'd first met Alice that she'd arrived in Winesap after fleeing from a violent husband or boyfriend. The bruises and poor Alice's general demeanor made the case for her. Sherry wouldn't be incredibly surprised to learn that there was currently a man in Alice's life encouraging or causing her to make very poor decisions. It could be the same man, or it could be a new one of a similar disposition: in Sherry's experience, there were women with an almost uncanny ability to escape one terrible relationship only in order to run headlong into a new, nearly identical one. The sort of man who'd give fragile little Alice a black eye was, statistically speaking, exactly the sort of man who might get involved with a homicide. In any case, though, that was all speculation: Sherry didn't have a shred of actual evidence that there was a man with little regard for the law in Alice's life who might have provided transportation for Alice to and from a murder scene—or, possibly, taken on the task of killing Alice's boss on her behalf. Finding out if there *was* such a person in her life might be difficult. Alice hadn't mentioned a man: therefore, if there was one, she didn't want Sherry to know about him. If Sherry wanted to rule out the possibility, she would have to snoop.

Sherry opened her eyes, got up, and found a notepad to write down her to-do list. Then she checked the clock. It was still early: just before ten. Plenty of time before lunch to go to the library, she thought. Then she frowned. She wasn't sure why she'd thought that. She had to go around town and talk to people: this was one occasion when the library probably wasn't going to be much help. Then she thought of something else, something that Sheriff Brown had said to her the day before and that she had somehow almost immediately forgotten. What was it? She could remember his face when he said it, now, how desperate he'd looked to make her listen. What had he said, though? She tried to put herself back in the moment: the chill of the jail cell, the squeeze of his hand on her wrist. Something like terror in his eyes.

What happened to the internet, Sherry?

TWENTY-ONE

She headed down to the library as fast as she could, feeling sure now that there was something that she needed to do there. Whatever it was that Sheriff Brown had said to her kept slipping in and out of her head, but she felt deeply convinced that there was something at the library that would help it to all make sense. Something that she'd forgotten about.

When she arrived, she started out at the card catalog, thinking that maybe something there would spark a memory. Nothing was sparked. Then she started prowling through the whole library, waiting to see if a specific shelf or display or book title would jog her memory. Nothing did, until she completed a full circuit of the front room and came to the door to the room that they never used. She almost walked right past it. Then she stopped, turned, and looked at it very carefully.

Why didn't they use this room?

She tried to think back, to remember if she'd ever been given an explanation for it. She thought as hard as she could. Nothing. No one had ever said a thing. No one had ever told her that they never used that room. She'd just—known it, somehow. Known that this was a room that was never used and a door that was never, under any circumstances, to be opened.

She reached out to try the door handle.

Reality shifted in its seat, straightened its jacket, and started the moment over.

She blinked, then frowned. She was standing in her favorite cozy corner in the library, the one near the room that they never used, and she couldn't remember why. She turned around to look at the armchair, just in case she'd set something down there that she'd come back to get. Something like a book. Something like her—

Her what? She remembered being back home in Florida, patting her pockets and checking her purse, making sure that she had her wallet, her keys, and her—

What happened to the internet, Sherry?

She turned back to face the door that was never opened, reached out, and tried the handle.

Locked.

She huffed out a frustrated little sigh. Of course it couldn't be that easy. She checked her own key chain first, on the off chance that she'd had the key the whole time. She hadn't. She moved on to her desk and systematically worked her way through the contents of every drawer. No luck. She sat down for a moment to think. Her predecessor, she'd been told, had been a very organized woman, but her systems of organization for anything other than books—books had always been meticulously dealt with based on library best practices—had made more sense to herself than they had to other people. She'd apparently had a particular penchant for packing things neatly away into old boxes and storing the boxes in the basement. These boxes, unfortunately, were generally unlabeled, since she had the ability to recall with perfect clarity that the Christmas lights were in a box with a picture of a television on it, while the supplies for the annual garden party were boxed up in packaging that had originally held a window air-conditioning unit. Sherry had never had the key to the unused room. It only made sense, then, that her predecessor would have been the last one to have it, and that she would have tidily put it away in a place that made sense to her before she left.

The basement it was, then.

Sherry had never liked going down into the basement. Maybe it was a relic of her Floridian childhood: she'd never even seen a basement in real life until she moved to New York, and there was still something about them that she found deeply unnerving. There was nothing normal about climbing into a pit in the ground to find the Christmas decorations.

The library basement was less threatening than a basement might be, at least, with patchy brown wall-to-wall carpeting on the floor and innumerable books destined for the gruesome annual cull known as the library book sale lining the walls. The unlabeled boxes full of mystery contents lined the wall closest to the staircase. Some brave soul—possibly Beth, judging from the handwriting—had made an attempt to label some of them with their contents (one read *snowman costume*, and another *clay supplies*) before giving up a few boxes in. Sherry skipped by those and settled on a plan of action, which was, essentially, "Pick up one box at a time and shake them to see if they rattle." If they rattled, she opened them up to check for keys. Most of them didn't contain keys. One of them, bafflingly, contained a large button collection. Maybe someone had done a craft activity involving buttons. She moved through a few more boxes, discovering a collection of assorted mysterious electrical cords, ancient

Magic Markers, and an assortment of cutlery. Then, finally, the jackpot: an old cookie tin that gave a particularly loud and resonant rattle, and, when opened, revealed a large collection of orphaned keys of all shapes and sizes.

She carried her new treasures upstairs, fighting against a mounting sense of unease and unmoored guilt, as if she was carrying something out of a shop without paying for it or trying to surreptitiously stick a flyer for a fringe political movement onto a public bulletin board. The feeling only got worse as she reached the door to the locked room, and increased in its pitch as she proceeded to grimly, one at a time, attempt to fit the keys into the keyhole.

She didn't even have to turn the seventh key in the lock to know that she'd found the right one. She could tell just from the surge of fear that hit her gut, the conviction that nothing would ever be right in the world until she dropped the key, ran away from the door, and never touched either again. She ignored the feeling. She pushed right through it. She turned the key in the lock and opened the door.

The computer lab.

It made sense immediately. There was no confusion this time, no sense of reality reordering itself to reject what she could see. Of course the library had a computer lab. There was the printer. There was the scanner. There was the neat row of monitors lined up down a long table against the wall. There was the computer lab, and if she turned one of the computers on, she'd be able to use the internet.

It was remarkable how easy it was. She didn't even have to think about it: she was navigating to Google in under two minutes and typing in Corey Thompson's name.

It took a while to find him. There were, apparently, a very

large number of Corey Thompsons in the world. She tried it in combination with his father's and brother's names, then just Alan's name with various terms related to his job, and finally struck gold with Alan's Facebook page.

It was unexpectedly wrenching to see it. Just Alan's ordinary life, before Sherry had entered it: pictures of him with his sons and grandchildren, and posts from people congratulating him on his retirement or wishing him a happy birthday. They'd continued all the way through him opening his antiques shop, then abruptly stopped. That gave Sherry another jolt. The problem wasn't Winesap, then: it had been a normal town not too long ago, where people remembered that it was the twenty-first century and that the internet existed. Things had only gotten truly weird when Sherry came to town.

From Alan's page it was easy enough to find his sons'. Eli had never been particularly active on his: most of the posts on his page were group shots that someone else had tagged him in. He apparently belonged to a running club in Connecticut. She clicked on their page and scrolled. They'd had an event—a five-mile "fun run," which didn't sound particularly fun to Sherry—on the day of Alan's death. She clicked through the photos. There was Eli, running in the middle of the pack. After the run, the group had gone to a brewery. No Eli in those pictures. The location of the run was about four hours from Winesap, which would have given Eli a long enough window to drive to Winesap and arrive with time to spare. She couldn't rule him out, though she did wonder what could have happened at a fun run to trigger the desire to drive across state lines and bludgeon your own father to death with a lamp. If he'd planned it ahead of time, it meant that he was calculating and coolheaded enough to know that he should stick to his usual schedule on the day in question to avoid suspicion. The thought made Sherry shiver.

She returned to his page and searched for any signs of his mother having an internet presence. Eventually she hit one via pictures from a family birthday party. Her page was much like her older son's: the only activity seemed to be requests for birthday donations to various worthy organizations and pictures of her looking poised and polished at various openings and galas shared by the pages of said organizations. She had, however, not been tagged in anything on the evening of her husband's murder.

Corey's page was easy to find from there, and of a very different character. He'd been extremely active on Facebook a decade earlier, posting lots of pictures of himself and updates about what he was doing, to the general interest and acclaim of his many friends. Then the posts tapered off, replaced at first with cross-posts from Instagram and then with nothing. She navigated over to Instagram, then spent a frustrating few moments trying to click on things before she was forced to create an account to look at anything. Her fingers typed in an email address and password without her having to think about it. For a username, she considered for a moment before typing in *imbrandon1992*. A Brandon born in 1992 seemed like the sort of person who might follow Corey on Instagram. She found a picture of a blandly handsome young man walking on a beach to serve for a profile picture. Then, after a bit more fussing, she was ready to go.

Corey's Instagram was very . . . illuminating. She'd rarely seen so much of a young man whom she'd only recently been introduced to. He certainly took very good care of himself. He also very obviously spent an enormous amount of money to keep up with his evidently very wealthy social circle. There were lots of pictures of him on boats and in beautiful houses in the Caribbean, to the point where it seemed that he spent very little time at home. This, Sherry thought, would be a good excuse to economize on housing and rent a modest studio as a home base, but Corey clearly had other ideas. The few pictures he posted of his apartment emphasized the wall of floor-to-ceiling windows overlooking a swath of Manhattan. She was looking at the comments under one of these photos from several weeks earlier when she saw a very familiar jawline in one of the profile pictures, next to the comment *Miss this view.*

She clicked through, and there he was, sprawling attractively in a chair somewhere outdoors, the lighting falling flatteringly on his cheekbones. The profile was set to friends only, and the area where he could describe himself was blank. He had several thousand followers. If she hadn't spent so much time staring at his twin's earnest face while he babbled nervously about exorcisms, she might have second-guessed herself, but as it was, there was no question in her mind that this was Todd. She checked the comment he'd made on Corey's post again. Next to it was the notation "9w." He'd been commenting on Corey's Instagram over two months ago and had been inside his apartment before that. When he'd said that they'd met once at a recent party before running into each other on the train, he'd been lying. Now she only had to figure out what the lie had been covering up. She clicked on the follow button, then minimized the window and stood. She would have to wait for him to accept her request, and she had to get to a lunch date.

Walking through Winesap felt stranger, now that she'd

been so forcibly relocated back to the second decade of the twenty-first century. She was suddenly conscious of the place as a stage set. She'd never been someone who paid much attention to cars, but even to her untrained eyes it was plainly evident that the vehicles of Winesap had emerged out of a time warp: the seventies, eighties, and nineties appeared to be well represented, but she couldn't see anything that looked much more contemporary. The people, too, were all dressed as if the most recent twenty years had never happened, though it was hard to pinpoint most of them as belonging to any particular era. Two young girls walked past in blue jeans and flannel shirts: Were they dressed up as if they were from the nineties, or were they simply wearing outfits that wouldn't have looked out of place on teenagers at any point over the past few decades? A man went by in a tweedy brown suit that looked as if it could have been from the seventies, but also might just have been the choice of a man who liked the idea of wearing tweed with leather elbow patches. Sherry looked down at herself: blue jeans, winter boots, blue hand-knitted sweater, heavy blue wool coat. Once again, nothing to mark itself out as being of any particular moment between 1970 and the present. Nothing to prompt questions or disturb the suspension of disbelief. Nothing, she realized abruptly, that couldn't possibly be seen on an extra in an episode of *Murder, She Wrote*.

She arrived at the diner exactly on time. Father Barry, predictably, had arrived early. She settled in across from him and made awkward small talk—it was hard not to be awkward when you suspected that someone's twin brother might be involved in some kind of dastardly criminal scheme—until Charlotte and Todd arrived together, bursting through the door in a cloud of conspiratorial laughter and settling into opposite sides of the booth: Charlotte next to Sherry and Todd next to his brother. Sherry tried not to make eye contact with poor Barry, and failed.

"I'm *starving,*" Charlotte said, with gusto, and snatched up a menu to peruse. She looked very refreshed and very happy. Sherry took the opportunity to peruse her own menu and avoid looking at Todd. From what she could see of him, he looked smug. Good for both of them, she supposed, but she wasn't sure she appreciated the ease and speed with which Todd had managed to insert himself into her inner circle.

"How did your visit to the antiques shop go?" Sherry asked, once they'd all ordered their food. "Did you find anything?"

Charlotte grimaced. "No," she said. "Alice said that the cops took her store key, so we had to, uh. *Find the door just coincidentally unlocked.*"

Todd gave a very nice smile and added helpfully, "I learned how to do that in high school. With a paper clip. My parents used to lock me out when I stayed out past curfew, and Barry always slept through it when I threw rocks at his window."

"I didn't sleep through it when you threw a rock *through* my window," Barry muttered.

Everyone ignored him. Sherry pressed Charlotte. "How about signs of a previous break-in? Did everything look normal to you?"

"Nothing looked too weird," Charlotte said. "It was a little hard to tell. We didn't turn the lights on in the shop because people would see it from the street. We turned them on in the back office, though, so we could see to look around. There was a safe, but Alice told us about that ahead of time and said that they kept cash in there for the register, nothing else. We looked through the desk but there was just electric bills and stuff."

"And I doubt that the accounts would have been in the safe if Alan had been planning on looking at them at home," Sherry said with a disappointed little sigh. "If he'd forgotten, he would have left them on the desk, not locked them up in the safe. So we're left with someone having taken them. Either the police or someone who didn't want them looked at." Like Alice, who worked for Alan and always seemed desperately short of money. Or like Corey, Alan's ne'er-do-well son who'd been helping him at the store and always needed money.

Or like Todd, who'd almost certainly slept with Corey at least once, more than two months earlier, had subsequently lied about it, had a previous fraud conviction, and had managed to involve himself in the investigation into Alan's death from almost the instant he'd arrived in Winesap.

She couldn't say any of this aloud to this group, of course. Todd had already clearly managed to wedge himself firmly into Charlotte's life, and he'd been part of Father Barry's this whole time. For all Sherry knew, Barry had been accidentally slipping him information about the investigation since it first started. Or, she realized with a jolt, Barry could have been sharing information *deliberately*. It wasn't as if she really, truly knew him that well. He'd just been kind to her when she'd needed help, and she'd immediately started acting as if they'd had years of close friendship. She would have to be more careful from now on. She'd always worked mostly alone, before this bunch came into her life. Starting from this lunch, she needed to play things much more carefully. No more running to her friends for advice and feedback. The demon wanted *her* to investigate, just her, and it was becoming apparent that she would have to take care of things alone either way.

"Sherry!" Charlotte said in Sherry's right ear, jolting Sherry out of her reverie. "I have something for you." The twins appeared to be having some kind of quiet argument; for the moment, she and Charlotte were unobserved.

Sherry sat up straighter in her seat. She did love a present. "Oh! What is it?" she asked, then smiled as Charlotte handed it over, pleased, if a little baffled. "Oh, goodness, it's *beautiful*."

It was a necklace, the sort of piece of impressive statement jewelry that she always admired on Charlotte but would look silly paired with her own usual modest little department store sweaters and blue jeans. She had no idea why Charlotte would give it to her.

"It's red branch coral," Charlotte said, seeming uncharacteristically bashful. "I was trying to come up with something I could do to help out with the demon problems, and I thought about my jewelry collection. Crystals have powers, right? So I called my witch friend and asked, and she said red coral is supposed to protect against evil, like, all over the world, in China and ancient Rome and the Americas and all through history, which I thought would probably cover our bases if our demon here is from, I don't know, ancient Macedonia or something. So, I picked this out, and she helped me do a blessing over it. It's vintage, so it's definitely actual coral. I figure it couldn't hurt if you wore it, right?"

"According to my cat," Sherry said, "it's mostly about whether we believe that it will help. Which I think I do. I think all of those people all over the world must have known something."

Charlotte looked relieved. "Me, too," she said, like a confession. "I mean—there's something about it that feels right." She cleared her throat. "My friend says to make sure that the coral's touching your skin. That helps it to work."

Sherry put on the necklace and tucked it in under her shirt. It was long enough to drape over her heart. The red of the coral was the same red as the berries she'd pulled from the yew branch to make her dagger, which was still tucked safely into her coat pocket. She put her hand into her pocket to touch it, and yelped as a painful surge of heat passed through her fingers and her chest.

"What?" Charlotte asked, clearly startled.

Sherry licked her lips, then smiled. "I think that it's working already," she said.

Charlotte didn't laugh or smile. Instead, she just nodded. "Good."

Their food arrived, bringing with it a wave of comforting ordinariness that made the strange, ancient power that Sherry was increasingly convinced that she really had managed to cook up out of a roadside shrub and some statement jewelry recede to a more comfortable distance. They all lapsed into eating paired with safe small talk. Todd was surprisingly voluble on the topic of the *best tuna melt in New York*, a subject in which he apparently had a particular interest. Sherry picked at her food for a while—uncharacteristically, she didn't have much of an appetite—then stood. "I have to go," she said. "Thank you very much for all of your help."

Charlotte and Todd were, at this point, too wrapped up in giggling with each other to notice her, but Father Barry frowned. "Are you all right, Sherry?"

Oh, he was good. No wonder she'd liked and trusted him so quickly. He could tell the second her mood shifted. "I'm fine," she said firmly. "Thank you, Barry." Then she added a quick, apologetic little, "If I need help, I'll—" She stopped. *Call you*, she'd been about to say. Call him on the smartphone that she now remembered had until recently always been in her purse, and which she could have used to very quickly perform many of the tasks she'd recently performed with endless phone calls and poring over microfiche. Where had all their phones gone? She strained to think, but she couldn't come up with anything. Maybe they were all neatly piled behind some door in Winesap that everyone knew they weren't supposed to open.

Barry was looking more worried than ever. She hastily finished her thought. "If I need help, I'll let you know."

He nodded. He had a look to him like he knew that something had shifted. "Good luck, Sherry."

She swallowed, nodded back, and left.

TWENTY-TWO

Sherry had only made it about halfway down the block when Father Barry caught up with her. "Sherry!"

She stopped, letting herself look mildly irritated. She had a long list of things that she needed to get *done*. Troublesome loose ends that she needed to stitch back together. First up was Jason and his not particularly convincing alibi. She needed to find out if any of his neighbors had noticed him leaving when he was supposed to be cozily ensconced at home with his lovely wife and daughters. "Yes?"

"You're shutting me out of what you're doing because of Todd, aren't you?"

Her face went warm. "I don't know him," she said after a second. Arguing the point seemed like a waste of time.

"But you know *me*," he said. Then he said, "Sherry, I love my brother. But I'm not going to tell him anything that you tell me in confidence. I'm a priest. I know how to keep my mouth shut."

For good or evil, Sherry thought. She was feeling uncharitable. She said aloud, "Why are you so interested in knowing what I'm doing, then? You weren't so excited to get involved in my demon problems a few days ago."

He sighed. "I don't *want* to get involved. But I can't just let an old—I can't just let a woman go talk to murderers by herself without telling anyone where she is. You could be lying dead somewhere and none of your friends would have any idea."

"You were going to say *an old lady*, weren't you?" Sherry asked, pleased to be able to score a point in the face of Father Barry's otherwise honestly fairly reasonable argument. He went slightly red again, which felt like enough of an admission of error that she could make a concession of her own. "I'm going to talk to Jason Martinez's neighbors first, to see if anyone can confirm or dispute his alibi. He says that he was home all night."

"Then let me go with you," Father Barry said. "He's one of my parishioners. If I ask about him, it will be less suspicious."

"It will be if you ask the questions that I want the answers to," Sherry said, though she had to admit to herself that it wasn't a completely terrible idea. She still wasn't sure that she wanted him tagging along. "If a priest showed up at my house and started asking questions about my neighbor's movements at night, I'd think that either he was a robber dressed up as a priest to case the joint, or that the priest was some kind of weird pervert."

"I would make it sound good," he said. "I'd say—that I was expecting to meet him that evening after dinner to counsel him about something, but I haven't seen him since, and I've been concerned about him. Then I could take it from there."

She considered that. "That sounds like a lot of lying, for a priest. We'll split the difference. I'll say that I'm involved in the investigation, and you wanted to come along as his spiritual adviser in case he's in crisis. Everyone knows I work with the police, and I'll have you for backup in case they don't want things to get back to the cops." That decided, she started marching toward the lake again, allowing Father Barry to trot along if he saw fit. She didn't want to wait any longer.

It was a pleasant walk down to the lake, at least, on the sort of glass-clear spring day when the air felt sharp enough to cut and the light glittered bright enough to dazzle on the water. The little houses that clustered around the lake looked shabbier than usual on this sort of day, with no leafy trees or flattering lighting to soften their flaws. They walked past one house with a collection of weather-faded plastic flowers and pinwheels sticking out of planters by the front door and a listing bathtub near the mailbox; one with peeling siding and a basketball hoop that had lost its basket; and a third that looked sleek and shiny and new, with a bright-red front door and neatly trimmed hedges. New money in town, maybe: young professionals who commuted into one of the nearby cities. In a few more years maybe all the plastic pinwheels would be gone forever.

It wasn't hard to find Jason's house: his rusty pickup was parked prominently out front, and she could see a pink plastic playhouse in the yard half-buried in the snow. Sherry nudged Father Barry to keep up and walked briskly as she passed the house, swinging her arms like a woman out for some afternoon exercise in the cold. Then she doubled back to knock on the neighbor's door.

No one was home. She tried a few more, until finally someone answered: a lady who might have been in her eighties bundled up in a big warm sweater with appliquéd flowers on the front. She gave Sherry the polite, fixed smile of someone who thinks that they're about to be asked to make a donation to something. "Can I help you?" Then she spotted Father Barry and beamed. "Oh! Good afternoon, Father! What a lovely surprise!"

"Good afternoon, Mrs. Sherman," Father Barry said. "It's so nice to see you. How's that ankle doing?"

Sherry tried not to look as impressed as she felt. He was still new in town and had probably about a hundred parishioners: most people wouldn't have been able to match one old lady's face to the right name and medical complaint this early in their tenure as parish priest. That is, if he had matched the right face to the correct failing joint, which it appeared he had: Mrs. Sherman was still smiling. "Oh, just about the same," she said. "Would you like to come in for a coffee?"

"I don't know if we have time today, Mrs. Sherman," Barry said. "We just wanted to stop by because I'm helping my friend Sherry look into something."

"Oh," Mrs. Sherman said, and directed a slightly suspicious glance toward Sherry. "You're the one who does the murders."

Sherry winced. "I *investigate* murders," she said. She didn't *do* them. She wasn't that sort of lady.

"We wanted to ask about one of your fellow parishioners," Barry said hurriedly. "Your neighbor, Jason Martinez. It seems like the police might be looking at him for Alan Thompson's murder, and I was hoping that one of his neighbors might be able to say whether or not they noticed him leaving home that night. I want to be able to tell the police that I don't think he possibly could have done it with a clear conscience." He was blushing slightly, but that somehow just made him look even more wholesome and sincere than he usually did. Sherry was impressed all over again. He hadn't even really technically *lied*.

Mrs. Sherman had the look of a woman who was fulsomely

appreciating an extremely sincere, wholesome, and square-jawed young priest. "How nice of you, Father," she said. "I don't know if I can help, though. I don't think I know Mr. Martinez."

"He's one of your across-the-street neighbors," Sherry put in. "A few doors down. The family with the two little girls and the playhouse in the front yard."

"Oh, him!" Mrs. Sherman said. "I know him and his wife to wave to, but I don't really *know* them. He's in trouble? They seem like such a nice family."

"We hope that he isn't going to be in any trouble," Barry said soothingly.

"We were wondering if you might have noticed him coming and going from the house the Saturday night before last," Sherry said. "It would have probably been between nine and midnight."

Mrs. Sherman was already shaking her head. "I went to bed very early that night. I'd been woken up at four in the morning by the neighbor's dog barking, so I was completely dead to the world by nine. I'm sorry I can't be more helpful."

Father Barry looked somewhat crestfallen but quickly recovered himself. "Oh, no, don't apologize," he said. "I knew it was a long shot that anyone would have noticed anything. People don't just watch their neighbors all night long. Thank you for taking the time to talk to us!"

Mrs. Sherman indicated that it was nothing and that she'd be more than happy for Father Barry to drop by anytime. Sherry cleared her throat. "Just one more thing," she said, and immediately felt self-conscious. She should have come with a raincoat and a cigar. "The dog that woke you up. Does it do that often?"

"*All the time,*" Mrs. Sherman said. "It's awful. It's one of those little ones, the little things that look like rats. It goes absolutely berserk every time anyone walks past the house. It hates pedestrians. I think it thinks they're all mailmen. There's *nothing* it hates more than the mailman. Once after a big storm he came to deliver the mail on skis and the thing nearly launched itself straight through a window to get at him. If it wasn't such a tiny dog I'd be scared for the poor man. That dog is *malevolent.*"

"Like a miniature Cujo," Sherry said. "I hope you got a good night's sleep on Saturday, at least."

"I did. Like I said, I passed out at nine and slept through until morning, which is unusual for me. Usually I'm up and down all night. Things like wind and the birds wake me up."

Sherry said a few polite things about how difficult that must be and how she sometimes struggled to get enough sleep herself, then shamelessly promised Mrs. Sherman, without consulting Barry, that Father Barry would be coming by for coffee soon, which allowed them to leave Mrs. Sherman feeling happy about the whole strange conversation. As they walked away, Sherry could hear muffled, high-pitched yaps coming from inside the house next door.

"Well," Sherry said eventually, "at least we know that Jason didn't *walk* to kill Alan."

"How?" Father Barry asked. "Wait, don't tell me. Because of the dog? It would have barked if someone walked past the house, and that would have woken up Mrs. Sherman?"

"Right," Sherry said. "Because the dog hates pedestrians. I didn't think that Jason would have walked to Alan's, anyway, though. He has a limp. I don't see why a man who's unsteady on his feet would choose a night with heavy snow falling to walk almost a mile to confront someone who betrayed his trust decades earlier, kill him, and then make history's slowest getaway. It would have been a stupid thing to do, and it would have set off the horrible dog, so it probably didn't happen. If he did it, he would have driven there."

"So we don't know any more than we did before," Father Barry said.

"Sure we do," Sherry said. "We know that Jason definitely didn't leave his neighborhood on foot, which means that if he was involved, someone might have seen a red pickup near the murder scene. That's something."

Barry seemed unconvinced. They knocked on a few more doors, anyway. Only three more people answered: one young man who'd been at work at a bar in Saratoga at the time, a stay-at-home mother to a toddler who'd been asleep on the living room couch while her husband contentedly ignored the toddler dumping an entire bottle of chocolate syrup onto the living room floor, and a furtive-looking teen girl who'd been listening to music in her bedroom for most of the evening and hadn't seen or heard a thing until Barry mentioned that it was connected to a murder investigation, at which point she'd *definitely* heard someone screaming. By the time they decided to give up and head back to the village, Father Barry was looking a little downcast. "Cheer up, Father," Sherry said. She was feeling surprisingly high-spirited herself. Just being out and about and asking questions made her feel a little more in control. "It's never as easy as you hope it's going to be, but you always end up knowing more than when you started."

"Very philosophical of you," Father Barry said.

"I think so, too," Sherry said modestly. "I have a few more things that I need to look into this afternoon. Will you be tagging along this whole time?"

Father Barry frowned. "Will it involve more interrogating strangers?"

"No," Sherry said. "It will mostly involve the internet."

"The what?" Father Barry asked, and Sherry distracted him by darting toward Jason's pickup truck, which they were currently walking past. Something had just occurred to her. She was crouching down in the snow behind the truck when Father Barry caught up to her. "*Sherry,*" he hissed. "He's going to look out the window and see you!"

Sherry popped up again, beaming all over her face. She felt triumphant. "That's fine," she said. "If he comes charging out of the house to confront me, I'll just tell him—"

She stopped. Caught herself short. She'd agreed to Barry coming along with her on this particular fact-finding mission, but she wasn't sure how much information she should continue to share. She didn't think that he would intentionally disrupt her investigation, but there was still the problem of Todd to consider. Until she was sure of where she stood with the disreputable Todd, she would have to be careful about what she said to his twin brother.

"What?" Barry asked. "You'll tell him what?"

"I'm not sure," she said. "I mean—I might be wrong. I'll tell you later." Then she took off walking again. Father Barry only badgered her about it very briefly before he gave up. When they arrived back on Main Street, he hesitated. "Are you going to talk to more people?"

"No," she said. "I'm going to the library to do some more research." She was going to go rooting around on social media some more, but it didn't seem wise to bring that up when it seemed that Father Barry still couldn't remember what the internet was. She also planned on going straight from the

library to Alan's house so that she could illegally break and
enter it again, a plan that seemed somewhat more likely to get
her in trouble than spending all afternoon in the library computer room. She thought that she could save Father Barry the
worry of having to hear about that part.

"Oh," he said, his shoulders relaxing. "That should be safe,
shouldn't it be? I need to work on my homily. I put it off until
the weekend last week and was up most of Saturday night trying to finish it before mass. I think people might have been
able to tell. It wasn't very good." He looked very anxious at the
thought.

Sherry wasn't usually the sort of person who gave spontaneous hugs, but in that moment, she really did want to hug
Father Barry. "I'm sure I'll be safe," she said. "Go work on your
homily. I'll see you soon."

They went their separate ways. Sherry went straight to the
library and walked past a few browsing patrons to enter the
computer lab. As soon as she reached the door, they all
snapped their faces away in unison, toward a book or a shelf
or the floor, anywhere but the door that led to the computers.
It was as if the director had shouted, "*Action,*" and they all had
to look away from the camera. It made Sherry's skin itch.

Once she was safely established at a computer with the
door closed firmly behind her, she was delighted to discover
that Todd had accepted her fake account's friend request on
Instagram. She scrolled through his posts. It took a while to
get through them: he generally didn't stay inactive for longer
than a few days. There was enough information available for
Sherry to form what she thought might be a fairly accurate
picture of Todd's life. A handsome, charming man with a large
social circle but not many close friends. A string of what might

be boyfriends or girlfriends, none of them lasting longer than a month or so. Lots of pictures from nightclubs, parks, nice restaurants, charming city streets, and the beautiful homes where he attended dinner parties. No pictures of his own home, which she suspected would be quite modest. No ostentatious displays of expensive purchases. No pictures that showed much of his body except when his being shirtless was appropriate for the occasion: here he was in a candid shot on the beach looking casually gorgeous while laughing with a friend. All very calculated and curated for effect: all very tasteful and pointedly not desperate. Nothing referencing his parents, though occasionally Barry would feature in childhood pictures of the two of them together with captions like, *Heading upstate to see this guy* or *Best friends since before birth*. It seemed that Barry's loyalty to his brother was genuinely mutual. There was even one picture of them as adults, with Barry in his priest's collar, with the caption *Barry and his evil twin*. The comments below were very heavy on the jokes about kneeling, confessing sins, et cetera. Poor Barry: he was like a vegan who was constantly being offered free filets.

She kept digging through the posts. Corey's apartment featured in one, as did the man himself in a group shot taken at some gallery opening from six months earlier. She clicked through to the profiles of the other people tagged in the picture. Nobody stuck out as particularly relevant, until she hit one well-dressed older gentleman with receding silver hair and an impressive set of white teeth. His profile contained a link to his website. MikeKaminskiAntiques.com.

Mike Kaminski, the antiques dealer who had seen Alan on his last day alive.

TWENTY-THREE

S herry frowned at the screen. It wasn't such a *massive* co-incidence, really. Todd knew Corey. Corey was Alan's son and did some work purchasing art for his antiques store. Mike Kaminski was a regular customer at said store, and both of them were involved in the wider world of art and antiques in New York. It was reasonable to think that they could have met at some point, running in such similar circles. It wasn't beyond the bounds of normal social behavior that Corey could have brought Todd to a party where Mike Kaminski also happened to be in attendance.

It wasn't a *massive* coincidence, but it was still a striking coincidence.

She clicked through Mr. Kaminski's website for a while, not really sure what she expected to find. A section of the shop for murder weapons, maybe. Something that would clarify things a little. Instead, all she found was a niggling sense of unease that she was forgetting something. It bothered her. She frowned her way through a few more sections of the website. She was scrolling crankily past first a selection of rewired midcentury table lamps, followed by some admittedly nice-looking area rugs, when it hit her.

The website didn't feature a single figurative drawing.

It was, yet again, far from damning. There were a fairly limited number of items on the website, clearly far from Mr. Kaminski's entire inventory, and the fine art selection was particularly slim. Still, on reflection, it was strange. Mr. Kaminski had a very clear personal sense of taste that came through in what he was offering for sale: lots of bold geometric shapes and saturated colors, and everything on a scale that would fit into only the largest of Hudson Valley summer homes. Here was an enormous Bakelite and chrome ceiling lamp, and there was an abstract impressionist canvas selling for almost five thousand dollars that would take up the better part of Sherry's living room wall. Nowhere was there anything like the modest little charcoal drawing that Alan had liked enough to bring home from the shop and hang on his own living room wall. Which was strange, because Alice had specifically mentioned Mr. Kaminski being annoyed that the set of drawings was missing one picture.

Sherry pulled out a notebook from her bag, returned to Instagram, opened up the profiles for each of the three men, and carefully noted down their movements on the days directly surrounding Alan's murder. Then she carefully checked for any other social media accounts and did the same, before scrolling further through the accounts to confirm that certain details lined up correctly. She followed links from profile to profile, googled names, and looked up records. An hour passed, then two. She was beginning to feel as if she had an idea of how it all fit together.

Next, she looked up the telephone numbers for several restaurants and bars in New York City, introduced herself as working with the Winesap Sheriff's Office, and asked if they could confirm that certain groups and individuals had been in their restaurants at the times in question. Finally, she called Mike Kaminski himself. He remembered her and was as helpful as ever, readily providing her with the names and numbers of some of the friends he'd been with on Saturday night and emailing her a picture of his receipt. That seemed to settle his location on the night in question but did nothing at all to clear him of involvement in whatever else the three of them might have been up to. She had a suspicion that there was a very neat explanation to many of the odd coincidences she'd been running into, but there was only one way for her to know for certain.

She really hoped she wasn't going to get arrested for breaking into what was technically now her own house.

Sherry had successfully left the computer room without accidentally causing a break in the fabric of reality—the library patrons all looked away again when she exited, as if she'd left the bathroom not only with her fly down but also with snakes for hair—and headed to the circulation desk. There was one last thing that she wanted to check before she headed to Alan's house, and it was in the file of cards for books that were currently checked out. She went immediately to the 700s, the arts-related section, and hit what she was looking for almost immediately: Alan had checked out multiple books on fine arts and art appraisal before he died, including one hefty encyclopedia of American artists of the twentieth century.

She wrote down the names of the books in her notebook, then headed for the exit. She'd almost made it out when she was waylaid by Mary, her elderly volunteer and favorite gossip provider. "*Sherry*," she said. "I'm *so* sorry about Alan. He was

such a wonderful man." Mary and Alan had both been involved with the local historical society, and Mary had known
Alan for longer than Sherry had.

"Thank you," Sherry said. "He really was." She was a little
surprised that she still believed that. He'd been terrible at his
job as a defense attorney and had fled his hometown in shame
when he'd been found out, had lied to her about his wife, had
spoiled his youngest son past the point of no return, and
might have mismanaged his business so badly that he hadn't
been able to figure out an extremely serious problem with its
operations until it was too late. He'd been kind, though. A
weak man, maybe, and an incompetent man, almost certainly.
Still, he'd been kind. It was more than you could say for lots
of people.

"I'm sorry to bring up gossip at a time like this," Mary was
saying now—though she didn't *look* very sorry—"but you'd
asked me to tell you if I heard anything else about the priest
and Mrs. Walker."

Sherry, who'd been glancing toward the door, perked up
immediately. "He's been back? Did Karen say something
to you?"

She nodded. "She said it was the strangest thing. For years
now Mrs. Walker has only ever asked people over in the afternoon to sit by her bed and have tea. But two weeks ago she
apparently was up and about trying on some of her nice old
dresses, and then she told Karen that she was having a guest
over for dinner on Saturday night and she wanted a full dinner
like she used to have for guests with courses and wine. It was
the priest. He came over at seven, and Karen said that he
stayed for hours. She went to bed at almost eleven and he was
still there. Mrs. Walker practically banished her from the

room after she was done serving, but Karen could hear her just laughing away until late. She was talking about what a wonderful time she had with him for days afterward. Isn't that strange? A priest coming to visit an old lady is one thing, but laughing and drinking wine with her until midnight?"

"Very strange," Sherry agreed. Another piece of the puzzle nestled right into its proper spot. "Thank you very much for telling me. That was very helpful." Then she left, hurrying on to her next destination.

The key to Alan's house was, remarkably, still under the gnome.

It really did seem as if some responsible person should have removed it by now. There it still was, though, glinting gold in the late afternoon sun. She let herself in, then started to search. She was much more systematic about it this time, now that she knew what she was looking for. First, she went to his expansive bookshelves and hunted through them for a while—Alan was very tidy, but he had absolutely no organizational system in place for his books—until she found the art books he'd checked out from the library. She pulled them out to look through them. No notes detailing his worries, alas, but lots of scraps of paper stuck between various pages to mark his place. This artist or that one. There was no clear pattern that Sherry could see. That didn't make it any less suggestive, in Sherry's mind. He hadn't just been trying to inform himself about art appraisal in general. It seemed to her that he had very specific things that he was trying to look up.

Next, his living room wall. The cowboy drawing. She took it down from its hook and looked at it more closely. Nothing immediately struck her, until the name in the cramped signature in the lower right corner caught her eye. The same as one of the names Alan had bookmarked. He'd been wondering about the provenance of his beloved new piece of art, just before he died. She checked the book again: the artist himself had died decades earlier.

She gave the drawing a gentle shake. Nothing. She turned it over to examine the frame. It was clearly very new, with fresh paper covering the back. No sticker from the shop that had done the framing work. Corey's work, most likely. She was picking delicately at the paper with a fingernail to see if it would come off when a shadow went past the window.

Sherry, absurdly, hit the floor. A moment later someone knocked on the door and called out, "Is someone in there? I'm calling the police!"

Sherry cursed quietly to herself and waited for the neighbor—she was fairly certain that this must be the same neighbor who had recorded her crimes on his security camera—to leave. Once he'd walked off, she shoved the library books and the drawing into her enormous bag and headed for the back porch. She'd be able to escape more discreetly that way. She was passing through the porch when something caught her eye, and she paused. Alan kept some of his outdoor things back here. A couple of cheap plastic sleds that his grandchildren played with when they came to visit. His snowshoes, two pairs: one old-fashioned wood-and-leather pair that he'd told her that he mostly kept for sentimental reasons—they were heavy and bulky to use—and the modern aluminum-and-plastic set that she knew he used regularly for his long winter tromps through the woods. Next to the snowshoes were two pairs of skis and one pair of ski boots.

Odd.

She leaned down and, as quickly as she could, tried to fit

one of the boots into the bindings for each pair of skis. One clicked into place almost immediately. The other wouldn't, no matter how much she wiggled it.

She straightened and looked around. There were no other ski boots on the porch. There was no more time to hunt for the missing pair, though: she had to go. She hurried back toward the library. It was after five now, so it would be closed, and if Sheriff Brown was looking for her, he'd look for her at home first. That gave her a little extra time. She felt as if finally she was in her element again, as if her brain was working right, as if she was, once more, the kind of amateur detective that she liked to read about in books.

She got to the library, let herself in, and went straight back into the computer room. She made a few last checks and took notes of what she found. She needed to be sure that she wasn't missing anything or mixing anything up. She took apart the picture frame, just to confirm exactly what she'd already been convinced was true, and put it back together again. She was about to try to pull off something ridiculous, something outrageous, something that she'd never done before. Something that she was very sure would catch her demon friend's attention.

She went to the front desk and started making phone calls. It took her a while. She didn't have the numbers for everyone she wanted. Alice, first, that was easy. Charlotte and Janine. Father Barry, who had Todd with him. She asked Todd to please contact the Thompsons. She called the diner and asked for Jason, shamelessly pretending that she was more formally associated with the police than she was to make sure that his boss would let him come in. Then she called the actual police.

"Sherry," Sheriff Brown said. "I was just at your house."

"I know," Sherry said. "I thought you might have been. I'm at the library. Could you please come here? In about"—she checked her watch—"thirty minutes?"

There was a long pause on the other end of the line. "Why?"

"To make an arrest," Sherry said.

Another pause. "Of who? You?"

"No," Sherry said. "Well, maybe, if you want to. For trespassing. But I want you to arrest Alan's murderer."

He sighed. It crackled through the receiver. "You've found him?"

"I really hope that I have," Sherry said. "If I haven't, you're going to be the least of my problems. Are you going to come?"

"Do I have a choice?" Sheriff Brown asked, and then hung up before she could come up with anything snappy to say in response.

Sherry sat in the comfortable chair near the computer room and tried not to fidget too much. She always got horribly nervous right before she pointed her finger at someone and said, "*You.*" There was always the same sickening lurch in her gut right as she named her suspect aloud for the first time, like the moments just before the roller coaster went over the first drop, when she inevitably, desperately thought, *I wonder if they'll stop the ride if I scream.*

They wouldn't stop the ride, of course. There were things that you just had to see through once you started them. This thing she was doing tonight was one of them. She'd started it off, and now she had to ride it all the way to the end.

There was a knock on the closed library door. Sherry answered it. It was Janine. God bless Janine. Sherry had been icing her out of the investigation a bit—she was just so *skeptical*—but of course she was the first to arrive when Sherry needed her. Now, having had the realization that the demon had trapped them all in a strange time warp, Sherry could suddenly recognize why she'd sometimes had the confusing urge to laugh when she saw Janine: while everyone else's outfits seemed to tend toward the blandly timeless, Janine was purely, delightfully late eighties: today she was wearing enormous white earrings and a turquoise turtleneck under her long white coat. Sherry gave her a big hug. "I think I've done something pretty stupid, Janine," she said into Janine's shoulder. She smelled like fancy old-fashioned perfume.

Janine hugged her gently back. "What did you do?"

"Called all of my suspects and asked them to come here," Sherry said. A small, hysterical little laugh escaped her chest. "Not *you*, you're moral support. Most of the rest of them are suspects. I'm pulling a Poirot."

"A what?" Janine asked, and pulled back to look at her. A moment later her heavily shadowed eyes went wide. "Oh, no. You mean the part at the end? When he calls everyone together and explains who did it?"

Sherry nodded. Janine sighed. "I really hope you know what you're doing, Sherry. Did you ask the sheriff to be here, at least?"

"I don't," Sherry said. "And I did."

Janine gave Sherry a look that told her *exactly* what she thought of Sherry trying to be clever. "So he's coming? That's something. We don't want to end up with bodies in the library."

"That was a Poirot, I think," Sherry said, with another helpless giggle. "Or a Miss Marple? I don't remember. But I'll try to make it the opposite. No bodies in the library this evening."

No bodies in Winesap, either, she hoped, if she managed to accomplish what she wanted to tonight. "Tea?"

She made two big pots of tea in teapots that were still rattling around the office from last year's garden party, spurred on by a bizarre compulsion to be a good hostess despite what she was planning. She set the tea things up in the meeting room. The rest of her guests and suspects started trickling in. Father Barry arrived, and Alice. The Thompsons showed up in one cautious bunch, with Todd there to lead them. Charlotte arrived and planted herself close to Sherry's side. Jason came in, looking baffled and anxious, his hands shoved deep into his pockets. Then, finally, the sheriff arrived, slipping quietly into the room as if he was hoping not to be noticed.

For a moment after he'd arrived, Sherry just stood there like an uncomfortable plus-one at a wedding. Then she pulled herself together and cleared her throat. "If you could all head into the meeting room in the back, please? Thank you."

They all shuffled in a murmuring mass into the back and took their seats; all except Jason, who leaned against the wall close to the door like he wanted to be prepared to make a fast escape. Janine sprang into action to help Sherry pass the teapots around. Some people refused it with looks of dramatic disbelief that anyone could drink tea under these circumstances, but others filled their cups. There was a muted clinking of spoons. Corey was the first to crack and speak. "What exactly are we doing here, Miss Pinkwhistle?"

Sherry gave a smile that she hoped looked calm and confident rather than like the bared teeth of a submissive chimpanzee. "I know that it's a little strange," she said, "but I've asked you all to come here today because one of you killed Alan Thompson."

TWENTY-FOUR

Everyone started talking at the same time. It was just like in an Agatha Christie. Sherry wondered whether that was from demonic interference. Probably not: probably the chaos that ensued after you'd just announced that you were pulling a Poirot was the natural, organic reaction from any normal group of people. "Oh, come on, seriously? Like some kind of Sherlock Holmes thing?" This was Corey again. "If you know who killed Dad, then why didn't you just call the police?"

"I did," Sherry said. "Sheriff Brown is right here with us." She gave him a nod and received a slightly reluctant-looking nod back. Then she spoke directly to the demon. "There's someone also in the room with us who I think may have been . . . involved with some of the strange things that have happened recently in Winesap. I hope that my doing this will encourage that person to speak with me, as we agreed they would."

Everyone was staring at her. Father Barry very discreetly made the sign of the cross. Sherry swallowed and thought her way back to every old-fashioned detective story she'd ever read or seen. They did this with flair, usually. She suspected that the demon liked flair very much. Fine: that's what she'd try to provide.

"It was very clear from the crime scene that Alan knew and trusted his killer," she began. "He invited them inside and made tea for them before he died. Everyone in this room knew Alan well enough for him to have willingly let them in late on a snowy Saturday night. Almost everyone in this room might have profited in one way or another from Alan's death. I wasn't short of motives in this case. The problem was that there were too many people who might have benefited from his getting sick or having an accident, but no clear individual who both had the opportunity to kill him last Saturday night, and who was truly desperate enough to follow through and kill a man who was in the process of serving them a cup of tea."

She let her eyes flick over the assembled people. Some looked away, some at the table. Jason looked fidgety and anxious. Alice looked close to tears. Mrs. Thompson was stonefaced; Eli was glancing around the room like he thought there might be secret cameras recording the scene. Corey was scowling. Todd gazed straight back at her, looking amused and engaged by the proceedings, as if he'd paid for a night at the murder mystery dinner theater and was already enjoying the show.

She continued. "In an investigation like this, the first people that the police look at are usually the victim's nearest and dearest. I'll begin in the same way, with Alan's wife and children."

"This is bullshit," Corey said. Sherry ignored him and continued.

"All of Alan's immediate family members profited enormously from his death. None of them were rich a month ago, but with Alan gone, all three of them are millionaires. Out of everyone here, Susan Thompson might have one of the strongest motives for wanting her husband dead. He broke up their marriage after many years together, then refused to come to what she felt would be equitable terms in their divorce. People sometimes kill their exes just for revenge, but in this case, she'd also finally be getting the money that he'd been denying her for years. She was also seen with Alan on the day that he died. There was also Eli, the older son. I got the sense that Eli must have been used to his father taking him for granted. There he was, working hard every day at the office to provide for his family, while his father regularly handed cash to his younger brother.

"The only problem with either of them as suspects is that they both have strong alibis. I made some phone calls this afternoon and was able to confirm that Susan Thompson attended a gala and Eli Thompson was enjoying beers with his running club in Connecticut. Though it might be theoretically *possible* that one of them managed to slip away, get up to Winesap, kill Alan, and then get back home again without anyone noticing, it seems *unlikely* that either of them could have done it in time."

She looked toward Corey. He was still scowling, his arms folded over his chest. It made him look much less attractive than he was in his Instagram pictures. "Corey Thompson," Sherry said, "was the son that his father worried about. He has a history of asking his father for money, and his father had a history of paying up. Alan was very happy when Corey started expressing interest in working with him for the antiques shop, and he was absolutely delighted when it seemed that Corey had a real aptitude for sourcing and framing fairly valuable pieces of fine art to resell. By the time Alan died, Corey was practically co-owner of the shop."

She took a sip of tea, then continued. "Corey has all of the million-dollar motivation for murder that his mother and brother have, on top of an interest in his father's business, and a very expensive lifestyle to maintain. What he lacks is an alibi. Is that accurate, Corey? Is there anyone who could confirm where you were on the night your father died?"

His scowl deepened. "No," he said shortly. "I was home alone. I'd been out late Friday night and didn't feel like doing anything."

"Thank you," Sherry said. "We've established that young Corey has motive, and he doesn't have an alibi. Those are two points against him. What *doesn't* exist is any evidence that he was here, in Winesap, at any time when he could have committed the crime. I'd therefore like to set him aside for now.

"Now that we've moved on from Alan's immediate family, we need to consider other people in his life who might have wanted to see him dead for one reason or another. Friends, lovers, employees. Alan had a few friends in Winesap, but none of them would have any reason to have a grudge against him, and none had any financial entanglements with him that I could discover. He also had an employee, Alice, and a—girlfriend. Me."

Her face felt hot. She continued, anyway. "I've claimed to have never known that Alan was still married, or that he'd left me his house in his will." She had to pause for a moment at the muted murmur in the room at that. "It would be reasonable to doubt me. Jealousy or desire to inherit a million-dollar estate would both be very convincing reasons for a woman to want to kill her boyfriend. I was also the last person to have seen Alan alive. For both of those reasons, I should probably be the biggest suspect in the case."

The room was very quiet. Janine leaned in closer to Sherry's side as if she was preparing to catch her if she suddenly collapsed. Sherry continued. "There's also Alice. On the day he died, Alan mentioned to me that he was unhappy with Alice's performance at work. Could he have fired Alice earlier that day? Alice had been struggling with money, and having been fired might keep her from being able to claim unemployment benefits."

"He didn't fire me," Alice said.

Everyone turned to look at her. Alice shrank back into her chair, visibly diminished by the attention. "He didn't," she said, almost in a whisper. "He said he felt like I was zoning out a lot lately. I said I would try to do better. That's all that happened."

"We only have your word for that, though it does fit with what Alan said to me," Sherry said, as kindly as she could under the circumstances. "What's more important is that you have a fairly strong alibi. Both of us do." She addressed the wider room. "Alan's estimated time of death was between ten and midnight. He dropped me off at home at about ten fifteen, and I walked across the street to talk to Alice before I went home and went to bed. She woke me up again at a quarter after midnight to ask me for my help after her power went out. Neither Alice nor I own a car. In good weather it takes about forty-five minutes to walk from where we live to Alan's house, and more than an hour to walk back. I couldn't have possibly killed Alan at ten and walked up to have a chat with Alice a few minutes later, and she couldn't possibly have talked to me, walked down there, talked to Alan, killed him, and walked back again all in under two hours in the middle of a blizzard.

Barring a conspiracy between the two of us, or between one of us and an unknown getaway driver, I'm prepared to set aside both Alice and myself as suspects for now."

"Oh, come *on*," Corey burst out. "You can't just rule yourself out as a suspect. Is everyone seriously letting her get away with this? This is *crazy*."

"I don't know," Todd said. "I think we should let her finish. Maybe at the end she'll reveal that she was the killer all along and tell the sheriff to slap the cuffs on her and haul her away." Todd, at least, seemed to be enjoying himself.

"Thank you, Todd," Sherry said. "I promise that I do have a point to make with all of this. Everyone should have some more tea, if they want it. We're just about to get into the complicated parts."

Someone gave a very quiet groan. Others took her advice. Tea was poured. "My next suspect is probably unfamiliar to those of you who don't live in Winesap," Sherry said. "Jason Martinez works at the diner here in Winesap. He met Alan many years ago, when Alan was working as a public defender in Schenectady. Jason was accused of murder, and Alan mishandled the case so badly that Jason was sent to prison for several years for a crime that he didn't commit."

This caused a small, brief commotion as Alan's family reacted. Alan really had done a good job of keeping it a secret: it was clear from their expressions that Alan's sons were both dismayed by the news. Todd was craning around to look at Jason, who was still standing by the door. "I didn't do it, though," Jason said. He was looking very steadily right back at Sherry. "You know that I didn't, Miss Pinkwhistle. I'm not a murderer. You know that."

She flushed again but didn't respond. She was going to

finish what she'd started no matter how guilty anyone tried to make her feel about it. "The motive, in this case, doesn't have to be explained. Revenge. We also know that Jason lives only about a mile and a half from Alan's house, so it wouldn't have taken him very long to get there and back. His only alibi comes from his own wife. So far, he still seems like a viable suspect, until we come to the old lady who lives across the street, and her neighbor's horrible Chihuahua."

"A mysterious hound!" Todd stage-whispered. Charlotte made a noise that sounded very much like she was struggling not to laugh.

Sherry ignored them. "Mrs. Sherman is elderly, but her hearing is excellent, and she's a very light sleeper. Her next-door neighbor has a small dog who frequently wakes her up by barking at pedestrians. On the night in question the dog didn't bark. Jason couldn't have left his house on foot that night, even if he'd *wanted* to choose the evening of his wife's birthday to struggle through a blizzard on foot in order to get revenge on a man who had wronged him—though very seriously—many years ago. If Jason Martinez killed Alan, he must have driven there."

"*So?*" Corey asked. "So he drove there, then."

"Yes, that's what I would have assumed," Sherry said. "Until I got a chance to look at his truck. The Martinez family only owns one vehicle. I'd noticed over the past two weeks that I kept hearing what I first thought was a motorcycle driving through Winesap about half an hour after the diner closed. When I walked past Jason's truck I checked to see if my hunch was right and saw that his muffler is missing. If it was missing on the night Alan was killed, his driving back and forth between ten thirty and midnight would have been more than loud enough to disturb his insomniac neighbor, but she went to bed at nine that night and slept through until the morning. Jason, did you try to get that muffler repaired any time before Saturday?"

Jason's entire body relaxed. He smiled, then stepped forward, pulled out a chair, and sat down at the table with everyone else. He even grabbed the nearest teapot and a cup. "Yeah," he said. "It fell off on the highway a few weeks ago. I went to my guy on Route 20 about it, but he had to order a part, so I've just been driving around like that. You can call him and ask, he'll have the records and everything."

"Thank you, Jason," Sherry said, and gave him a small smile. Then she said to the room, "It might not hold up in a court of law, but considering that we don't have any other evidence to suggest that Jason was with Alan that night, on top of his wife insisting that he was home, I feel confident in crossing Jason off of my suspect list."

"At this rate you're going to run out of suspects," Todd said. "Unless the surprise twist at the end is going to be that it was the butler who did it all along."

"Oh, don't worry about that," Sherry said pleasantly. "I still have a few suspects left to go through. Like you, for example."

Todd raised his eyebrows. *"Me?"*

Sherry nodded, smiled politely, and continued, addressing the whole room again. "This is the point when this case gets complicated. There were other crimes being committed beyond the murder, and they involve three people, two of whom are in the room with us right now: Corey Thompson and Todd McCarthy. The third, Mr. Mike Kaminski, lives and works down in the city."

"I'm not listening to this," Corey said, and stood as if he was planning on storming out. Then his mother's hand shot out and caught his wrist.

"I think that you should, Corey."

Corey went very red and settled silently down into his seat again. Susan Thompson gave Sherry a short nod. "Go ahead, Sherry."

Sherry's throat felt oddly tight. "Thank you, Susan," she managed, and swallowed. "I first started thinking that something strange might be going on when Alan told me about how incredibly well Corey had been doing at finding art for the shop. It just seemed unlikely that someone would be able to so consistently find pieces that would be snapped up for hundreds or thousands of dollars up here in little Winesap. It wasn't quite strange enough to make a fuss over, though. Corey wasn't bringing back any Van Goghs. Everything was just on this side of reasonable. That's what I thought at first. That's what Alan thought, too, until the day that he started getting suspicious.

"I'm not sure what first made Alan think that something wasn't right, but he definitely suspected that there was something strange going on in his shop. Before he died, he'd been clearly worried about something involving the business, he'd checked out a number of books on art appraisal and contemporary American artists from the library, and he'd been poring over the books for the shop. I think he was looking for inconsistencies between the pieces that were coming in, their provenance, and the prices that Corey was asking for them. And there *were* inconsistencies. But what, exactly, was going on?"

She took a gulp of tea, partially to wet her dry mouth and partially so she could take a moment to get her thoughts together before she continued to speak. "As I said, there were three people involved, though it took me a while to establish a connection. I first noticed that something was off when Todd, Father Barry's twin brother, arrived in town appearing to already know Corey Thompson, Alan's son. They claimed that they'd met only very recently at a party and coincidentally bumped into each other again on the train up to Saratoga. I very quickly learned that this was a lie. They've known each other for at least six months, on what seems to have been fairly intimate terms. Why would they feel the need to lie about that? Both of them are single. Corey's family have known that he's gay since he was very young. There's no obvious reason for them to want to downplay their connection unless they have something else to hide. I decided to dig into that."

"Maybe I just value my privacy, Sherry," Todd said. "I don't like letting everyone on the planet know more than they need to know about my personal life."

"Yes, I'd noticed that about you," Sherry said. "Corey posts practically everything he does on the internet, but you keep things much more private. I did learn a few things about you, though. You have a very colorful criminal record, for such a young man. That one romance scam that got you in the papers was very clever. Cruel, but clever."

Todd shrugged. "That was years ago," he said. "I was young, broke, and stupid. I've grown up since then."

"You've definitely gotten less stupid," Sherry said. "From what I've seen. Anyway. While I was digging, I found something else interesting: you've known Mike Kaminski for many years. Mr. Kaminski," she said to the room, "is an antiques dealer, and the man who seems to have purchased a large percentage of the items that Corey brought into the shop. Alice, who works in the shop, mentioned to me that he was recently very annoyed when he learned that Alan had taken home one of the pictures in a set of small, realistic charcoal drawings of Western scenes that Mr. Kaminski had wanted to purchase. I didn't think anything about that, really, until I looked into his shop and realized that nothing that he sells looked even remotely similar to small charcoal cowboy drawings. So why was he so desperate to purchase a full set of them?

"I looked into him some more and learned something interesting. Mr. Kaminski has a criminal past of his own. Specifically, many years ago he served eighteen months in prison for possession of cocaine with intent to distribute. The police suspected him of involvement with a larger organization but couldn't make the charges stick."

She looked around the room. Corey was stiff in his chair, his eyes fixed rigidly on the table. Todd was relaxed, comfortable, still watching Sherry as if he was having a night at the theater.

"Here's what I think happened," Sherry said. "Todd met Corey some time ago. Maybe six months ago, maybe a year or more. He learned that Corey was a talented artist who wasn't doing much with his skills and was living far, far beyond his means. He learned that Corey took frequent trips to the Caribbean on a wealthy friend's yacht. He learned that Corey's father ran a small antiques store up in Winesap, where Todd's twin brother, Barry, just happened to be preparing to take over as the parish priest. Todd himself was unemployed, increasingly aware that relying on older ladies and gentlemen to pay for his incidentals was a way of life with an expiration date, and looking for a new route to easy cash. He was friends with Mike Kaminski, who he knew still had connections in the drug trade. I suspect that Mr. Kaminski never stopped selling cocaine: as he got into the antiques and design business and started socializing with the people whose homes he helped to decorate, he merely restricted his sales to his own circles, and the police don't pay much attention to what rich people and their pet artists do at parties. Todd, being in the same circles, would have been aware of this.

"Eventually Todd came up with a scheme: Mr. Kaminski would reach out to his contacts to find a source of cocaine in the Caribbean. Corey, with money he'd asked for from his father plus possibly a contribution from Todd, acquired the drugs on his next trip with his friend. At some point he would have also gotten very busy creating convincing-enough-looking framed works of art by moderately well-known dead artists that he would bring to his father's shop, along with other works of art that he had purchased elsewhere and would be much more moderately priced. The fake pieces would then be purchased by Mr. Kaminski, who would distribute the drugs down in the city. The goal was to make pieces of art that an ordinary person wandering into an antiques store in Winesap would never consider purchasing for the marked price, but that could, plausibly, be sold for that much to enthusiasts or discerning resellers like Mr. Kaminski. They did it this way just in case Alan got curious or suspicious and started looking up the artists whose works he was supposedly selling: he'd find out that, yes, this artist existed, and that similar-looking works of theirs sold for a similar price. He'd be unlikely to pursue it any further after that. The whole thing fit together perfectly: the money coming to Corey would be laundered through the shop, and Mr. Kaminski had his own business to make everything look nice and reasonable on his end. Todd probably negotiated a cut from Corey's share. The one thing that they didn't think to factor in was the fact that Alan, who loved Westerns, would like one of his son's charcoal drawings so much that he'd willingly pay the shop the massively inflated price to bring it home with him and hang it on his living room wall."

There was a box of tissues on the table. Sherry pulled a tissue from the box and used it to grip the framed charcoal drawing in her bag and hand it across the table to Sheriff Brown. "Sheriff," she said, "would you please open up the back of the drawing?"

The sheriff did so silently, peeling away the paper and then popping out the cardboard backing. Behind the cardboard, packed tightly into the frame, were dozens of small plastic bundles of white powder.

TWENTY-FIVE

I think that you're very likely to find Corey Thompson's fingerprints on the bags," Sherry said.

"Mom—" Corey started. His mother squeezed his wrist again.

"Not until you have a lawyer with you," she said, and fixed Sherry with her cool blue stare. "That's drug trafficking," she said. "Not a murder."

"I know," Sherry said. "I'm getting to the murder bit." Then she winced. That had sounded incredibly insensitive. "Sorry," she said, and then quickly moved on. "Alan was suspicious of what was going on in his shop, and he had a substantial amount of cocaine hidden in a picture frame hanging on his living room wall. I don't think that he'd found the drugs, but I also think that it would have seemed like a ticking bomb to the men involved in the scheme. Any one of them would have had a strong motivation to go see Alan that night to try to shut him up permanently." She regretted that turn of phrase as soon as she said it. It was hackneyed. She cleared her throat. "Which of them could have done it? Of the three of them, Mr. Kaminski is the one with the strongest and most obvious alibi. He was in Manhattan that evening, enjoying scotch and cigars with six other men. There are photos of them together, the cigar lounge confirmed that he was there that night, and he happily sent me copies of his receipts. So much for Mr. Kaminski.

"What about Todd McCarthy? He doesn't seem to have a clear alibi for that night on first glance. He was, in fact, one of my top suspects, until I heard that Father Barry has been spending lots of time with wealthy old ladies late into the evenings recently."

Father Barry practically jolted out of his chair. "*What?* I didn't—"

Sherry interrupted him. "Father, did you receive a message from Mrs. Walker or her assistant, Karen, recently?"

He blinked, then nodded. "A few weeks ago, I think. I'd gone to visit with her a few times, then one day I got a letter saying that she wouldn't be able to see visitors for a while because her health had taken a turn for the worse, and that she'd call if anything changed. I thought it was a little strange when the whole point is for me to minister to the sick, but I didn't want to be pushy."

"I thought it might have been something like that," Sherry said. "At first, I took it at face value as slightly odd behavior for a priest. Then I met Barry's twin, and I heard that Father Barry had been at a very rich old lady's house until nearly midnight on the night Alan was killed. Just before I heard this, Father Barry himself mentioned to me that he'd been up late that night feverishly trying to finish writing a homily for the next morning. I suspect that the person visiting Mrs. Walker that night was, in fact, Todd, and that his alibi for Alan's murder is that he was too busy trying to defraud an old lady at the time to be the person responsible."

"*Todd,*" Barry said.

Todd laughed. It was a small, muted laugh, but still definitely a laugh. "Sorry," he said, and straightened in his chair. He was still twinkling a little around the eyes. "I was with Mrs. Walker that night," he said. "Barry had complained about her to me before, so I thought it would be fun to take over from him and do a little ministering of my own. She had a great time. It's not illegal to pretend to be your twin brother as a prank when all you do is cheer up a lonely old hypochondriac for a few hours."

"Hm," Sherry said. She didn't really know what else to say. He was, as far as she knew, technically correct. Impersonating a police officer was a crime: impersonating a priest was not. "And you can prove that you were at Mrs. Walker's house all evening?"

"You can always ask her," he said. "Ask her if she told Father Barry a story about pretending she didn't recognize Truman Capote at a party in 1976. Actually, ask her to tell you the whole story. It's a good one."

"I'll do that," Sherry said, aiming for severity and possibly missing. Todd had a terrible history of taking advantage of people who'd been taken in by his charm, but the charm itself was fairly hard to deny. "That's two of the three eliminated, then. The one man involved in the little drug ring who doesn't have an alibi is also the one man most closely linked to both Alan and the crimes, who would have the most to lose, and who Alan would allow into his home without hesitation at any time of the day or night." She looked straight at Corey then, and waited.

Corey had gone very, very pale. His mother was gripping his arm again. "We're leaving," she said, moving as if to stand up. "And calling our lawyer."

"I wouldn't leave just yet," Sherry said. She was surprised by how firmly she said it. It came out confidently enough that Susan sat firmly back down in her seat as if she'd been admonished by the teacher.

"Corey doesn't have an alibi," Sherry said. "On the other hand, there's no evidence that he was in his father's house that night at all. In fact, there's a very major piece of evidence that suggests that he *wasn't* there, and it's the same piece of evidence that's made his involvement in his little drug ring so obvious." She pointed across the table to the picture frame. "He was the person who framed that picture. Anyone who knew Alan well would have known that: Alan was very proud of what a craftsman Corey had turned out to be. If, at any point, someone discovered the cocaine packed into the back, it would be very obvious who was responsible. So why on earth would Corey kill his father in order to cover up his own involvement in a drug ring, but leave behind the piece of evidence that would have motivated the killing in the first place? To say nothing of all of that cocaine. It doesn't make any sense."

The entire room jolted slightly in their seats when quiet, responsible Eli Thompson slammed his hand down onto the table.

"That's *enough*," he said, and then took a deep breath. "I'm sorry, Miss Pinkwhistle. But this has been a really hard week for our family. I need you to get to the point."

Sherry's cheeks heated. "I was getting there," she said, and took a second to collect herself before carrying on. "As I was saying. It wouldn't make any sense for Corey to leave that picture behind—or, at least, to leave the cocaine inside of it. That bothered me, when I went back to Alan's house today. There were actually two other things that also bothered me when I went back to look at the crime scene again with all of my suspects firmly in mind. One thing that was missing, and two things that were there and shouldn't have been." She ticked them off on her fingers. "Missing: the financial records from Alan's shop that he said that he'd wanted to go over that night. Present: a pair of skis, with no ski boots to fit them, and a picture with hundreds of dollars' worth of cocaine stuffed into the frame."

Everyone in the room was staring blankly at her. She soldiered onward. "The missing books weren't taken away by the police, and Alan himself had planned on working on them that night. Either he hid them away because he was worried about someone taking them, or someone *did* take them. Why would someone take the books away? Presumably because they contained information that would look bad for the person who took them. Corey might fit there: all of those fake art sales would have been recorded. But how about those skis?"

Sherry stood up then. She hadn't planned on it. She was just too full of nervous energy to sit any longer. "Those skis bothered me. They didn't fit Alan's ski boots, and Alan was a very tidy, organized kind of guy. Everything in its place. When guests left things behind at his house, he'd stick little notes onto them to remind himself who they belonged to and that he needed to return them. So why was there a pair of skis in his porch with no ski boots to fit them? The answer, I think, makes all three of those puzzling objects fit into one story." She put her hands onto the table to try to stop them from shaking. "Alice Murdoch killed Alan Thompson, and it was partially my fault."

There was a wave of noise from the gathered crowd: it

crested quickly, then subsided just as fast, leaving the room in complete silence. Sherry started to pace now, her words coming faster. "Everyone in this room thinks of themselves as the protagonist of their own story. I'm no exception. I'd been thinking of myself as the hero of this show, as the detective main character, and so I didn't manage to really think about how things that I'd seen from my perspective could have looked very different from across the street.

"Here's what I think happened. Alice had been short of money for a long time. She worked long hours at the antiques shop, but she still barely made enough to cover her bare essentials every month. She knew that Alan was well off, and she knew that he was careless about keeping track of the finances for the shop. She probably felt a little resentful. Why should Alan live the high life off of her labor while she was practically drowning? She started to steal from the register. Not much, I don't think. Ten or twenty dollars here or there. Maybe she'd tell Alan that a customer had haggled for a discount, or that someone had handed her a ten instead of a fifty, but I think that she usually just fudged the math a little when she cashed out in the evenings. She probably got away with it for a while, until Alan started acting more interested in the books than he'd been before.

"That would have made her anxious. She would have worried that she was about to be fired, which would have impacted her behavior. Alan definitely noticed something: on the day he died he spoke to her about how she'd seemed distracted at work. I think that he might have already known that she'd been stealing a few dollars here or there, and that was his way of gently warning her that she needed to cut it out. That would have been like him. He was a very gentle, nonconfrontational man. Besides, he had much bigger problems to worry about: he was trying to figure out if his son had gotten his business mixed up in a full-on criminal enterprise. Alice's petty theft would have seemed like a pretty minor issue in comparison, and he'd want to give her the chance to quietly clean up her act before he'd consider firing her or getting the police involved.

"If that is what he was trying to communicate to her, then it would have gone over her head. Alice Murdoch isn't a young woman who's had much experience with gentle, forgiving, indirect men. She's someone who's always on high alert for danger. That's where I came in. That night, when I came by to give her the leftovers from my dinner with Alan, I mentioned how he'd been poring over the books. I only said it because I was gushing about my evening and how sorry I felt for poor Alan having to work late. Alice heard it as a threat. She was the protagonist to her own story: it never would have occurred to her that Alan could be concerned about something more important than her stealing cash from the register. She didn't know anything about Corey and Todd and their little upstate cocaine ring. She just panicked, thinking that she might be about to lose her job, and decided she needed to get to Alan to talk to him before he really dug into the books and realized that her math errors were always in the same direction.

"Here's another point where I failed to think beyond my own perspective. Alice and I provided each other's alibis that night. Neither of us own cars, and I knew for a fact that there was absolutely no way that I could have gotten down to Alan's and back in a blizzard within that two-hour window. What I completely failed to do is consider the fact that *Alice isn't me*. I'd seen skis in her front porch, but they'd been mixed up with all sorts of other things that I thought were just pieces of junk she'd accumulated. *I* don't know how to ski, and I was in the habit of thinking of Alice as this sort of hapless young thing who needed my help with everything. It didn't occur to me that she might be very good at something that I couldn't do at all. She is, though. I did a little digging into her background this afternoon and found some pictures of her in high school, working as an instructor for children at a ski resort."

Sherry stopped pacing then and turned to face her audience again. "From there, it's simple. Alice skied down the hill to Alan's house to talk to him. It would have taken a fraction of the time it would have taken her to walk: maybe only five minutes or so. He invited her in and made her tea, which is exactly the sort of thing that you would do for Alice if she showed up at your house seeming agitated late at night. She was probably pacing around the living room, trying to figure out what she should say to keep her job. He came in with the tea and said something that spooked her. Maybe something about how he was going to have to talk to the police soon. Alan was the protagonist of his story, as well. He was so wrapped up in thinking about Corey that it wouldn't occur to him that she might think he was threatening *her*. Whatever he said or did, as he was leaning over with the tea, she grabbed a brass table lamp and hit him on the back of the head."

Susan Thompson made a small, wounded sound. Sherry swallowed and pressed on. "She probably didn't mean to kill him. She was probably shocked. She thought quickly, though. She grabbed the account books but left the picture full of cocaine on the wall: she would have had no idea that there was anything special about it. She couldn't ski back up the hill again, and carrying the skis back would have slowed her down and made her look suspicious if anyone saw her, so she put her skis with Alan's so that they blended right in. Then she hurried back up the hill to her house, where she deliberately blew the power out so she'd have an excuse to come over to my house and establish an alibi."

"I didn't," Alice said. Her voice was small and wavering, but she spoke up, anyway. "I didn't do any of that. You just made it all up. Just because you saw some random skis, and you can't find some papers from the shop. That's not proof."

"She's right," Sheriff Brown said. "If it happened like you said, then she's had days to dump the evidence."

"I've thought about that, yes," Sherry said. "But there's a problem. Where would Alice dispose of the evidence? The accounts from the shop could be burned at the kitchen stove, maybe, but then there's the ski boots. She couldn't exactly flush them down the toilet. Tossing them into the woods somewhere risks them getting found."

"Just throw them away," Sheriff Brown said. "They could be under a foot of trash in the landfill by now."

"You'd think so," Sherry said. "But this is Winesap. There aren't sanitation workers who come to take the garbage away," she added, for the benefit of the city people present. "You have to drive your trash to the landfill on your own. The problem for me and Alice is that neither of us has a car, so we have to get someone else to do it. I have a guy who I'd hired to take mine away once a week, and when Alice arrived, I just paid him extra to start picking hers up as well. Normally he'd actually have come to get our garbage right about now."

"But now?" Sheriff Brown asked.

She allowed herself a small smile. "I called an hour ago to

cancel the pickup. If Alice tried to throw those boots away, they should still be in a garbage bag sitting next to her mailbox."

Alice gave a small, despairing groan and buried her face in her hands. "*Sherry*," she said. "*I thought that we were friends.*"

TWENTY-SIX

Somehow, the ordinary mechanisms of reality creaked, groaned, and began to move.

Sheriff Brown was the first to stand up and do something. He called out for his backup—the willing young man in question had apparently been waiting in the other room—and told him to go get Alice's garbage from where it had been left by her mailbox. The young man asked whether or not he would need a warrant for that, to which the sheriff, not very politely, replied that if you needed a warrant to pick up garbage, they would have to have a judge riding shotgun in all of the great state of New York's garbage trucks. Then he told Alice that he was bringing her in to the station for questioning. She didn't fight, didn't argue. There was a placidity to her. "I have a daughter," she said, before she was led away. "She's three. She's staying with my mom now. If Alan had called the cops on me and I got arrested, there's no way I could have gotten custody again."

Sherry didn't say anything in response. Instead, she watched, silent, as Sheriff Brown led Alice away. She had a plan. There was someone else for her to talk to. Poor, frightened little Alice. Poor everyone in Winesap. All of this had come to them along with Sherry's arrival in Winesap. She had a chance, tonight, to put it right.

The others, exchanging nervous glances, filed out after her. There was an atmosphere of strained uncertainty in the room. Usually in books and television shows the scene ended after the most dramatic point of confrontation, so no one had to figure out how to gracefully leave a gathering after someone was accused of murder and then marched away in handcuffs. There was a lot of polite, embarrassed mumbling. Jason was the first to leave, his head held high. Eli and Mrs. Thompson flanked Corey as if they were either his jailers or his bodyguards. Sheriff Brown would be visiting him in his bed-and-breakfast soon, Sherry assumed. Not that she cared that much either way. Drugs could cause a murder, but she was only concerned with the murder part. Corey was no longer her problem to solve. Todd left as well, after a brief, tense exchange with his twin. This whole evening, she thought, had managed to profoundly strain more than one family.

She herself didn't move. She felt less *worn-out* by her performance than *enervated*, as if it was beyond her to do so much as get up out of the chair she'd dropped into once the sheriff led Alice out. She just watched, still and quiet, as the room emptied out until only her friends were left. Father Barry, Charlotte, and Janine all hovered nearby, watching her as if they expected something else to happen.

She had to rally herself to speak. "You should all go home," she said. "It must be getting late."

Janine was frowning. "Only if you come home with me," she said. "The spare room has clean sheets on the bed."

"That's a great idea," Charlotte said immediately. "You look kind of . . . gray."

"Thanks," Sherry said automatically. "I'm fine. I just—need a minute. Could you all give me a minute? Please?" She was conscious of begging a little. "I just want a minute alone to . . . think." They wouldn't stop *looking* at her. She just needed them to leave her alone. She had a date.

Now they were all frowning. Janine was the first to step in again, in her brisk, no-nonsense way. "Right," she said. "I'm going to run to the diner to get you a hot chocolate and a grilled cheese sandwich. I'll bring it back here, you can eat it, and then you can come home with me. Father Barry, Charlotte, maybe the two of you could wait in the other room until I get back, in case Sherry needs something? No, Sherry, don't argue, I'm sure they'll be happy to wait for twenty minutes."

"We will be," Barry said immediately. "I think we might be able to find something to read if we need to pass the time."

Sherry made a small snorting noise by way of acknowledging that he had made a joke, then subsided back into just sitting there and staring dully into the air just past her face. *Leave*, she thought. She dimly noticed her friends exchanging worried glances. Then they retreated, and she was, finally, alone.

"You owe me an explanation," she said to the air. "A deal's a deal."

A portion of the air at the corner of the room began to thicken into something else. Like water or fog. She watched it, feeling her muscles tighten. *Run*, she thought. She didn't run. Instead, she waited, until the strange figure in the room with her finished taking shape. A tall woman with thick dark hair down to her waist. A loose green dress. Bare feet. A wide, lovely smile.

"Caroline?" she found herself saying, even though of course it wasn't. Caroline was much older now, and had never really been this beautiful. This was Caroline as she'd always existed in Sherry's imagination. Her lovely, charming, bewitching liar of a best friend.

"Of course," the spirit said. Her voice wasn't quite Caroline's, either. The face of the creature looked young, but the voice sounded old. Not old like Sherry was. Old like an abandoned well. "Isn't it always Caroline with you, Sherry?"

Throughout her entire ridiculous Poirot performance, Sherry had somehow managed to never take off her coat. She was glad she was wearing it now. It was cold. "I don't know what that's supposed to mean," she said. Then she said, "Who are you? What do you want? Why are you doing this?"

"I'm not who," the demon said. "I am, only, and have been, and will be, and all I want is a little amusement."

"What?" Sherry said. She felt like she must be very slow.

"I liked the stories," the creature said, almost dreamily. "The ones that woman wrote. And then the ones on the television. They were such clever stories. You had to guess who did it, and it was never who you thought it was going to be, and then at the end the mustache man explained everything. Like you did, just now. I liked that very much. You did such a good job, like the mustache man."

"Poirot," Sherry said. "I thought you might like that. So—you just like stories? Mystery stories?"

"They pass the time," the spirit said. "There's so much time, isn't there? It piles up. You little persons, you think I care about you. You think that I care about your immortal souls. *Those* aren't interesting. I've never even seen one. They don't pass any time at all, and I have so *much* of that."

"You were bored," Sherry said.

"*Yes*," the creature said. It looked pleased that she understood. "I'm so *bored*. And I ran out of stories. There's so much more time than stories. All I had was time. Time and a little bit of power over the minds of the little persons. So I decided to make my *own* stories."

"I'd wondered," Sherry said. "It seemed like that. Like a play. But why Winesap?"

"Because of you, of course," the demon said. "You were perfect. A librarian, that's perfect. I wanted a librarian. I had to look a long time to find you. A librarian who knows about the stories. A librarian who knows how to act in one. Not this very clever kind with the purple hair on the head and the silver ring in the nose. The *proper* kind, like in a book. That's the kind I wanted. Just like you. You felt so special when you got to help with a murder. You felt like you were really *alive*. A nice old lady librarian who'd run away to a nice little town to get away from what she'd done, but you didn't *really* feel guilty. You were just afraid of getting into trouble. You *loved* getting to do a murder with your Caroline. All I did was give you more of it. More murder, and more Caroline, and more getting to feel *so* important. Didn't you like it?" it asked, as if it was genuinely expecting a response in the affirmative.

Sherry's face was so hot. It felt ridiculous to blush at what a demon said, but she couldn't keep from blushing. "What are you talking about? *More Caroline?* I haven't seen her in years."

"But she's always there, in your little stories," the demon said. "Most murders are so *boring.* They don't have a feminine touch. One man shoots another man over drug money, and the police catch him twenty minutes later while he's still running down the street with the gun in his hand. That's not a story. That's just an *incident.* That's not what *your* stories are like. There's always a Caroline in yours. A woman who needs to be saved, or a woman who needs to be punished, and always all sorts of plots and schemes and lies. Caroline was very good at lies. They kept you from being bored, just like my stories. You didn't let her go, when you left her, so now I've given you more of what you loved so much about her. All of the Caroline that you need."

"But *you* made all of this happen," Sherry said. "I didn't take over this town and trap everyone here and make everyone forget what year it is and force people to murder each other. That was *you*, not me."

"I didn't *force*," the demon said. It sounded offended. "I never *forced*. I just *suggested*. I hinted to the little persons what they *could* do. It was up to them what they *did*. And then I let you solve the murders. The only thing I forced was no killing in the library. I wouldn't like that. To get blood on the stories. It would make it harder to read them."

"Oh," Sherry said. "That makes sense." Then she said, "I'm not doing this anymore, you know."

"Yes, you are," the demon said, very pleasantly. "You're good at it. You like it. You'll keep solving the murders and making the stories. We won't be bored ever again."

It felt as if it would be easy to agree. The demon wasn't wrong, not really. Sherry did like it. She *loved* it. And she was good at it. The trouble was all that death. The demon had threatened her into investigating before, but she knew the truth now. Nudges. The point of the murders was her investigations. The stories. If the investigations stopped, the killings would have no point. She could make Alan's murder the last of its kind, in Winesap, if she was brave enough. She didn't feel brave enough. When she opened her mouth to speak, she felt surprised even while she was doing it. "I can't," she said. "I'm sure that you understand. You said before that I'm like that detective in those stories you like. I'm like him in more than one way. I don't approve of murder."

"I don't care about you," the demon said, and it was closer to her. It didn't step closer. It just was. "I said that I *didn't* force," it said. "But I can. And I will."

Sherry lifted her chin. Her legs were shaking. "Try it," she said.

The demon climbed into her.

It was a strange feeling, to have your entire self erased. It started from her childhood. Her mother vanishing, and her father. Opening presents under a pink plastic Christmas tree. Trying out for a solo in the recital and not getting it. Digging in the grass of the backyard. Pushing broccoli to the very edge of her plate. Big things. Little things. The demon rifled through them and then discarded them. Her first kiss. Her wedding day in a modern Methodist church that she'd always thought was ugly. In the car with Caroline, the rain pounding on the windshield. Everything but the most essential parts for the character it needed her to play. The nice librarian in the small town. The tea and toast. The marmalade cat. The circle of quirky but loyal friends. No will, and no fury. No capacity to notice the endless, pointless deaths.

The demon settled into her skin and flexed its new muscles. It stretched, and popped her neck. "I can do this whenever I want," it said, with Sherry's mouth. "Wouldn't you rather just be good for me, instead of making me take charge like this?"

Sherry couldn't quite remember how this had happened, or why. For a long moment she didn't think anything or feel anything at all. Then something in a secret little corner of her brain pinged. "Do I have to investigate?" she asked. Her words slurred together. The demon had tightened up her tongue. "I can investigate. I'm good at investigating."

The demon sighed through her mouth. "Ah," it said. "Did I take too much of the mind away? It's so easy to break the little persons." It loosened its grip on her then. She could move her fingers again. "You *are* good at investigating," it said, warmly and sweetly. "Won't you keep doing it, Sherry?"

Sherry didn't reply. She was still wearing her coat. She put one of her newly freed hands into the pocket and closed her fingers around her yew dagger. She didn't have time to consider what she was about to do. *Hear me, protect us, deliver us from evil.* Sherry could only hope that she had been able to make it sharp enough. "No," she said. Then she yanked the dagger out of her pocket and, before either the demon or her own instincts could stop her, used both hands to stab it as hard as she could through her shirt, through the coral necklace, and into her own chest.

There was a blaze of pain, and even greater heat, heat that rushed through her hand and the dagger and into the necklace and her chest, a burn that circled her throat and poured straight into her heart. A howl came out of her mouth. She crashed down heavily onto one knee. The demon was tearing out of her like a Band-Aid being ripped off tender skin. Black wind was pouring out of her nose and mouth. It shrieked, then it giggled. *"Oh, clever,"* it whispered. *"Clever little person. You know the old stories, too. The old ones and the new ones. A wand of yew, and a sacrifice of blood, and a stake in a dark creature's heart. I'll abide by the rules, little person. The stories are no good if the rules aren't followed."* Sherry's whole body felt cold. The demon was still laughing. *"What a good ending it is,"* it said. *"Until next time, little friend."*

The room was suddenly quiet. Sherry's shirt felt wet.

"Ouch," she said aloud, just as someone kicked through the meeting room door, and she passed out.

TWENTY-SEVEN

The next few weeks were very, very strange, despite being the most ordinary weeks that anyone in Winesap had lived through in years.

She woke up in the hospital, feeling groggy, nauseous, and as if more time had passed than she would have preferred. It was very dark outside, and Father Barry was asleep in a chair in the corner. She tried to clear her throat, which turned into a cough, which made her head pound. Father Barry woke with a small start, looked toward her, and sighed. "You're awake!"

"So are you," she said. "How long was I out?"

"Just a few hours," he said. "Asleep, not unconscious. You were awake when I brought you here. They think you have a concussion, so that's probably why you don't remember."

She'd expected, *You lost a lot of blood.* She'd remembered the blazing heat and the stickiness of the blood on her shirt. She pressed a hand to her chest where she remembered having stabbed herself with the yew wand. It was a little tender, maybe, like there might be a bruise there. She blinked at him. "What happened, exactly?"

He hesitated. "I told the hospital that I was waiting for you to get your things together in the next room, then heard a crash, and went in to find you on the floor. They said that you probably fainted from low blood sugar and banged your head. You were . . . acting confused, so they decided to keep you overnight for observation."

"Acting confused," she repeated. "Do you mean—"

"Talking about how you'd stabbed yourself to get rid of the demon," he said.

"Oh," she said. Her face was warm. "You just said—what you told the hospital. Was that the same as what actually happened?"

He gave his head a quick, hard shake. "There were voices," he said quietly. "Not just you. There was someone else." He paused. "*Something* else. I couldn't open the door, even though you hadn't locked it. Then we heard this—horrible howling sound, so I kicked the door in."

"Wow," she said, smiling despite its making her head hurt more. "Charlotte must have liked that."

Father Barry turned pink. "She probably would have liked it better from my brother," he said, and cleared his throat. "They were here earlier, by the way. Charlotte and Janine. Then they left to go get your cat and some of your things from your house. Janine said she had a key. You're not supposed to exert yourself too much after a concussion, so we don't want you walking up and down that hill for a while. Janine said that you can stay in her spare room for as long as you need, and Charlotte has volunteered to take the cat if he's too much for you."

"He's no trouble," Sherry said. "As long as he doesn't talk." Then she went abruptly teary. "You're all being so nice."

"We're your friends," he said, and then smiled slightly. "And this sort of thing is technically part of the job description."

"That's true," she said. She felt as if she was slurring again.

Her eyelids were drooping. "Ministering to the possessed. And the dispossessed. After you've exorcised them."

"Is that what *dispossessed* means?" Father Barry asked. He stood up. "Get some sleep, Sherry. Janine will come get you in the morning, and I'll stop by to check on you."

"In the morning," Sherry mumbled, and fell asleep.

When she woke up again it was the morning, and a nurse desperately wanted to check her blood pressure. She permitted the woman to do so. Then Sheriff Brown walked in, holding his hat in his hand. He looked . . . different, somehow. Sherry wasn't sure if she could put her finger on how, exactly. *Relaxed*, maybe. Or maybe *at ease*. Like a seasoned performer who had finally reached the end of a long run of a particularly grueling show. "Sherry," he said. "I just wanted to let you know that we've cleared up the source of the poisoning."

"The what?" Sherry asked, baffled.

"You know," Sheriff Brown said, in the tone of voice of a man who really, truly *needed* Sherry to know. "The poisoning. The"—he paused for a fraction of a second—"ergot poisoning."

"The ergot poisoning," she repeated. "You mean—"

"Yes. The bakery got a delivery of tainted flour. And you know how popular those doughnuts are. The whole village lost its mind. We all thought—"

"That all of those people had been killed?" Sherry asked, her heart giving a leap up toward her chin.

"Oh, no," Sheriff Brown said hurriedly. "No, they're, ah, they're definitely dead. They died in the bus crash. Remember? That terrible bus crash?" Something in his expression caught and held her. *Please*, it seemed to say. *Please, say that you remember the bus crash.*

"Of course," Sherry said, after she took the moment she

needed to bite down on her cheek to keep herself from crying. "The—bus crash. With all of those people from Winesap on it. They were going . . ."

"Down to the city. To see a Broadway show."

"Right," Sherry said. "Of course. Alan did love going to see shows. How silly of me to have forgotten. It must have been the bump on the head. And then we all thought that there had been a string of murders? Because of the . . . ergot poisoning."

"Exactly," Sheriff Brown said. "It was all just a series of tragic accidents. It'll take a while to get it all sorted out. All of those people who I—who were arrested."

"Of course," she said. "But it will all get sorted out?"

He gave a firm nod. It seemed to her that he was blinking less than he normally would. "Yes, definitely. Since it was all down to the bus crash. Followed by the mass hallucination caused by ergot poisoning. The prosecutor's office is already working on it. They'll all be exonerated. There will probably be some sort of payout from the state, even."

"Good, good," Sherry said, and then looked him in the eye. "Isn't it nice. That there was such a tidy explanation for all of this, after all."

He looked straight back at her. "Yes, Sherry. It's very nice. I'm very glad that we won't need to look into any of those deaths any further. It's all over now. We can leave it alone."

"Right," she said. "I understand. Thank you for coming to see me and letting me know. About the source of the poisoning, I mean."

"You're welcome," he said, and put his hat back on. "And, Sherry—thanks. To you, too."

A bit of an impish impulse seized her for a moment. "What for?"

He gave her a long look. "For your donation to the police athletic league fundraiser. That was a really generous check. It will make a real difference to the kids."

She smiled despite herself. "Oh," she said. "You're welcome."

"Goodbye, Sherry."

"Goodbye, Peter," she said. She supposed she would have to write that check once she went home.

Her friends kept all their promises. Janine came to pick her up as soon as she was given the green light to leave, and Charlotte came by with Sir Thomas in his cat carrier a few hours later. The doctor at the hospital who discharged her had told her that she needed full rest for the next few days, body and brain both, so that was exactly what she did. It was wonderful that doing exactly what she felt at a bone-deep level she needed to do was now medically necessary.

On the first full evening of her doctor-ordered convalescence, she was enjoying a post-dinner doze—she had eaten wonton soup while sitting up in bed, which had felt like a level of decadence worthy of an unusually louche Roman emperor—when she was jolted awake by a familiar voice very close by her ear. "Are you awake, Mistress Pinkwhistle?"

Sherry said something that, if it could be spelled, would probably be spelled something like "*Unggblaughah?!*" and sat up again. Lord Thomas was sitting at the foot of her bed. He was wearing a green ribbon tied in a bow around his neck. She stared at him for a moment, goggle-eyed. "I am now," she said finally. "How did you get that ribbon on your neck?" *She* hadn't put it on him.

"I wear this ribbon in celebration of your great triumph

against the Ancient One!" the cat said in a voice so plummy you could use it to glaze a duck.

"Oh," Sherry said. "That's nice. But how did you *get it on*?" For some reason this was, at the moment, striking her as the really pressing point.

"By various methods," the cat said airily. "And now, thanks to our mutual efforts, I am free of her influence!"

"Oh," she said again. "That *is* nice. I'm happy for you." She meant it. The possibly evil spirit of possibly actual Lord Thomas Cromwell had, despite her best efforts, grown on her a little, in the same way that a shockingly pink mold had grown over a casserole that she'd put off clearing out of her fridge over the past few frantic weeks of demon hunting. All sorts of strange things could change in your life while you were fighting evil spirits. "What will you do next?"

"I will slip this mortal form and disport myself among the fairy folk, for a time," Lord Thomas said.

". . . Oh," Sherry said cautiously. "Like . . . a vacation?"

"*Yes!*" Lord Thomas said, and started kneading his little paws on her duvet. "How prettily you put it, Mistress Pink-whistle! I shall *go on vacation.*"

"That's great," Sherry said sincerely. "I hope you get a nice tan. So you won't be in my cat anymore?"

"I will vacate your cat entirely, so that you may stroke him at your pleasure," Lord Thomas said. "Although," he added, "if you have need of me, you need merely call my name with true intent, and I shall fly to your side. I now owe you a modest debt, Mistress Pinkwhistle."

"Should I call *Lord Thomas Cromwell*?" Sherry asked, feeling very clever, "or your *true* name?"

The cat's voice changed then. The silly TV-movie-Tudor

voice disappeared. Its voice now was a hiss and a meow, a mouse's dying squeak and the rustle of tall grasses. "You may not have my true name, mistress," it said. "But call me with intent, and I will come. Farewell to you, Mistress Pinkwhistle, giver of tuna cans, scratcher of ears, opener of the kitchen door to release me from my bondage."

"Goodbye," Sherry said. Her cat gave a slow blink. Then he rolled himself up into a ball and went to sleep. She watched him for a while. Then she went to sleep, too.

The next few days passed in the same way. She lay in bed, and listened to quiet music, and petted Lord Thomas's soft, warm sides until he stretched and purred. He didn't have a single rude thing to say. Why would he? Cats couldn't talk, after all. No one was murdered. An utterly horrified Janine demanded to know who'd been letting her leave her house in shoulder pads and bright-blue eye shadow. Sherry stopped ever seeing Charlotte without a cell phone either in her hand or very close to it. It came to Sherry's attention that, in the usual course of things, running the library involved a shocking number of extremely boring budget talks and board meetings that the demon had apparently dispensed with as not essential for plot purposes. Winesap went about its business like a nice, sleepy little rural town should.

Eventually, Sherry was well enough to move back into her house and get back to ordinary things again. She worked a few shifts at the library (poor Connie was still tasked with all of the meetings, for now), beat back the new spring weeds that were starting to sprout in the garden, and made a few cautious ventures into Alan's house to attempt to start organizing his things. She reached out to Eli to find out if he or his children wanted anything from the house. He didn't reply, so she did her best to start sorting out the things that might have sentimental value and organize them tidily away into the basement. She'd told herself that she didn't want Alan's house, that she'd never move in, but that was a lie. It was a beautiful house, it was much closer to the library, and it had been left to her by someone she'd loved. She could admit that now. She'd loved Alan, in her own way, and he seemed to have loved her back. It was too late to have realized it. It was something, at least.

One morning, as she sat in her living room dawdling over a cup of tea and a novel, her old landline started to ring.

That was strange. Ever since the demon left, everyone had gone back to using their cell phones as if they'd never stopped, even though she'd had to exchange numbers with her newer friends. Father Barry sometimes texted her memes, which she always found funny even when she didn't get the joke, because a priest sending memes reminded her of the time she'd seen a small dog in Manhattan wearing four tiny red leather shoes. Probably because of its lack of capacity to send memes as well as call people, her landline had been quiet for days. But now it was ringing. It was a number she recognized. Once she'd left the fog that the demon had created, she'd been able to search the internet to try to find where the number she'd used to call Caroline was from, and had learned that the number was from Eastern Europe: further research suggested that she might be using an internet service for calling and changing the country code to mask her location. It was a comfort, in a way, to think that whatever Sherry's best friend's flaws had been, the woman had never been stupid.

She answered it. On the other end of the line, Caroline said, "Sherry? Is that you?"

Sherry was lucky that her landline's cord was long enough for her to sit down hard in her armchair without pulling it out of the wall. She did so. "Caroline?"

Caroline gave that familiar laugh of hers. Her laugh that said they were both in on the joke. Then she said, "Wow, Sherry, I've *missed* you."

"I've missed you, too," Sherry said. "That's why I called. I've been thinking about you all the time. I know you probably don't want to tell me too much, but—how are you?"

That was all it took. It wasn't surprising, really. Caroline had always loved to talk about herself, and she'd always taken it for granted that Sherry would listen in wide-eyed fascination to every word that she said. And she wasn't wrong about that, was the embarrassing thing. Sherry always had orbited Caroline like a wayward bit of space station. Not now, though. Not exactly. She was listening as attentively as ever, but she wasn't letting herself get caught up in the narrative as Caroline spoke, as much as she would have enjoyed letting herself sit back and be swept away with the dark river, and the thick rubbery leaves of the trees, and the sudden shock of a macaw against the sky. Caroline talked about music, and rice and beans with a view of the beach, and meeting hippies and travelers and American retirees who'd settled in the same place that she'd chosen.

Caroline was very careful not to name a single person or place, but Sherry had expected that. Sherry listened. Sherry asked questions. *Do you ever sit on the beach to watch the sunset? I hate how dark it is here all winter. Is it any brighter there? Does it rain much? Have you had any trouble communicating with the locals?* She also took very, very careful notes. The way that Caroline described the monkeys. How long it took her to walk to the beach, and how long into town. The types of bars and restaurants she mentioned. The distance she had to travel to get to a store that sold the kinds of foods she missed from home. Sherry wrote it all down, as quickly and precisely as she could, until eventually Caroline stopped mid-sentence and said, "Oh, God, I'm going to be late! I'll call you back soon, Sher. Love you!"

"I love you, too," Sherry said to the dead air on the other end of the line. Caroline had hung up on her. Then she packed up her notebook and headed down to the library.

The computer room was open again, and constantly bustling now, full of people industriously scanning family photos or printing out boarding passes in preparation for their long-anticipated first trips to Italy or Cancún. It felt nice, somehow, to be able to walk past that now always-open door and go straight to the books. Travel guides, encyclopedias, atlases, and books on the tropical rain forests. It didn't take long to start narrowing things down. Everything had already pointed to Costa Rica, and everything that Caroline had said only confirmed that assumption. She could watch a sunset from the beach, so the west coast, and the proximity to the beach and presence of certain types of monkeys eliminated any highland areas. The amount of rainfall eliminated one popular expat destination, and the relative sleepiness that Caroline described knocked out another.

From there, she moved to the internet, where she refined her search further. This was where things got grueling. She'd had to pay very close attention to the things that Caroline had said that were likely to be core facts and not lies. How long she rode her scooter to get to the shops. The general size of the neighborhood she went to when she wanted to chat with other

Americans. The types of food served at her favorite restaurant, and the drinks at her favorite bar. Eventually she managed to narrow the possibilities down to a few likely options. Then, before she logged out of her computer to give a library patron a chance to use it, she looked up a phone number.

Detective Daniel Ortiz sounded tired when he answered the phone. Sherry resisted the urge to be too apologetic for disturbing him. "Detective Ortiz? This is Sherry Pinkwhistle. You probably don't remember me, but you interviewed me six years ago about the Howard Hastings murder case. I was friends with his wife, Caroline."

Detective Ortiz sounded instantly more alert. "I remember you, ma'am. How can I help you?"

"I just wanted to tell you," she said, "that I've managed to speak to Caroline on the phone. I think she's living in Costa Rica, probably somewhere along the Whale Coast. There's one town in particular I think is the most likely option, but there are also a few other possibilities if she wasn't being completely accurate about the place."

"Wait, hold on a second," Detective Ortiz said, and there was a brief pause. Sherry imagined him searching a cluttered desk for a pen. "Okay. Where?"

Sherry listed off the names, which she'd neatly written down in her notebook. Detective Ortiz thanked her. "If she calls again, let me know right away."

"I will," Sherry said, and said her goodbyes and hung up before sitting back in her chair. She wasn't sure exactly how she felt. A little guilty, maybe. A little guilty, and vastly, enormously relieved. She hadn't truly realized how heavy it all had been until it was gone, and now, suddenly, she was free. She'd gone back to that first murder case. She'd done her best to really, truly help solve it. Now it was someone else's problem to deal with. Maybe she was a bad friend. Maybe Caroline had never deserved such a good one.

She left the library and started heading home. The little rented house was still home, for now, but the walk was pleasant. Somehow, without her noticing, spring had truly arrived. There were tulips in people's front yards. The sight of them made her think of something.

She called Janine first. "Would you like to go down to Albany with me?" she asked.

"Why?" Janine asked.

"I want to get takeout from a restaurant someone told me about and have a picnic in the park and look at the tulips before the crowds get there in a few weeks and the petals all fall off," Sherry said. "Will you come?"

Janine agreed. So did Charlotte, who agreed to go before having even been told what the plan was, and so did Barry, who extracted a promise to also go to the food co-op so he could buy some very expensive-sounding ingredients for a very complicated-sounding recipe he'd been wanting to make.

The picnic all organized, Sherry retrieved the wad of cash that she'd gotten from Caroline and kept hidden away for all these years. She put it into an envelope, which she addressed to Alice's mother, with a brief, anonymous note saying that the money was to be spent on Alice's little girl's education. Next, she went to the bank and withdrew the exact same amount from her own account, money that she'd saved up over the past few years of quietly working in Winesap and punishing herself for what she'd done wrong. It was hers, earned fairly: she had nothing left to feel guilty about. Or maybe she did. All those people who'd spent months in jail because of her investigations, all the people she could have saved by taking their deaths as seriously as she *should* have instead of as if it was all an elaborate game. It was strange, though: she couldn't work herself up to the shame that used to come so easily to her. Maybe Sheriff Brown was right. Maybe it really was all over. Or maybe Barry was rubbing off on her, and she was just ready to forgive herself a little. She tucked the money into her purse. Then she called a cab.

A few hours later, she was driving off the lot of the local used car dealership in an ancient sea-green Cadillac. It was the sort of car that her ex-husband would have thought was an embarrassing thing for an old lady to drive around in. It was the sort of car that Sherry would have been embarrassed to buy. Not anymore. She was done with that now. She needed a car, and she liked this one, so now this one was hers.

Her friends' reactions told her that she'd made the right decision. When she beeped the horn outside Charlotte's apartment and Charlotte saw the car, she gave a gratifying little scream of delight, like a character in a movie. Barry patted the hood and beamed at it like it was a friendly dog. Even Janine, when she saw it, gave a big, startled smile and said, "How fun!" before she climbed into the passenger's seat. Then they set off all together, the windows rolled down to let in the breeze and very modern pop music that Sherry was pleased to not recognize playing on the radio. She'd had more than enough of staying in Winesap and listening to only the timeless, inoffensive music that that demon had allowed to be played. She wanted to be lost, and baffled, and fully aware of being completely out of touch and behind the times. "Is *this* what the kids are listening to now?" she asked aloud more than once when something particularly terrible started to play. She loved every second of it.

When she finally found a parking spot near the restaurant, Janine gave her a skeptical look. "*Here?*" It was, admittedly, not the most glamorous-looking stretch of street.

"Here," Sherry said firmly, and got out, with Barry jumping out to tag along and help her gather up all the bags of containers from the friendly young man behind the counter. The restaurant was fairly spartan inside, with white walls and round tables topped with lazy Susans, but the smells wafting out of the bags made Sherry's mouth start to water. She'd ordered what had felt like half the menu, or at least everything that she thought that they realistically might be able to eat on a blanket in the park: dumplings in chili oil, dandan noodles, cucumber with garlic sauce, spicy beef tongue and tripe salad: as many of the things that she could think of that Alan had told her about while thinking that she'd never tried anything like it before. He'd wanted her to experience something new and good. This could be that, in a way. She'd eaten Sichuan food before, but not from this restaurant, with these three friends, while looking at tulips in the park on a nice late April afternoon.

She drove them to the park, and they walked to a spot by a bank of frilly pink and orange tulips with a good view of the fountain behind them, with its imposing Moses striking water from the rock. They scooped food onto paper plates, and Sherry poured prosecco into enamel mugs she'd found in Alan's camping supplies as everyone started to eat. There were exclamations over the food: there wasn't anything like it closer to Winesap. Janine, who hated having to look for parking and rarely ventured into any of the local cities, asked, "How did you even find that place?"

"Alan told me about it," Sherry said. "He'd been wanting to bring me there for a while, but he never had the chance."

Everyone went quiet for a moment. Sherry passed around the camping mugs. "To Alan," she said, holding up her mug of prosecco.

"To Alan," her friends said back. They all clinked mugs. Janine was the first to speak up. "I know that I didn't know him as well as you did, Sherry, but I remember back when Alan first moved to Winesap—"

They just talked about him for a while, then. About Alan, but also about Winesap, and all the strange, horrible, unreal things that had happened that they hadn't been able to think about too deeply. Sherry laughed a lot, then got a little teary. She ate too many noodles and drank exactly the right amount of prosecco. Eventually, the conversation shifted to other things: the vacation to southern France Janine was planning, and the dinner party Father Barry had invited them all to. (There would, he promised Charlotte, be eligible bachelors present, though his brother wouldn't be among them. The police hadn't been able to directly tie Todd to the cocaine ring, but he'd been lying low at a friend's goat farm in Vermont, anyway.) Charlotte waxed enthusiastic for a while about her plan for a new exhibit in the gallery featuring work made by inmates at the women's prison not far from Winesap. Then, abruptly, she said, "Hey, Sherry? Remember my witch friend I told you about? The one who got in the car accident and helped me bless your necklace?"

"Of course," Sherry said. "Poor thing, how is she?"

"She's fine," Charlotte said, taking a sip of her drink.

"Insurance ended up paying for most of it. I had a really weird conversation with her the other day, though."

"Weird how?" Sherry asked, immediately interested. Charlotte lived in Winesap. At this point, they all had a high threshold for weird.

"This is going to sound crazy," Charlotte said.

"Not to us," Barry said, just as Sherry said, "Really?" and Janine gave a skeptical "Hm!"

They all laughed. Charlotte laughed, too. "Yeah, okay. So, she knows about the Winesap stuff, right? Like, I've been keeping her up to date, so she knows about everything that happened, and about you, Sherry, and how you kind of fixed everything. And the thing is, she's friends with a, uh, *coven* of witches in New Orleans, and they've all been sending her messages saying that they think there's . . ." She winced slightly, and said, almost apologetically, "A vampire? Attacking people around town? And she was wondering if maybe you'd be able to . . . consult with her a little? About what you do when you have . . ."

"Demon problems?" Father Barry asked.

"Right," Charlotte said. "Some *serious*-sounding demon problems."

Familiar-sounding demon problems, Sherry thought. Not in the vampire aspect, but in how thematic it was. Cozy murder mysteries in a quaint little town in rural upstate New York. Vampires in Louisiana. *Until next time*, the demon had said.

She shouldn't get involved. She didn't need to get involved.

"I don't know anything about vampires," she said slowly. "But . . ."

Charlotte leaned forward slightly. The water trickled in the fountain. A squirrel chirped in a tree above them. A big brown pit bull made an enthusiastic lunge for their picnic before abruptly being hauled back by his extremely apologetic owner. There were so many beautiful things in the world to enjoy that had absolutely nothing to do with murder, mystery, or disturbing occult plots.

And yet.

"But," Sherry said again. Her heart was beating a little faster. She had expected more time to pass before the demon creature showed up again, but here it was. It hadn't come to her this time. It had chosen somewhere far away for its new playground, and it hadn't invited Sherry. She wasn't the sort of sexy leather-clad figure that would fit into the southern gothic vampire romance or urban fantasy genres that she suspected her demonic friend was riffing off this time. Too bad. The demon had wanted a sweet old lady to star in its cozy mysteries. It had ended up with something else. "Things always slow down a little at the library, at this time of year," she said, and pressed her hand lightly to her chest, where she'd been ready and willing to stab herself in the heart the last time she'd kicked this obnoxious demon's ass right back to where it had come from. "And I'm sure we have some good books about vampire myths and New Orleans history. I might have a little time to do some extra reading."

Acknowledgments

As usual, lots of people helped out with this book. Thank you to my agent, Bridget Smith, and my editor, Jessica Wade. Eternal gratitude to the rest of the team at Penguin who worked on this book, including Gabbie Pachon, Liz Gluck, Stephanie Felty, Jessica Plummer, and Katie Anderson. Many thanks also to Sara Hopkins, who kindly provided answers to some preliminary questions about the librarian life that the demon and I then mostly flagrantly ignored for plot reasons (sorry, Sara!), and to my sister Rosemary, who provided answers to questions about medicine and Catholicism that I probably also ignored for reasons related to either laziness or terrible organizational skills (sorry, Rosemary!). Thanks to my staunch coworking companions: Mary-Ellen, Kellen, and Chloe. Thanks to Mom for watching the baby while I frantically type, to Dad for working as an entire volunteer publicity and hype squad, to Ah Du for life support, and to my sister Ellen for being my "Are babies supposed to do this????" texting buddy. Also, thanks very much to Miss Baby: you make being that cute look easy.

C. M. Waggoner grew up in rural upstate New York, where she spent a lot of time reading fantasy novels in a swamp. She studied creative writing at SUNY Purchase and lived in China for eight years before moving to Albany, New York, where she now lives with her husband and daughter. She is the author of three books: *Unnatural Magic, The Ruthless Lady's Guide to Wizardry*, and *The Village Library Demon-Hunting Society*. When she's not writing or reading, she enjoys cooking, trying to learn how to draw, and going on extremely long walks. You can voice your complaints to the management (or sign up for her mailing list) on her website, or hunt her down on social media.

VISIT C. M. WAGGONER ONLINE

CMWaggoner.com
C.M.Waggoner
CMWaggoner2

Ready to find
your next great read?

Let us help.

Visit prh.com/nextread

Penguin
Random
House